Pra

'Unputdownable! Bear [...] h great ferocity'   Sir Ranulph [...]

'This debut thriller by the adventurer Bear Grylls is enthralling. Grylls excels in describing the trials and tribulations of tramping through uncharted Amazon rainforests . . .'   *The Times*

'[A] fast and furious debut novel'   *Press Association*

'An impressively strong fiction debut from one of the best known TV faces of survival and outdoor adventure, Bear Grylls makes full use of his military and survivalist background to deliver a rip-roaring and vividly colourful *Boy's Own*-style thriller'
Irish Independent

'A modern-day conspiracy to raise Hitler's Third Reich from the ashes'   *Mail on Sunday*

'*Ghost Flight* is a great adventure story: huge spiders, deadly piranhas, unforgiving terrains, evil Nazis, and death at every turn. What's not to like? Jason Bourne meets Ban Hope with a dash of Indiana Jones in an adventure series set to continue'
Buzz Magazine

By Bear Grylls

Novels
Ghost Flight
Burning Angels

Non-Fiction
Facing Up
Facing the Frozen Ocean
Born Survivor
Great Outdoor Adventures
Living Wild
To My Sons
Mud, Sweat and Tears
A Survival Guide for Life
True Grit
Your Life – Train For It
Extreme Food
Fuel for Life
How to Stay Alive

Mission Survival
Gold of the Gods
Way of the Wolf
Sands of the Scorpion
Tracks of the Tiger
Claws of the Crocodile
Rage of the Rhino
Strike of the Shark
Lair of the Leopard

GHOST FLIGHT

BEAR GRYLLS

ORION

An Orion paperback

First published in Great Britain in 2015
by Orion Books
This paperback edition published in 2018
by Orion Books,
an imprint of The Orion Publishing Group Ltd,
Carmelite House, 50 Victoria Embankment
London EC4Y 0DZ

An Hachette UK company

1 3 5 7 9 10 8 6 4 2

A CIP catalogue record for this book
is available from the British Library.

ISBN 978 1 4091 8113 2

Typeset by Input Data Services Ltd, Somerset

Printed and Bound in Great Britain by Clays Ltd, St Ives plc

MIX
Paper from
responsible sources
FSC® C104740

www.orionbooks.co.uk

This book is dedicated to my late grandfather,
Brigadier William Edward Harvey Grylls, OBE,
15/19th King's Royal Hussars and
Commanding Officer of Target Force.

Gone but not forgotten.

ACKNOWLEDGEMENTS

Special thanks to the following: literary agents at PFD Caroline Michel, Annabel Merullo and Tim Binding for their unfaltering support and perceptive comments on early drafts. Thanks to Laura Williams, Associate Agent at PFD, as ever for all her Herculean efforts. To Jon Wood, Jemima Forrester and all at my publisher, Orion – Susan Lamb, Sophie Painter, Malcolm Edwards, Mark Rusher, Gaby Young and everyone on 'Team Grylls'.

To Hamish de Bretton-Gordon OBE MD CBRN, Avon Protection, for his advice and expert input on chemical, biological and nuclear weapons and defence and protection measures. To Chris Daniels, and all at Hybrid Air Vehicles, for their insight and guidance on all things Airlander. To Dr Jacqueline Borg, foremost expert on brain-related disorders, including ASD. To Anne and Paul Sherrat, for their incisive advice and criticism on all things Nazi and Eastern Bloc.

And the final, biggest thank you, of course, to Damien Lewis for helping build on what we discovered together in my grandfather's war chest, marked 'Top Secret'. Bringing those documents to life in the way you have is pure brilliance.

AUTHOR'S NOTE

My grandfather, Brigadier William Edward Harvey Grylls, OBE, 15/19th King's Royal Hussars – and Commanding Officer of Target Force, the covert unit established at Winston Churchill's request towards the end of WW2. The unit was one of the most clandestine bands of operators ever assembled by the War Office, and it was predominantly charged with tracking down and protecting secret technologies, weapons, scientists and high-ranking Nazi officials, to serve the Allied cause against the world's new superpower and enemy, the Soviets.

No one in our family had any idea of his covert role as Commanding Officer of T Force until many years after his death and the release of information under the Official Secrets Act seventy-year rule – a process of discovery that inspired the writing of this book.

My grandfather was a man of few words, but I remember him so fondly from when I was a child growing up. Pipe smoking, enigmatic, dry humoured and loved by those he led.

To me, though, he was always just Grandpa Ted.

Harper's Magazine, October 1946
SECRETS BY THE THOUSANDS
By C. Lester Walker

Someone wrote to Wright Field Airbase recently, saying he
understood this country had got together quite a collection of
enemy war secrets . . . and could he, please, be sent everything
on German jet engines. The Air Documents Division of the
Army Air Forces answered:

'Sorry – but that would be fifty tons.'

Moreover, that fifty tons was just a small portion of what is
today undoubtedly the biggest collection of captured enemy
war secrets ever assembled. If you always thought of war secrets
– and who hasn't? – as coming in sixes and sevens . . . it may
interest you to learn that the war secrets in this collection
run into the thousands, that the mass of documents is
mountainous, and that there has never before been anything
quite comparable to it.

....

Daily Mail, March 1988
THE PAPERCLIP CONSPIRACY
By Tom Bower

The Paperclip Conspiracy was the climax of an astonishing
battle between the Allies in the aftermath of the war to seize
the spoils of Nazi Germany. Just weeks after Hitler's defeat,
men classified as 'ardent Nazis' were chosen by senior officers
in the Pentagon to become respectable American citizens.

1

While in Britain political controversy inhibited plans to hire incriminated Germans in the drive for economic recovery, the French and Russians took on anyone regardless of their crimes, and the Americans, through a web of deceit, sanitised the murderous record of their Nazi scientists.

The proof of German technical prowess is overwhelmingly established in the hundreds of reports written by Allied investigators, who do not shy away from describing the Germans' 'astonishing achievements' and 'superb invention'.

Hitler does indeed have the last laugh on his enemies.

....

The Sunday Times, December 2014
VAST SECRET NAZI 'TERROR WEAPONS' SITE UNCOVERED IN AUSTRIA
By Bojan Pancevski

A secret underground complex built by the Nazis towards the end of the Second World War that may have been used for the development of weapons of mass destruction, including a nuclear bomb, has been uncovered in Austria.

The vast facility was discovered last week near the town of St Georgen an der Gusen. It is believed to be connected to the nearby B8 Bergkristall underground factory that produced the Messerschmitt Me 262, the first operational jet-powered fighter, which posed a brief threat to Allied air forces in the war's closing stages. Declassified intelligence documents as well as testimony from witnesses helped excavators identify the concealed entrance.

'This was a gigantic industrial complex and most likely the biggest secret weapons production facility of the Third Reich,' said Andreas Sulzer, an Austrian documentary film-maker who is in charge of the excavations.

Sulzer assembled a team of historians and found further evidence of scientists working on the secret project, which was managed by SS General Hans Kammler. Kammler was in charge of Hitler's missile programmes, including the V-2 rocket used against London in the latter stages of the war.

He was known as a brilliant but ruthless commander, who had signed off the blueprints for the gas chambers and crematoria at the Auschwitz concentration camp complex in southern Poland. Rumours persist that he was captured by the Americans and given a new identity after the war.

Sulzer's excavation was stopped last Wednesday by local authorities, who demanded a permit for research on historic sites. But he is confident that digging can resume next month. 'Prisoners from concentration camps across Europe were hand-picked for their special skills – physicists, chemists or other experts – to work on this monstrous project, and we owe it to the victims to finally open the site and reveal the truth,' said Sulzer.

1

His eyes opened.

Slowly.

Peeling apart eyelash by eyelash, straining against the thick crust of blood that fused one with the other. Cracks sprung a fraction at a time, like broken glass over bloodshot eyeballs. The brightness seemed to scorch into his retina, as if a laser was being focused on to his eyeballs. But who by? Who were the enemy . . . his tormentors? And where in God's name were they?

He couldn't remember the slightest damn thing.

What day was it? What year was it, even? How had he got here – wherever here might be?

The sunlight hurt like hell, but at least his sight was returning to him, little by little.

The first concrete object that Will Jaeger became aware of was the cockroach. It swam into focus, looking blurry, monstrous and alien as it filled his entire vision.

As far as he could tell, his head seemed to be lying sideways on a floor. Concrete. Covered in a thick brownish scum. With his head at this angle, the cockroach appeared to be approaching as if it was about to crawl right inside his left eye socket.

The beast flicked its feelers towards him, at the last moment drifting out of sight, scuttling past the tip of his nose. And then Jaeger felt it claw its way up the side of his head.

The cockroach stopped somewhere around his right temple

– the one that was lying furthest from the floor, fully exposed to the air.

It started feeling around with its front legs and mandibles.

As if it were searching for something. *Tasting something.*

Jaeger felt it begin to chew; biting into flesh; insect jaws carving their way in. He sensed the hissy, hollow clacking of the roach's serrated mandibles, as they ripped away shreds of rotten meat. And then – as the scream left his lips soundlessly – he sensed that there were dozens more swarming over him . . . as if he were long dead.

Jaeger fought down the waves of nausea, one question crashing through his brain: *why couldn't he hear himself scream?*

With a superhuman effort he moved his right arm.

It was just the barest fraction, but still he felt as if he were trying to lift the entire world. Each centimetre that he managed to raise it, his shoulder socket and elbow joint screamed out in agony, his muscles spasming with the puny effort he was forcing from them.

He felt like a cripple.

What in God's name had happened to him?

What had they done to him?

Gritting his teeth, and focusing on the sheer force of will, he drew the arm towards his head, dragging his hand across his ear, scrabbling at it, desperately. The fingers made contact with . . . legs. Scaly, spiny, insect-savage legs, each twitching and pulsing as it tried to force the cockroach body deeper into his ear hole.

Get them out of there! Get them out! Get them OUUUUTTT!

He felt like vomiting, but there was nothing in his guts. Just a shitty dry film of near-death, which coated everything – his stomach lining, his throat, his mouth; even his nostrils.

Oh shit! His nostrils. They were trying to crawl in there too!

Jaeger cried out again. Longer. More despairing. *This is not the way to die. Please, not like this . . .*

Again and again his fingers scrabbled at his bodily orifices, the roaches kicking and hissing their insect anger as he prised them free.

At long last the sound started to bleed back through to his senses. First, his own desperate cries echoed through his bloodied ears. And then he became aware of something mixed in – something more chilling even than the scores of insects that were intent on feasting on his brains.

A human voice.

Deep-throated. Cruel. A voice that revelled in pain.

His jailer.

The voice brought it all flooding back. Black Beach Prison. The jail at the end of the earth. A place where people were sent to be tortured horribly and to die. Jaeger had been thrown in here for a crime he'd never committed, on the orders of a crazed and murderous dictator – and that was when the real horrors had begun.

Compared to waking to this hell, Jaeger preferred even the dark peace of unconsciousness; anything rather than the weeks he'd spent locked away in this place worse than damnation – his prison cell. His tomb.

He willed his mind to slip away again, back towards the soft, formless, shifting shades of grey that had sheltered him before something – what was it? – had dragged him up to this unspeakable present.

The movements of his right arm became weaker and weaker. It dropped to the floor again.

Let the cockroaches feast on his brains.

Even that was preferable.

Then the thing that had woken him hit again – a rush of cold liquid to the face, like the slap of a wave at sea. Only the smell was so different. Not the ice-pure, bracing aroma of the ocean. This smell was fetid; the salt tang of a urinal that hadn't seen a lick of disinfectant for years.

His tormentor laughed again.

This was real sport.

Chucking the contents of the toilet bucket in the prisoner's face – what could be better?

Jaeger spat out the foul liquid. Blinked it away from his burning eyes. At least the blast of putrefying fluid had driven the roaches away. His mind searched for the right words – the choicest expletives that he could fling in his jailer's face.

Proof of life. A show of resistance.

'Go and . . .'

Jaeger began to speak, croaking out the kind of insult that would for sure secure him a beating with that same flex hose that he had learned to dread.

But if he didn't resist, he was done for. Resistance was all he knew.

Yet he didn't get to finish those words. They froze in his throat.

Suddenly, another voice cut in, one so familiar – *so brotherly* – that for several long moments Jaeger felt certain he had to be dreaming. The incantation was soft at first, but growing both in power and in volume; a rhythmical chant replete somehow with the promise of the impossible . . .

'*Ka mate, ka mate. Ka ora, ka ora.*

Ka mate, ka mate! Ka ora, ka ora!'

Jaeger would know that voice anywhere.

Takavesi Raffara; how could he be here?

When they'd been teammates playing the British Army at rugby, it had been Raff who'd led the haka – the traditional Maori pre-match war dance. Always. He'd rip off his shirt, ball his fists, and ripple forward to get eyeball-to-eyeball with the opposing team, hands thumping his massive chest, legs like pillared tree trunks, arms like battering rams, the rest of his team – Jaeger included – flanking him, fearless, unstoppable.

His eyes had bulged, tongue swollen, face frozen in a rictus of warrior challenge as he'd thundered out the lines.

'*KA MATE! KA MATE! KA ORA! KA ORA!*' Will I die? Will I die? Will I live? Will I live?

Raff had proven equally relentless when standing shoulder-to-shoulder on the battlefield. The ultimate fellow warrior. Maori by birth and Royal Marines Commando by destiny, he had soldiered with Jaeger across the four corners of the earth, and he was one of his closest brothers.

Jaeger swivelled his eyes right, towards the source of the chanting.

Out of the corner of his vision he could just make out a figure standing on the far side of the cell's bars. Massive. Dwarfing even his jailer. Smile like a shaft of pure sunlight breaking through after a dark storm seemingly without end.

'Raff?' The single word was rasped out, ringing with a barely suspended disbelief.

'Yeah. It's me.' That smile. 'Seen you looking worse, mate. Like that time I dragged you out of that Amsterdam bar. Still, best get you cleaned up. I've come to get you, mate. Get you out of here. We're flying BA to London – first class.'

Jaeger didn't respond. What words were there? How could Raff be here, in this place, seemingly so close at hand?

'Best get going,' Raff prompted. 'Before Major Mojo your buddy here changes his mind.'

'Yah, Bob Marley!' Jaeger's tormentor forced a mock joviality from behind evil slits of eyes. 'Bob Marley – you the real joker man.'

Raff grinned from ear to ear.

He was the only man Jaeger had ever seen who could smile at someone with a look that could freeze the very blood. The Bob Marley reference had to refer to Raff's hair – worn long, in braids, the traditional Maori way. As many had learned on the rugby field, Raff didn't take well to anyone disrespecting his choice of head apparel.

'Unlock the cell door,' Raff grated. 'Me and my friend Mr Jaeger – we're leaving.'

2

The jeep pulled away from Black Beach Prison, Raff hunched over the wheel. He handed Jaeger a water bottle.

'Drink.' He jerked a thumb at the back seat. 'There's more in the cooler. Get as much down you as you can. You need to rehydrate. We've got one hell of a day ahead of us . . .'

Raff lapsed into silence, his mind on the journey that lay before them.

Jaeger let the quiet hang in the air.

After weeks in that prison, his body was a mass of burning. Every joint screamed with agony. It seemed like a lifetime had passed since he'd been thrown into that cell; since he'd travelled anywhere in a vehicle; since his body had been exposed to the full blast of Bioko's tropical sunlight.

He flinched in pain with every jolt of the vehicle. They were following the ocean road – a narrow stretch of blacktop that led into Malabo, Bioko's one major town. There were precious few surfaced roads in the tiny African island nation. Mostly, the country's oil wealth went into funding a new palace for the President, or another of his fleet of giant yachts, or to further inflating his Swiss bank accounts.

Raff gestured at the vehicle's dash. 'Pair of shades in there, mate. You look like you're struggling.'

'Been a while since I've seen the sun.'

Jaeger flicked open the glove compartment and pulled out what looked like a pair of Oakleys. He studied them for an instant. 'Fakes? You always were a bloody cheapskate.'

Raff laughed. 'Who dares wins.'

Jaeger let a smile creep across his battered features. It hurt like hell to do so. He felt as if he hadn't smiled in a lifetime; as if the smile was cracking his face right in two.

In recent weeks Jaeger had come to believe he was never getting out of that prison cell. No one who mattered had even known he was there. He'd become convinced that he would die in Black Beach, unseen and forgotten, and that, like countless corpses before, his would be thrown to the sharks.

He couldn't quite fathom it – that he was alive and free.

His jailer had let them out via the shadowed basement – the place that housed the torture cubicles – sliding wordlessly past blood-spattered walls. The place where the trash was dumped, plus the bodies of those who'd died in their cells and were ready to be thrown into the sea.

Jaeger couldn't imagine what kind of deal Raff had cut, to enable him to walk.

No one walked from Black Beach Prison.

Not ever.

'How did you find me?' Jaeger let his words fall heavy into the silence.

Raff shrugged. 'Wasn't easy. Took a few of us: Feaney, Carson, me.' He laughed. 'You glad we bothered?'

Jaeger shrugged. 'I was just getting to know Major Mojo. Nice guy. The kind you'd want to marry your sister.' He eyed the big Maori. 'But how *did* you find me? And why . . .'

'Always there for you, buddy. Plus . . .' A shadow fell across Raff's features. 'You're needed back in London. An assignment. We both are.'

'What kind of assignment?'

Raff's expression grew darker still. 'I'll brief you when we're out of here – 'cause there ain't gonna be no assignment until we are.'

Jaeger took a long pull on the water. Cool, clear bottled water

– it tasted like sweet nectar compared to what he'd been forced to live off in Black Beach.

'So what's next? You got me out of Black Beach; doesn't mean we're off Hell Island. That's what they call it around here.'

'So I heard. Deal I cut with Major Mojo – he gets his third payment once you and I are on our flight to London. Only we won't be making that flight. The airport: that's where he'll grab us. He'll have a reception party waiting. He'll claim I busted you out of Black Beach, but he recaptured us. That way, he gets two paydays – one from us, and a second from the President.'

Jaeger shuddered. It was the President of Bioko – Honore Chambara – who'd ordered his arrest in the first place. A month or so back there had been an attempted coup. Mercenaries had seized the other half of Equatorial Guinea – Bioko being the country's island capital – the half that lay just across the ocean, forming part of the African mainland.

In the aftermath, President Chambara had rounded up all foreigners on Bioko – not that there were many. Jaeger had been one of them, and a search of his digs had turned up the odd memento from his time as a soldier.

As soon as Chambara had heard, he'd figured Jaeger had to be in on the coup; *their man on the inside.* Which he wasn't. He was here in Bioko for an entirely different – and innocent – set of reasons, but there was no convincing Chambara. On the President's orders, Jaeger had been thrown into Black Beach Prison, where Major Mojo had done his best to break him; to force him to confess.

Jaeger slipped on the shades. 'You're right – we'll never make it out of here via the airport. You got a Plan B?'

Raff threw him a look. 'Way I heard it, you were here working as a teacher. Teaching English. At a village in the far north of the island. I paid them a visit. A bunch of fishermen there figure you're the best thing that ever happened on Hell Island. Taught their kids to read 'n' write. More than President Chugga ever did.' He paused. 'They've readied a canoe so we can make a break for Nigeria.'

Jaeger thought about it for a second. He'd spent close to three years on Bioko. He'd got to know the local fishing communities well. The journey across the Gulf of Guinea by canoe – it was doable. Maybe.

'It's thirty klicks, or thereabouts,' he volunteered. 'The fishermen do it now and then – when the weather's set fair. You got a map?'

Raff gestured at a small flight bag lying at Jaeger's feet. Jaeger reached for it, painfully, and rifled through the contents. He found the map, unfolded it and studied the lie of the land. Bioko lay in the very crook of the armpit of Africa – a tiny island thick with jungle, no more than a hundred kilometres long by fifty kilometres wide.

The nearest African country was Cameroon, lying north and west of there, with Nigeria set further to the west again. A good two hundred kilometres south lay what had been, until recently, the other half of President Chambara's domain – the mainland part of Equatorial Guinea – that was, until the coup plotters had seized it.

'Cameroon's closest,' Jaeger remarked.

'Cameroon? Nigeria?' Raff shrugged. 'Right now, anywhere's better than here.'

'How long till nightfall?' Jaeger queried. He'd lost his watch to Chambara's thugs, long before he'd been dragged into his Black Beach cell. 'Under cover of darkness, we might just make it.'

'Six hours. I'm giving you one hour max at the hotel. You spend it scrubbing all that shit off, and necking water – because no way are you gonna make it unless you rehydrate. Like I said, big day still to come.'

'Mojo knows which hotel you're staying at?'

Raff snorted. 'No point trying to hide. Island this size – everyone knows everything. Come to think of it, reminds me a bit of home . . .' His teeth flashed in the sunlight. 'Mojo won't cause us any trouble – not for a good few hours. He'll be checking if his money has cleared – by which time we'll be long gone.'

Jaeger drank the bottled water, forcing gulp after gulp down his parched throat. Trouble was, his stomach had shrunk to the size of a walnut. If they hadn't beaten and tortured him to death, the starvation diet would have done for him pretty soon, that was for certain.

'Teaching kids.' Raff smiled, knowingly. 'So what were you really up to?'

'I was teaching kids.'

'Right. Teaching kids. You got nothing whatsoever to do with the coup?'

'President Chugga kept asking me the same question. In between the beatings. He could use a man like you.'

'Okay, you were teaching kids. English. In a fishing village.'

'I was teaching kids.' Jaeger stared out the window; the smile had fallen from his face completely. 'Plus, if you've got to know, I needed somewhere to hide. To think. Bioko – the asshole at the end of the universe. I never thought anyone would find me.' He paused. 'You proved me wrong.'

The hotel pit stop had done Jaeger a world of good. He'd showered. Three times. By the third, the water that swirled down the plughole was just about clean.

He'd forced a dose of rehydration salts down him. He'd sliced off his beard – a five-week growth – but stopped short of shaving. There hadn't been the time.

He'd checked himself over for breaks; miraculously, there didn't seem to be many. He was thirty-eight years old, and he'd kept himself fit on the island. A decade in the military elite prior to that – he'd been pretty much at the peak of physical condition when they'd thrown him into his cell. Maybe that was why he'd emerged from Black Beach comparatively unscathed.

He figured he had a couple of broken fingers; ditto his toes.

Nothing that wouldn't heal.

A quick change of clothes and Raff had them back in the SUV, heading east out of Malabo into the thick tropical bush. At first he drove hunched over the wheel like an old granny – 30 mph top speed. He did so to check for a tail. The few who were lucky enough to own a car in Bioko all seemed to drive like the proverbial bat out of hell.

If a vehicle had stuck to their backside, it would have stood out a mile.

By the time they turned on to the tiny dirt track threading towards the north-east coast, it was clear that no one was following.

Major Mojo had to be banking on them leaving via the airport. In theory, there was no other way off the island – not unless you wanted to take your chances amongst the tropical storms and the sharks that circled Bioko, ravenously.

And there were precious few who ever did that.

3

Chief Ibrahim gestured towards the Fernao village beach. It was close enough for the sound of the surf to echo through the thin mud walls of his hut.

'We have readied a canoe. It is provisioned with water and food.' The chief paused and touched Jaeger's shoulder. 'We will never forget, especially the children.'

'Thank you,' Jaeger replied. 'I won't, either. You've all saved me in more ways than I can explain.'

The chief glanced at a figure standing at his side – a young, finely muscled man. 'My son is one of the best seamen in all Bioko . . . You are sure you will not let the men ferry you across? You know they would gladly do so.'

Jaeger shook his head. 'When President Chambara finds out I'm gone, he'll take revenge any way he can. Any excuse. We say our goodbyes here. It's the only way.'

The chief rose to his feet. 'It has been three fine years, William. Insh'Allah you will make it across the Gulf and from there to your home. And one day, when the curse of Chambara finally is lifted, insh'Allah you will come back and visit.'

'Insh'Allah,' Jaeger echoed. He and the chief shook hands. 'I'd like that.'

Jaeger glanced momentarily at a line of faces that ringed the hut. Kids. Dusty, scuffed up, semi-naked – but happy. Maybe that was what the children here had taught him – the meaning of happiness.

His eyes returned to the chief. 'Tell them why for me, but only when we're good and gone.'

The chief smiled. 'I will. Now go. You have done here many good things. Go with that knowledge, and with lightness in your heart.'

Jaeger and Raff made their way towards the beach, threading through the cover of the thickest groves of palm trees. The fewer people who saw them make their getaway, the fewer who were likely to suffer any reprisals.

It was Raff who broke the silence. He could tell how much it pained his friend to abandon his young charges.

'Insh'Allah?' he queried. 'The villagers round here – they're Muslim?'

'They are. And you know what – these people, they're some of the best-hearted I ever met.'

Raff eyed him. 'Three years alone on Bioko Island, and bugger me if the mighty Jaeger-bomb has gone soft.'

Jaeger flashed his friend a wry smile. Maybe Raff was right. Maybe he had.

They were approaching the pristine white sands of the beach when a figure ran up beside them, panting breathlessly. Barefooted, bare-chested, and dressed only in a pair of raggedy shorts, he looked to be no more than eight years old. The expression on his face was one of panic approaching terror.

'Sir, sir!' He grabbed Jaeger's hand. 'They are coming. President Chambara's men. My father – someone radioed through a warning. They are coming! To find you! To take you back!'

Jaeger crouched down until he was at the boy's eye level. 'Little Mo, listen: no one's taking me back.' He slipped off the fake Oakleys and pressed them into the kid's hand. He ruffled the boy's dusty, child-wiry hair. 'Let's see them on, then,' he prompted.

Little Mo slid the sunglasses over his eyes. They were so large that he had to hold them in place.

Jaeger grinned. 'Dude! You look awesome! But keep them

hidden – at least until Chambara's men are gone.' A pause. 'Now, run. Get back to your father. Stay inside. And Mo, tell him from me – thanks for the warning.'

The kid gave Jaeger one last hug, full of reluctance at their parting, before he scuttled off, tears pricking his eyes.

Jaeger and Raff melted into the cover of the nearby bush. They crouched low, whisper-distance close, Jaeger grabbing Raff's wrist so as to do a quick time check.

'Around two hours to last light,' he murmured. 'Two options . . . One, we make a break for it right now, in broad daylight. Two, we hide up and sneak away come nightfall. From what I know of Chambara, he'll get his fast patrol boats out scouring the ocean, in addition to whatever force he's sending direct to the village. It's no more than forty minutes by boat from Malabo: we'll barely have hit the water before they're on top of us. Which means . . . no choice: we wait for nightfall.'

Raff nodded. 'Mate, you've been here three years. You got the local knowledge. But we need a hiding place where no one will ever think to look for us.'

His eyes scanned their surroundings, coming to rest upon the dark and brooding vegetation lying at the far end of the beach. 'Mangrove swamp. Snakes, crocs, mosquitoes, scorpions, leeches and waist-deep shitty mud. Last place anyone sane would ever want to hide.'

Raff delved deep in his pocket, pulling out a distinctive-looking knife. He handed it to Jaeger. 'Keep it handy, just in case.'

Jaeger slipped it open and felt across the five-inch semi-serrated blade, testing it for keenness. 'This another fake?'

Raff scowled. 'With weaponry, I don't cut corners.'

'So, Chambara's men are on their way,' Jaeger mused, 'no doubt to drag us back to Black Beach. And we've got one blade between us . . .'

Raff pulled out a second, identical knife. 'Trust me, even getting these through Bioko airport was a miracle.'

Jaeger gave a bleak smile. 'Okay, one blade each: we're unstoppable.'

The two men flitted through the palm grove towards the distant swampland.

From the outside, the maze of wild, tangled roots and branches looked impenetrable. Undeterred, Raff dropped to a belly-crawl and squirmed his way ahead, slipping through impossible gaps, unseen creatures slithering out of his way. He didn't stop until he was a good sixty feet inside, Jaeger crawling closely behind him.

The last thing Jaeger had done on the beach was grab some old palm fronds and scuttle backwards across the sand, wiping their footprints away. By the time he'd wriggled his way deep inside the mangroves, every last sign of their passing had been swept clean.

The two men proceeded to immerse themselves in the evil-smelling black mud that formed the base of the swamp. By the time they were done, just their heads remained above the surface, and even those were coated in a thick film of muck and filth. The only thing that picked them out from their surroundings was the whites of their eyes.

Jaeger could feel the dark surface of the swamp bubbling and seething with life all around him. 'Almost makes me homesick for Black Beach,' he muttered.

Raff grunted an acknowledgement, the flash of his teeth the only thing that revealed his position.

Jaeger's eyes roved around the latticework of wood that formed a tight-woven cathedral above their heads. Even the largest mangrove was no thicker than a man's wrist, rising to little more than twenty feet in height. But where the roots thrust out of the mud and were washed daily by the tide, they grew arrow straight for a good five feet or more.

Raff reached for one and sawed through it at ground level, using the serrated edge of his knife to do so. He made a further cut at around four feet, handing the length of wood to Jaeger.

Jaeger flashed him a questioning look.

'Krav Maga,' Raff growled. 'Stick-fighting skills with Corporal Carter. Ring any bells?'

Jaeger smiled. How could he forget?

He took his blade and began to hone one end of the hard, tough wood, tapering it into an arrow-like point.

Slowly, a short, sharp stabbing spear took shape.

Corporal Carter had been the doyen of weaponry, not to mention hand-to-hand combat. Both he and Raff had trained Jaeger's unit in Krav Maga, a hybrid martial art first developed in Israel. A blend of kung fu and raw street fighting, it taught you how to survive in real-life situations.

Unlike most martial arts, Krav Maga was all about bringing a battle to an end as quickly as possible, by doing maximum damage to your enemy. Systemic damage was what Carter had always called it: damage designed to be terminal. There were no rules, and all moves were aimed at hitting the most vulnerable parts of the body – the eyes, nose, neck, groin and knee. And hard.

The golden rules of Krav Maga were speed, aggression, surprise; plus to strike first and to improvise weaponry. You fought with whatever came to hand – planks of wood, metal bars, even broken bottles.

Or a sharpened wooden stake fashioned from a mangrove root.

Chambara's men appeared shortly before dusk.

There were two dozen of them in one truck. They moved on to the far end of the beach, fanning out to search it from end to end. They paused at each of the dugout canoes, turning them over as if they expected their quarry to be hiding underneath.

It was the obvious place to lie low – which had made it a complete no-no as far as Jaeger and Raff were concerned.

The soldiers from the Bioko armed forces loosed off rounds from their G3 assault rifles, blasting holes in the bottom of several of the boats. But there was little order to their actions, and Jaeger made careful note of which canoes hadn't received a burst of bullets.

It didn't take the soldiers long to find the canoe packed with provisions. Orders were screamed across the sand. A pair of camouflage-clad figures hurried into the village, returning a minute later with a diminutive form slung across their shoulders.

He was dropped in the sand at the force commander's feet.

Jaeger recognised the commander, a large, overweight man, from one of his many visits to Black Beach, where he'd overseen the interrogations and the beatings.

The commander proceeded to boot the prostrate form in the ribs.

Little Mo let out a muffled scream.

It echoed pitifully across the dusky beach.

Jaeger clenched his teeth. The chief's boy had been like a son to him as well. He'd been a smart pupil, but with a goofy smile that had always made Jaeger laugh. Plus he'd proved an ace at beach soccer, their favourite pastime once the daily lessons were done.

But it wasn't just that that had bonded the two of them. In so many ways, Little Mo reminded Jaeger of his own boy.

Or at least the son he'd once had.

4

'MR JAEGER!' The call rang out, cutting through Jaeger's dark thoughts.

'Mr William Jaeger. Yes, I remember you, you coward. And as you see, I have the boy.' A massive hand reached down and pulled Little Mo up by the roots of his hair, until he was balanced on the very tips of his toes. 'He has one minute left to live. ONE MINUTE! You white bastards show yourselves, NOW! Or this boy takes a bullet between the eyeballs!'

Jaeger locked eyes with Raff. The big Maori shook his head. 'Mate, you know the score,' he whispered. 'We show ourselves we damn the entire village – ourselves and Little Mo with it.'

Wordlessly, Jaeger flicked his eyes back to the distant figures. Raff was right, but the image of the kid dancing on his tiptoes as the big commander gripped him punched into Jaeger's brain. It flipped his mind back to a long-buried memory – to a remote mountainside and a shredded, knife-torn length of canvas . . .

Jaeger felt a massive arm upon him, powerful; restraining. 'Easy, buddy, easy,' Raff whispered. 'I mean what I'm saying. Show yourself now, we're all dead . . .'

'The one minute is up!' the commander screamed. 'COME OUT! Now!'

Jaeger heard the sharp, steel-on-steel *clatch-clatch* of a round being chambered. The commander whipped his pistol up, shoving the muzzle hard into Little Mo's temple. 'I COUNT FROM TEN. Then, make no mistake, you British bastards, I fire!'

The commander was facing the sand dunes, flashing his torch across the tussocks of grass and hoping to spot Raff and Jaeger.

'Ten, nine, eight . . .'

A new voice rang out over the darkening beach, the childish cries cutting across the commander's words. 'Sir! Sir! Please! *Please*!'

'Seven, six, five . . . Yes, boy, plead to your white friend to save you . . . Three . . .'

Jaeger felt his big Maori friend pinning him to the mud, as his mind darted in horror between distant memories: to a savage attack on a dark and frosted mountainside; to blood amongst the first winter snows. To the moment his life had imploded . . . To right now; to Little Mo.

'Two! One! IT IS *FINISHED*!'

The commander pulled the trigger.

A single muzzle flash threw the beach into stark light and shadow. He loosened hold of the boy's hair, letting the tiny body crumple to the sand.

Jaeger turned his head in agony and pressed it tight against the mangrove roots. Had Raff not been restraining him, he would have burst out of hiding, knife and sharpened stake at the ready, murder blazing in his eyes.

And he would have died.

He wouldn't have given a damn.

The commander barked out a series of staccato orders. Camouflaged figures dashed in all directions, some back into the village, others to either end of the beach. One came skidding to a halt at the edge of the swamp.

'So, we continue with our little game,' the commander announced, still searching in all directions. 'And so we fetch the next child. I am a patient man. I have all the time in the world. I am quite happy to shoot every last one of your pupils, Mr Jaeger, if that is what it takes. Show yourself. Or are you the poor white coward I always thought you were? Prove – me – wrong.'

Jaeger saw Raff make the move. He stole forward silently,

gliding through the mud on his stomach like a giant ghostly snake. For the briefest of moments he glanced over his shoulder.

'Want to go in a blaze of glory?' he whispered.

Jaeger nodded grimly. 'Speed. Aggression . . .'

'Surprise,' Raff completed the mantra.

Jaeger slithered forward, following the path that Raff made. As he did so, he marvelled at the big Maori's ability to move, to hunt, silently – like an animal; a natural-born predator. Over the years Raff had taught Jaeger so many of those skills: the total belief and the focus it took to stalk and kill.

But still Raff remained the master; the best there ever was.

He melted out of the swamp like a formless shadow, just as another hapless child was hauled on to the beach. The commander started booting the child in the guts, his men grinning at the cruel spectacle that was unfolding.

It was now that Raff seized his moment. Enshrouded in the darkness, he stole towards the lone guard nearest the swamp. In one swift move he slipped his left arm around the sentry's neck and mouth in an iron chokehold, blocking off any possibility of a cry, jerking the chin upwards and to the side. At the same instant his right arm snaked around in a savage thrust, sinking the blade of his knife up to the hilt through the man's throat, before punching forward to slice through the artery and the windpipe.

For several seconds Raff gripped the stricken sentry, as his life drained into his lungs, drowning the man in his own blood. Silently, he lowered the body to the sand. An instant later he was back at the swamp, the dead man's assault rifle gripped in hands thick with blood.

He crouched low, widening the narrow exit for Jaeger.

'Come on!' he hissed. 'Let's go!'

Jaeger sensed the movement from the corner of his eye. A figure had materialised out of nowhere, his assault rifle rising to aim, Raff bang in his line of fire.

Jaeger let fly with his knife.

The movement was instinctive. The blade whispered through the dusk air, twisting as it flew, and sliced deep into the figure's guts.

The gunman screamed.

His weapon went off, but the shots sprayed wide, punching wildly off target. As the echoes of the gunfire died away, Jaeger rose and sprinted forward, wooden stake raised in one hand.

He'd recognised the gunman.

He leapt, slamming the spear into the man's chest. He felt the sharpened stake split apart ribs and slice through muscle and sinew, as he forced it in with all his strength. By the time he'd grabbed the fallen man's assault rifle, he had him pinned to the sand – the stake driven clean through the side of his chest and shoulder.

Major Mojo, Jaeger's erstwhile tormentor, was screaming and writhing like a stuck pig – but he wasn't going anywhere, that was for sure.

In one smooth move Jaeger lifted the rifle, flicked off the safety and opened fire. The muzzle spat burning bursts of tracer, as rounds ripped through the darkness.

Jaeger aimed for the torso. Head shots were fine for a day out on the ranges, but in a live firefight you went for the guts every time. It was the biggest target, and few ever survived a stomach wound.

He swept his weapon across the beach, seeking out the figure of the commander. He saw the village kid struggling to break free, and darting into the safety of the nearby palm grove. Jaeger unleashed a savage burst, and watched the commander turn and run. He saw his tracer fire tearing up the commander's heels and ripping into his torso.

He sensed the fear and indecision ripple through the enemy's ranks as their leader went down, screaming in fear and in the agony of his death throes.

They were like a decapitated snake now.

This was the moment to seize the advantage.

'Mag change!' Jaeger yelled, as he grabbed a full magazine from his former jailer's pocket and rammed it home. 'Go! Go! Go!'

Raff needed no second urging.

In an instant he was on his feet, charging forward, screaming out his war cry, Jaeger hammering out the covering fire. As the dark, fearsome Maori giant tore ahead, Jaeger saw the first of the enemy break and run.

Raff made thirty yards, then sank to his knee, opening up in a barrage of aimed shots. He yelled at Jaeger in turn: 'GOOOOOOOOOO!'

Jaeger rose from the sand, weapon in his shoulder, all his pent-up rage and fury focused into the fight. He sprinted forward, only his eyes and his bared teeth showing white among the dark film of swamp filth that coated him from head to toe, thundering across the open beach, his muzzle spitting fire.

Within moments, the last of President Chambara's soldiers had broken rank and run. Raff and Jaeger chased them through the palm grove with aimed bursts, until not a single enemy figure was visible anywhere.

Seconds later, the dark stretch of sand had fallen silent – apart from the groans of the dying and the wounded.

Wasting no time, the two men sought out the chief's canoe and dragged it towards the surf. The big, thick-skinned dugout was unwieldy on dry land, and it took all their strength to man-handle it into the waves. They were just about to push off when Jaeger signalled Raff to wait.

He scuttled through the waves and crossed the beach to where a figure lay pinned to the blood-soaked sand. He wrestled the wooden stake free, hoisted the wounded man on to his shoulders and returned the way he'd come, dumping the semi-conscious form of his jailer in the centre of the craft.

'Change of plan!' he yelled at Raff, as they ran the vessel deeper into the surf. 'Mojo's coming with us. Plus we head east and due south. Chambara's men will presume we've pushed north, for Cameroon or Nigeria. It'll never cross their minds we've gone the opposite way, back into their country.'

Raff leapt aboard the canoe and reached to help Jaeger. 'Why would we head back into President Chugga's hellhole?'

'We make for the mainland. It's twice the distance, but they'll never think to follow. Plus it isn't Chambara's territory any more, remember? We link up with the coup plotters and take our chances with them.'

Raff grinned. '*Ka mate! Ka mate! Ka ora! Ka ora!* Let's bloody go!'

They paddled the boat further out to sea, Jaeger taking up the chant, and were quickly swallowed by the moon-washed darkness.

5

'Okay, gentlemen, you will be pleased to know you check out. A couple of calls was all it took. Your reputations, it seems, go before you.'

The accent was broad South African, the figure in front of them squat and stocky, with the beefy, bearded red face of a Boer. The physique spoke of a youth spent playing rugby, drinking hard and soldiering in the African bush, before age and gout got the better of him.

But Pieter Boerke wasn't here for the fighting. He was the coup leader, and he had a force of far younger, fitter men to lead the charge.

'You're still planning on taking Bioko?' Jaeger remarked. 'The Wonga coup pretty much never even got started . . .'

Several years back there had been a previous attempt to remove President Chambara from power. It had turned into something of a debacle, earning the derisive nickname 'the Wonga coup'.

Boerke snorted. 'I run a very different operation. This is the Gotcha coup. Chambara's finished. The international community, the oil companies, the people of Bioko – everyone wants him gone. Who wouldn't? The guy is an animal. He eats people – mostly his favourite prisoners.' He eyed Jaeger. 'Bet you're glad you made it out of Black Beach when you did, eh?'

Jaeger smiled. It still hurt to do so, after three days of being battered by tropical storms and washed by sea spray as they crossed the Gulf of Guinea.

'I've got C-130s in-loading weapons as we speak,' Boerke continued, 'flying shuttle runs out of Nigeria. We're building up for the big push. Come to think of it, I could use a couple of extra hands – guys like you who know the lie of the land.' He eyed the two men. 'Fancy joining us?'

Jaeger glanced at Raff. 'According to my big Maori friend here, we've got business back in the UK.'

'Unfortunately,' Raff growled. 'After tasting a little of President Chugga's hospitality, I'd love to go kick his front door in.'

'I bet you would.' Boerke let out a bark of a laugh. 'Last chance, guys. I could use you. Really I could. I mean, you broke out of Black Beach. No one does that. You fought your way off the island with a couple of toothpicks and a bottle opener between you. Made a three-day voyage here by canoe. Like I said, I could use you.'

Jaeger held up his hands. 'Not this time. I'm done with Bioko.'

'Understood.' Boerke got to his feet, a bundle of energy pacing back and forth behind his desk. 'So, I can get you out of here on the next C-130. You hit Nigeria, you'll be slipped aboard a BA flight direct to London, no questions asked. Least I can do for you, after delivering that little shit to us.'

He jerked a thumb over his shoulder. The heavily bandaged form of Major Mojo was slumped in one corner of the room. After three days at sea and the injuries that he'd suffered, the man was barely conscious.

Raff eyed him, contemptuously. 'I'd appreciate it if you could give him the same kind of treatment that he gave my friend here, with interest. That's if he lives.'

Boerke flashed a smile. 'No problem. We got a lot of questions to ask him. And remember, we're South Africans. We don't take prisoners. Now, anything else I can do for you guys before we go our separate ways?'

Jaeger hesitated for an instant. His instinct told him that he could trust the South African, plus they shared the brotherhood of warriors. In any case, if he wanted to get money to Chief Ibrahim, Boerke was about his only option right now.

He pulled a slip of paper from his pocket. 'When you've taken Bioko, can you get this into the hands of the chief of Fernao village? It's a numbered Zurich bank account, complete with access codes. There's a sizeable amount of money in there – what Raff paid Mojo to bust me free. The chief's son died because of us. Money will never bring him back, but maybe it's a start.'

'Consider it done,' Boerke confirmed. 'But one thing. By bringing that shit Mojo here, you did a very good thing. He knows Chambara's defences inside out. If one Bioko child had to die to secure that kind of inside knowledge, that's regretful. Let's hope his death will bring life to many.'

'Maybe. Let's hope so,' Jaeger conceded. 'But he wasn't one of your kids; your star pupil.'

'Trust me, when Chambara's gone, every single kid on Bioko will have a far brighter future. Hell, man, that country should be rich. It has oil, gas, minerals – the lot. Sell off Chambara's yachts, raid his foreign bank accounts – we'll be making a good start. Now, is there anything else?'

'Maybe there is one thing . . .' Jaeger mused. 'You know, I was there for three years. That's a lot of time in a place like Bioko. Long story short, I got digging into the island's history. Second World War. Towards the end of the war, the British launched a top-secret operation to spy on an enemy vessel. The *Duchessa*. A cargo ship anchored in Malabo harbour. We went to extraordinary lengths to do so. Question is, why?'

Boerke shrugged. 'Search me.'

'Apparently the ship's captain had filed a manifest with the Bioko port authorities,' Jaeger continued. 'It was incomplete; it listed six pages of cargo, but the seventh page was missing. Rumour has it the seventh page is secreted in the Malabo Government House vault. I tried everything I could to get hold of it. When you take the capital, maybe you can grab a copy for me?'

Boerke nodded. 'No worries. Leave me email and phone details. But I'm curious. What do you think she was carrying? And why the interest?'

'I got sucked in by all the rumours; kind of grabbed me. Diamonds. Uranium. Gold. That's what they say. Something that could be mined in Africa; something the Nazis needed desperately to help them win the war.'

'Most likely uranium,' Boerke suggested.

'Maybe.' Jaeger shrugged. 'But the seventh page – that would prove it.'

6

The MV *Global Challenger* lay at anchor on the Thames, a heavy sky glowering low and sullen above the masthead. The black taxi that had ferried Raff and Jaeger from Heathrow airport pulled up at the kerb, tyres coming to rest in a grey puddle slick with oil.

It struck Jaeger that the taxi fare was enough to furnish an entire Bioko classroom with books. And when Raff didn't tip the cabbie quite as much as he'd evidently been expecting, he sped off without a word, splashing the puddle over the tops of their shoes.

London in February. Some things never changed.

He'd slept nearly the entirety of the two flights – mainland Equatorial Guinea to Nigeria in a noisy C-130 Hercules cargo aircraft, and then on to London. They'd flown the Lagos to London leg in the absolute lap of luxury, but from experience Jaeger knew that first class came with caveats.

Always.

Someone was footing the bill for those BA flights, and at seven grand a pop it was no small change. When he'd pressed Raff on the subject, the big, easy-going Maori had seemed oddly reticent. Clearly someone wanted Jaeger back in London badly and money was no object, but Raff didn't want to talk about it.

Jaeger figured he was good with that. He trusted the man absolutely.

By the time they'd hit London, Jaeger was starting to feel the cumulative effects of five weeks' incarceration in Black Beach

Prison, plus the battles and escape that had followed. He made his way up the *Global Challenger*'s gangplank, limbs creaking like an old man, just as the heavens opened.

A former Arctic survey ship, the *Global Challenger* was the headquarters of Enduro Adventures, the business that Jaeger had founded upon leaving the military, along with Raff and one other fellow warrior. That man – Stephen Feaney – was standing at the top of the gangplank, half obscured by the falling rain.

He held out a hand in greeting. 'Never thought we'd find you. You look like shit. Seems like it was only just in time.'

'You know how it is.' Jaeger shrugged. 'That big Maori bastard – President Chambara was just about to cook and eat him. Someone had to drag him out of there.'

Raff snorted. 'Like hell!'

There was laughter. The three men shared the briefest of moments as the rain hammered across the open deck.

It was good – sweet – to be back together again.

Soldiering at the elite level always had been a young man's game. Jaeger, Raff and Feaney had been where few others had been and done things few ever imagined possible. It had been the ultimate adventure, but it had taken its toll.

A few years back, they'd decided to quit while they were still ahead. They'd taken their skills learned at the taxpayer's expense and used them to set up their own business. Enduro Adventures – motto: 'Planet Earth is our playground' – was the result.

Jaeger's brainchild, Enduro was an outfit dedicated to taking wealthy individuals – businessmen, sportsmen and a sprinkling of celebrities – on some of the world's most challenging wilderness experiences. Over time, they'd built it into a lucrative concern, attracting big personalities on some of the most incredible adventures planet Earth had to offer.

But then, practically overnight, Jaeger's life had fallen apart and he'd disappeared off the map. He'd become Enduro Adventure's invisible man. Feaney had been forced to take over the money-making side of things, and Raff the business end of expeditioning – although it was neither man's natural milieu.

Jaeger, a captain, was the only former officer among the three of them. Back in the military, he'd commanded D Squadron, a sixty-man SAS unit. He'd worked closely with senior command and could move easily in high-end business circles.

Feaney was older, and he'd come up the hard way through the ranks, ending up serving as Jaeger's sergeant major. As for Raff, his drinking and fighting had always made promotion something of a challenge, not that the big Maori had ever seemed to mind.

The last three years had proven something of a challenge for Enduro Adventures, left bereft of its figurehead. Jaeger knew that a part of Feaney resented him for his Bioko disappearing act. But had the same horror befallen Feaney, Jaeger figured he'd very likely have struggled too. Time and experience had taught him that every man had his breaking point. When Jaeger's had been reached, he'd fled to the last place on earth anyone would ever look for him – Bioko.

7

Feaney led the way inside. The *Global Challenger*'s boardroom was a shrine to adventure, the walls plastered with mementoes from far-flung corners of the earth: the flags of half the world's militaries; badges and berets of elite units few even knew existed; racks of deactivated weaponry, including a gold-plated AK-47 hailing from one of Saddam Hussein's palaces.

But it was also a powerful tribute to the wonders of planet earth: photos of some of the most wild and extreme biomes – bone-dry, wind-blasted desert; ice-blue snow-capped mountains; a charcoal jungle canopy pierced by burning shafts of sunlight – graced the walls, along with scores of photographs of the teams that Enduro Adventures had led into such places.

Feaney rattled the door of the fridge behind the bar. 'Beer?'

Raff grunted. 'After Bioko, I could murder the lot.'

Feaney handed him a bottle. 'Jaeger?'

Jaeger shook his head. 'No thanks. I was dry on Bioko. Not for the first year. But the two after that. One beer, you'll be scraping me off the ceiling.'

He grabbed a water, and the three men settled around one of the low tables. They talked for a while, catching up on all that had gone down in each other's absence, before Jaeger brought the focus back to the heart of the matter – the reason why Raff and Feaney had gone to the ends of the earth to find him, and bring him home.

'So, this new contract – fill me in. I mean, Raff told me some of it, but you know how the Maori is: he can talk a glass eye to sleep.'

Raff plonked down his beer. 'I'm a fighter, not a talker.'

'A drinker, not a lover,' Jaeger echoed.

They laughed.

Three years' absence, and Jaeger had returned a different man from the young warrior-expeditioner who had disappeared. He was darker. Quieter. More closed. Yet at the same time there were occasional flashes of the easy humour and charm that had made him such a fine frontman for Enduro Adventures.

'Well I guess you've figured as much,' Feaney began, 'but the business – Enduro – struggled after you did your—'

'I had my reasons,' Jaeger interjected.

'Mate, I'm not saying you didn't. God knows we all—'

Raff held up a big meaty hand for silence. 'What Feaney's trying to say is – we're all good. The past is the past. And the future – for us lot – it's this shiny new contract. Only, in recent weeks it's become coated in some real evil shit.'

'It has,' Feaney confirmed. 'This is the short version. A month or two back I was contacted by Adam Carson, who you'll remember from his days as Director of Special Forces.'

'Brigadier Adam Carson? Yeah.' Jaeger nodded. 'How long was he with us? Two years? A capable commander, but I never warmed to him much.'

'Me neither,' Feaney agreed. 'Anyhow, after the military, he was headhunted by some media outfit. He's ended up as the MD of a film company name of Wild Dog Media. Not as weird as it may sound: they specialise in remote area filming – expeditions, wildlife, corporates; that kind of thing. Employ a lot of ex-forces types. Perfect kind of people for us to partner with.'

'Sounds like,' Jaeger confirmed.

'Carson had a proposition for us – a lucrative one. An air wreck has been discovered deep in the Amazon. Second World War-era most likely. The Brazilian military found it when doing aerial surveillance along their far western border. Suffice to say, it's in the absolute bloody middle of nowhere. Anyhow, Wild Dog were competing for the opportunity to discover what exactly the wreck might be.'

'It's in Brazil?' Jaeger queried.

'Yeah. Well no, actually. It's kind of parked on the very border – where Brazil, Bolivia and Peru meet. Seems it's got one wing in Bolivia, one wing in Peru, with its arse end halfway towards Copacabana beach. Put it this way: whoever left it there didn't give a shit about international borders.'

'Reminds me of our time in the Regiment,' Jaeger commented drily.

'Doesn't it just. There was a turf war for a while, but the only military with the capacity to do anything about it was the Brazilians – and it was a big ask, even for them. So they sent out feelers to see if an international team could be put together to uncover its secrets.

'Whatever the aircraft is, she's massive,' Feaney continued. 'Carson can brief you more, but suffice to say she's a mystery wrapped inside an enigma inside a . . . or however the saying goes. Carson proposed sending in an expedition to film the entire thing. Big TV event, to be broadcast worldwide. Raised a massive budget. But there were rival offers, and the South Americans were arguing amongst themselves.'

'Too many chiefs . . .' Jaeger ventured.

'Not enough Indians,' Feaney confirmed. 'Talking of which, the region where the wreck lies – it's also home to one very unfriendly Amazon Indian tribe. The Amahuaca, or some such name. Never been contacted. Very happy to stay that way. And keen to loose off arrows and blow-darts at anyone who strays into their domain.'

Jaeger raised one eyebrow. 'Poison-tipped?'

'Don't even ask. As expeditions go, this one's a real peach.' Feaney paused. 'So, now's where you come in. The Brazilians are taking the lead. It's all need-to-know, and they've kept the exact location of the wreck a tight secret, so no one can pull a fast one. But Bolivia is to Brazil what France is to Britain, and let's just say the Peruvians are the Germans. No one trusts anyone on this thing.'

Jaeger smiled. 'We like the former's wine, the latter's cars, but that's about it?'

'You got it.' Feaney took a pull on his beer. 'But Carson's smart. He managed to swing the Brazilians his way, and all down to one thing. You lead the Brazil missions. You trained their anti-narcotics squads – their special forces. Seems you made a real lasting impression, as did Andy Smith, your second-in-command. You they do trust. Absolutely. You know best why.'

Jaeger nodded. 'Is Captain Evandro still with them?'

'Colonel Evandro, as he now is. He's not only still with them, he's Brazil's Director of Special Forces. You pulled some of his best men out of the shit. He's never forgotten. Carson promised that either you or Smith would lead this. Preferably both of you. That swung the colonel our way, and he brought the Bolivians and Peruvians onside.'

'Colonel Evandro's a good man,' Jaeger remarked.

'Seems like. Leastways, he doesn't forget. Hence why Carson – and Enduro – got the gig. Hence why we came looking for you. And seems like we were just in time, by all accounts.' Feaney eyed Jaeger for a moment. 'Anyway, it's a big contract. Several million dollars. Enough to turn Enduro's fortunes around.'

'Sweet.' Jaeger glanced at Feaney. 'Maybe too sweet?'

'Maybe.' Feaney's face darkened. 'Carson set about recruiting a team. International; split male and female – to appeal to the TV side of things. There were scores of volunteers. Carson was inundated. At the same time, we couldn't get the slightest trace on you. So Smithy agreed to head the thing up alone, seeing as though you had . . . well . . . fallen off the edge of the earth.'

Jaeger's expression remained inscrutable. 'Or gone to Bioko to teach English. Depends on how you look at it.'

'Yeah. Anyhow . . .' Feaney shrugged. 'All was set fair for the Amazon; the expedition of a lifetime was green for go; everyone was looking forward to a mind-blowing discovery.'

'Then the TV execs had to put their oar in,' Raff growled. 'Just kept pushing, pushing – the greedy bastards.'

'Raff, mate, Smithy *agreed*,' Feaney protested. 'He agreed it was the smart thing to do.'

Raff went to fetch another beer. 'Still got a bloody good man—'

'We don't know that!' Feaney cut in.

Raff slammed the fridge door. 'Yes we bloody do.'

Jaeger held up his hands. 'Whoa . . . Easy, guys. So, what happened?'

'On one level, Raff's right.' Feaney picked up the thread again. 'The TV people demanded extra; a pre-deployment chapter, if you like. Andy Smith was to take the recruits to the Scottish hills; put them through their paces. Kind of like a mini-SAS selection course: weed out the weaker recruits, and all to be filmed.'

Jaeger nodded. 'So they went to the Scottish hills. What's the issue?'

Feaney glanced at Raff. 'He doesn't know?'

Raff placed his beer down, very deliberately. 'Mate, I pulled him out of Black Beach half dead; we fought our way off Hell Island with two bloody penknives between us; then we battled our way through sharks and tropical storms. You tell me when was the right time?'

Feaney ran a hand across his close-cropped hair. He glanced at Jaeger. 'Smithy led the team to Scotland. It was the West Coast in January. The weather was atrocious. Evil. The police found his body at the bottom of the Loch Iver ravine.'

Jaeger felt his heart miss a beat. *Smithy dead*? He'd had a weird feeling that something bad must have happened, but never this. Not to Smithy. Utterly solid and reliable, Andy Smith was the guy who'd always had his back. Never lost for a wisecrack, no matter how bad the odds, there were few friends that came closer.

'Smithy fell to his death?' Jaeger demanded, incredulous. 'Impossible. The man was bloody indestructible. He was a master on the hills.'

The room fell silent. Feaney stared at his beer bottle, trouble clouding his eyes. 'The cops say his blood alcohol level was way off the scale. They say he drank a bottle of Jack Daniel's, went up on the hills and stumbled to his death in the darkness.'

Jaeger's eyes flashed dangerously. 'Bullshit. Smithy drank even less than I do.'

'Mate, that's exactly what we told them. The police. But they're sticking to their story: death by misadventure, with more than a hint of suicide.'

'Suicide?' Jaeger exploded. 'What in God's name would Smithy have need to kill himself for? Wife and kids like that? Dream mission like this to lead? Come on: *suicide*. Get real. Smithy had everything to live for.'

'You'd best tell him, Feaney.' It was Raff, and his voice was tight with barely suppressed anger. '*Everything*.'

Feaney visibly braced himself for what was coming. 'When Smithy was found, his lungs were half full of water. Cops claim he'd lain all night in the lashing rain and breathed it in. They also claim that the fall killed him pretty much instantly. Clean broke his neck. Well, you can't breathe in water when you're dead. The water had to have got in there whilst he was still alive.'

'So what're you saying?' Jaeger glanced from Feaney to Raff and back again. 'You saying he was *waterboarded*?'

Raff curled his fingers around his beer bottle, knuckles white. 'Lungs half full of water. Dead men don't breathe. Go figure. Plus, there's more.' He glanced at Feaney, the bottle twisting under his tightening grip.

Feaney reached below the table and pulled out a plastic folder. He removed a photo, sliding it across to Jaeger.

'Police gave it to us. We went to the morgue anyway, to double-check. That mark; that symbol – it was carved into Andy's left shoulder.'

Jaeger stared at the image, an icy chill running up his spine. Cut deep into his former second-in-command's skin was a crudely stylised eagle. It was standing on its tail, cruelly hooked beak thrown to its right and wings stretched wide, talons grasping a bizarre circular form.

Feaney reached forward, stabbing a finger at the photo. 'We can't place it. The eagle symbol. Doesn't seem to mean much of anything to anyone. And trust me, we've asked.' He glanced at Jaeger. 'Police argue it's just some arbitrary pseudo-military image. That Smithy did it to himself. Self-harm. Part of the case they're building for suicide.'

Jaeger couldn't speak. He'd barely registered Feaney's words. He was unable to tear his eyes away from that image. Somehow the sight of it eclipsed even the horrors he'd suffered in Black Beach Prison.

The longer he stared at that dark eagle symbol, the more he felt it burn into his brain. It summoned terrible memories hidden deep within him.

It was so alien yet so familiar somehow, and it threatened to drag those long-buried memories back to the surface, kicking and screaming.

8

Jaeger grabbed the heavy bolt-croppers and clambered over the fence. Luckily, the security at east London's Springfield Marina never had been too hot. He'd left Bioko with the clothes he stood up in. He'd certainly had zero time to grab his keys – including those that opened the gates leading into the marina.

Still, it was his boat and he saw no reason why he shouldn't break into his own home.

He'd brought the bolt-croppers at a local store. Before leaving Raff and Feaney he'd asked them – plus Carson, Wild Dog Media's MD – for forty-eight hours. Two days in which to decide if he was up for taking over from where Smithy had left off – leading this seemingly ill-fated expedition into the Amazon.

But despite the time he'd asked for, Jaeger knew he really wasn't kidding anyone. Already, they had him: for so many reasons, he just couldn't refuse.

First off, he owed Raff. The big Maori had saved his life. Unless Pieter Boerke's mercenary forces had liberated Bioko in record time, Jaeger would have perished in Black Beach Prison – his passing unnoticed by a world from which he had so utterly withdrawn.

Second, he owed Andy Smith. And Jaeger didn't leave his friends hanging. Not ever. There was no way Smithy had taken his own life. He intended to triple-check, of course. Just to be absolutely certain. But he sensed that his friend's death had to be linked to that mystery air wreck lying deep in the Amazon. What other reason – *what other motive* – was there?

Jaeger had an instinctive feeling that Smithy's killer was amongst the expedition team. The way to find them had to be to join their number and flush them out from the inside.

Thirdly, there was the aircraft itself. From the little that Adam Carson had been able to tell him over the phone, it had sounded intriguing. Irresistible. Like the Winston Churchill quote Feaney had attempted – it absolutely was a riddle, wrapped in a mystery, inside an enigma.

Jaeger found the draw of it utterly compelling.

No. He was already decided: he was going.

He'd asked for the forty-eight hours for entirely different reasons. There were three visits he intended to make; three investigations to undertake – and he would be doing so without breathing a word to anyone. Maybe the last few years had left him deeply distrustful. Unable to put his faith in anyone any more.

Maybe the three years in Bioko had rendered him something of a loner; too at home with his own company.

But maybe it was also better – *safer* – that way. It was how he would survive.

Jaeger took the path that skirted around the marina, his boots crunching through the slick, rain-soaked gravel. It was late afternoon by now, dusk settling over the marina, cooking smells drifting across the still winter water.

The scene – the brightly painted boats, smoke curling lazily from funnels – was all so out of kilter with the leafless, washed-out February greys of the canal basin. Three long years. Jaeger felt as if he'd been away a lifetime.

He came to a halt at the mooring two before his own. The lights were on in Annie's barge, the old wood-burning stove puffing and smoking wheezily. He climbed aboard, poking his head unannounced through the open hatchway that led into the galley.

'Hi, Annie. It's me. You got my spare keys?'

A face looked up at him, eyes staring fearfully wide. '*Will*?

My God . . . But where on earth . . . We all thought . . . I mean, we were worried that you'd . . .'

'Died?' Jaeger flashed a smile. 'I'm no ghost, Annie. I've been away. Teaching. In Africa. I'm back.'

Annie shook her head, confused. 'My God . . . We knew you were a still-waters-run-deep type. But three years in Africa . . . I mean, one day you were here. The next gone, without a word to anyone.'

There was more than a little injury in Annie's tone, not to mention resentment.

With his grey-blue eyes and dark hair worn longish, Jaeger was handsome in a chiselled, slightly gaunt and wolfish way. There was barely the faintest streak of silver to his head of hair, and he looked younger than his years.

He'd never shared many personal details with the others on the marina – Annie included – but he'd proven to be a reliable and loyal neighbour, not to mention one who was always on the lookout for his fellow boaties. The community prided itself on being close. That was part of what had drawn Jaeger to it; that, plus the promise of having a home base with one foot in the heart of London, the other in the wide-open countryside.

The marina lay on the River Lee, in the Lee Valley which formed a ribbon of green that stretched north into open meadows and rolling hills. Jaeger would return here after a day's work on the *Global Challenger* and pound the riverside paths, running the tension out of his system and some much-needed fitness back in.

He'd never had much need to cook: Annie was forever pressing him with home-made goodies, and he particularly loved her smoothies. Annie Stephenson: single, early thirties, pretty in a skittish, hippyish way – he'd long suspected she had a crush on him. But Jaeger had been resolutely a one-woman man.

Ruth and the boy: they were his life.

Or at least they had been.

Annie – much as she'd proven a wonderful neighbour, and

much as he'd enjoyed teasing her about being such a hippy – had never stood a chance.

She rummaged around and handed him his keys. 'I still can't believe you're back. I mean – it's great to have you back. That's what I mean. You know, Tinker George – he was just about to grab your bike and claim if for himself. Anyhow, the stove's hot.' She smiled. Nervous, but tinged with a hint of hope. 'I'll bake a celebratory cake, shall I?'

Jaeger grinned. He could look so young and boyish on those rare moments when the darkness fell away from him. 'You know something, Annie – I've missed your cooking. But I'm not going to be around for long. Few things I need to get sorted first. Plenty of time for a slice of cake and a catch-up after.'

Jaeger stepped ashore, passing by Tinker George's barge. He allowed himself a wry smile: typical of the cheeky bastard to be eyeing-up his motorbike.

Moments later he climbed aboard his own vessel. He kicked away the piles of fallen leaves and bent at the entrance. The thick security chain and padlock were still very much in place. It was about the last thing he had done – chaining up the barge – before he'd left London, catching a flight to the ends of the earth.

He gripped the chain in the bolt-cropper's jaws, tensed his aching limbs, and snap! – it fell away. He slipped Annie's spare key into the main lock, and pulled open the split doors that gave access to the interior. His was a Thames barge. Wider and deeper than your average narrowboat, they tended to offer the space to indulge in a little luxury.

But not Jaeger's.

The interior was strikingly sparse. Utterly functional. Devoid of all but a few personal effects.

One room formed a makeshift gym. Another a spartan bedroom. There was a tiny kitchen, plus a living area with a few worn rugs and cushions scattered across the wooden floor. But the majority of the interior was given over to desk space, for it was from here that Jaeger preferred to work whenever the hectic commute into head office – the *Global Challenger* – could be avoided.

He didn't linger for long. He grabbed a second set of keys hanging on a nail and stepped outside. Lashed in the prow of the boat and firmly sheeted over was his Triumph Tiger Explorer. The motorbike was an old friend. He'd bought it second-hand to celebrate passing SAS selection a good decade or more ago.

He untied the sheeting and rolled it aside. He bent over a second security chain, cut it, and was just about to straighten up when he detected a faint noise; just the barest hint of a heavy footfall in wet, greasy gravel. In an instant he'd wrapped a loop of the thick chain around his hand, leaving a generous two feet hanging free, the heavy padlock swinging on one end.

He spun around, the makeshift weapon poised like a medieval ball-and-chain.

A giant figure loomed in the darkness. 'Thought I'd find you here.' The eyes flicked down to the chain. 'Figured on a warmer welcome, though.'

Jaeger let the tension drain out of his bunched muscles. 'Fair enough. Brew? I can offer you three-year-old milk and stale tea bags.'

They stepped inside. Raff glanced around the barge. 'Blast from the past, mate.'

'Yeah. We spent some good times here.'

Jaeger busied himself over the kettle, then handed Raff a mug of steaming tea. 'Sugar's hard as rock. Biscuits're soft as shit. Presume you'll take a pass.'

Raff shrugged. 'Tea's good.' He glanced out the open door at the Triumph. 'Planning on taking a spin?'

Jaeger was giving nothing away. 'You know how it is: live to ride.'

Raff delved into his pocket and handed Jaeger a slip of paper.

'Smithy's family – their new address. No point going to the old one. They've moved twice in the past three years.'

Jaeger's face remained an unreadable mask. 'Any particular reason? The moves?'

Raff shrugged. 'He was making good money working for us. For Enduro. He kept upsizing. Needed the extra room. Planning on having another kid, so he said.'

'Not exactly suicidal behaviour.'

'Not exactly. Need a hand with the bike?'

'Yeah, thanks.'

The two men manoeuvred the Triumph across a makeshift gangplank and on to the riverside path. Jaeger could feel that the tyres had gone half flat. They'd need a good burst of air. He returned to the boat and fetched his biking gear. Waterproof Belstaff jacket. Boots. Thick leather gloves. His open-faced helmet. Lastly he grabbed a scarf and an ancient pair of what looked like Second World War flying goggles.

Then he pulled out a drawer, turned it upside down and ripped off the envelope that was taped to the underside. He checked inside: £1,000 in cash, just as he'd left it.

Jaeger pocketed the money, locked up and rejoined Raff. He plugged in an electric compressor and reinflated both tyres. He'd left the bike with a solar charger wired to it. Even in the depths of winter it provided enough of a trickle charge to top up the battery. The engine turned over a few times, then roared into life.

Jaeger wrapped the scarf around his lower face, pulled on his helmet, then dropped the goggles over his eyes. They were special to him. Precious. His grandfather, Ted Jaeger, had worn them during the Second World War when serving with some sneaky-beaky outfit. He'd never spoken much about it, but from the photos that had graced his walls, it was clear that he'd taken his open-topped jeep into a whole lot of remote, battle-torn terrain.

Jaeger often wished he'd asked more about it when Grandpa

Ted was still alive; about what exactly he'd got up to during the war. And after the last few hours, Jaeger found himself regretting not having done so many times over.

He climbed aboard the Triumph, eyeing Raff's empty mug. 'Leave that on the boat, will you.'

'Yep.' Raff hesitated, then reached out a massive paw, placing it on the bike's handlebars. 'Mate, I saw that look in your eyes when you clocked Smithy's photo. Wherever you're going, whatever you're planning – be careful.'

Jaeger stared at Raff for a long moment. But even as he did, his gaze seemed turned inwards. 'I'm always careful.'

Raff tightened his hold on the bars. 'You know what – at some point you've got to start trusting someone. None of us knows what you went through. We wouldn't even pretend to. But we are your mates. Your brothers. Don't ever forget that.'

'I know.' Jaeger paused. 'Forty-eight hours. I'll be back with an answer.'

Then he blipped the throttle, accelerated across the darkened gravel and was gone.

9

Jaeger made only the one stop on the drive west – at a Car-phone Warehouse to pick up a pay-as-you-go smartphone. He'd kept the Explorer at a steady 80 mph on the M3, but it was when he hit the A303 turn-off and the smaller Wiltshire roads that he finally began to immerse himself in the ride.

During the long motorway slog his mind had drifted. Andy Smith. Friends like that didn't come easy. Jaeger could count those he had – Raff included – on the fingers of the one hand. And now there was one fewer, and Jaeger was damned if he wasn't going to find out exactly how and why Smithy had died.

Those Brazilian anti-narcotics training missions had been some of the last on which they had served together. Jaeger had left the military shortly thereafter, to found Enduro Adventures. Smithy had stayed in. He'd argued that he had a wife and three young kids to provide for, and he couldn't risk losing his regular military pay.

It was on their third Brazilian training mission that events had taken an unexpected turn. In theory, Jaeger and his men were there purely to train the Brazilian special forces – the Brigada de Operacoes Especiais; the Brazilian Special Operations Brigade (B-SOB). But over time, bonds had been forged, and they'd come to revile the drugs traffickers – the narco gangs – almost as much as the B-SOB boys did.

When one of Captain Evandro's B-SOB teams had gone missing, Jaeger and his men had taken matters into their own hands. It had become the longest foot patrol in Brazilian special-forces history. Jaeger had led it, with an equal number of B-SOB operators accompanying. They'd located the narco gang's deep jungle hideout, studied it for several days, then launched a blistering assault.

In the ensuing bloodbath, the bad guys had been wiped out. Eight of Captain Evandro's twelve men had been rescued alive – which in the circumstances was a result. But in the process, Jaeger himself had come close to losing his life, and it was Andy Smith's bravery and selfless actions that had saved him.

And like Captain Evandro, Jaeger was not one to forget.

He eased the Explorer down the exit road signposted to Fonthill Bishop. He hit the outskirts of the picture-postcard village of Tisbury and flicked his eyes right, towards a house set a little back from the road. Its windows were lit up a faint yellow – mournful eyes blinking on to a fearful outside world.

The Millside: Jaeger had recognised the address the moment Raff had handed it to him.

Thatched, mossy, cottagey, creepers climbing hither and thither, with its own stream and a decent half-acre of land – Smithy had always had his eye on the place, ever since he'd moved into the area to be closer to his former commander and best friend, Will Jaeger. Evidently he'd finally got the house of his dreams – only Jaeger would have been a good two years into his disappearing act by then.

He pushed onwards out of the village, taking the winding, switchback lane leading towards Tuckingmill and East Hatch. He eased the bike beneath the railway bridge that carried the main line to London – the one he often used to take, when the weather was too cold and wet to countenance the long motorbike ride.

Momentarily his headlight caught the sign for New Wardour Castle. He turned right, pulled up a short length of lane and in through the modest stone gateposts.

His tyres hit the grand sweep of the gravel drive, the ranks of chestnut trees to either side like ghostly sentinels. An imposing country house, Wardour had been purchased as a near wreck by a school friend. Nick Tattershall had made a fortune in the City, using the money to restore New Wardour Castle to its former glory.

He'd split it into several apartments, keeping the largest for himself. But just as the work was nearing completion, Britain had hit one of her cyclical recessions and the property market had tanked. Tattershall had risked losing everything.

Jaeger had stepped in and purchased the first – still to be completed – apartment, his vote of confidence luring other buyers in. He'd got it at a knock-down price, so acquiring a piece of real estate the likes of which he could never normally have afforded.

In time, it had proven the perfect family home.

Set in the heart of a beautiful, sweeping expanse of parkland, it was utterly private and peaceful – yet only a couple of hours' ride or train journey from London. Jaeger had managed to split work between here, the Thames barge and the *Global Endeavour*, never spending long away from the family.

He parked the bike in front of the imposing limestone facade. He slipped his key into the communal lock, stepped across the cool, marbled entranceway and made for the staircase. But even as he took the first of the stone steps, his legs felt weighed down with bittersweet memories.

So many good times had been had here.

So much happiness.

How could it all have gone so wrong?

He paused at the door to his apartment. He knew what awaited. He steeled himself, turned the key in the lock and stepped inside.

He flicked on the lights. Most of the furniture had been covered with dust sheets, but once a week his faithful cleaner, Mrs Sampson, came to dust and to hoover, and the place was scrupulously clean.

Jaeger paused for an instant. Right before him on the wall was a massive painting – a striking orange-fronted bird: the rufous-bellied thrush, one of the national symbols of Brazil. Painted by a well-known Brazilian artist, it had been a gift from Captain Evandro – his way of saying a very special thank you.

Jaeger loved the painting. It was why he'd placed it on the wall opposite the entrance, so it was the first thing you saw as you walked in.

When he'd left for Bioko, he'd asked Mrs Sampson not to sheet it over. He didn't quite know why. Maybe he'd expected to be back sooner, and he'd wanted to know that the bird would be there, as always, waiting to greet him.

He turned left and stepped into the wide expanse of the living room. No point in throwing open the massive wooden shutters; it had long been dark outside. He flicked on the lights, and his eyes came to rest upon the indistinct form of the writing desk pushed against one wall.

He stepped towards it and very gently pulled the dust sheet aside.

He reached out with one hand, his fingers touching the face of the beautiful woman in the photo frame. His fingertips lingered, momentarily frozen to the glass. He sank to his haunches, until his eyes were level with the desk.

'I'm back, Ruth,' he whispered. 'Three long years, but I'm back.'

He let his fingers drift down the glass, coming to rest upon the features of a young boy, standing somehow protectively at his mother's side. Both were dressed in 'Save the Rhino' T-shirts; they'd purchased them on a family holiday to East Africa's Amboseli National Park. Jaeger would never forget the midnight walking safari the three of them had taken, along with their Masai guides. They'd trekked across the moonlit savannah amongst herds of giraffe, wildebeest and, best of all, rhinos, the family's favourite animal.

'Luke – Daddy's back . . .' Jaeger murmured. 'And God only knows how much I've missed you guys.'

He paused, a heavy silence echoing off the walls. 'But, you

know – there's never been the slightest hint; not the vaguest proof of life. If you could just have sent me something; the barest sense of a sign. Anything. Smithy kept watch. He was eyes-on. Always. He promised to let me know.'

He picked up the photo and cradled it. 'I went to the ends of the earth to try to find you. I'd have gone to the ends of the universe, even. Nowhere would have been too far. But for three long years there's been nothing.'

He ran a hand across his face, as if brushing away the pain of those long missing years. When it came away, his eyes were damp with tears.

'And I guess if we're honest – if we're truthful with each other – maybe it's time. Time to say a proper goodbye . . . time to accept that you really are . . . gone.'

Jaeger bowed his head. His lips brushed the photograph. He kissed the woman's face. Kissed that of his son. Then he placed the picture back on the desk, laying it gently on the dust sheet.

Face up, so he could see both of them, and remember.

10

Jaeger padded across the living room to the far side, where double doors opened on to what they'd dubbed the music room. One wall was shelved high with racks of CDs. He chose one – Mozart's Requiem. He slipped it into the CD deck, flicked the power switch and it started to play.

The lilting melodies brought everything flooding back; all the family memories. For the second time in as many minutes, Jaeger found himself having to fight back the tears. He couldn't allow himself to break down; to properly grieve. Not yet.

There was something else – something deeply, deeply troubling – that he had come here for.

He dragged the battered steel trunk out from its place beneath the music stand. For a moment his eyes lingered on the initials stencilled on the lid: W. E. J. – William Edward 'Ted' Jaeger. His grandfather's war chest, which he'd gifted to Jaeger shortly before he died.

As the Requiem swelled to a first crashing crescendo, Jaeger thought back over the times Grandpa Ted had sneaked him into his study, allowing Jaeger to share a pull on his tobacco pipe, and enjoy a few precious moments – grandfather with grandchild – rifling through this very trunk.

Grandpa Ted's pipe, eternally clamped between his teeth. The smell: Player's Navy Cut and whisky-steeped tobacco. Jaeger could almost see the scene now – the occasional smoke ring blown by his grandfather dancing soft and ethereal in the light of his desk lamp.

Jaeger flicked open the clasps and hinged back the trunk's heavy lid. On top lay one of his favourite mementoes: a leather-bound file, stamped in faded red lettering: *TOP SECRET*. And below that: *Officer Commanding No. 206 Liaison Unit*.

It had always struck Jaeger as odd that the contents of the file had never quite lived up to the promise of the cover.

Inside were booklets of Second World War radio frequencies and codes, diagrams of main battle tanks, blueprints of turbines, compasses and engines. It had proven utterly fascinating to a child; but as an adult, Jaeger had realised that there was nothing in there with much relevance to the file's cover, or warranting such excessive secrecy.

It was almost as if his grandpa had put together the file's contents to fascinate and entertain an adolescent boy, but to give nothing of any sensitivity – of any real value – away.

After his grandpa's death, Jaeger had tried to research the No. 206 Liaison Unit, to better trace its history. But there was nothing. The National Archives; the Imperial War Museum; the Admiralty: every archive that should have contained some form of record – if only a war diary – was devoid of any mention.

It was almost as if the No. 206 Liaison Unit had never existed; as if it were a ghost squadron.

And then he'd found something.

Or rather, Luke had.

His eight-year-old son had proven equally fascinated by the contents of the trunk – his great-grandpa's heavy commando knife; his much-lived-in beret; his battered iron compass. And one day Jaeger's son's hands had dug deep, to the very bottom of the trunk, and found what had been for so long hidden.

Working feverishly, Jaeger did similarly now, emptying the contents on to the floor. There was so much Nazi memorabilia in there: an SS Death's Head badge, skull fixed in an enigmatic smile; a Hitler Youth dagger, its hilt displaying a picture of the Führer; a necktie of the Werewolves – the diehard Nazi resistance set up to fight on after the war proper had been lost.

Occasionally Jaeger had wondered if his grandfather had grown too close to the Nazi regime, so much of its memorabilia had he seemingly hoarded. Whatever he had done during the war, had it somehow brought him perilously close to the evil and the darkness? Had it seeped into him, making him its own?

Jaeger didn't believe so, but he'd never been able to have those kind of conversations before his grandfather had unexpectedly passed away.

He paused at a distinctive-looking book, one that he'd almost forgotten was in the trunk. It was a rare copy of the Voynich manuscript, a richly illustrated medieval text written entirely in a mystery language. Strangely, that book had permanently graced the desk in his grandfather's study, and it had come to Jaeger along with the trunk's contents.

It was another of the things that he had never got to raise with his grandfather: why this fascination with an obscure and unintelligible medieval manuscript?

Jaeger removed the heavy book, revealing the false wooden bottom built into the trunk. He'd never worked out if his grandfather had left the document in there by accident, or if he had done so deliberately, hoping that his grandson would one day find the concealed compartment.

Either way, it had been there, hidden amongst a bunch of war mementoes, waiting three decades or more to be discovered.

Jaeger's fingers delved below the wooden boards, found the latch to the compartment and flicked it open. He felt around and pulled out the fat, yellowing envelope, holding it before him with hands that were visibly shaking. A part of him absolutely did not want to look inside, but a greater part knew that he had to.

He pulled out the document.

Typeset, stapled along one side, it was just as he had remembered it. Across the top of the cover in the thick gothic script synonymous with Hitler's Nazi regime was one word, in capitals: *KRIEGSENTSCHEIDEND*

Jaeger's German was practically non-existent, but via a German–English dictionary he'd managed to translate the few words on the document's cover. *Kriegsentscheidend* was the highest security classification ever awarded by the Nazis. The nearest British equivalent would be 'Beyond Top Secret – Ultra'.

Below that was typed: *Aktion Werwolf* – 'Operation Werewolf'.

Below that again, a date, which needed no translation: 12 February 1945.

And finally, *Nur fur Augen Sicherheitsdienst Standortwechsel Kommando* – 'For Sicherheitsdienst Standortwechsel Kommando eyes only'.

The Sicherheitsdienst was the security service of the SS and the Nazi party – the apex of evil. Standortwechsel Kommando translated as 'the Relocation Commando', which meant practically nothing to Jaeger. He'd googled both mystery references, 'Operation Werewolf' and 'Relocation Commando', in English and in German.

They had turned up nothing.

Not one single reference out there anywhere in the ether.

That was about as far as his investigatory efforts had got, for the darkness – and his flight to Bioko – had descended shortly thereafter. But it was clearly a document that had been of extremely high sensitivity at the time of the war, one that had somehow fallen into his grandfather's hands.

Yet it was the page that followed which had triggered Jaeger's memories, drawing him from London to Wiltshire, back to his – largely abandoned – family home.

He turned the cover with a heavy sense of foreboding.

Looking up at him from the title page was a stark image stamped in black. Jaeger stared at it, his mind reeling. Just as he'd feared, his memory hadn't lied or played tricks on him.

The dark image was that of a stylised eagle standing on its tail, wings outstretched below a cruelly curved beak – its talons gripping a circular symbol etched with unreadable markings.

11

Jaeger sat at his kitchen table, his gaze turned inwards.

Before him were ranged three photographs: one, that of Andy Smith's body, eagle symbol carved deep and bloody into his left shoulder; two, a photo that Jaeger had taken on his smartphone of the eagle symbol on the inside cover of the Operation Werewolf document.

And the third – the photo of his wife and child.

During his time in the military, Jaeger hadn't exactly been the marrying type. A long and happy marriage and a life in special forces didn't often go together. Every month was a new mission – pitting himself against a sun-blasted desert, a sweaty jungle or an ice-clad mountain. There had been little time for prolonged romances.

But then the accident had happened. During a high-altitude freefall jump over the African savannah, Jaeger's 'chute had malfunctioned. He was lucky to have survived. He'd spent months in hospital with a broken back, and though he'd fought his way back to physical fitness, his days in the SAS had been numbered.

It was during that time – the long year's recovery – that he'd first met Ruth. They were introduced via a mutual friend and at first they hadn't got along at all well. Ruth, six years his junior, a university graduate and a diehard wildlife and environmental campaigner, had assumed Jaeger to be her polar opposite.

As for Jaeger, he'd presumed a tree-hugging type like her would despise an elite soldier like him. It was down to a mixture of his razor-sharp, teasing humour and her feisty attitude, coupled with her striking good looks, that they'd gradually grown to appreciate each other . . . and eventually to fall in love.

Over time they'd realised they shared a common bond – a burning love of all things wild.

Ruth was three months pregnant with Luke on the day of their wedding, at which Andy Smith had been best man. And via Luke's birth and the months and years that followed, they'd experienced the miracle of having brought a mini version of their two selves into this world.

Every day with Luke and Ruth had been a wonderful challenge and an adventure, which made the void of their dark loss all the more impossible to bear.

For close to an hour Jaeger stared at those three images – a mouldering yellow Nazi document and a police photo of an alleged suicide victim, both displaying that same eagle symbol; and the photo of Ruth and Luke – trying to fathom the connection that lay between them. There was a feeling he couldn't shake that somehow that eagle symbol was linked to the death – no: the *disappearance* – of his wife and child.

In some unknowable way – some way that he couldn't for the life of him seem to grasp – there was a disturbing sensation of cause and effect here. Call it a soldier's sixth sense, but he'd learned to trust that inner voice of his over the years. Or maybe this was all complete bullshit. Maybe three years in Bioko and five weeks in Black Beach Prison had finally got the better of him, the paranoia eating into him like a dark and corrosive acid, rotting his mind.

Jaeger had almost no recollection of the night his wife and son had been ripped out of his life. It had been a still winter's evening, one of a crisp, breathtaking serenity and beauty. They'd been camped out on the Welsh hills, the sweep of the starlit sky wide and wild above them. It was the kind of place where Jaeger had been at his happiest.

The fire had died to ashes and the last conscious thought

Jaeger had had was of crawling into the tent, zipping together the sleeping bags, and his wife and son wrapping close to him for warmth. He'd been left half dead himself – the tent pumped full of a toxic gas that had rendered him utterly defenceless – so the lack of any further recollection was hardly surprising. And by the time he'd come to, he was lying in intensive care, his wife and child many days gone.

Yet what he couldn't fathom – what terrified him – was the way in which that eagle symbol seemed to dig into those long-buried memories.

The army shrinks had warned him that the memories would be in there somewhere. That one day they would very likely start to resurface, like driftwood washed ashore by a storm-lashed sea.

But why was it this – this dark eagle symbol – that threatened to reach so deep and drag them back to the light?

12

Jaeger had spent the night alone in the apartment.

He'd had the dream again; the one that had for so long haunted him after Ruth and Luke had disappeared. As always, it had taken him right up until the moment of their being snatched away from him – the images crisp and clear as if it were only yesterday.

But the instant the dark terror struck, he'd woken, moaning, in a tangle of sweat-soaked sheets. It tortured him – this inability to go there, to remember, even in the comparative safety of his own dreams.

He was up early.

He grabbed a pair of running shoes from the wardrobe, and set out to pound the frost-kissed fields. He headed south, following an easy slope that led across a shallow valley, crowned by the woodland of Grove Coppice on the far side. He hit the track that steered a wide loop through the trees, and upped his pace, settling into a familiar ground-eating rhythm.

This had always been his favourite part of the circuit – the thick wood shielding him from prying eyes, the tall ranks of pines deadening any sound of his passing. He let his mind settle into the beat of the run; let the meditative pulse of his footfalls quieten his troubled consciousness.

By the time he burst into the sunlight once more, at the northern end of Pheasant's Copse, he knew exactly what he had to do.

Back at Wardour Castle, he showered quickly, then powered

up his desktop. He sent a quick message to Captain – now Colonel – Evandro, hoping that his email address remained the same. After the usual niceties, he popped the question: who were the other parties that had bid against Wild Dog Media to undertake the coming expedition?

In Jaeger's mind, if there were people out there with a motive to murder Andy Smith, surely the rival bidders had to be first amongst them.

That done, he gathered up the precious photo of his wife and child, replaced the secret papers in their hiding place in Grandpa Ted's war chest, locked the apartment and fired up the Triumph. He took a leisurely ride down Hazeledon Lane; it was early and he had time to kill.

He parked at Tisbury's Beckett Street Delicatessen. It was nine o'clock, and they were just opening for business. He ordered poached eggs, hickory-smoked bacon and black coffee. As he waited for the food, his eye was drawn to the newspaper rack. The headline across the nearest paper read: *Central African coup: President Chambara of Equatorial Guinea captured.*

Jaeger grabbed it and flicked his eyes over the story, relishing the news along with the excellent breakfast.

Pieter Boerke had been bang on: his Gotcha coup had delivered all that he had promised. Boerke had somehow managed to ferry his men across the Gulf of Guinea during the height of a tropical storm. He'd chosen to do so deliberately, for local intelligence – most likely Major Mojo's – had suggested that Chambara's forces would be stood down due to the appalling weather.

Boerke's men had struck from out of a howling, rain-lashed devil of a night. Chambara's guards had been taken by utter surprise, their resistance fast crumbling. The President had been caught as he tried to flee the country in his private jet, at Bioko airport.

Jaeger smiled. Maybe he would be getting the seventh page

of the *Duchessa*'s manifest, after all – not that it particularly seemed to matter now.

Fifteen minutes later, he pressed a finger on to a doorbell. He'd left the Triumph in the village and walked up the hill, having first phoned through a warning to Dulce that he was coming.

Dulce. *Sweet*. Smith's wife had certainly proven true to her name.

Smith had met her in Brazil, during their second training mission, Dulce being a distant cousin of Colonel Evandro. Marriage had followed a whirlwind romance, and Jaeger couldn't say that he blamed Smithy for grabbing his girl.

Five foot nine; dark, smouldering eyes and burnished skin – Dulce was smoking hot. She was also the perfect marriage material, as Jaeger had made clear in his best man's speech, while at the same time gently reminding Dulce of Smithy's bad habits but enduring loyalty.

The door to the Millside opened. Dulce stood there, striking as ever, a brave smile on her shadowed features. But there was no hiding the grief that lay raw and fresh just below the surface. Jaeger handed her the hamper that he'd purchased from the delicatessen, plus a hastily scribbled card.

She made coffee, while Jaeger filled her in on the short version of his three missing years. He'd maintained contact with her husband, of course, but it had been mostly one-way – Smithy reporting by email that nothing had been heard of Jaeger's missing wife and child.

The deal Jaeger had cut with his closest friend was that his whereabouts would remain a closely guarded secret until he chose otherwise. There had been one caveat: if Smithy died or was otherwise incapacitated, his lawyer would release details of Jaeger's whereabouts.

Jaeger figured that was how Raff and Feaney had found him, but he hadn't troubled to ask. With Smithy dead, it was all pretty much an irrelevance now.

'Was there anything?' Jaeger asked, as the two of them shared some of Dulce's *pasteis de nata*, a Brazilian delicacy, across the kitchen table. 'Anything that might have suggested he was unhappy? That he'd take his own life?'

'But of course not!' Dulce's eyes flashed with a spark of Latino anger. She always had had a fiery side. 'How can you ask? We were happy. He was so happy. No. Andy would never have done what they say he did. It is just not possible.'

'No money worries?' Jaeger probed. 'No grief with the kids at school? Help me here. I'm floundering around trying to find something.'

She shrugged. 'There is nothing.'

'He wasn't drinking? He'd not hit the bottle?'

'Jaeger, he's gone. And no, *amigo*, he wasn't drinking.'

Her eyes met his. Pained. Smoky. Storm-laden.

'He had a mark,' Jaeger ventured. 'Kind of like a tattoo. On his left shoulder?'

'What mark?' Dulce looked blank. 'He had nothing. I would know.'

Jaeger realised then that the police hadn't shown her the photo of the dark eagle carved into her husband's shoulder. He didn't exactly blame them. It was already traumatic enough for her; she didn't need to be confronted with the full gory details.

He moved swiftly on. 'This expedition into the Amazon, how was he about it? Any trouble with the team? With Carson? The film company? Anything?'

'You know how he was about the jungle: he loved it. He was so excited.' A pause. 'There was maybe one thing. It troubled me more than it did him. We used to joke about it. I met the team. There was this woman. A Russian. Irina. Irina Narov. Blonde. She thinks she is the world's most beautiful woman. We didn't hit it off.'

'Go on,' Jaeger prompted.

She reflected for a moment. 'It was almost as if she thought she was the natural-born leader; that she was better than him. Like she wanted to take it – take the expedition – away from him.'

Jaeger made a mental note to get some deep background checks made on Irina Narov. He'd never heard of someone committing murder for such tenuous a reason. But hell, a lot was arguably at stake here: with global TV exposure, the promise of international fame and the potential fortune to follow.

Maybe there was a motive after all.

Jaeger pressed north, the Triumph eating up the miles.

Somehow, oddly, the visit to Dulce had settled him. It had confirmed what he'd known in his heart – that all had been good in Andy Smith's life. He hadn't killed himself; he'd been killed. Now to trace the murderers.

He'd left Dulce promising that if she or the kids needed anything – *anything* – she only had to call.

It was a long drive from Tisbury to the Scottish borders.

Jaeger had never quite understood why his great-uncle Joe had chosen to move there, so far from friends and family. He'd always felt that the man was hiding, but from what exactly he didn't know. Buccleuch Fell, east of Langholm, lying below Hellmoor Loch – you could hardly find a more remote and tucked-away location and still be on planet earth.

The Triumph was a hybrid road/off-road bike. By the time Jaeger turned on to the track that led up to Uncle Joe's Cabin, as they'd always called it, he was very glad of it, too. He hit the first dusting of snow, and as the track climbed higher so the conditions worsened.

Lying between Mossbrae Height and Law Kneis – each a 1,500-foot peak – the cabin nestled in a rare clearing in a vast expanse of forest, at close to a thousand feet. Jaeger could tell from the thick layer of snow that no one had driven this way for many a day now.

He had a box of groceries strapped to the bike's rack – milk, eggs, bacon, sausages, porridge oats, bread. He'd done a pit stop at Westmorland services, one of the last before he'd turned off the M6. By the time he pulled into Great Uncle Joe's clearing, he was using both his feet to stabilise the bike, as it slewed through humped snowdrifts a foot deep or more.

In the summer, this place was something close to paradise. Jaeger, Ruth and Luke had found it hard to keep away.

But in the long months of the winter . . .

Three decades back, Great Uncle Joe had bought this land off the Forestry Commission. He'd built the cabin pretty much single-handedly – though it was far too sumptuous to warrant the name. He'd diverted a stream on to the land, and excavated a series of small lakes, one cascading into the other. All around had been landscaped into an eco-paradise, complete with shaded corners for growing vegetables.

With solar panels and a wood-burning stove, plus wind-generated power, it was close to self-sufficient. There was no phone and no mobile signal, so Jaeger hadn't been able to call through in advance. A thick stream of white smoke billowed from the steel chimney pipe that ran up the side of the cabin; the firewood came free from the forest, and generally the cabin stayed toasty.

At ninety-five years of age, Great Uncle Joe had need of the warmth, especially when the weather turned as bad as it had now.

Jaeger parked up, crunched through the snowdrifts and hammered on the door. He had to knock a good few times before a voice could be heard from inside.

'All right, all right!' There was the sound of the door being unbolted and then it swung wide.

A pair of eyes peered out from beneath a mop of snowy-white hair. Beady, shining, full of life, they seemed to have lost none of their sharpness over the intervening years.

Jaeger held out the box of groceries. 'I thought you might be needing these.'

Great Uncle Joe stared at him from under craggy brows. Since Grandpa Ted's death, Uncle Joe, as Jaeger called him, had taken on the role of honorary grandpa, and very good at it he'd proven too. The two of them were close.

Uncle Joe's eyes lit up as he recognised the unexpected visitor. 'Will, my boy! Needless to say, we weren't expecting you . . . But in. In. Come in. Get out of those wet things and I'll put the tea on. Ethel's out. Gone for a stroll in the snow. Eighty-three and still going on sixteen.'

It was typical Uncle Joe.

Jaeger hadn't seen him for pushing four years. He'd sent the odd postcard from Bioko, but with precious little news; just to let them know that he was still alive. And now here he was, unannounced, on their doorstep, and Joe had taken it firmly in his stride.

Just another day on Buccleuch Moor.

For a while they did the necessary; exchanging respective news. Jaeger related the story of his time in Bioko, made short. Great Uncle Joe told of the last four years in Buccleuch – no great changes there. Then Joe asked about Ruth and Luke. He didn't feel able not to, although he knew in his heart of hearts that if Jaeger had heard anything, he'd have been amongst the first to know.

Jaeger confirmed that their disappearance was as much of a mystery now as ever it had been.

The catching-up done, Joe fixed Jaeger with one of his looks – half steely inquisition, half light-hearted teasing. 'So, don't try telling me you rode all this way in the depths of winter just to bring an old man some groceries – much that they are appreciated. What're you really here for?'

In answer, Jaeger reached inside his Belstaff jacket and pulled out his phone. He flipped through to the photo of the eagle symbol – the one displayed on the Operation Werewolf document.

He laid it in front of Joe on the kitchen table.

'Forgive the new-fangled technology, but does that image mean anything to you?'

Great Uncle Joe fiddled around in his cardigan pocket. 'I'll need my glasses.'

He picked up the phone at arm's length, and angled it this way and that. He was clearly unfamiliar with the technology, but as his eyes made out the image, a change came over him as dramatic as it was unexpected.

In a matter of moments the colour had drained from his face completely. He'd turned as white as a ghost. His hand shaking, he slowly set the phone down on the table. When he glanced up, there was a look in his eyes that Jaeger had never seen before, and never expected to see, for that matter.

Fear.

13

'I . . . I half expected . . . I always feared . . .' Great Uncle Joe gasped, gesturing towards the sink for some water.

Jaeger hurried to fetch some.

The old man took it in a hand that was trembling, and drank, spilling half of it across the kitchen table. When his eyes met Jaeger's again, all life seemed to have been sucked out of them. He glanced around the room, almost as if the place was haunted; as if he was trying to remember where he was, to anchor himself in the here and now, the present.

'Where in the name of God did you get it?' he whispered, gesturing at the image on the phone. 'No, no – don't answer! I *dreaded* that this day might come. But I'd never imagined it would come through you, my boy, and after all you have suffered . . .'

His eyes drifted to some distant corner of the room.

Jaeger didn't know quite what to say. The last thing he'd ever wanted was to cause this dear old man any discomfort; any distress. What right did Jaeger have to do so in the twilight of Joe's years?

Great Uncle Joe shook himself out of his reverie. 'My boy, you'd best come into the study. I'd not like Ethel to overhear any of . . . well, of this. In spite of her forays into the snow, she's not as robust as she once was. We none of us are.'

He levered himself to his feet, gesturing at the glass. 'Can you manage my water?'

He turned towards his study, and as he led the way, he

appeared as Jaeger had never seen him before. He was stooped – almost bent double – as if he had all the world's troubles piled upon his shoulders.

Great Uncle Joe sighed deeply, the sound like a dry wind rustling through the mountains. 'You know, we thought we could go with our secrets to the grave. Your grandfather. Me. The others. Honourable men; men who knew – who understood – the code. Soldiers all – who knew what was expected of us.'

They'd locked themselves away in his study, whereupon Great Uncle Joe had asked to know everything – every minute detail; every happening – that had led up to the present moment. Once Jaeger had finished talking the old man had remained quiet, entombed in his thoughts.

When finally he had broken his silence, it was almost as if he was holding a conversation with himself, or with others in the room – the ghosts of those who had long passed away.

'We thought – we had hoped – the evil was gone,' he whispered. 'That we could each go to our final resting place with our souls at peace, our consciences clear. We imagined that we had done enough, all those years ago.'

They were sitting in a pair of worn and comfy leather armchairs half facing each other, the walls around them hung with mementoes of the war. Black and white photos of Great Uncle Joe in uniform; tattered flags; iconic insignia; his commando fighting knife; his battered beige beret.

There were only a few exceptions to the war theme. Joe and Ethel had never had any children. Jaeger, Ruth and Luke – they had been the adopted family. A few photos – mostly of Jaeger and his family holidaying at the cabin – cluttered the desk, along with a distinctive-looking book, one that seemed so out of place amongst the war memorabilia.

It was a second copy of the Voynich manuscript, seemingly identical to the one that lay in Grandfather Ted's war chest.

'And then this boy comes here, this precious boy,' Great

Uncle Joe continued, 'with . . . with that. *Ein Reichsadler*!' The last words were spat out with vehemence, as the old man's gaze fixed upon Jaeger's phone. 'That damn cursed damnation! From what the boy says, it seems as if the evil has returned . . . In which case, am I empowered to break the silence?'

He let the question hang in the air. The thickly insulated walls of the cabin tended to deaden any sound, yet still the room seemed to resonate with a dark warning.

'Uncle Joe, I haven't come to pry—' Jaeger began, but the old man held up a hand for silence.

With a visible effort he seemed to drag his focus back to the present. 'My boy, I don't think I can tell you everything,' he murmured. 'Your grandfather, for one, would never have countenanced it. Not unless the circumstances were utterly desperate. But you deserve to know *something*. Ask me questions. You must have come here with questions. Ask, and I will see what I can tell.'

Jaeger nodded. 'What did you and Grandpa do during the war? I did ask when he was alive, but he never volunteered much. What did you do that meant he ended up with documents like that,' he gestured at the phone, 'in his possession?'

'To understand what we did in the war you must first understand what we were up against,' Great Uncle Joe began quietly. 'Too many years have passed; too much has been forgotten. Hitler's message was simple, and it was terrifying.

'Remember Hitler's slogan: *Denn heute gehort uns Deutschland, und morgen die ganze Welt*. Today Germany belongs to us: tomorrow, the entire world. The One Thousand Year Reich was to be truly a global empire. It was to follow the model of the Roman Empire, with Berlin renamed Germania and serving as the capital of the entire world.

'Hitler argued that the Germans were the Aryan master race, the Übermensch. They would employ *Rassenhygiene* – racial hygiene – to cleanse Germany of the *Untermensch* – the subhumans – after which they would be invincible. The *Untermensch* were to be exploited, enslaved and killed off with impunity. Eight, ten, twelve million – no one knows for sure how many were exterminated.

'We tend to think of it as the Jews only,' Great Uncle Joe continued. 'It was not: it was anyone who was not of the master race. *Mischlings* – half Jews or mixed race. Homosexuals; communists; intellectuals; non-whites – and that included Poles, Russians, southern Europeans, Asians . . . The *Einsatzgruppen* – the SS death squads – set about exterminating them all.

'And then there were the *Lebensunwertes Leben* – the "life unworthy of life" – the disabled and the mentally ill. Under Aktion T4, the Nazis began to kill *them*, too. Imagine it! *The disabled*. Killing off the most vulnerable in society. And you know the means they employed to do so – they collected the *Lebensunwertes Leben* in a special bus upon some excuse or other, and drove them around the city pumping in exhaust fumes as they gazed out of the windows.'

The old man glanced at Jaeger, a haunted look etched across his features. 'Your grandfather and I, we saw so very much of it with our own eyes.'

He took a sip of his water. Made a visible effort to collect himself. 'But it wasn't just about extermination. Above the gates of the concentration camps they displayed a slogan: *Arbeit macht frei* – work makes you free. Well, of course, nothing could have been further from the truth. Hitler's Reich was a *Zwangswirtschaft* – a forced-labour economy. In the *Untermensch* he had a vast army of slave labourers, and they were worked to death in their millions.

'And you know the worst of it?' he whispered. '*It worked*. In Hitler's terms at least, the plan worked. The results spoke for themselves. Extraordinary rocketry; cutting-edge guided missiles; cruise missiles; super-advanced aeronautics; jet-powered flying wings; stealth submarines; unheard-of chemical and biological weapons; night-vision equipment – in almost every field the Germans scored a string of firsts. They were light years ahead of us.

'Hitler had an absolutely fanatical belief in technology,' he continued. 'Remember – with the V-2 they were the first to put a rocket into space; not the Russians, as is commonly believed today. Hitler truly thought that technology would win them the war. And trust me – bar the nuclear race, which we won more by dint of luck than design – by 1945 it almost had done.

'Take the XXI stealth submarine. It was decades ahead of its time. By as late as the seventies we were still trying to copy and equal its design. With three hundred XXI U-boats, they could have thrown a stranglehold around Britain and forced us into surrender. By the end of the war, Hitler had a fleet of a hundred and sixty ready to prowl the seas.

'Or take the V-7 rocket. It made the V-2 look like a child's toy. It had a range of three thousand miles, and weaponised with one of their secret nerve agents – sarin or tabun – it could drop death from the skies on all our major cities.

'Trust me, William, they came that close – if not to winning the war, to achieving their *Tausendjahriges Reich*, then at least to forcing the Allies to sue for peace. And if we had done, it would have meant that Hitler – Nazism; this ultimate evil – would have survived. For that was all he and his core group of fanatics cared about – safeguarding their *Drittes Reich*, to rule for a thousand years. They came that close . . .'

The old man sighed wearily. 'And in so many ways it was our job – your grandfather's and mine – to try to put a stop to them.'

14

Great Uncle Joe reached into his desk drawer and rummaged around. He pulled something out, unwrapped the tissue paper and handed it to Jaeger. 'The original badge of the SAS. A white dagger; *WHO DARES WINS* beneath it. It was worn with our parachutist's wings, which together became the famous winged dagger of today's unit.

'As you've no doubt surmised, your grandfather and I served in the SAS. We soldiered in North Africa, the eastern Mediterranean and finally in southern Europe. There's nothing so revelatory about that. But understand, my boy, that our generation just didn't speak about such things. That's why we kept our unit insignias – and our war stories – tucked away and hidden.

'It was in the autumn of 1944, in northern Italy, that we were both injured,' he continued. 'A behind-enemy-lines operation; an ambush, a bloody firefight. We were evacuated to hospital, first in Egypt and then to London. You can imagine – neither of us was much inclined to take it easy recuperating. When the opportunity arose to volunteer for a top-secret unit – well, we jumped at the chance.'

Great Uncle Joe glanced at Jaeger, uncertainty clouding his eyes. 'Your grandfather and I were sworn to secrecy. But . . . well, in light of all this . . .' He waved a hand at Jaeger, the phone. 'Your grandfather was more senior in rank; by then he'd been promoted to colonel. In January 1945 he was appointed Commanding Officer, Target Force. I became one of his staff officers.

'Make no mistake, my boy, I've never spoken about this before. Not even to Ethel.' The old man took a moment to collect himself. 'Target Force was one of the most secretive units ever formed. That's why you've doubtless never heard of us. We had a very specific mission. We were charged to hunt down the Nazis' foremost secrets: their war technology; their *Wunderwaffe* – their extraordinarily advanced war machines; plus their top scientists.'

Now that the old man had started, he didn't seem to want to stop. The words tumbled from his lips, as if he was desperate to unburden himself of the memories; the secrets.

'We were to find the *Wunderwaffe* ahead of the Russians, who were – even then – seen as the new enemy. We were given a "black list" of key sites: factories, laboratories, testing grounds, wind tunnels, plus the scientists and foremost experts, that were not at any cost to fall into Russian hands. The Russians were advancing from the east; it was a race against time. One that we largely won.'

'That's how he came upon the document?' Jaeger queried. He hadn't been able to resist posing the question. 'The Operation Werewolf report?'

'It's not a report,' Great Uncle Joe murmured. 'It's an operational plan. And no, actually. A document of that level of secrecy – deniable; emanating from the deep black – that was way beyond even our remit; beyond even Target Force.'

'So where—' Jaeger began.

The old man waved him into silence again. 'Your grandfather was a fine soldier: fearless, intelligent, morally incorruptible. During his time with T Force he realised something so shocking, so utterly dark, that he rarely spoke of it. There was an operation beyond T Force: one formed in the deniable, black world. Its mission was to spirit away the most high-profile and undesirable Nazis – the absolute untouchables – to places where we could still profit from them.

'Needless to say, your grandfather was appalled when he

learned of it. Horrified.' Great Uncle Joe paused. 'Most of all, he knew how wrong it was. How it would corrupt us all if we brought the worst of the evil into our living rooms. He believed *all* the Nazi war criminals should stand trial at Nuremberg . . . But now we move into realms wherein he swore me to absolute secrecy.' He cast a momentary glance at Jaeger. 'Am I to break my word?'

Jaeger placed a comforting hand on the old man's arm. 'Uncle Joe, what you've told me already – it's far more than I ever knew, or hoped to know.'

Great Uncle Joe patted his hand in return. 'My boy, I appreciate your patience, your understanding. This . . . this is far from easy . . . At war's end your grandfather re-joined the SAS. Or rather, there was no SAS by then. Officially it was disbanded immediately after the war. Unofficially, Winston Churchill – the greatest leader a country could ever have wished for – kept the unit alive, and thank God that he did.

'The SAS had always been Churchill's baby,' he continued. 'After the war he ran the unit secretly, completely off the books and from a hotel in central London. They set up clandestine bases all across Europe. Their aim was to wipe out those Nazis who had escaped the dragnet; to hunt them down, especially those who were responsible for such terrible abuses during the war.

'You'll perhaps have heard of Hitler's *Sonderbehandlung* – his Commando Order? It decreed that all captured Allied special forces should be handed over to the SS for special treatment – in other words, torture and execution. Hundreds disappeared into what the Nazis called the *Nacht und Nebel* – the night and fog.'

Great Uncle Joe paused for a moment, the effort of reaching so far into the darkness proving an exhausting one.

'Churchill's secret SAS set about hunting down those Nazis still at large. All of them – no matter what their level of seniority. The *Sonderbehandlung* came direct from Hitler himself.

The very top people in the Nazi regime were right in your grandfather's sights, and that put him in direct conflict with the people tasked to spirit those selfsame men to safety.'

'So we were fighting against ourselves?' Jaeger queried. 'One part trying to finish off the very worst of the evil, the other trying to safeguard them?'

'Quite possibly,' the old man confirmed. 'Quite possibly we were.'

'How long did this go on for?' Jaeger queried. 'Grandpa Ted's – Churchill's – secret war?'

'With your grandfather, I don't think it ever stopped. Not until the day he was . . . he died.'

'So all that Nazi memorabilia,' Jaeger ventured. 'The SS Death's Heads; the Werewolf insignia – he acquired it in the course of the hunt?'

Uncle Joe nodded. 'He did. Trophies, if you like. Each speaking of a dark memory, of an evil snuffed out, just as all should have been.'

'And the Operation Werewolf document?' Jaeger prompted. 'He came across that in the same way?'

'Possibly. Probably. I really can't say.' The old man shifted uneasily in his seat. 'I know precious little about it. And needless to say, I didn't know your grandfather had kept a copy. Or that it had passed to you. I've only ever heard mention of it once or twice, and then only in whispers. Your grandfather – he doubtless knew more. But he took his deepest, darkest secrets to the grave. An early grave, at that.'

'And the *Reichsadler*?' Jaeger ventured. 'What does that signify? What does it stand for?'

Great Uncle Joe stared at Jaeger for a long moment. 'That *thing* on your phone – that's no ordinary *Reichsadler*. The standard Nazi eagle sits above a swastika.' The old man glanced again at Jaeger's phone. 'That – it's markedly different. It's the circular symbol below the eagle's tail that you need to pay special attention to.' The old man shuddered. 'Only one . . . organisation has ever used such a symbol, and it did so *after* the war, when the world was supposedly at peace and Nazism dead and buried . . .'

It was warm in the study, the heat from the wood-burner in the kitchen drifting through and keeping it toasty, but even so, Jaeger detected a dark chill that had crept into the room.

Great Uncle Joe sighed, a haunted expression etched across his eyes. 'Needless to say, I haven't seen one in, well, close to seventy years. And I've been happy not to.' He paused. 'There. Now I worry that I've gone too far. If I have, your grandfather and the others – they must forgive me.'

He paused. 'There is one other thing I feel compelled to ask: do you know how your grandfather died? It's part of the reason I moved up here. I couldn't bear to be around the area where we had been so happy as children.'

Jaeger shrugged. 'Only that it was unexpected. Untimely. I was only seventeen – too young for anyone to tell me much.'

'They were right not to tell you.' The old man paused, turning the SAS cap badge over and over in his frail hands. 'He was seventy-nine years of age. As fit as a fiddle. Feisty as ever, of course. They say it was suicide. A hosepipe through the car window. The engine left running. Poisoned by the exhaust fumes. Overburdened by traumatic memories of the war. What complete and utter rubbish!'

Bitter anger was burning in Uncle Joe's eyes now. 'Remind you of anything? Hosepipe through the car window? I'm sure it does! He wasn't of course a *Lebensunwertes Leben* – one of the disabled; one of the Nazis' "life unworthy of life".'

He glanced at Jaeger despairingly. 'But what better way for them to take their revenge?'

Jaeger gunned the bike, the powerful 1200 cc engine howling with the throaty soundtrack of a Triumph at speed on a de-serted, night-dark highway. Yet as he headed south on the M6, he was feeling far from triumphant. Indeed, his visit to Great Uncle Joe had left him reeling.

It was the old man's final revelation that had really hit him.

Grandfather Ted had been found dead in his fume-filled car, apparently having suffocated to death from the exhaust fumes. The police had argued that self-harm and suicide were most likely the cause of death. Chillingly, a distinctive image had been carved into his left shoulder: a *Reichsadler*.

The parallels with Andy Smith's death were unnerving.

Jaeger had left it as long as he could before leaving the cabin. He'd helped Ethel in from the snow. Shared a supper of smoked kippers with the two of them. Seen them both to bed, his great uncle seemingly more exhausted and troubled than Jaeger had ever known him. And then he'd made his excuses and hit the road.

He'd promised Raff, Feaney and Carson a decision in person, within forty-eight hours. The clock was ticking, especially as he had one last stop-off to make on the long journey back to London.

He'd left the cabin deep in the snowy woods hoping that in their isolation, Joe and Ethel were at least safe. But for the whole of the long drive south, Jaeger felt as if the ghosts of the past were chasing him through the darkness.

Hunting him through the *Nacht und Nebel* – the night and the fog.

15

'Feast your eyes on those!' Adam Carson tossed a sheaf of aerial photos on to the desk.

Clean-cut, square-jawed, razor-sharp, slick, a gifted orator – Carson had been born one of life's winners. Jaeger didn't particularly like him. He'd respected him as a military commander. But did he trust him? He'd never really been sure either way.

'The Cordillera de los Dios: the Mountains of the Gods,' Carson continued. 'An area almost the size of Wales – totally unexplored jungle. Ringed by massive peaks – fifteen, sixteen thousand feet – and shrouded in mist and rain. You've got savage tribes, waterfalls as high as cathedrals, caves that run for miles and miles, plus plunging ravines and perilous river gorges. Probably a herd of *Tyrannosaurus rex*, to boot. In short, it's a veritable Lost World.'

Jaeger studied the images, flicking through them one by one. 'Sure looks a long way from Soho Square.'

'Doesn't it.' Carson shoved a second set of aerial photos in Jaeger's direction. 'And if you've any residual doubts, take a look at those. Isn't she a beauty? A mysterious, dark, sensual beauty of a beast. A siren of the air, calling to us from across two thousand miles of jungle, not to mention all the years.'

Jaeger eyed the images. The mystery air wreck sat among a sea of emerald green, being all the more noticeable in that the forest in her immediate vicinity was bleached white as snow. Dead. Leafless branches reaching skywards like myriad skeletal fingers, the carcass of the jungle picked clean and laid bare.

'Forest of bones,' Jaeger muttered, indicating the area of die-back all around the mystery aircraft. 'Any idea what did that?'

'None.' Carson smiled. 'Must be something pretty toxic, but there are any number of potential candidates. You'll be taking NBC suits, plus respirators, obviously. You'll need proper protection – that's if you *are* going.'

Jaeger ignored the dig. He knew that everyone was waiting on his answer. The forty-eight hours were up. That was why they'd gathered here at Wild Dog Media's plush Soho offices – Adam Carson, a handful of TV executives, plus the Enduro Adventures team.

Apparently, anyone who was anyone in TV had to have a base in Soho, a glitzy slice of central London where the great and the good of the media seemed to gather. Carson, typically, had gone for gold, hiring a suite of offices in Soho Square itself.

'The aircraft looks remarkably intact,' Jaeger pointed out. 'Almost as if she *landed* there. Do we have any idea where she was flying to and from, and in what year?'

Carson slid across a third set of photos. 'Close-ups on her markings. You'll see they're badly weathered, but it appears she was decked out in US Air Force colours. Suffering that kind of weathering, she's clearly been lying there for decades . . . Everyone suspects she's Second World War-era. But if she is, she's utterly unique: a phenomenon, decades ahead of her time.

'Compare her to a C-130 Hercules.' Carson glanced at the TV execs. 'The C-130's a modern transport aircraft used by most NATO forces. Our mystery aircraft is a hundred and twelve feet nose to tail, as opposed to a C-130's one hundred feet – so that makes her longer than a modern day C130. Plus she's got six engines, as opposed to four, and a far wider wingspan.'

'So she'd carry a far heavier payload?' Jaeger queried.

'She would,' Carson confirmed. 'The only vaguely comparable Allied Second World War plane is the Boeing B-29 Super-fortress, of the type that dropped the atom bombs on Hiroshima and Nagasaki. But this aircraft's shape is utterly different – far more aerodynamic and streamlined – plus the B-29 was far smaller. And that pretty much sums up the enigma: what the devil is she?'

Carson's smile grew wider; more confident, almost cocky. 'She's been dubbed "The Last Great Mystery of World War Two". And indeed she is.' He was in full-blooded salesman speak now, playing to his audience. 'So all we need is the right man to lead the mission.' He glanced at Jaeger. 'Are you up for it? Are you on?'

Jaeger did a quick scan of the faces gathered around him. Carson: uber-confident that he'd got his man. Raff: inscrutable as ever. Feaney: face tinged with worry, Enduro Adventures fortunes very much hanging in the balance. Plus the assorted TV execs. Early thirties; sloppily – *trendily?* – dressed; looking anxious – their TV extravaganza resting on a knife edge.

And then there was Mr Simon Jenkinson, the archivist. In his late fifties, he was by far the oldest in the pack, his demeanour like a hibernating honey bear, all salty beard, jam-jar glasses, and moth-eaten tweedy jacket, his dreamy head stuck very much in the clouds.

'And you, Mr Jenkinson,' Jaeger prompted. 'I understand you're the expert in the room? You're a member of LAAST – the Lost Aircraft Archaeological Society Trust – as well as being an expert on all things Second World War? Shouldn't we hear what you think she might be?'

'Who? Me?' The archivist glanced around as if waking from a long sleep. His whiskers twitched worriedly. 'Me? Hear from me? Probably not. I'm not good at group discussions.'

Jaeger laughed good-naturedly. He'd warmed to the guy immediately. He liked his lack of pretension, of guile.

'We are in something of a hurry,' Carson cut in, glancing around at the TV execs. 'Makes sense to talk to the archivist once we've dealt with the key agenda item, don't you think – which is, are you on for this, or not?'

'Whenever I make a decision, I like it to be an informed one,'

Jaeger countered. 'So, Mr Jenkinson, your best guess. What's it to be?'

'Well, erm – if I might be so presumptuous . . .' The archivist cleared his throat. 'There is one aircraft that conforms to the specifications of this one. The Junkers Ju 390. German, obviously. A pet project of Hitler's, as it happens. She was intended to spearhead the Amerika Bomber project – Hitler's programme to fly transatlantic bombing raids against America, towards the end of the war.'

'So did they?' Jaeger queried. 'New York? Washington? Were they ever bombed?'

'There are reports of such missions,' Jenkinson confirmed. 'None absolutely verified. But suffice to say, the Ju 390 had the specifications to achieve it. She boasted in-flight refuelling capabilities, and the pilots operated her using cutting-edge Vampir night-vision equipment, which rendered night into near-daylight – meaning they could take off and land in utter darkness.'

Jenkinson tapped a finger on one of the aerial photos. 'And you see that: the Ju 390 was fitted with a dome atop the fuselage, for celestial observations. The aircrew could navigate over vast distances using the stars, and without resorting to radar or radio. In short, she was the perfect warplane for making covert, untraceable flights halfway around the world.

'So, yes, if they'd wanted to drop sarin nerve gas on New York, it was quite within her capabilities.' Jenkinson glanced around the room nervously. 'Erm . . . sorry. That last bit. The sarin on New York bit . . . Got a little carried away there. Are you all still with me?'

There was a series of nods in the affirmative. Oddly for Simon Jenkinson, he seemed to have his audience absolutely gripped.

'Fewer than a dozen Ju 390s were ever built,' he continued. 'Fortunately, the Nazis lost the war before the Amerika Bomber programme could become a frightening reality. But the odd thing is, none of the Ju 390s were ever traced. At war's end they . . . well, they disappeared. If it *is* a Ju 390, it'll be a first, obviously.'

'Any idea what a German warplane would be doing in the heart of the Amazon?' Jaeger prompted. 'And painted with American markings?'

'Not a clue.' The archivist grinned self-deprecatingly. 'In fact, I must confess that's what's been preoccupying me, while locked away in the vaults. There's no record anywhere that I can find of such an aircraft ever having flown to South America. As for it being in United States Air Force markings: well, the mind boggles.'

'If there was such a record, you'd have found it?' Jaeger queried.

The archivist nodded. 'As far as I can tell, she's the plane that never was. A ghost flight.'

Jaeger smiled. 'D'you know something, Mr Jenkinson, you're wasted in the archives. You should be dreaming up ideas for TV programmes.'

'The plane that never was,' Carson echoed. 'The ghost flight. Pure genius. And Will, doesn't that just quicken your appetite for the mission?'

'It does,' Jaeger confirmed. 'So, I've got one final question and one caveat, after which I guess I'm on.'

Carson spread his hands invitingly. 'Fire away.'

Jaeger let the question fall like a bomb into the room. 'Andy Smith – any news on why he was murdered?'

Carson's face remained an inscrutable mask, just the faintest twitching of a muscle in his cheek revealing how the question had unnerved him. 'Well, it's death by misadventure or suicide, as far as the police are concerned. So, whilst it's certainly cast a malaise over the entire expedition, it's one from which we will recover and move forward.' A beat. 'And the caveat?'

In answer, Jaeger slid a folder across the table. It contained a number of glossy brochures, each with a space-age-looking airship displayed on the front. 'I called in at Cardington Field

Hangar, Bedford, this morning, the headquarters of Hybrid Air Vehicles. I guess you know Steve McBride and the other people there?'

'McBride? Yes, indeed,' Carson confirmed. 'A good, solid operator. But what's your interest in HAVs?'

'McBride assures me they can get a Heavy Lift Airlander 50 – their largest – standing orbit over that patch of the Amazon.' Jaeger turned to the TV execs, two of whom were British, and one – the money man – an American. 'Put simply, the Airlander 50 is a modern-day airship. Helium-filled, as opposed to hydrogen, so utterly inert. In other words, she's no Hindenburg: she won't explode in a ball of flame.'

'Four hundred feet long and two hundred wide,' Jaeger continued, 'the Airlander is designed for two things. One: persistent wide-area surveillance – keeping watch on whatever's going on below. Two: lifting major loads.'

He paused. 'The Airlander's got a sixty thousand kilogram payload. McBride figures a warplane of these kinds of dimensions will weigh in at around half of that, so some thirty thousand kilos – maybe pushing fifty thousand if she's loaded with cargo. If we deploy an Airlander 50, she can keep a watch over us and we can lift out that aircraft all in one go.'

The American TV exec slapped the table excitedly. 'Mr Jaeger – Will – if you're saying what I think you're saying, that is a simply awesome proposition. *Awesome.* If you guys can go in, track this thing down, secure it and lift it out all in the one hit – hell, we'll double our contribution to the budget. And correct me if I'm wrong, Carson, but we're forking out the lion's share here, right?'

'You are, Jim,' Carson confirmed. 'And why not use an Airlander? If McBride says he can make it work, and you'll be so good as to cover the extra budget items, let's not just go in and find her; let's go in there and bring her home!'

'One query,' one of the British execs cut in. 'If as you say this Airlander can hover over the jungle and lift out the aircraft, why can't it drop you guys direct on to it? I mean, the plan right now is for you to parachute into the jungle several days' trek away and move in overland. Wouldn't the Airlander save you all the trouble?'

'Good question,' Carson replied. 'Three reasons why not. One: you never drop a team directly on to the site of an unknown toxic threat. It'd be close to suicidal to do so. You move in from a safe location to identify and assess the threat. Two: look at the terrain above the wreck: it's a mass of dead, broken, jagged branches. We drop the team on to that, we'll lose half of them speared in the treetops.

'And three,' Carson nodded at the American network executive, 'Jim wants a parachute drop for the drama it adds to the show; for the cameras. That means dropping on to a clear, open, safe patch of ground. Hence why they need to go in as planned, using that one landing zone that we've been able to identify.'

16

An early lunch was served in the boardroom – an outside catering company brought in trays racked with cold bites, each covered in a cling-film wrapping. Jaeger took one look and decided he wasn't feeling hungry. He worked his way around the room, until he had the archivist cornered somewhere reasonably private.

'Interesting,' Jenkinson remarked, studying a piece of particularly rubbery-looking sushi. 'Amazes me how we end up eating the old enemy's food . . . I take my own sandwiches into the archives. Mature cheddar cheese and Branston pickle.'

Jaeger smiled. 'Could be worse: they could have served us sauerkraut.'

It was Jenkinson's turn to chuckle. 'Touché. You know, there's a part of me that's almost envious of you going in to find that mystery aircraft. Of course, I'd be next to useless in the field. But, well – you'll be making history. Living it. Unmissable.'

'I could find you a place on the team,' Jaeger suggested, a touch of mischief creeping in. 'Make it a condition of my going.'

The archivist choked out a piece of raw fish. 'Oops. Sorry. Revolting, anyway.' He wrapped it in a paper napkin and placed it on a convenient shelf. 'No, no, no, no, no – I'm more than happy sticking to my vaults.'

'Talking of vaults . . .' Jaeger mused. 'Just for a moment forget what you absolutely know. I'm after some pure conjecture here. Based on all you've seen and heard, what do you actually think that mystery aircraft is?'

Jenkinson's eyes moved nervously behind his thick glasses. 'I don't normally do conjecture. Not my usual currency. But since you ask . . . Only two possible scenarios make any kind of sense. A, it's a Ju 390, and the Nazis painted it with US markings so as to sneak around undetected. B, it's a top-secret American warplane, one that no one's ever heard of.'

'Which is the more likely scenario?' Jaeger prompted.

Jenkinson eyed the soggy napkin on the shelf. 'B is about as likely as me ever liking sushi. Option A: well, you'd be surprised how common such skulduggery was. We captured their aircraft; they captured ours. We painted them in enemy colours and sneaked about up to all kinds of dodgy business. They did likewise.'

Jaeger raised one eyebrow. 'I'll bear that in mind. Now, slight change of subject. Got a puzzle for you. A riddle. Figured you probably enjoy a good riddle – but I'd like you to keep this one just between the two of us, okay?'

'Never happier than when I'm trying to solve a good riddle,' Jenkinson confirmed, a gleam in his eye, 'and especially one that I have to keep a strict secret.'

Jaeger lowered his voice. 'Two old men. Veterans of the Second World War. Served in secret units. All very sneaky-beaky. Each keeps his study decked out wall-to-wall with war memorabilia. There is one exception: each has on his desk an obscure ancient manuscript written entirely in an unintelligible language. Question is, why?'

'You mean, why would they each have one?' Jenkinson rubbed his beard pensively. 'There's no evidence of a wider interest? No reference works? No similar texts? No history of a wider study of the phenomena?'

'Nothing. Just the one book. That's it. Sat on the desk in each of the old men's studies.'

Jenkinson's eyes twinkled. He was clearly enjoying this. 'There is something called the book code.' He pulled out an old envelope from his jacket pocket and began scribbling. 'The beauty is its absolute pure simplicity; that, and the fact that it's totally unbreakable – unless, of course, you happen to know which book each person is referring to.'

He scribbled down an apparently random sequence of numbers: 1.16.47/5.12.53/9.6.16/21.4.76/3.12.9.

'Now, imagine you and one other person each has the same edition of a book. He, or she, sends you those numbers. Starting with the first sequence, 1.16.47, you turn to chapter one, page sixteen, line forty-seven. It starts with an I. Next, chapter five, page twelve, line fifty-three: starts with a D. Chapter nine, page six, line sixteen: starts with an I again. Chapter twenty-one, page four, line seventy-six: O. Chapter three, page twelve, line nine: T. Put it all together and what have you got?'

Jaeger spelled out the letters. 'I-D-I-O-T. Idiot.'

Jenkinson smiled. 'You said it.'

Jaeger couldn't help laughing. 'Very funny. You've just blown your invite to the Amazon.'

Jenkinson chuckled silently, his shoulders rocking back and forth as he did so. 'Sorry. It's just the first word that came into my mind.'

'Watch it. You're digging yourself a deeper grave.' Jaeger paused for a second. 'But let's say the book's written in an unknown language and writing system. How does it work then? Surely that would make the code unworkable?'

'Not if you have a usable translation. Without the translation you'd have a five-letter word that was utterly unintelligible. Without the translation, it'd be pure nonsense. But with the translation it adds another layer of encoding, that's all. Both individuals have to have both books to hand, of course, in order to decode the message. But it's a stroke of genius, actually.'

'Can such a code be broken?' Jaeger ventured.

Jenkinson shook his head. 'Very difficult. Next to impossible. That's the beauty of it. You need to know which book the two users are referring to, and in this case have access to the translation too. Makes it almost impossible to crack – that's unless you capture the two old men and beat and torture it out of them.'

Jaeger eyed the archivist curiously. 'That's a dark mind you have there, Mr Jenkinson. But thanks for the insight. And keep digging for any trace of our mystery flight.' He scribbled his email and phone details on the bottom of Jenkinson's envelope. 'I'd be keen to hear of anything you turn up.'

'Absolutely.' Jenkinson smiled. 'Glad to see someone's taking a real interest at last.'

17

'Two-way mirror,' Carson announced. 'We use it for assessing which characters will appeal most to TV audiences. Or at least, that's the bullshit theory.'

He and Jaeger were standing in a darkened room, before what appeared to be a long glass wall. On the far side was a group of individuals enjoying a cold lunch buffet, apparently oblivious to the fact that they were being watched. Carson's patter had changed markedly. He'd slipped back into what he clearly figured was buddy-buddy soldier speak.

'You wouldn't believe the crap I've been put through pulling this team together,' he continued. 'TV executives – they wanted freaks, glamour and eye candy. Top ratings material, as they call it. I wanted tough ex-military types who'd stand at least a chance of making it through. That little lot,' he jerked a thumb at the glass, 'is the bloody result.'

Jaeger indicated the trays of sandwiches that the expedition team was busy tucking into. 'So why don't they get the revolting—'

'The sushi? Perks of being management,' Carson cut in darkly. 'We get the obscenely expensive, indigestible food. So, I'll talk you around the team, and then I suggest you go say a few cute 'n' cuddly words of introduction.'

He pointed out a figure through the glass. 'Big guy. Joe James. New Zealander. Former Kiwi SAS. Lost one too many of his mates along the way; plagued by PTSD, hence the long greasy hair and Osama Bin Laden beard. Looks like a biker crossed with a homeless bum, which the TV execs love, of course. But never judge a book by its cover: he remains a tough and resourceful operator, or so I'm told.

'Two: chiselled black dude. Lewis Alonzo. Former US Navy SEAL. Works as a bodyguard these days, but misses the adrenalin rush of combat. Hence volunteering for the present fun and games. About the most reliable bloke you've got. Don't whatever you do lose him in the Amazon. As the Yank made clear in the meeting, they're footing the lion's share of the bill. They need Americans on the team – preferably ones performing some world-beating heroics – to play to a US audience.

'Three: the French broadcaster Canal Plus has stumped up a sizeable chunk of the budget, hence the elegant-looking French bird. Sylvie Clermont. Served with the unfortunately named CRAP – *Commandos de Recherche et d'Action en Profondeur*. Think SAS minus the Special. She wore Dior all through the trials in the Scottish hills. Looked bloody good in it, too. Probably doesn't wash much – French birds tend not to – but I figure I could forgive her that . . .'

Carson laughed at his own joke. He glanced at Jaeger, as if expecting him to share in the humour. He didn't get even a hint of a smile in return. He shrugged – undeterred; skin as thick as a hippo – and ploughed on.

'Four: Asian-looking guy. Hiro Kamishi – Japanese broadcaster NHK's choice. Hiro by name, hero by nature. A former captain in the Tokusha Sakusen Gun – the Japanese special forces. Fancies himself as a modern-day samurai; a warrior of the higher path. He's made a name for himself as a war historian, largely due to Japanese guilt over the Second World War. Personally I don't know what there is to feel guilty about. We won. They lost. The end.'

Carson laughed at his own joke again, no longer bothering to seek endorsement from Jaeger. The message was clear: I run the show around here, and I'll say what I bloody well like and like what I bloody well say.

'Five and six: couple of long-haired dudes barely started shaving – Mike Dale and Stefan Kral. An Aussie and a Slovak. They're Wild Dog Media's camera crew, so you don't need to worry much about them. They've worked in remote and conflict-prone areas and should be able to look after themselves. The upside: they'll be behind the cameras filming the show, so should keep well out of your way. The downside: you're almost old enough to be their father.'

Carson guffawed. It was clearly his favourite joke of the show so far.

'Seven. Peter Krakow. Polish–German. ZDF, the German broadcaster's esteemed choice. Krakow is former GSG9. What else is there to say? He's a Kraut. He's got the character of a woodlouse and the sense of humour of a worm. He's a dour, down-the-line Teutonic type. If that aircraft is German, you can rely on Krakow to keep reminding you.

'Eight: hot-looking Latino chick. Leticia Santos – foisted on us by the tree-hugger brigade. Brazilian *chica* now working for FUNAI, the Brazilian government's Amazon Indian agency. She was formerly with the B-SOB – your buddy Colonel Evandro's Brazilian special forces. She's got a new mantra now: hug an Amazonian Indian. But she's the nearest the colonel has to having a man on your mission.

'And finally, number nine – come in, please, your time is up! *If only*. Yeah, I'm talking about the striking-looking blonde. Smokin' hot. Irina Narov. Former officer in Russia's Spetsnaz, now taken up American citizenship and lives in New York. Narov is ice cool. Highly capable. Decidedly easy on the eye. Oh yeah, and never to be found without her knife. Or crossed. Needless to say, the TV execs love her. They figure Narov will blow the ratings through the roof.'

Carson turned to Jaeger. 'With your good self – makes a round ten. So, what d'you reckon? The team to die for, eh?'

Jaeger shrugged. 'I presume it's too late to change my mind and pull out?'

Carson's smile split his face from ear to ear. 'Trust me, you're going to love it. You're the perfect character to mould them into one cohesive team.'

Jaeger snorted. 'There is one thing. I'd like Raff as my 2iC. Safe pair of hands to backstop operations and help me handle that bunch of crazies.'

Carson shook his head. 'No can do, I'm afraid. As a soldier's soldier there's no one better. But he's hardly the most erudite of individuals, nor easy on the eye. The TV execs are dead set on the team as assembled. That means you've got the delightful Irina Narov – the honorary American – as your right-hand . . . well, woman.'

'It's a deal-breaker?'

'It is. It's the blonde bombshell or bust.'

Jaeger turned back to the two-way mirror, eyeing Irina Narov for a long moment. Oddly, he had the sensation that she knew he was watching – as if she could feel his gaze burning through the glass.

18

It was first light.

Approaching time to fire up the Lockheed Martin C-130J Super Hercules and take to the skies. The rest of Jaeger's team was locked and loaded. Good to go. They were strapped into the aircraft's fold-down canvas seats, plugged into the on-board oxygen-breathing system, and psyching themselves up for what they knew was coming – the plunge from the roof of the world into the unknown.

Now was the time when Jaeger took a last few moments for himself, just as the mission – or in this case, the expedition of a lifetime – was about to get airborne.

They were poised to go wheels-up.

Green-lit. Green for go.

No turning back. Committed beyond all reason.

These were the final minutes before the struggle for survival would become all-consuming. Jaeger headed further down the airstrip, seeking a few seconds' privacy – no doubt the last he'd get in the days and weeks that lay ahead. He'd done this in the world of the military elite. He did it now, as he steeled himself to lead this expedition deep into the Amazon.

They were flying out of Brazil's Cachimbo airport, which lay in the heart of the Serra do Cachimbo – the Smoking Pipe Mountains. Cachimbo was equidistant between Rio de Janeiro on the Atlantic coastline and the far western extremities of the Amazon – making it the midway point in Brazil to their intended destination.

It was all too easy to forget how massive Brazil was as a country, or how vast was the Amazon basin. Some 2,000 kilometres east of Cachimbo lay Rio de Janeiro; some 2,000 kilometres west lay that mystery warplane, in the furthest reaches of the rainforest. And pretty much everything in between was dense jungle.

Reserved exclusively for military operations, Cachimbo airport was the perfect launching point for their insertion into that real-life Lost World. As a bonus, Colonel Evandro, the B-SOB commander, had decreed that there would be no filming prior to take-off. He'd argued it was too sensitive, due to all the special missions he ran out of Cachimbo. In truth, he'd done so at Jaeger's request, for Jaeger was sick to death with having a camera stuck up his nose 24/7.

The camera crew had been with the expedition team for the best part of two weeks now, filming their every waking moment and desperate to catch the barest hint of any unfolding drama. Jaeger was far from used to the constant in-your-face intrusions.

To make matters worse, he'd had Irina Narov to deal with – his supposed deputy, and, as he saw it, the chief suspect in Andy Smith's murder. While the rest of his team had seemed to welcome Jaeger's presence among them, Narov had done little to hide her hostility.

The blonde Russian bombshell seemed to resent his presence from the get-go, and her abrasiveness had begun to get on his nerves. It was almost as if she had expected to lead things once Andy Smith had been done away with; as if somehow her ambitions had been thwarted.

Jaeger's broken toes and fingers, courtesy of Black Beach Prison, were still paining him. They were strapped tight with bandages, and he reckoned he was fit enough to make it through whatever was coming – as long as he could avoid Narov sticking the knife in when his back was turned. He couldn't quite fathom her hostility, but he figured in the cauldron of the jungle all would be revealed.

There had been one other expedition dynamic that hadn't

escaped his notice. From the very start sparks were flying between Leticia Santos, the Brazilian team member, and Irina Narov. Jaeger figured it was a classic case of two beautiful women and an all-too-predictable catfight.

Yet a part of him couldn't help but think that although they were jealous of each other, somehow he was the source of their jealousy and the tension.

He forced the thought from his mind. It had rained during the night and he caught the distinctive smell of a fresh, cool tropical downpour falling upon hot, sun-baked earth. It was unmistakable. It transported him back to his first time in 'the trees', as the SAS referred to the jungle.

Jungle training was a core part of SAS selection – the brutal trial that each soldier was required to pass before making it into the unit. From day one in the trees, Jaeger had realised he had a natural affinity with jungle living. He figured it was the dense undergrowth, the mud and the rain that struck a chord – reminding him of messing about outdoors as a kid with his father. Trying to survive endless days of mud, rain and low, claustrophobic jungle forced a man to improvise, and Jaeger liked to wing it – to be forced to think smart on the move.

He closed his eyes and breathed deeply, the moist, musty, earthy air filling his lungs.

This was the time he took to tune in to his inner voice, his warrior's sixth sense.

He'd always listened to it, ever since those days spent scrambling over the hills around his childhood home in rural Wiltshire, or the weekends camped in the forest, surviving off his wits and the wild.

Under his father's guidance he'd learned to catch trout with his bare hands – running his fingers through the gently rippling water, moving them slowly along the fish's cold, scaly sides, 'tickling' it into submission, before whipping it on to the riverbank lightning-fast. He'd learned how to set snares for rabbits and to build a watertight basha – a shelter – out of what you could find in your average British woodland.

Back then the inner voice had proven itself worthy of his attention, reminding him of the natural order of the wild. And as an elite soldier in later years, that same instinct had served to put steel in his soul. During Officer Week on SAS selection, he'd gone against the plan of every other candidate, to universal ridicule – but the inner voice had felt strong and he'd trusted it. He'd been proven right when he was one of only two officers to pass selection that brutal winter.

That inner voice had always served to centre him.

Or at least it had done until now.

For some strange reason this endeavour had Jaeger seriously spooked, which didn't make a blind bit of sense. The coming expedition wasn't some kind of mission deep behind enemy lines, outnumbered and outgunned. He couldn't put his finger on exactly what was eating him.

Most likely it was Andy Smith's death, and everything that had followed.

Prior to flying out of the UK, Jaeger had attended Smithy's funeral, but even as he'd stood alongside Dulce and the children paying his respects, it had felt wrong in his guts. Afterwards, he'd caught a beer with Raff at the wake. It was there that the big Maori had shared with him one crucial detail about the way in which Andy Smith had died.

There had been no sign of forced entry to his hotel room. As far as the police were concerned, he'd let himself out of his own accord, climbed the hills in a drunken stupor and leapt to his death. But if it wasn't suicide, then Andy had clearly made no attempt to stop his killers from entering his hotel room.

That suggested that he knew them.

It suggested that he knew them and trusted them.

They'd been staying at the remote Loch Iver Hotel, in the midst of a storm-lashed January. It had been pretty much empty of guests, bar the expedition members – and that in turn suggested that the killer had to be amongst Jaeger's team.

In short, he or she was very likely in their midst.

Jaeger had his suspicions as to who it might be. But he'd kept quiet, largely because he hadn't wanted to alert any of the team to the fact that he or she might be a suspect. Other than Irina Narov, the only ones he hadn't warmed to were the cocksure and gobby Mike Dale, plus Stefan Kral – the camera crew – but it made zero sense for them to be Smithy's murderers.

With his inherent distrust of all things media, Jaeger had found Dale and Kral to be all mouth and no substance. In return, they'd clearly found him distinctly spiky and uncooperative whenever they'd stuck their camera in his face. Andy Smith would surely have proven more easy-going, malleable film material, so they'd be the last people to want him killed off.

Every which way he looked at it, Jaeger remained convinced that the answer as to how and why his friend had been murdered – for he felt convinced it *was* murder – lay somewhere deeper in the jungle on the coming expedition. He felt an urgent need to get going now. It was time to get boots on the ground and to prove this thing once and for all.

Jaeger wasn't in the habit of doing things by halves. Once he'd agreed to lead the expedition, he'd thrown himself into it wholeheartedly. He'd had to pick up from where Smithy had left off and hit the ground running. The frenetic preparations had consumed his every waking moment, leaving precious little time for anything else.

He'd only just managed to grab a quick phone call with his parents prior to departure. A few years back they'd retired to Bermuda – to permanent sunshine, the odd hurricane and the joys of tax-free living. During a rushed call he'd told them the basics: that he was back from Bioko; there was no news on Ruth and Luke; he was off to the Amazon on an Enduro Adventures expedition; plus he wanted to come and visit, to ask them more about Grandpa Ted's life, and also about how he'd died.

He'd promised his parents he'd get out to see them soon and signed off the call. He'd left his suspicions about Grandpa Ted's death unsaid. It felt wrong to raise them over an echoing phone line. Such a conversation needed to be held face-to-face. As soon as he was finished in the Amazon, he'd catch a flight to Bermuda.

Jaeger and his team had been in Brazil for a week now, hosted by Colonel Evandro and his B-SOB teams. Over that time the Brazilian warmth – both of character and of climate – had soothed the worst of his fears. Gradually the lurking sense of darkness that had gripped him in the UK had faded from his mind.

It was only now – as they prepared to head deeper into the Amazon proper – that those worries had started crowding in again.

19

Cachimbo airstrip lay deep in a densely forested valley, an impenetrable carpet of lush, tangled vegetation marching up the slopes to either side. The first rays of sunlight were starting to blaze above the ragged jungle horizon – lasers burning away the wisps of mist that clung to the treetops. The fierce tropical sun would soon burn off the cool dawn.

Those in Jaeger's line of work said that there were only ever two kinds of reaction to the jungle: it was either love or hate at first sight. Those who hated it saw it as dark, alien and foreboding. Claustrophobic. Fraught with danger. But with Jaeger it had always been the opposite. He was drawn irresistibly to the wild, thrusting, exuberant riot of life – the awe-inspiring tropical forest ecosystem.

He was thrilled by the idea of a wilderness devoid of all trappings of human civilisation. And in truth, the jungle was neutral. It was neither inherently hostile nor friendly to humankind. Learn its ways, tune into its resonance, become at one with its essence, and it could prove a fantastic friend and refuge.

That being said, the pure, simple remote wildness of the Cordillera de los Dios – the Mountains of the Gods – was unlike anything else on this earth. And then of course there was that mystery aircraft, lying hidden in the Cordillera's remote heart.

From above him what looked like a harpy eagle emitted a lonely, high-pitched screech. There was an answering cry from atop one of the tallest of the forest giants. It was an 'emergent' – a massive tropical hardwood towering some 150 feet above the dark and shadowed recesses of the forest floor. Its thrusting crown had broken through the canopy, reaching high in the battle for sunlight.

There it stood, bathed in the first rays of a glorious dawn.

King of all it surveyed.

The topmost branches offered the perfect vantage point from which the eagle could hunt his prey. Jaeger scanned the tree's spreading vegetation, which was dusted with a delicate pink blush of flowers. It alone was in full bloom. It drew the eye – a patch of iridescent colour surrounded on all sides by a sea of deep greens.

He spotted the nest.

The eagles were a breeding pair.

No doubt there were hungry chicks to feed.

For a moment, Jaeger imagined himself as that eagle, soaring high over the jungle on wings some seven feet across. He saw himself diving over that remote and distant wilderness where the mystery aircraft lay hidden. With an eagle's vision he could track a mouse moving on the forest floor from several hundred yards away. Spotting the site of that air wreck – the bare, skeletal branches drained of life and stripped clean of vegetation – was child's play.

In his mind's eye he glided overhead, the scene below him looking so unnatural. Still. Lifeless. Ghostly, even.

What had caused the forest to die like that?

What secrets – *what dangers* – did that mystery aircraft harbour?

Watching the eagles, Jaeger was reminded of the *Reichsadler*. In the hectic whirl of the last few days he'd had little time to dwell upon that cruel eagle symbol; that prophetic darkness. Odd how such a magnificent bird could represent both evil and wild freedom and beauty.

It was Sun Tzu, the ancient Chinese master of warfare, who'd first coined the phrase *know your enemy*.

In the military, Jaeger had made that his mantra.

He was used to facing an enemy that he knew and understood well. One that he'd studied hard, using satellite images, surveillance photos and briefings from the world's foremost intelligence agencies. Using signals intercepts. Employing humint – human intelligence – assets on the ground: a spy, or a source within the bad guys' camp.

Before any mission he would assure himself that he knew his enemy intimately, so much the better to defeat him. But right here and now they were going in to face a whole plethora of potential dangers, none of which they knew or understood.

Whatever the risks were, they remained unknown.

Whoever the enemy might be, they were faceless.

Strangers.

No doubt about it, that was what had Jaeger spooked – rushing into this nameless and unknowable peril.

But at least now he'd got it straight in his head.

At least now he knew.

Having reached that realisation, Jaeger felt somewhat reassured. He turned to face the aircraft. He heard the high-pitched whine as the starter motors fired up the first of the giant turbines. Slowly, ponderously, the massive hook-bladed propellers began to turn as if they were mired in thick treacle.

A Land Rover was tearing down the rutted dirt track that sat alongside the runway. Jaeger guessed someone was coming to drive him back to the waiting plane. It pulled to a halt and the unmistakable figure of Colonel Evandro jumped out.

Six foot two, dark-eyed, lithe and athletic-looking despite his age, the B-SOB colonel had lost none of his presence during the years since Jaeger had first served alongside him. He had opted to put himself through the hell of SAS selection so that he could better shape his unit in the British regiment's image – and Jaeger admired him greatly for it.

'Time to head for the hold,' he announced. 'Your team – they're making their final preparations for getting airborne.'

Jaeger nodded. 'You sure you won't be coming with us?'

The colonel smiled. 'Truthfully? I would love nothing more. Pen-pushing is hardly my milieu. But with rank and command comes all the usual bullshit.'

'Best I get going, then.'

The colonel held out his hand. 'Good luck, my friend.'

'You think we'll be needing it?'

He eyed Jaeger for a long moment. 'It is the Amazon. Expect the unexpected.'

'Expect the unexpected,' Jaeger echoed. Wise words.

Together they climbed into the Land Rover and tore back along the track towards the waiting Hercules.

20

Jaeger paused at the aircraft's cockpit. A head poked out of the side window high above him.

'Weather's holding good over the DZ,' the pilot called down. 'Wheels up in fifteen. You good with that?'

Jaeger nodded. 'Tell you the truth, I can't wait. I hate the waiting.'

The aircrew was all American, and by their poise and bearing Jaeger figured they were ex-military. The Hercules C-130 had been chartered by Carson from some private air-freight company, and Jaeger had been assured that these guys were the best in the business. He had every confidence that they'd get him to the exact spot in the sky where he and his team needed to jump.

'You got any tunes you want playin'?' the pilot queried. 'Like, for P-Hour?'

Jaeger smiled. P-Hour stood for Parachute Hour, the moment when Jaeger and his team would hurl themselves off the tail ramp into the howling void.

It was a long-standing tradition amongst airborne units that they'd blast out some music as they prepared for the *go-go-go*. It boosted the adrenalin and got the pulse hammering as they waited to freefall into war; or, as in this case, on a mystery journey into a modern-day Lost World.

'Something classical,' Jaeger suggested. 'Wagner maybe? What've you got on the system?'

Jaeger's chosen jump music had always been something of

that nature. It was counter-culture, as far as his mates saw it, but the old stuff always served to centre him. And on this one he sure was going to need some centring.

He would be leading the jump, so as to guide those coming after. And he wasn't going to be jumping alone.

Irina Narov had joined the team late – too late for Andy Smith to take her through the necessary HAHO refresher course. HAHO stood for High Altitude High Opening, a form of parachute insertion that enabled a force to drift for miles into their target. It was their chosen means of insertion for the expedition.

Jaeger was going to have to make a tandem HAHO jump, leaping into the void at 30,000 feet with another person – Irina Narov – strapped to his torso. He figured he needed a dose of calming music like never before.

'I got AC/DC's "Highway to Hell",' the pilot announced. 'Led Zeppelin's "Stairway to Heaven". ZZ Top and Motörhead. I got some Eminem, 50 Cent and Fatboy. Take your pick, buddy.'

Jaeger delved into his pocket, pulled out a CD and tossed it up to the pilot. 'Try that. Track four.'

The pilot glanced at the CD. '"Ride of the Valkyries".' He snorted. 'Sure you don't want "Highway to Hell"?'

He broke into a burst of song, fingers drumming on the skin of the Hercules in time to AC/DC's lyrics.

Jaeger smiled. 'Let's save it for the pick-up, eh?'

The pilot rolled his eyes. 'You Brits – you need to let your hair down. We'll get you guys enjoyin' yourselves yet!'

Jaeger sensed that the 'Ride of the Valkyries' – the theme tune to the iconic Vietnam War movie, *Apocalypse Now* – was going to prove uniquely fitting to the present mission. It was also a halfway house to the pilot's chosen blast, and in Jaeger's book it was always good to keep your aircrew happy.

The pilot and his crew had the difficult task of getting ten bodies kicked out of the aircraft's hold at exactly the right point in the sky, one that would get them on to their target – a tiny patch of clear ground some ten kilometres straight down.

Right now, the pilot pretty much held Jaeger's life – and those of his team – in his hands.

Jaeger moved around to the aircraft's rear and climbed aboard. He let his eyes wander around the dark interior of the hold. It was lit here and there by the eerie red glow of low-level lighting. He counted nine jumpers, ten with himself included. In contrast to what he was accustomed to in the military, he knew none of them well. They'd had a few days' preparation and that was all.

His team was fully geared up. Each was dressed in a thick and cumbersome Gore-Tex survival suit, one specially designed for HAHO jumps. It was a pain having to wear them, for as soon as they hit the steamy jungle they'd be roasting hot. But without such protection they'd freeze to death during the long drift under the parachutes through the thin and icy blue.

At their 30,000-foot jump altitude they'd be a thousand feet higher than the peak of Everest, in the permanently frozen death zone. The temperature would be minus fifty degrees centigrade and the winds at that altitude – the same as commercial airliners flew at – would be fearsome. Without their specialist survival suits, masks, gloves and helmets, they'd freeze to death in the blink of an eye, and they were going to be under their parachutes for far longer than that.

They couldn't jump from a lower height for the simple reason that the complex glide map to get them on to their exact drop zone required them to drift beneath their chutes for forty-odd kilometres, and you could only achieve that kind of distance when dropped from 30,000 feet. Plus doing a HAHO had the added advantage of maxing out the drama for the TV cameras.

In the centre of the Hercules' hold lay two giant toilet-roll-shaped containers. These para-tubes were so heavy that they were mounted on a set of rails that ran the length of the floor. Two of Jaeger's most experienced jumpers – Hiro Kamishi and Peter Krakow – would strap on to the tubes just prior to the jump, so as to parachute them into the landing zone.

They were packed with the team's inflatable canoes and ancillary equipment – stuff too bulky and heavy to carry in the rucksacks. Kamishi and Krakow would be 'riding the tube', as the saying went. The physical strain of doing so would be horrific, but Jaeger had a quiet confidence in the two of them.

His own task was even more challenging. But he told himself that he'd jumped tandem dozens of times before, and that he shouldn't stress about getting Irina Narov down in one piece.

He took up a position facing his team. They were spread along the seats lining one side of the Hercules. On the opposite side sat the PDs – the parachute dispatchers, whose job it was to get them safely out of the aircraft.

With the various elements of the expedition spread halfway around the world, all would need to work to a standardised time. What Jaeger was about to do was exactly what he'd have done were this a military operation. He went down on one knee and rolled back his left sleeve.

'Heads-up,' he announced, having to yell above the noise of the aircraft's turbines. 'Confirming Zulu time.'

A row of figures fought with their bulky suits as they struggled to make their timepieces visible. Ensuring everyone had correctly synchronised their watches would be absolutely vital to what was coming.

Their team and the airship orbiting above them would at times be operating in the Bolivian time zone. The C-130 aircrew was flying out of Brazil, which was one hour ahead of Bolivia, while the Wild Dog Media production HQ in London was two hours ahead again.

It would be pointless Jaeger calling in an extraction aircraft at mission's end if either they or it arrived at the rendezvous three hours late, due to time differences. Zulu time was the accepted global standard upon which all militaries operated – and the expedition would be doing the same from here on in.

'In thirty seconds it'll be 0500 Zulu,' Jaeger announced.

Each of the figures had their eyes glued to the second hands on their watches.

'Twenty-five seconds and counting,' Jaeger warned. He glanced up at the team. 'All good?'

There was a series of gestures in the positive. Eyes glowed with excitement from behind bulky oxygen masks. When doing a HAHO jump, you had to breathe a forced-air mixture, pressurised pure oxygen being pumped into your lungs. You had to start doing so before take-off, to reduce the danger of getting altitude sickness, which could rapidly disable or kill.

The masks prevented any chat, but still Jaeger felt heartened. His team looked more than ready to get down and dirty in the Cordillera de los Dios.

'0500 Zulu in ten seconds . . .' he counted. 'Seven . . . four, three, two: mark!'

On his call, each of the team nodded their acknowledgement. They were good – synchronised to Zulu time.

No one was wearing anything other than a quality timepiece, but none had anything particularly flashy either. The golden rule was the fewer buttons and gizmos the better. The last thing you wanted was a watch with a million functions. Bulky knobs and dials had a habit of either breaking or getting snagged. 'Keep it simple, stupid' were words of advice ingrained in Jaeger from his SAS selection days.

He himself wore a bog-standard dull green British Army watch. It was low-luminosity, so it wouldn't show up in the dark, and it had zero reflective or chromed metal – nothing to glint in the sunlight when you least wanted it to. During his time in the military he'd worn that watch for another reason too: it didn't mark him out as anything other than a regular soldier.

If you were captured by the enemy, you didn't want anything on your person that might distinguish you as being particularly special. In fact, he and his men used to sanitise themselves completely before any mission – cutting out all labels from clothing, and not carrying a single piece of ID or mark of unit or rank.

Like every soldier in his squadron, Jaeger had trained to be the grey man.

Well, almost.

Just as now, he'd made one exception to the rule. He'd always carried two photos, laminated and hidden in the sole of his left boot. The first was of his childhood dog, a mountain collie that had been a gift from his grandfather. She was immaculately trained, totally devoted, and she used to follow him everywhere. The other was of Ruth and Luke, and a big part of Jaeger refused to let their memory go now.

Carrying such photos was a big no-no on any mission, but some things mattered more than the rules.

21

Watches synched, Jaeger stepped towards his parachute pack. He wriggled into the harness, pulled the straps taut, then closed the heavy metal chest buckle with a solid thunk. Lastly, he tightened the restraining loops around his thighs. He now had the equivalent of a large sack of coal strapped to his back, and this was only the beginning.

When they'd first pioneered HAHO jumps they'd done so using a system whereby the jumper's heavy rucksack was strapped to his back along with his chute. But that had made the jumper overwhelmingly backside-heavy. If for any number of reasons he lost consciousness during the jump, having all the weight on his back would invert him during the freefall.

The parachute was set to open automatically at a certain altitude, but if the jumper had blacked out and was falling on his back, it would open beneath him. He would drop through his own chute, which would wrap around him like a bundle of damp washing, and jumper and chute would plummet to earth like a stone.

Thankfully, Jaeger and his team were using a far newer system – the BT80. With the BT80, the heavy rucksack hung in a tough canvas bag, strapped to the jumper's front. That way, if he blacked out, the weight would force him to fall front-first, with his face towards the earth. When the chute was triggered automatically, it would open above him – an absolute lifesaver.

The PDs fussed around Jaeger, tightening straps and making minute adjustments to the load he was carrying. This was vital.

On a jump such as this, they'd drift under the chutes for anything up to an hour. If the weight was unbalanced or the straps loose, the whole lot would shift and swing about, rubbing flesh bloody and raw, and throwing the descent off-balance.

The last thing Jaeger needed was to hit the jungle with a sore and shredded groin or shoulders. In the hot and humid conditions, wounds would fester. Any such injury could spell endex – end of expedition – for the victim.

Jaeger pulled on his chunky para-helmet. The PDs strapped his personal oxygen tank to his chest and passed him his mask, which was linked to his oxygen canister by a ribbed rubber tube. He pressed the mask into his face and took a sharp intake of breath, to check that it made a good, airtight seal.

At 30,000 feet, there was little if any oxygen.

If the breather system failed for just a few seconds, he'd be a dead man.

Jaeger felt a wild rush of euphoria – the pure, cold oxygen surging into his brain. He pulled on his leather gauntlets, followed by thick Gore-Tex overgloves, to protect against the biting cold once under canopy at high altitude.

He'd jump with his weapon – a standard Benelli M4 combat shotgun with a folding stock – slung over his left shoulder, barrel downwards, and strapped to his person. It was always possible that during the jump you'd lose your backpack, in which case it was vital to still have your main weapon securely to hand.

Jaeger wasn't expecting a hostile force to be present on the ground this time, but there was that uncontacted tribe to contend with – the Amahuaca Indians. The last sign they'd given of their presence was when they'd shot poison-tipped arrows at a group of gold prospectors who'd strayed into their forest domain.

The miners had fled for their lives, barely living to tell the story.

Jaeger didn't exactly blame the Indians for defending their territory so resolutely. If all the outside world ever brought them was illegal gold mining, and most likely logging as well, his sympathies lay fully with the Indians – for mining and logging would cause pollution and the destruction of their forest home.

But it meant that any outsider who trespassed into the Indians' territory – Jaeger and his team included – was bound to be seen as hostile, especially when they were dropping from the heavens right into the very heart of the tribe's world. Truth was, Jaeger had no real idea what sort of enemy, if any, they might encounter once they hit the ground, but his training had taught him to always be prepared.

Hence why he had chosen the shotgun as his weapon. It was perfect for close-quarter combat in dense jungle. It fired off a wide cone of lead shot, so being able to see and target your enemy amongst the darkness and the vegetation wasn't essential.

You just swung the muzzle in the general direction and let rip.

22

In truth, Jaeger hoped to hell that if they did run into that tribe, it would prove a peaceful meeting. There was a part of him that thrilled to the prospect: if anyone understood the mysteries of the rainforest, these Amazonian Indian people would – their knowledge gained over countless centuries being the key to unlocking its ancient secrets.

Strapped into his bulky gear, Jaeger shuffled over and took his seat.

He was closest to the ramp. Poised to be first out.

Narov was next in line beside him.

Strapped up, bulked out and weighed down like this, he felt like some kind of abominable snowman. It was hot and claustrophobic, and he hated the waiting.

The aircraft's ramp whined closed.

The hold became a dark tunnel of shadow.

Like a giant steel coffin.

They had a four-hour flight ahead of them, so if all went to plan they would be over the drop zone at around 0900 hours Zulu. They'd pile out of the aircraft, ten figures clad in khaki green, faces daubed with dark camo cream, suspended beneath their matt-black parachutes.

They would be invisible, and inaudible, to any watchers as they hit the ground. It would all be high drama, which would be great for the TV cameras. But Jaeger just felt better going in low profile and unseen.

The aircraft jerked forward and began to taxi along the

sun-blasted runway. Jaeger felt it slow, and then the turbines screamed to a fever pitch as it spun around on the spot, facing the direction for take-off. He felt a surge of adrenalin as the engines roared ever louder, the pilot doing his last-minute checks before releasing the brakes.

Inside the hold, the air was thick with the fumes of burning avgas, but all Jaeger could smell and taste was the heady rush of pure oxygen. Rigged up in all his HAHO gear – suit, gloves, harness, oxygen tank, parachute pack, helmet, mask, goggles – he felt horribly constrained. Trapped even.

It was hard to keep any sense of perspective.

The oxygen tended to push you into a heightened state of being – like having a massive alcohol high, but without the worry of the after-party hangover.

There was a sharp change in the howl of the turbines and the C-130 surged forward, accelerating powerfully. Seconds later, Jaeger felt it lift off and claw its way into the muggy skies. He reached behind him and plugged into the aircraft's intercom, so he could tune in to the pilot's chat.

It always served to calm him when preparing for a jump.

'Airspeed one hundred and eighty knots,' the pilot's voice intoned. 'Altitude fifteen hundred feet. Rate of climb . . .'

At this point, the only threat to getting in there was a storm forming over the jungle. At 30,000 feet, conditions were pretty much predictable – ice cold, windswept, but stable – whatever the weather at lower altitudes. Yet if a tropical storm blew up at ground level, it could make the landing impossible.

If there was anything more than a fifteen-knot crosswind, they'd have trouble putting down. Parachutes would be dragged sideways, their human cargo with them, and it would be doubly hazardous with their chosen landing point being so menaced by dangers on all sides.

A mighty river – the Rio de los Dios – cut through the jungle, twisting this way and that as it went. On one particularly tortuous stretch it had deposited a long, slim sandbar, which remained devoid of practically all vegetation. It was one of the few patches of clear ground in the vast expanse of jungle, hence why they'd chosen it as their point of touchdown.

But it left precious little room for error.

At one limit of the slender sandbar lay the riverbank, marked by a towering wall of jungle. If any bodies were blown off course that way, they would smash into the trees. If forced in the other direction, they'd get swept into the Rio de los Dios, the heavy weight of their kit dragging them under.

'Altitude three thousand five hundred,' the pilot's voice announced. 'Airspeed two hundred and fifty knots. Climbing to cruise height.'

'See that break in the jungle?' the navigator cut in. 'We follow that river due west for the next hour or so.'

'Got it,' the pilot confirmed. 'And ain't it a beautiful morning.'

As he listened in on the chat, Jaeger felt a rush of nausea hit his throat. As a rule, he didn't get airsick. It was getting wrapped, strapped and trapped in all the HAHO gear that he found so debilitating.

During HAHO training he'd had to undergo a series of tests to check his resistance to high altitude, low oxygen levels and extreme disorientation. He'd been placed inside a compression chamber, which had taken him up in stages to the kind of conditions encountered at 30,000 feet.

With each 3,000-foot rise in altitude, he'd had to rip off his oxygen mask and yell out his name, rank and serial number, before slamming the mask back on again.

That he'd found pretty much okay.

But then he was placed in the dreaded centrifuge.

The centrifuge was like a giant washing machine on steroids. He was spun around and around, faster and faster, until he was on the verge of passing out. Before losing consciousness you 'greyed out', your vision fading into a fractured kaleidoscope of grey. You needed to know when you were about to grey out, so you could recognise it on a real jump and get yourself out of the spin.

The centrifuge had been pure, puke-inducing horror.

They'd given Jaeger a video as a keepsake. Greying out was far from pretty. Your eyes bugged out like a wasp dosed with fly-killer, your face became hollowed out and skeletal, your cheeks flapped and sucked, your features distorted all to hell.

The centrifuge had come close to tearing Jaeger down and breaking him apart. A man who thrilled to the open wild, he'd hated crawling into that enclosed metal drum – that suffocating steel coffin of a machine. It had felt like a prison. Like his own grave.

Jaeger detested being locked up or in any way unnaturally constrained.

Just like now, trussed up in all this HAHO gear and waiting to make the jump.

He leaned back and closed his eyes, willing himself to sleep. It was the first rule of elite soldiering that he'd ever learned: never refuse the chance of a meal or a sleep, for you never knew when you might be getting your next.

Sometime later he felt a hand shake him awake. It was one of the PDs. For a moment he figured it had to be showtime, but when he glanced along the line of jumpers, no one seemed to be making ready for the exit.

The PD leaned closer and yelled in his ear. 'Pilot's coming aft to have a word.'

Jaeger glanced forward, seeing a figure step around the navigator perched on his fold-down seat at the rear of the cockpit.

The pilot must have handed the aircraft's controls to his co-pilot, Jaeger figured. He approached and leaned over, yelling to make himself heard above the roar of the engines. 'How you doin' back here?'

'Sleeping like a baby. Always a pleasure to fly with true professionals.'

'Always good to catch a few zees,' the pilot confirmed. 'So, something's kind of come up. Thought I ought to warn you guys. No idea what it means, but . . . Shortly after take-off, I got this sense we were being followed. Once a Night Stalker, always a Night Stalker, if you know what I mean.'

Jaeger raised one eyebrow. 'You were with the SOAR? The 160th?'

'Sure was,' the pilot growled, 'before I got too old and stiff to soldier any more.'

The 160th Special Operations Aviation Regiment – otherwise known as the Night Stalkers – was America's foremost covert airborne operations unit. On several occasions when deep behind enemy lines with the bad guys breathing down his neck, Jaeger had found himself calling upon a SOAR combat search-and-rescue helicopter.

'There's no finer unit,' Jaeger told the pilot. 'Respect for you guys. Many a time you pulled us out of the shit.'

The pilot delved into his pocket and drew out a military coin. He pressed it into Jaeger's hand.

It was about the size and shape of a large piece of chocolate money, of the type that Jaeger used to give Luke at Christmas in his stocking. Christmas had been a very special time for the Jaeger family; until their last – which had been mired in utter darkness. The memory of it caused Jaeger a momentary stab of pain.

The SOAR coin felt cold, thick and heavy in his hand. It had the unit's badge displayed across one face, with their motto on the other: *Death Waits in the Dark*. It was a tradition in the American military to give your unit coin to a fellow warrior, one for which the British military sadly didn't have an equivalent.

Jaeger felt honoured to have that coin, and he was determined to carry it through the coming expedition.

'So, I did a three-sixty-degree scan,' the pilot continued. 'Sure enough, some kind of small civilian aircraft had powered over the horizon and was keeping track with us. The longer it stayed there, hanging in my blind spot, the more certain I was we had a tail. It's still there, keeping maybe a good four miles back, and we're an hour-twenty into the flight.

'Figure from its radar signature it's somethin' like a Learjet 85,' the pilot continued. 'Small, fast, ultra-slick private passenger jet. You want me to dial them up and ask them what the hell they're doing sticking their nose up our ass?'

Jaeger thought about it for a second. Typically, an aircraft behaving like this one would be on a surveillance mission – trying to discover what the guys in front might be up to. Many a war had been won or lost on the strength of who had the best intelligence, and Jaeger for one never liked to be spied on.

'Any chance it's a coincidence? Maybe a commercial flight that happened to be on the same vector and cruise speed as us?'

The pilot shook his head. 'Not a hope. Learjet 85 cruises at up to forty-nine thousand feet. We're at thirty thousand – jump height. Pilots always fly at different altitudes, to de-conflict the airspace. And a Learjet cruises a good hundred knots faster than a Herc.'

'Any way they can cause us trouble?' Jaeger queried. 'With the jump?'

'Learjet versus a Super Hercules.' The pilot guffawed. 'I'd like to see 'em try.' He eyed Jaeger. 'But he's hanging back and sticking in our blind spot. Make no mistake – we got us a tail.'

'Let's just leave them thinking we don't know they're there. Gives us more options that way.'

The pilot nodded. 'Guess so. Keep 'em guessing.'

'Maybe it's a friendly agency?' Jaeger suggested. 'Keen to see what we're up to here?'

The pilot shrugged. 'Could be. But you know what they say: presumption is the mother of all screw-ups.'

Jaeger smiled. That had been one of their favourite sayings in the SAS. 'Let's assume whoever's tailing us isn't Santa Claus with a sleighload of presents. Keep a close eye. Let me know if anything changes.'

'Got it,' the pilot confirmed. 'Meantime, we'll keep it straight and steady, so you can grab some more zees.'

23

Jaeger leaned back and tried to sleep, but he felt strangely restless. Any which way he looked at it, he didn't have a clue what to make of that unidentified plane. He stuffed the pilot's Night Stalkers coin deep into his pocket, his hand brushing against a folded piece of paper. He'd almost forgotten it was there.

Shortly before leaving Rio de Janeiro, he had received an unexpected email. It was from Simon Jenkinson, the archivist. With Jaeger taking neither laptop nor smartphone on the coming expedition – they'd have zero chance of electricity or a mobile signal where they were heading – he'd printed out a copy.

He ran his eye over the message again now.

You asked me to keep you posted if I turned up anything interesting. Kew Archives just opened a new file under the 70-year rule: AVIA 54/1403A. When I saw it I couldn't believe it. Mind-blowing. Scary, almost. Strikes me as being something the authorities would never have allowed released if censors were doing their job properly.

I've asked for a copy of the entire file, but it usually takes an age. I will email over full documents once I have them. I managed to sneak a few photos via iPhone of the highlights. One is attached. Key name is Hans Kammler, or SS Oberst-Gruppenführer Hans Kammler as he was during the war. Make no mistake, Kammler is the key.

The National Archives, based in Kew, west London, contained vaults of documents from the workings of the British government reaching back over many centuries. You were free to go and view them in person, but you had to order copies of any you wished to take away and study further. It was strictly forbidden to copy them yourself.

The fact that Jenkinson had sneaked photos via his iPhone impressed Jaeger greatly.

Clearly the archivist had hidden reserves of steel.

Or maybe the documents had just seemed so extraordinary – so 'mind-blowing', as Jenkinson had put it – that he hadn't been able to resist breaking a few rules.

Jaeger had downloaded Jenkinson's attached photo. It had shown a blurry image of an intelligence briefing from Britain's wartime Air Ministry. Across the top was stamped in red: *MOST SECRET – ULTRA: To be kept under lock and key and never to be removed from this office*.

It read:

Signal intercept, 3rd February 1945. Translates as follows:

From the Führer to Special Plenipotentiary of the Führer, Hans Kammler, SS Oberst-Gruppenführer and General of the Waffen SS.

Subject: Führer's Special Task – reference *Aktion Adlerflug* (Operation Eagle's Flight).

Status: *Kriegsentscheidend* (beyond top secret).

Action: Kammler, as Führer's plenipotentiary, is to take command of all German Air Ministry departments, personnel, both flying and non-flying, allotment and development of aircraft, and all other supply matters including fuel and ground organisation, including airfields. Kammler's Reichssportfeld HQ to be headquarters for all allocation of equipment and supplies.

Kammler to be put in charge of programme to move vital armament industries beyond enemy reach. Kammler to form relocation commando reporting centres, equipped with Squadron 200 (LKW Junkers) tasked with removal of armaments systems, evacuation and transport, with a view to appropriate redistribution to pre-identified safe havens.

Jenkinson had added an explanatory note to the effect that the LKW Junkers was an alternative Nazi designation for the Ju 390.

Jaeger had googled the word 'plenipotentiary'. As far as he could discern, it meant a special emissary granted extraordinary powers. In other words, Kammler had been Hitler's right-hand man and go-getter, empowered to do whatever was necessary.

Jenkinson's email was tantalising. It seemed to suggest that Hans Kammler had been tasked to remove the Nazis' key weaponry at the end of the war, putting it out of reach of the Allies. And if Jenkinson was right, the means to do so may well have been a squadron of giant Ju 390 warplanes.

Jaeger had emailed Jenkinson asking for a sense of what the entire Kammler file might signify. But he'd received no reply, or at least not before he'd boarded the flight into the heart of the Amazon. He had had to reconcile himself to getting no further clarification – or at least not until the expedition was complete.

'P-Hour minus twenty.' The pilot's announcement broke Jaeger's reverie. 'Weather reports good and clear; approach course unchanged.'

There was a bitterly cold draught blowing through the aircraft's hold. Jaeger bashed his frozen hands together to try to work some life into them. He'd kill for a steaming cup of coffee right now.

The Super Hercules was some 200 kilometres east of their release point. Via a bunch of mind-boggling calculations – taking into account the wind speed and direction at 30,000 feet and all altitudes in between – they'd calculated the exact point in the sky from which they needed to jump.

From there, it would be a forty-kilometre glide into the sandbar.

'P minus ten,' the pilot intoned.

Jaeger got to his feet.

To his right he saw a line of figures likewise levering themselves off their seats, stamping stiff legs to drive out the cold. He bent and clipped his heavy rucksack on to the front of his parachute harness, using a series of thick steel clips – carabiners – to do so. When he jumped, the pack would be left hanging from his chest, suspended on a pulley system.

'P minus eight,' the pilot announced.

Jaeger's pack weighed in at thirty-five kilograms. He had a similar weight of parachute gear strapped to his back. Plus he was carrying fifteen kilos of weaponry and ammo, and the oxygen-breathing system.

Approaching ninety kilos in all.

More than his own bodyweight.

Jaeger was five foot nine and lithe with it, every inch honed and toned muscle. People tended to think of elite forces types as being monsters, true man mountains. Sure, there were some – like Raff – who were simply massive, but a greater proportion were like Jaeger: leopard-slim, fast and deadly.

The lead PD stepped back so they could all see him. He flashed up five fingers: *P minus five*. Jaeger couldn't hear the pilot any more; he'd unplugged from the intercom system. From now on the jump would all be done via hand signals.

The PD held up his right fist and blew into it. His fingers opened as he did so, like a spreading flower. He held up five fingers, flashing them twice. It was the signal for wind speed at ground level: ten knots. Jaeger breathed a sigh of relief. Ten knots was doable for making the landing.

He busied himself tightening straps one last time and double-checking his gear. The PD flashed three fingers in front of his goggled face: three minutes to the jump. It was time to link up with Irina Narov for the tandem.

Jaeger turned to face the rear of the Hercules. He shuffled ahead, lifting his heavy rucksack with one hand and using the other to hold himself steady against the aircraft's side. He needed to get as near to the ramp as possible before his fellow jumper was strapped on.

From up ahead he heard a dull and hollow thunk. It was followed by a mechanical whine and an icy inrush of air. The ramp had cracked open and begun to lower, and with each foot a howling gale blew ever more powerfully into the hold.

As he moved closer to the churning slipstream, Jaeger half expected to hear the first notes of Wagner blasting out of the aircraft's speakers. It was around now that the pilot would normally start the music.

Instead he caught a burst of wild and savage guitar riffs, followed an instant later by the thumping percussion of drums. Then the high-pitched manic voice of the lead singer of an iconic heavy rock band cut in . . .

It was AC/DC's 'Highway to Hell'.

The pilot was a Night Stalker all right: he'd clearly decided they were going to do this his way.

The maniacal chorus struck up just as the lead PD manhandled a figure towards Jaeger: Irina Narov – ready for the strap-on.

Highway to hell . . .

The pilot – plus the song's very title – seemed to be suggesting that Jaeger and his team were on a one-way trip to damnation.

Were they? Jaeger wondered. Were they heading into hell?

Was that where this mission was taking them?

He hoped and prayed that a far better fate awaited them in the jungle.

Yet a part of him feared they were jumping into the worst kind of torment amongst the Mountains of the Gods.

24

Jaeger did his best to blank the crazed, frenzied singing from his head. For a moment he locked eyes with the tall, finely muscled Russian woman standing before him. She looked to be in perfect shape: there didn't appear to be an ounce of excess weight anywhere on her sparse frame.

Jaeger didn't know exactly what he expected to read in her gaze.

Apprehension? Fear?

Or maybe something approaching panic?

Narov was ex-Spetsnaz, about the nearest the Russians had to the SAS. By rights, as a former Spetsnaz officer she should be shit hot. But Jaeger had known many a top soldier crap out when on the brink of diving off the ramp into the freezing, screaming blue.

At this kind of height the curvature of the earth would be clearly visible, stretching away to the pencil-slim horizon. Jumping off a C-130's ramp was daunting enough at the best of times. When doing so from the very outer reaches of earth's atmosphere it was a total leap of faith, and it could be terrifying as hell.

But as he looked into Narov's ice-blue eyes, all Jaeger could detect was an unreadable, inscrutable calm. A surprising emptiness filled them; a resolute stillness – almost as if nothing, not even a 30,000-foot dive into the churning void, could reach her.

She flicked her gaze away from his, turned her back on him and adopted the position.

They shuffled closer.

On a tandem, you jumped both facing the same direction. Jaeger's parachute should be enough to stem their combined fall, giving them an expanse of shared silk to glide under all the way to the touchdown. The PDs standing to either side proceeded to strap the two of them together, vice-tight.

Jaeger had tandemed up scores of times before. He knew he shouldn't be feeling as he was – awkward and uncomfortable at having another human being in such close proximity to his person.

Before now he'd always tandemed with a fellow elite operator; a brother warrior. Someone he knew well and would gladly fight back-to-back with, if ever the shit went down. He felt far from comfortable getting strapped skin-tight to a total stranger, and a woman.

Narov was also the person in his team that he least trusted right now: his chief suspect for Andy Smith's murder. Yet he couldn't deny it – her striking good looks were getting under his skin. However much he might try to zone out such thoughts and tune into the jump, it just wasn't happening.

It wasn't helped by the music – AC/DC's wild lyrics pounding into his skull.

Jaeger glanced behind him. It was all happening fast now.

He could see the PDs rolling the two para-tubes forward on the rails that ran the length of the hold. Kamishi and Krakow shuffled ahead, and bent as if in prayer over the bulky containers. The PDs proceeded to strap the para-tubes to their chest harnesses. The two jumpers would roll the tubes ahead and leap out with them, just seconds after Jaeger and Narov were gone.

Jaeger turned back to face the sun-whipped void.

All of a sudden the screeching racket from the aircraft's speakers seemed to stop dead. 'Highway to Hell' had been cut short. There was a few seconds' wind-blasted silence, before Jaeger heard a new burst of sound. In the place of AC/DC's hell track, a uniquely powerful and evocative piece of music began to pulsate through the C-130's hold.

It was unmistakable.

Classical.

Jaeger allowed himself a smile.

The pilot had needled him for a while there, but he'd come good in the end. It was Wagner's 'Ride of the Valkyries' after all – and for the final few seconds before jump time.

Jaeger and the music went back a long way.

Before joining the SAS, he had served as a commando in the Royal Marines. He'd got himself jump-trained, and it was the 'Ride of the Valkyries' that had been played during the ceremony when he'd gained his parachute wings. Many a time he'd hurled himself out of a C-130 along with his fellow SAS blades, Wagner's classic composition blaring out over the speaker system.

It was the unofficial anthem of British airborne units.

And it was as fine a track as any to be jumping to, on a mission such as this.

As he steeled himself for the exit, Jaeger gave a moment's thought to the aircraft that had been on their tail. The C-130 pilot had made no further mention of it. Jaeger guessed it had disappeared – maybe calling off the pursuit as the Hercules had crossed the border into Bolivian airspace.

It certainly couldn't be about to interfere with the jump, or the pilot wouldn't be letting them go.

He blanked it from his mind.

He nudged Narov forward, shuffling as one towards the open ramp. To either side the PDs strapped themselves to the air-frame to avoid being torn out by the howling gale.

The secret to making a HAHO jump was to always keep a grasp on your spatial awareness; to know exactly where you were positioned within the stick of parachutists. As lead jumper, it was vital that Jaeger held them tight. If he lost someone he couldn't exactly use his radio to call them back; the turbulence and wind noise made communications impossible during the freefall.

Jaeger and Narov came to a halt at the very lip of the ramp.

Figures lined up aft of them. Jaeger felt his heart beating like a machine gun, as the adrenalin surged and burned through his veins. They were on the very roof of the world up here, the realm of the starry heavens.

The PDs did a final visual check on each of the jumpers, ensuring that no straps were snagged or tangled, or hanging free. With Jaeger it was a case of doing so by feel, making sure that all Narov's points of contact with him were attached good and tight.

The lead PD started yelling the final instructions. 'Tail off equipment check!'

'TEN GOOD!' the rearmost figure cried.

'NINE GOOD!'

As each figure called out his ready status, he thumped the one in front. No thump on the shoulder and you knew the guy behind was in trouble.

'THREE GOOD!' Jaeger felt a whack from the jumper to his rear. It was Mike Dale, the young Aussie cameraman who'd be filming him and Narov as they piled off the aircraft's open ramp, with a miniature camera strapped to his helmet.

Before the words could freeze in his throat, Jaeger forced himself to yell: 'ONE AND TWO GOOD!'

The line shuffled more tightly together. Too much separation in the sky and they'd risk losing each other in the freefall.

Jaeger glanced at the jump light.

It began to flash red: *get ready*.

He glanced ahead, peering over Narov's shoulder. He felt a few strands of her loose hair whipping into his face, the stark oblong of the ramp silhouetted against the bright, snarling maw of the heavens.

Outside was a whirlwind of pure, raging, blinding light.

He felt the wind tearing at his helmet and trying to rip the goggles from his face. He got his head down and steeled himself to drive forward.

Out of the corner of his eye he saw the red light burn green. The PD stepped back: 'GO! GO! GO!'

Suddenly Jaeger was thrusting Narov forward, driving her ahead and then diving into thin air. As one they tumbled into the snarling emptiness. But as they left the open ramp, Jaeger felt something catch momentarily, the force of it snagging and then tearing loose, serving to throw them violently off balance.

He knew instantly what had happened: they'd made an unstable exit.

They'd been thrown off-kilter and they were going into a spin.

This had the potential to be really bad.

Jaeger and Narov were sucked through the churning maw of the aircraft's slipstream, the violent turbulence throwing them over and over faster than ever. Spat out of the aircraft's wake, they began to plummet towards earth, twisting round and round like some giant crazed spinning top.

Jaeger tried to focus his mind on counting out the seconds before he could risk opening the chute.

'Three thousand and three, three thousand and four . . .'

But as the voice counted out the beats inside his head, he realised things were rapidly worsening. Rather than stabilising, the spin just seemed unstoppable. It was the nightmare of the centrifuge all over, only now it was happening at 30,000 feet and for real.

He tried to gauge how fast they were rotating – to see if he could risk pulling the chute. The only way to do so was by counting how rapidly the air around them turned from blue to green to blue to green and back again. Blue meant facing the sky, green meant the jungle.

Blue-green-blue-green-blue-green-bluuue-greeeeeen-blueeeennnnn . . . Aaarrgggh!

Right now Jaeger was struggling to remain conscious, let alone get a grip on the view.

25

The jump plan called for them all to link up in the free-fall, and to pull their chutes on Jaeger releasing his. That way they'd descend pretty much as one, gliding into the landing zone good and tight. But being in tandem and with the spin catapulting them across the heavens – already they were starting to lose the others.

They plummeted towards earth, spinning faster and faster with the fall. As the air speed increased so did the G-forces, the wind tearing at Jaeger's head like a raging hurricane. He felt as if he were strapped on to some giant out-of-control superbike, which was powering down a corkscrew-shaped tunnel at pushing four hundred kilometres an hour.

With the wind-chill factor, the temperature had to be minus 100 degrees. And as the spin became ever more violent Jaeger could sense the grey-out creeping into the edges of his frozen eyeballs.

His vision blurred and fuzzed. He felt himself gasping for breath; for oxygen. Burning lungs struggled to drag in enough gas from the bottle. His sensory awareness – the ability to judge where he was, or even who he was – was rapidly slipping away.

Beside him his combat shotgun was slamming about like a baseball bat, the folding butt cracking blows into his helmeted head. It had been fastened tight to his side, but somehow it had been ripped loose in the freefall, and it was making them even more unstable.

Jaeger was on the verge of losing consciousness now.

And he didn't want to imagine what state Narov was in.

With his pulse juddering inside his skull and his mind reeling from the dizziness and disorientation, Jaeger forced his scrambled mind to focus. *He had to stabilise their fall.* Narov was relying on him, as was every jumper in the stick.

There was only one way to stop the spin.

Now to do it.

He drew his arms in close to his chest, then flung both them and his legs into a rigid star shape, bracing his back against the unbearable forces that were threatening to tear him limb from limb. Muscles screamed against the pain and the pressure. He let out a piercing cry of agony as he held the pose and tried to anchor the two of them in the razor-thin air.

'*Aaaaaarrggghhhhh!*'

At least no one would ever hear him scream, for they were alone on the very roof of the world up here.

With arms and legs thrust out rigid to make four anchors, his body arched through the hopelessly light atmosphere. The frozen air howled all around him as his limbs locked with the pain. If only he could hold the star shape for long enough to stabilise their crazed corkscrew descent, they might just get through this alive.

Gradually, slowly, agonisingly, Jaeger began to sense the revolutions decreasing.

Finally, he and Narov stopped spinning.

He forced his frazzled mind to concentrate.

He was facing the blinding blue.

Blue meant sky.

He let out a string of curses. *Wrong way up.*

The two of them were dropping at a murderous speed with their backs to the earth. Every second brought them 300 feet nearer to a pulverising impact, as they plummeted towards the thick jungle. But if Jaeger pulled the chute in their present position, it would open below them. They would fall through it, tearing towards earth like a pair of corpses entombed in a shroud of tangled silk.

They'd smash into the forest at pushing four hundred kilometres an hour.

Dead men.

Or rather one man and one woman, locked in a killer embrace.

Jaeger changed position, forcing his right arm in close to his side. He threw his opposite shoulder over, trying to flip the two of them around. He needed to get them facing green. Urgently.

Green meant earth.

But for some reason all the manoeuvre seemed to achieve was the very worst result of all – the violent twist sending them back into the spin.

For a moment he was on the very brink of panic. His arm reached involuntarily for the release cord of his chute, but he forced himself to stay his hand. He forced himself to remember how they'd tested this repeatedly with a specially made dummy, during trial jumps.

If you opened the chute in the spin, you were asking for trouble. Big time.

The lines would wrap themselves up tight, like a kid spooling up spaghetti on a fork. Not good news.

As the spin intensified, Jaeger knew that the full grey-out was almost upon him. This was meltdown time. It was like the centrifuge on steroids, only at extreme high altitude and with no off button. His vision started to blur and fuzz, his mind drifting further and further away from him. He was on the verge of blacking out.

'Focus!' he snarled.

He cursed himself, trying to free his head of the blinding confusion. 'FOCUS! *FO-CUS.*'

Every second was precious now. He needed to flick himself back into the star shape, and get Narov to do the same. They'd stand a far better chance of stabilising like that.

There was no way of communicating with her, apart from

body language and hand gestures. He was about to grab her arms and signal what he wanted when his frazzled senses realised that she had started struggling violently against him.

Amidst all the blinding confusion, something flashed silver-bright through the clear and glistening air.

A blade.

A commando-style knife.

Thrusting towards him, ready to drive into his chest region.

In an instant Jaeger knew what was happening. It was impossible, but it was for real. Narov was preparing to stab at him with her knife.

Carson's warning flashed through his mind: *Never to be found without her knife. Or crossed.*

The blade drove at him in a savage thrust.

Jaeger managed to block it with a parry of his right arm, using the tough altimeter that he had strapped to his wrist to take the impact. The blade glanced off the thick glass, nicking into his Gore-Tex sleeve as it did so.

He felt a jabbing stab of pain in his right forearm.

She'd cut him with the first blow.

For a few desperate moments he continued to block and parry, as Narov slashed wildly with the blade, again and again and again.

She swung once more, stabbing much lower this time and clearly going for his guts. Jaeger's arm – frozen like a block of ice – was a split second too slow.

He failed to parry the thrust.

He tensed for the punching agony of a blade slicing deep into his abdomen. It didn't much matter where she stabbed him.

If she opened him up here, plummeting to earth at a thousand feet or more every three seconds, he was a dead man.

26

The knife came at him in a swift, driving thrust.

But oddly, as it disappeared from view around the base of his stomach, Jaeger felt no pain. No pain at all. Instead he felt the first of the straps that held Narov to him break open, as the blade sliced through it.

Her arm reached forward, drove backwards, and again the razor-sharp knife struck home, sawing apart the tough canvas and nylon.

Once she was done slicing through the right-hand straps, Narov swapped sides. She jabbed backwards with the blade several further times, cutting away frenziedly at the left-hand ones.

A few final jabs and she was done.

With that, Irina Narov, the wild card on Jaeger's team, spun away from him.

The moment she tore herself free, Jaeger saw her snap her arms and legs out into a star shape. As her limbs slowed her fall and she began to stabilise, Jaeger whirled past. Moments later there was a crack from above like the sails of a ship catching the wind, and a parachute flared in the sky.

Irina Narov had pulled her emergency chute.

Released of the dead weight of a second body, Jaeger's odds of survival were suddenly far better than the near-zero they'd been five seconds ago. For a few long moments he struggled desperately to bring his own spin under control, fighting to stop the wild corkscrewing and to stabilise himself.

He was pushing two minutes into the freefall when he finally risked jerking the release cord – sending 360 square feet of the finest silk billowing out behind him.

An instant later he felt as if a giant hand was reaching over and yanking him violently upwards by the shoulders. Decelerating from a monster freefall like this was akin to driving a car into a brick wall at colossal speed and all the airbags going off at once.

Jaeger had gone from facing an imminent, onrushing, life-ending impact with the jungle to knowing that his parachute had saved him. Or rather, that Irina Narov's slick handiwork with her knife had pretty much rescued the both of them. He glanced upwards, to check that his canopy was good. He reached with his hands, grabbed the steering toggles and gave them a series of sharp pumps, releasing the half-brakes and allowing the chute to fully fly.

Thank God it felt okay.

From the swirling, sickening maelstrom and earsplitting wind noise of the freefall, Jaeger's world had transformed itself into one of pure calm stillness. Just the occasional flap of wind ruffled the slider panel above him. For a moment he concentrated on bringing his heartbeat under control, and on properly clearing his head, so he could relax into the glide.

He risked a glance at his altimeter. He was at 1,800 feet. He'd just completed a 28,000-foot death ride towards earth. It had taken six seconds for his chute to open fully. He'd deployed it less than ten seconds away from ploughing into the earth at pushing 200 kph.

It had been that close.

At that speed there wouldn't have been a great deal left of him to scrape up from amongst the ferns and the rotting wood, so that his mates could bury his remains.

Jaeger stole a brief moment to scan the sky.

Apart from Narov, there wasn't another jumper to be seen.

He flicked his aching, bloodshot eyes downwards, searching

the velvety green canopy below. It was drifting up to meet him and not a clearing was there anywhere to be seen.

He figured he and Narov had to be thirty-plus kilometres away from their intended landing zone. The plan had been to open their chutes at 28,000 feet, and glide the forty-odd kilometres into that sandbar. But with their unstable exit and the murderous spin that had followed, all of that was now defunct.

Apart from the unarguably spirited and tough Narov, Jaeger had lost every other member of his team.

They were two lone parachutists drifting through the hot, steamy air, with nowhere to put down.

It didn't get a lot worse.

For a moment Jaeger wondered if it had been his weapon that had snagged on the ramp of the Hercules, sending them into that near-fatal spin. But how could the PDs have missed it? It was their job to ensure that every jumper was free of obstructions; that nothing was hanging loose that might snag. And beyond that, he knew he'd properly tightened his shotgun prior to making the jump.

Jaeger had worked with countless PD crews over the years. Invariably, they were the ultimate professionals. They knew they held the jumpers' lives in their hands, and that one tiny mistake could prove fatal. It was only by sheer luck – and, he had to admit it, Narov's quick thinking – that both of them were still alive.

It didn't make any sense for the PDs to have let his weapon flap loose on exit. It just didn't compute. In fact, there was one hell of a lot that didn't add up thus far. First Smithy had died – or rather, been murdered. Then they'd had that unidentified aircraft on their tail. And now this.

Had one of the PDs deliberately tried to sabotage their jump? Jaeger just didn't know, but he was starting to wonder what else could possibly go wrong.

As it happened, a great deal – for right now he had the mother of all problems to deal with.

After chute-opening, touchdown was the next most dangerous moment – always – and especially when you had absolutely nowhere clear on which to put down. A parachute jump instructor had once warned Jaeger that it wasn't the freefall that killed people – it was the ground that did.

Jaeger had gained a few hundred feet on Narov, once she'd cut away from him in the spin. They were reduced to a team of two now. The key priority was to keep together for the touchdown, and whatever might come thereafter. Jaeger focused on trying to slow himself, so she could catch him.

Above him, Narov executed a series of sharp left turns, as she corkscrewed downwards under her chute, rapidly losing height with each rotation. Jaeger kept trimming his own parachute, feathering his brake lines to slow his wind speed and fall.

After a few seconds he sensed a faint ruffling in the air beside him, and there was Narov. Their eyes met across the space between them. In spite of their epic mid-air 'knife fight', she seemed as cool as a cucumber. It was as if nothing untoward had happened.

Jaeger tried a thumbs-up.

Narov reciprocated.

He signalled that he'd lead her in to make the landing. She gave a curt nod. She dropped behind him and took up a position a few dozen metres above. They had just a few hundred feet to go now.

Fortunately, Jaeger had trained for what was coming – impact into a jungle canopy. It was far from easy to get it right. Only the most experienced jumpers could manage it. But from the trick that Narov had pulled when she'd cut free during the spin, Jaeger figured she'd stand as good a chance as any.

He searched the terrain below for a patch of canopy that seemed thinner than the rest; somewhere they could maybe break through. Most parachutists who dropped into dense jungle hadn't intended to be there at all; they were airmen bailing out of an aircraft that had either been shot down, or had suffered some kind of mechanical problem – maybe run out of fuel.

They'd hit the canopy with no idea how to approach it, nor any training on how to survive. They'd normally suffer injuries in the impact – broken arms or legs. But worse would follow. Whilst the jumper might break through, the parachute rarely if ever did. It would snag on the topmost branches, leaving the parachutist suspended in mid-air, hanging just below the treetops.

And that very often proved the death of them.

A jumper so trapped had three options. Remain suspended in his chute, and hope for some kind of rescue. Cut himself free, with a sixty- to eighty-foot drop to the forest floor below. Try to reach a branch, if one was near enough, and climb to the ground.

More often than not, jumpers chose to remain hanging in their chutes, for the other options were approaching suicidal. Injured, disorientated, suffering from shock and dehydration, and plagued by ravenous insects, they'd stay there waiting to be rescued.

Most took a long few days to die.

Jaeger didn't fancy that for himself, or for Irina Narov, either.

27

Through the swirling mist he caught sight of a patch of lighter yellowish-green amidst the dark carpet of old growth that stretched to the distant horizon. Fresh vegetation. That new growth should be more leafy, springy and yielding; less likely to break and snap into jagged branch ends, like spear tips.

Or so Jaeger hoped.

He glanced at his altimeter – the one with which he'd fended off what he'd feared were knife thrusts intended to disembowel him.

Five hundred feet to go.

He reached forward and pushed down the two metal levers on his rucksack's attachment. He felt the heavy pack drop away as the rope let it fall ten metres below him.

The last thing he did as the forest canopy raced up towards him was to punch a button on his wrist-mounted GPS – his global positioning system. Before the forest claimed them, he got it to waypoint – to mark – their exact position, for he figured they'd not be getting another chance to do so any time soon.

In the final few seconds prior to impact he concentrated on trimming the chute with the left and right toggles, so as to get himself down over that lighter patch of green.

He saw the mass of the canopy rushing up to meet him. He pulled back hard on both toggles, flaring and slowing his chute. If he could just hold it back from the stall, this was the way to burn off the speed and to ease his way through.

A moment later he heard the cracking thump as the thirty-five-kilo rucksack piled into the topmost branches, smashing them apart and disappearing from view.

Jaeger lifted his legs, bent his knees, and clenched his arms protectively over his chest and face. An instant later he felt his boots and knees penetrate the vegetation as he followed the rucksack through. Sharp branches ripped at his butt and then his shoulders before he shot past into the open darkness below.

He cannoned off some thicker branches, gasping with pain from the impact, and plummeted for several feet, before his chute ploughed into the canopy above, bringing him up short. He felt winded by the sudden deceleration. A swirling fog of leaves, broken twigs and plant matter whirled around him as he fought for breath. But as he swung backwards and forward like a pendulum, Jaeger counted his blessings a thousand times over.

He was uninjured, and he was still very much alive.

There was a second crash from above, and moments later Narov appeared beside him, likewise swinging wildly to and fro.

Slowly the atmosphere around them cleared.

Shafts of blinding sunlight streamed in through the holes they'd punched in the canopy, sunbeams dancing in the air.

In the ringing silence it was as if every living being in the jungle was holding its breath, as if shocked that two such alien creatures could have dropped in on their world.

The swaying of the chutes slowed.

'You okay?' Jaeger called across at Narov.

After all they'd been through, it sounded like the understatement of the century.

Narov shrugged. 'I am alive. You are evidently alive. It could be worse.'

Like how exactly? Jaeger felt like asking. But he held his counsel. While Narov's English was fluent enough, her Russian accent remained strong, her way of speaking oddly flat and unemotional.

He jerked his head upwards, in the direction of the freefall. He tried a winning smile. 'For a moment there I thought you were trying to kill me. With the knife.'

She stared at him. 'If I had wanted to kill you, I would have killed you.'

Jaeger chose to ignore the taunt. 'I was trying to stabilise the two of us. Something snagged us at the exit, tearing my weapon loose. I almost had it sorted when you cut yourself free. Talk about a lack of faith.'

'Maybe.' Narov eyed him for a brief second, her face a blank mask. 'But you failed.' She glanced away from him. 'Had I not cut free, we would both now be dead.'

There wasn't a lot Jaeger could say to that. He wriggled about in his harness, trying to get a good look at the terrain beneath them.

'Anyway, why would I want to kill you?' Narov continued. 'Mr Jaeger, you need to learn to trust your team.' She eyed the jungle canopy. 'So, the question now is – how do we get down from here? We didn't exactly train for this in the Spetsnaz.'

'Not like you train for cutting away from your tandem in the spin?' Jaeger queried. 'That knifework – that was pretty slick.'

'I have never trained for doing that. But there was nothing else; no other option.' Narov paused. '"Any mission, any time, any place: whatever it takes." The motto of the Spetsnaz.'

Before Jaeger could think of a suitable reply, there was a tearing crack from above, like an explosion. A heavy branch crashed downwards, tumbling to the forest floor below. An instant later Narov lurched a good few feet lower, as one of the panels of her damaged chute tore apart, giving way under the pressure.

She glanced up at Jaeger. 'So, do you have any idea as to how we get down? Other than falling? Or do I have to get us out of this one too?'

Jaeger shook his head in frustration. God, but this woman was trying. Yet after her mid-air performance with the knife, he was beginning to doubt whether she was Smithy's murderer after all. It had been the perfect opportunity for her to slip her blade into Jaeger and kill him, and yet she hadn't.

No harm in testing her further, though, Jaeger reflected. 'There is maybe a way to get us out of this.' He gestured at the tangled mess of their parachutes in the canopy. 'But first I'm gonna need that knife of yours.'

He had his own blade strapped to his person. It was the Gerber knife that Raff had given him in Bioko. It had a special meaning for him now, for it was the blade with which he'd saved his good friend's life. He wore it in a sheath slung diagonally across his chest. But he wanted to see if Narov would willingly hand over the weapon that had so nearly sliced his guts out.

She didn't so much as hesitate. 'My knife? But don't drop it. It's an old friend.' She reached for the long blade, unclipped it, took the point in her hand and launched it across the short distance between them.

'Catch,' she called, as it flashed through the sunlight and the shadows.

The knife that Jaeger caught looked strangely familiar. For a moment he turned it over in his hands, the slender seven-inch tapered stiletto blade glinting in the sunlight. There was no doubt about it: it was similar to the one lying in Grandpa Ted's trunk, back in Jaeger's Wardour Castle apartment.

When Jaeger had turned sixteen, his grandfather had allowed him to unsheathe that knife, while the two of them puffed away contentedly on his pipe. The smoky, aromatic scent came back to Jaeger now, as did the name of the knife: it was stamped on the dagger's hilt.

He checked Narov's blade, then glanced up at her appraisingly. 'Nice. A Fairbairn–Sykes fighting knife. Second World War vintage, if I'm not mistaken.'

'It is.' Narov shrugged. 'As you SAS proved back then, very good for killing Germans.'

Jaeger eyed her for a long moment. 'You think we'll be killing Germans? On this expedition?'

Narov's answer – thrown back at him defiantly – echoed Great Uncle Joe's dark words, and it was uttered in what sounded like fluent German: '*Denn heute gehort uns Deutschland, und morgen die ganze Welt.*' Today Germany belongs to us: tomorrow, the entire world.

'You know, it's unlikely there are going to be any left alive on that aircraft.' A hint of sarcasm had crept into Jaeger's tone. 'After seventy-odd years in the depths of the Amazon – I'd say next to impossible.'

'*Schwachkopf!*' – idiot! Narov glared at him. 'You think I don't know that? Why not do something useful, Mr Expedition Leader, and get us out of this mess you got us into?'

28

Jaeger outlined to Narov what he had in mind.

The emergency chute that Narov had been forced to pull was a smaller, less substantial piece of kit than his own BT80. It looked to have been badly torn when she ploughed into the treetops, which was why Jaeger proposed getting them stabilised under both canopies, forming one strong point from which they could lower themselves to the ground.

After he was done explaining, they proceeded to cut their rucksacks free, which until now had been left hanging suspended on the lines below. The heavy packs crashed through the layers of vegetation, each landing with a clearly audible thud on the forest floor far below. There was no way to complete the series of manoeuvres that he had in mind with thirty-five kilos of kit hanging on a line below their feet.

Next he got Narov to swing towards him, and he did likewise, each using their canopy like an anchor. With arms gripping the lines above, they twisted this way and that, until each was able to grab for the other at the furthest reach of their pendulum-like oscillation.

Jaeger's legs felt for Narov's body, hooked around her hips and held tight. Then his arms grabbed for her torso and he clipped her chest harness tight to his. They were now locked together at the point midway between their two chutes.

But in contrast to the tandem jump, they were joined face to face, attached via a thick carabiner – a D-shaped metal ring with a spring-loaded clip. Jaeger found the position and the close proximity decidedly uncomfortable, particularly as he was boiling up in the heat – the thick and cumbersome survival suit plus the rest of the HAHO gear serving to roast him alive.

But hell, anything to get them down in one piece.

Using a second carabiner, he locked the parachutes firmly together at the base of their rigging – the narrowest point of each. He then took out a length of Specter paracord – a high-tensile khaki cord about as thick as your average washing line, but with an extraordinary strength. It had a 500-pound breaking strain, but Jaeger doubled it over anyway, just to be certain.

He threaded it twice through a belay device – a climber's abseiling tool – to provide added friction, tying the upper end on to the parachutes. The rest of the paracord he uncoiled carefully below him, letting it fall the one hundred feet or so to the earth below. Finally, he clipped the belay device on to the carabiner attached to his chest harness, so that he and Narov were attached to the makeshift paracord rope.

They were now hanging in their chutes, whilst at the same time being attached to them independently via the paracord rig that Jaeger had just assembled. Now came the crunch moment: it was time to cut out of their parachutes, and for Jaeger to perform a free abseil, so lowering them to the ground.

Both he and Narov ripped off helmet, masks and goggles, letting them fall to the forest floor. Jaeger was sweating like a pig after all the exertion. He could feel the perspiration running down his face in rivulets, soaking the front of his clothing where he was clipped skin-tight to Narov.

It was like a wet T-shirt competition – only up close and personal – and he felt as if he could trace every minute contour of her body.

'I sense that you are uncomfortable,' Narov remarked. Her voice had an odd, matter-of-fact, mechanical ring to it. 'Such close proximity can be necessary for several reasons. One: practical necessity. Two: to share body warmth. Three: sex. This now is for reason number one. Stay focused on the job.'

Blah, blah, blah, Jaeger thought. *Trust me to end up trapped in the jungle with only the ice maiden for company.*

'So, you tricked me into your embrace,' Narov continued flatly. She pointed upwards. 'Whatever you next have in mind, I suggest you hurry.'

Jaeger looked where she indicated. Three feet above his head there was a gigantic spider. It was about the size of his hand, and it appeared semi-luminous and silvery in the half-light – its body plump, its legs like eight emaciated fingers groping towards him.

He could see its bulbous, evil red eyes glaring, the chomping moist maw of its jaws moving hungrily. It lifted its front legs, waving them aggressively, as it edged ever closer. Worse still, he could see its fangs – presumably tipped with poison – poised to strike.

He whipped up Narov's knife, ready to slash it to pieces, but her hand stopped him.

'Don't!' she hissed.

She pulled out her back-up blade and, without bothering to unsheathe it, slid the narrow end beneath the spider's hairy body and flipped it into the air. It spun around and around, torso glinting as it caught the sunbeams, then tumbled downwards, jaws hissing in anger at having been thwarted.

Narov didn't take her eyes off the treetops. 'I kill only when I need to. And when it is wise.'

Jaeger glanced where she was looking. There were scores more of the arachnids crawling towards them. In fact, their parachute rigging seemed to be alive with the things.

'*Phoneutria,*' Narov continued. 'Greek for murderess. We must have hit a nest as we came through.' She glanced at him. 'Rearing up with their front legs is a defensive posture. If you cut one, the body gives off a scent that warns its siblings, and then they really attack. The venom contains the PhTx3 neurotoxin. A nerve poison. Symptoms are very similar to a nerve gas attack: loss of muscle control and breathing, followed by paralysis and asphyxiation.'

'Whatever you say, Dr Death,' Jaeger muttered.

She glared at him. 'I will fend them off. You – you get us down from here.'

Jaeger reached behind her with the commando knife and began to cut through the thick band of canvas-like material that joined her parachute harness to its rigging. As he sliced away, he saw Narov's knife dart forward and flick a second and a third spider away.

She fended off more and more of the things, but he figured she must have missed one. It came pulsing towards him, front legs rearing up, fangs just inches from his bare hand. Acting on instinct, he flicked the knife towards it, the razor-sharp stiletto point jabbing at its underside. As the blade nicked it and drew blood, the spider balled up, rolling away and plummeting towards the forest floor.

The instant it did so, Jaeger sensed a clicking, clacking alarm signal pulse through its scores of fellow arachnids, as they sensed that one of their number had been blooded.

As one, they surged forward to attack.

'Now they really come!' Narov hissed.

She unsheathed her blade and lunged to left and right, stabbing at the hissing mass of arachnids. Jaeger redoubled his efforts. After a final few slashes, he succeeded in cutting Narov free, her weight dragging her down at an alarming rate before the carabiner locking her to Jaeger's harness pulled her up short.

For a split second he tensed for his canopy giving way under the extra weight, but luckily it held fast. He reached above his head, hacked at his rigging savagely, and a moment later it too gave way.

Both he and Narov broke free, as if they were falling.

For a second or two he let them plummet – the paracord rope hissing through the belay plate – until he judged they were well out of reach of the army of deadly arachnids. Then he closed his grip on the length of paracord and snatched it vertically downwards, pulling it tight.

The friction against the belay plate served to slow and halt their fall. They were now dangling on the paracord line some thirty feet below their chutes, which were now a seething mass of enraged and highly toxic spiders.

Phoneutria. Jaeger would be very happy never to see another as long as he lived.

He'd hardly had time to indulge the thought before the first of the writhing silvery blobs launched itself after them. It plunged vertically downwards, trailing out its own rope – a thin thread of spider's silk – behind it.

In response, Jaeger released the paracord and he and Narov plunged into the fall once more.

29

They'd barely dropped a dozen feet when they were brought to a halt with a sickening jerk. A broken strap in Narov's HAHO suit had got trapped in the belay device, jamming it.

Jaeger cursed.

He grabbed the material with his free hand and tried to rip it free. As he did so, he felt something soft and bony land in his hair with an angry, bubbling hiss.

A razor-sharp blade slashed just millimetres above his scalp.

Jaeger sensed the knife tip tear into the *Phoneutria* – the arachnid balling up in agony, losing its grip and tumbling off his head into thin air. Again and again Narov's blade chopped through the shadows as she fought off the spiders and Jaeger struggled to free the stubborn strap.

Finally, he managed to pull it clear of the belay, and they jerked back into the abseil.

'They don't give up easily,' he grunted, as he let the paracord zip through the belay system.

'They do not,' Narov confirmed.

She held up one arm in front of his face. It hadn't escaped Jaeger's notice that she was left-handed. There was a horrible-looking reddish-black welt spreading across the upper surface of her left hand, and he could see two distinct bite marks.

Her eyes were awash with pain. 'If you cut one *Phoneutria*, they all attack,' she reminded him. 'Victims describe the pain of a bite as like having fire running through your veins. It is quite accurate.'

Jaeger was speechless.

Narov had been bitten by one of the spiders that had dropped on them, yet she hadn't even cried out. More to the point, was he about to lose one of his expedition members, and before they'd even got started?

'I've got the anti-venom.' He glanced downwards. 'But it's in my backpack. We've got to get you down, and fast.'

Jaeger jerked his right hand upwards as far as it would go. The paracord rope hissed through the belay device faster than ever, and the two of them plummeted towards the ground at full speed. He was glad of his gloves, for the doubled-over paracord was still razor-thin to hold.

He made sure his boots hit first, taking the impact for the two of them. Normally he'd have used the rope and belay system to slow them to a halt before they touched down. But it had been a race against the *Phoneutria*, and they were out of time. He had to get his hands on the venom antidote.

They landed in the sullen gloom.

Very little of the sunlight that filters through the jungle canopy makes it to the forest floor. Some ninety per cent of the available illumination is sucked up by the mass of hungry vegetation layered above – making it semi-dark at ground level.

Until Jaeger's eyes adjusted to the low light levels, it would be hard to spot any dangers – *like spiders*.

He was pretty certain no *Phoneutria* would be able to follow them the full length of the fall, but – once bitten, twice shy. He glanced upwards. In the odd shaft of sunlight that penetrated the forest depths, he could just make out a score of silken threads glinting ominously, each lowering a glistening bundle of venomous death.

Unbelievably, the *Phoneutria* were still coming, and by the looks of it, Narov was pretty much incapable of moving out of their way.

As the spiders zipped downwards, Jaeger dragged her a few yards away from the abseil line. Then he unstrapped his shotgun, levelled it in the general direction of the *Phoneutria* and opened fire. The repeated retorts of the blasts in quick succession were deafening: *Kaboom! Kaboom! Kaboom! Kaboom!*

The Benelli had a pump action and a seven-round magazine, each loaded with 9 mm lead shot. A tidal wave of pellets tore into the arachnids.

Kaboom! Kaboom! Kaboom!

The last rounds erupted with the horde of *Phoneutria* practically sitting on the end of Jaeger's gun barrel, the shot turning them into instant spider purée. That was what Jaeger loved about the Benelli: you just pointed it in the general direction and let rip – although he'd never once envisaged using it against spiders.

The last echoes of the thunderous blasts reverberated around him, the sound thrown back from the massive tree trunks to either side. He could hear the panicked screams of what sounded like a troop of primates, high in the treetops. Very quickly the monkeys made themselves scarce, moving fast through the branches in the opposite direction.

The noise of the gunshots had been deafening and strangely ominous.

No doubt about it, Jaeger had just telegraphed their arrival to anyone or anything that might be listening . . . But to hell with it – he'd needed something with real firepower to deal with the tide of *Phoneutria*, and the combat shotgun was most definitely built for the job.

He threw the weapon across his back and cut Narov free from the abseil line. He dragged her out of the way, boots scuffing through rotten leaf matter and thin sandy soil, and laid her against the wall of a buttress – one of several inverted V-shaped roots that snaked out from the base of a massive tree.

The rainforest was a castle built upon sand – the soil below the jungle being wafer thin. In the intense humidity and heat, dead vegetation tended to rot swiftly, the nutrients released being rapidly recycled by both plants and animals. As a result, most of the forest giants sat on a web of buttresses, their root systems penetrating just inches into the poor soil.

Having propped Narov against one, Jaeger ran back to fetch his backpack. He was a qualified medic – one of his specialist skills learned in the military – and he was familiar with the effects of a neurotoxin such as this: it killed by attacking the nervous system, doing so in such a way that the nerve endings were permanently being fired, hence the horrific twitching and convulsing that Narov was starting to exhibit.

Death usually resulted from the inability of the muscles involved in breathing to keep functioning properly. Your body ended up literally suffocating itself to death.

The treatment required the nerve agent antidote ComboPen to be injected three times in quick succession. That would treat the symptoms of the poisoning, but Narov might also need pralidoxime and avizafone to help get the muscles that controlled her breathing functioning properly again.

Jaeger grabbed his medical pack and felt around for the syringes and phials. Luckily it was well padded, and most seemed to have survived the fall. He readied the first shot of ComboPen, raised it above his head and thumped the big needle of drugs into Narov's system.

30

Five minutes later, the treatment was done. Narov was still conscious, but she was nauseated, her breathing shallow, and she was twitching and spasming badly. It had been only a matter of minutes from her receiving the bite to Jaeger getting the antidote into her, but even so, there was still a chance that the spider toxins could kill her.

Having helped her out of her bulky HAHO gear, Jaeger urged her to drink as much as she could from the water bottle that he placed at her side. She needed to keep herself hydrated, as the fluids would help flush the worst of the toxins from her system.

Jaeger himself stripped down until he was wearing just a pair of tough cotton combat trousers and a T-shirt. His clothes were soaked in sweat and still it was pouring off him. He figured the humidity here had to be plus-ninety per cent. Despite the intense tropical heat, very little perspiration would ever evaporate, for the air was already saturated with water vapour.

For as long as they were in the jungle they'd be soaked through, and it was best just to get used to it.

Jaeger paused to collect his thoughts.

It had been 0903 Zulu when they'd plunged into the canopy at the end of the monster freefall. They'd been a good hour getting down from the treetops. It was around 1030 Zulu by now, and by anyone's reckoning they were in a whole world of hurt – one that he'd never even come close to envisaging when he'd sketched out the worst-case scenarios prior to departure.

One of his SAS instructors had once told him how 'no plan

survives first contact with the enemy'. Shit, that was true – and especially when it came to freefalling into the Amazon from 30,000 feet with a Russian ice queen strapped to your person.

He turned his attention to his rucksack. It was a seventy-five-litre green Alice Pack – a US-manufactured Bergen designed specifically for the jungle. Unlike many large packs it had a metal frame, which kept it a good two inches or more off the back, allowing for the worst of the sweat to run off – so reducing the risk of prickly heat, or hips and shoulders rubbing raw.

Most large packs tended to have a wide body and pouches sticking out the side. As a result, they were broader than a man's shoulders, and would tear and snag on undergrowth. The Alice Pack was thinner at the top and wider at the bottom, with all pouches attached to the rear. That way, Jaeger knew that if he could squeeze through, then his pack would follow.

The pack was lined with a tough rubber 'canoe bag', which rendered it waterproof and gave it enough buoyancy to float. As an added bonus, it provided an extra layer's cushioning to help deal with a hundred-foot drop like the one it had just suffered.

Jaeger rifled through the contents. As he'd feared, not everything had survived the fall. His Thuraya satellite phone had been stuffed into one of the rear pockets, for ease of access. It had a cracked screen, and when he tried to power up, nothing happened. He had a spare packed in one of the para-tubes that Krakow and Kamishi had jumped with, but that wasn't a great deal of good to them right here and right now.

He pulled out his map. Fortunately, as maps tended to be, it was pretty much indestructible. He'd had it laminated, to semi-waterproof it, and it was already folded to the correct page. Or at least it would have been the correct page: trouble was, he and Narov had put down anywhere up to forty kilometres or more away from their intended landing point.

Using his rucksack as a seat, he propped himself against the buttress root, and rearranged his map to what he figured had to be the correct page. Folding your map was actually a big no-no in the military. It instantly let the enemy know what your focus was, if you were captured. But Jaeger wasn't on operations here; this was meant to be a civilian jungle expedition, after all.

From his wrist GPS he retrieved the waypoint that he'd fed into it just moments before he'd plunged into the jungle canopy.

It furnished him with a six-figure grid: 837529.

He plotted the grid on the map – and immediately saw exactly where they were.

He took a moment to consider their predicament.

They were twenty-seven kilometres north-east of their intended landing point – the sandbar. Bad, but he guessed it could have been worse. Between them and it lay a wide bend of the Rio de los Dios. Presuming that the rest of the expedition team had made it to the sandbar as intended, the river lay between them and Jaeger and Narov's present position.

There was no way around that river, and Jaeger knew it. Plus twenty-seven kilometres through dense jungle with a casualty wasn't going to make for any holiday, that was for certain.

The agreed procedure if anyone failed to make the landing zone was for the rest of the team to wait there for forty-eight hours. If the missing person(s) wasn't there by then, the next rendezvous point was a distinctive bend in the river, approximately a day's journey downstream, with two more RV points each set a further day's travel downriver.

The Rio de los Dios flowed in the direction they needed to go to reach the air wreck – another reason why they'd decided to make that sandbar their landing point. Travelling on from there by river should have proven a comparatively easy means to move through the jungle. But each successive RV was set further to the west, which put it further away from Jaeger and Narov's present position.

The sandbar was nearest, which meant they had forty-eight hours in which to make it. If they failed, the main body of the expedition would move off more or less due west, and Jaeger and Narov would very likely never catch them.

With his Thuraya satphone kaput, Jaeger had no way of making contact with anyone to let them know what had happened. Even if he could somehow get it working, he doubted he could get a signal. The satphone required clear sky to see and acquire satellites, without which no message could be sent or received.

Presuming they made it over the Rio de los Dios, they would then face a further daunting trek through the heart of the jungle. Plus there was one other major problem that Jaeger was aware of – apart from the near-impossibility of Narov undertaking such a journey.

Colonel Evandro had treated the exact whereabouts of the air wreck with strictest confidence, to protect its location. He'd only been willing to pass the GPS coordinates to Jaeger in person, shortly before their departure on the C-130. Jaeger had in turn agreed to keep the location to himself, in large part because he harboured doubts about who exactly he could trust on his team.

He'd planned to brief the rest of the team on their exact route once they had boots on the ground at the sandbar – at which point they were pretty much all in this together. But when Jaeger had set the emergency RV procedure, he'd never imagined it would be *him* who failed to make the landing zone.

Right now, no one else knew the coordinates of the air wreck, which meant they could only proceed so far without him.

Jaeger glanced at Narov. Her condition seemed to be worsening. One arm was cradling the hand where she'd been bitten. Her face was slick with sweat, and her skin had taken on a sickly, deathly pallor.

He put his head back against the buttress root and took a few deep breaths. This wasn't simply about the expedition any more: it was about life and death now.

It was a survival situation, and the decisions he made would doubtless dictate whether he and Narov got through this alive.

31

Narov's white-blonde hair was tied off her face with a sky-blue headband. Her eyes were closed, as if she'd fallen asleep or lost consciousness, and her breathing was shallow. For a moment he was struck by how beautiful she looked, not to mention vulnerable.

Suddenly her eyes opened.

For an instant they stared into his – wide, blank, unseeing; an ice-blue sky torn with storm clouds. And then, with a visible effort, she seemed to pull her mind back into focus; back to the agonising present.

'I am in pain,' she announced quietly, between gritted teeth. 'I will not be going anywhere. You have forty-eight hours to find the others. I have my backpack: water, food, weapon, knife. Get going.'

Jaeger shook his head. 'That won't be happening.' He paused. 'I get bored by my own company.'

'Then you *are* a damn *Schwachkopf.*' Jaeger saw the hint of a smile flicker through her eyes. It was the first time he'd seen her show any hint of emotion, apart from a thinly veiled animosity, and it threw him. 'But it is hardly surprising you get bored by your own company,' she continued. 'You *are* boring. Handsome, yes. But also very boring . . .'

The hint of laughter in her eyes died in a spasm of convulsions.

Jaeger suspected he knew what she was trying to do here. She was trying to provoke him; to drive him to the point where he would abandon her, just as she had suggested. But there was one thing she didn't appreciate about him yet: he didn't leave his friends hanging.

Not ever. And not even the crazy ones.

'So this is what we're going to do,' he announced. 'We're going to leave all but the bare essentials, and Mr Boring here is going to carry your sorry arse out of here. And before you protest, I'm doing so because I need you. I'm the only one who knows the coordinates of the air wreck. If I don't make it, the mission's over. I'm now going to give the coordinates to you. That way, you get to take over if I go down. Got it?'

Narov shrugged. 'Such heroics. But you will never make it. All you will do is part me from my backpack, and without water and food I will die. Which makes you not just boring, but stupid also.'

Jaeger laughed. He was half tempted to reconsider and leave her. Instead, he got to his feet and dragged together the rucksacks so he could sort out the bare essentials: a medical pack; forty-eight hours' food for the two of them; poncho to sleep under; ammunition for his shotgun; map and compass.

He added a couple of full water bottles, plus his lightweight Katadyn filter, to get them drinkable water, fast.

He took his rucksack and packed two canoe bags into the bottom, followed by lighter gear. The heavier items – food, water, knife, machete, ammo – he threw on top, so that as much of the load as possible would lie high on his shoulders.

The rest of their kit would be left where it was, no doubt for the jungle to claim.

Gear sorted, he heaved the Bergen on to his back, slinging both his shotgun and Narov's weapon over his shoulder so they lay across his front. Lastly, he placed the three most crucial items – two full water bottles, his compass and map – in the pouches he had strapped around his waist on a military-style belt kit.

That done, he was ready.

His GPS worked on a similar system to the satphone – from

satellites. It too would be next to useless under the thick forest canopy. He would have to cross almost thirty kilometres of trackless jungle via a process known as pacing and bearing, a means of navigation as old as the hills.

Thankfully, in this age of modern technology, it was a skill that the SAS still relied upon, and had all of its members master.

Before reaching for Narov, Jaeger gave her the air wreck's co-ordinates – making her repeat them back to him several times over to ensure she had them memorised. He knew it would help her mentally if he reminded her that he needed her.

But there was a part of him that wondered if he really would make it: such a distance across such terrain, carrying such a weight – it would kill most men.

He bent down and took hold of Narov, raising her up in a fireman's lift until she was face down across his shoulders. Her stomach and chest were directly on top of his pack, so that it took much of her weight, just as he'd intended. He tightened the belt and chest straps of the Bergen, drawing it closer to his torso, so that the load was spread across his entire body – hips and legs included.

Lastly, he took a bearing on his compass. He fixed his eyes on a distinctive tree lying a hundred feet ahead of him, marking that as his first point to head for.

'Okay,' he grunted, 'so this isn't how it was supposed to happen – but here goes.'

'No shit.' Narov grimaced with the pain. 'Like I said, boring and stupid.'

Jaeger ignored her.

He set off at a steady pace, counting his every footfall as he went.

32

The noise of the forest closed all around Jaeger – the cries of wild animals high in the canopy; the beat of a thousand insects pulsating from the bush; the rhythmic croaking of a chorus of frogs, signalling that wetter ground lay somewhere in front of him.

He could sense the humidity rising and the sweat pouring off of him. But something else was niggling at him – something beyond the precariousness of their present predicament. He felt as if they weren't alone. It was an irrational feeling, but one he just couldn't seem to shake.

He did all he could to leave as little sign as possible of his passing, for as time went on he felt more certain than ever that they were being watched – the eerie sensation burning into the back of his neck and shoulders.

But movement was painfully difficult, especially with the weight he was carrying.

In so many ways, the jungle was by far the toughest of all environments to operate in. In the snows of the Arctic all you really had to worry about was remaining warm. Navigation was simplicity itself, for you'd nearly always manage to get a GPS signal. In the desert, the key challenges were staying out of the heat and drinking enough water to keep you alive. You'd move at night and lie up during the day in the shade.

By contrast, the jungle offered a plethora of dangers – ones that nowhere else could equal: fatigue, dehydration, infections, trench foot, disorientation, sores, bites, cuts, bruises, disease-bearing insects and ravenous mosquitoes, wild animals, leeches and snakes. In the jungle you were forever fighting the close, suffocating terrain, while the Arctic and desert were wide open.

And then of course there were the killer spiders – and hostile tribes – to contend with.

Jaeger was reminded of all this as he weaved his way through the dense undergrowth, the ground slippery and treacherous underfoot. His nostrils were assailed by the heavy scent of dark, musty decay. The terrain was dropping away from him as they approached the Rio de los Dios. Soon they'd hit the northern bank of the river – at which point the fun and games would really begin.

The higher you climbed in the jungle the easier the terrain tended to get – for it was invariably drier underfoot and the vegetation thinner. But sooner or later the Rio de los Dios had to be crossed, and that meant dropping down into denser, boggier ground.

Jaeger took a moment to catch his breath and survey the route ahead.

Straight ahead lay a deep ravine, which no doubt drained water into the Rio de los Dios during the rains. It looked wet and marshy underfoot, the ground starved of any sunlight. The gully was thick with medium-sized trees, each boasting a crop of vicious spikes that protruded several inches or more from the trunk.

Jaeger knew those spine-covered trees well. The spikes weren't poisonous, but that didn't matter much. He'd fallen against one once, during a jungle training exercise. The tough wooden spines had pierced his arm in several places, the wounds quickly turning septic. Ever since, he'd called them the 'bastard trees.'

Strung between those perilous trunks were thick vines, each armed with cruelly hooked thorns. Jaeger pulled out his compass and took a quick bearing. The ravine led due south, the way that he needed to go, but he figured it was best avoided.

Instead he took a bearing west, fixed his eyes on a tall, mature stand of hardwood trees and proceeded to head that way. He'd box his way around the ravine, then turn south a little further on, which should bring him directly to the river. Every twenty minutes he allowed himself to put Narov down, both for a breather and to grab a slug of water. But never longer than two minutes and then he was on his way again.

As he climbed, he shrugged Narov's weight higher on to his shoulders. He wondered for an instant how she was holding up. She'd not said a single word since they'd set out. If she'd lost all consciousness, the river crossing would be next to impossible, and Jaeger would be forced to come up with a different plan of action.

Fifteen minutes later, he skidded down a shallow slope, coming to a stop at a solid-looking wall of vegetation. On the far side he could just make out a moving mass – the odd glint of sunlight flashing through to him.

Water. He was almost at the river.

Mature jungle – vegetation that had remained undisturbed for centuries – generally consisted of a high forest canopy, with relatively sparse growth on the forest floor. But where such virgin rainforest had been disturbed – like having a high-way slashed through it, or here where a river carved into its depths – secondary vegetation would spring up in the clearings formed.

The Rio de los Dios cut a tunnel of sunlight through the jungle, and on either side it was a riot of dense, tangled bush. The vegetation that loomed before Jaeger was like a dark and impenetrable cliff face – high forest giants, fringed with smaller palm-like bushes, with tree ferns and vines reaching right to the forest floor. Next to impossible to negotiate with his load.

He turned east, following the riverbank until he hit the ravine that he'd boxed his way around. At the point where it plunged into the river, the terrain was largely swept clear of vegetation, leaving a tiny rocky beach no wider than your average English country lane.

It was enough. From there they could launch their river crossing – if Narov was still capable of making it.

He lifted her off his shoulders and lowered her to the ground. There was little sign of life, and for a horrible moment Jaeger feared that the spider toxins had claimed her as he'd carried her through the jungle. But when he felt for her pulse, he noticed the odd shiver and spasm ripple through her limbs, as the *Phoneutria* venom tried to work its way deeper into her system.

The shakes were nowhere near as bad as they'd been at first, so the antidote was clearly working. But still she seemed dead to all his attentions; comatose to the world. He lifted her head, supporting it with one hand as he tried to get some liquid into her. She gulped down a few mouthfuls, but still there was no sign of her opening her eyes.

Jaeger reached for his backpack and pulled out his GPS unit. He needed to check if it could see enough sky to acquire a usable signal. It bleeped once, twice, and thrice, as satellite icons flashed on to the screen. He checked their position, the grid provided by the GPS proving that his navigation had been bang on.

For a moment he stole a glance at the river, contemplating the crossing that lay before them. It was a good five hundred yards across, maybe more. The dark, sluggish water was interrupted here and there by slender mudbanks, which barely broke the surface.

Worse still, on one or two of them Jaeger spotted what he'd most feared to find here: the sleek forms of giant lizard-like creatures, sunning themselves in the mid-morning heat.

The beasts before them were the largest predators the Amazon had to offer. Crocodiles.

Or more accurately, this being South America – caimans.

33

The black caiman – *Melanosuchus niger* – can grow to five metres in length, and weigh anything up to 400 kilos, so more than five times a man's bodyweight. Immensely powerful, and with skin as thick as a rhino, they have no natural predators.

Hardly surprising, Jaeger reflected. He'd once heard the animal described as 'a croc on steroids', and they really didn't come any bigger or more aggressive. Note to self, Jaeger thought: be wary.

Still, he reminded himself that the black caiman had relatively poor eyesight, mostly adapted for hunting in the dark. They could barely see underwater, and especially not in rivers as silt-laden as this one. They had to get their heads above the surface to attack – and that meant they made themselves visible.

More commonly, they used their sense of smell to guide them to their prey. For a moment, Jaeger checked where Narov had nicked him with her blade as he'd tried to parry her knife thrusts during their crazed freefall. The wound had long ago stopped bleeding, but it would be best to keep it out of the water.

In the absence of any alternative plan, he pressed on with the only one he had. He opened his rucksack and pulled out the canoe flotation bags. He emptied out the pack's remaining contents and divided them between the two liners, so the weight was shared evenly.

Next he placed one of the liners inside his pack, inflated it, and closed it, folding the seal over twice and clipping it tight on to itself, before inflating and sealing shut the second liner.

Using the fastenings on his pack, he proceeded to strap it and the canoe liner together. He then took his and Narov's weapons and tied a longish length of paracord to each, attaching the loose ends to the two corners of his makeshift flotation device with quick-release knots.

That way, if either weapon fell in, he'd be able to retrieve it again.

Next he selected a thick bamboo from a grove that grew near the water's edge. He felled it with his machete, and cut the trunk into five-foot lengths. Using the sharp blade, he split two lengths of the bamboo in half, to make four cross poles. He then placed four lengths of whole bamboo in a row, lashed the cross struts to these with paracord, and tied it all together to make a simple frame, which in turn was roped to the flotation bags.

He dragged the makeshift raft into the shallows and sat astride it, testing for strength. It took his weight comfortably, floating high on the water, just as he'd intended. That done, he figured he was ready.

He had little doubt that it could manage Narov's weight.

He moored the craft and paused to filter some water. It was always smart to keep your bottles full, especially with the amount he was sweating. Using the Katadyn, he sucked up dirty brown river water via the intake tube, the filter jetting clear, crisp liquid into his bottle. He drank as much as he could before refilling both bottles.

He was just finishing when a fatigued voice cut through the clammy heat: fragile; tight with pain; hoarse with exhaustion.

'Boring, stupid . . . and half crazy.' Narov had come to, and she'd been watching him test his raft. She gestured to it weakly. 'No way do you get me on that. It is time to accept the inevitable and go on alone.'

Jaeger ignored the remark. He placed the weapons to either side of the craft, facing forwards, then returned to Narov, squatting down before her.

'Captain Narov, your carriage awaits.' He gestured at the

makeshift raft. He could feel his guts twisting with the thought of what lay ahead, but he did his best to suppress it. 'I'm going to carry you down and place you aboard. It's reasonably stable, but try not to thrash about. And don't knock the weapons overboard.'

He smiled at her encouragingly, but she could barely respond.

'Correction,' she whispered. 'Not half crazy: *clinically insane*. But as you see, I am in no fit state to argue.'

Jaeger lifted her up. 'That's my girl.'

Narov scowled. She was clearly too finished to think of a suitable retort.

Jaeger laid her gently across the raft, warning her to keep her long legs well tucked in. She curled up into a foetal position, the craft sinking a good six inches under her weight, but still most of it remained above the surface.

They were good to go.

Jaeger waded into deeper water, pushing the raft ahead of him, thick mud squelching underfoot. The water felt lukewarm and oily with sediment. Every now and then his boot encountered a lump of rotting vegetation – most likely a tree branch – embedded in the heavy silt. As he clambered over them, they threw up long lines of bubbles – gases from their decay rushing to the surface.

When the water was up to chest height, Jaeger kicked off. The current was stronger than he'd expected, and he didn't doubt that they'd be carried fast downstream. But it was what lurked in the water that made him so keen to get the river crossing over with.

34

Jaeger kicked across the first open stretch of water, keeping both hands on the raft. Narov lay before him, curled into a ball, unmoving. It was crucial that he kept going straight and steady. If the raft were spun violently or became unbalanced, she would tumble off, and would be as good as dead in the water.

She was too far gone to fend for herself, or even to swim for it.

Jaeger's eyes scanned the river to either side. He was almost level with the surface, giving him a weird, otherworldly perspective. He figured this was what it must be like to be one of the Rio de los Dios caimans, cruising the waters mostly submerged and hunting for their prey.

He searched to left and right, checking for any that might be heading their way.

He was twenty yards from the mudbank ahead when he sighted the first. It was the movement that drew his eye. He watched as it slithered into the river a good hundred yards or so upstream. Ungainly on land, the massive creature moved with a deadly grace and speed as it entered the water, and Jaeger felt every muscle tensing for the fight.

But instead of heading downstream, towards them, the caiman turned its snout northwards, nosing its way upriver for a good fifty yards or more. Then it climbed out on to a mudbank and went back to what it had been doing earlier – sunbathing.

Jaeger heaved a sigh of relief. That was one caiman that clearly wasn't feeling hungry.

A few moments later he felt his boots touch the bottom. Wading now, he pushed the raft up on to the first patch of land – a stretch of boggy sediment a dozen feet across. He moved to the front of the craft, and began to haul it onwards, his limbs burning with the effort. With each step his legs sank up to the knees in the black, clinging mud.

Twice he lost his grip completely, falling on to his hands and knees and getting splattered all over in stinking filth. For a moment he was reminded of the swamp that he and Raff had hidden in on Bioko island. Difference was, there had been no giant caimans to contend with there.

By the time he reached the edge of the deeper water again, he was covered from head to toe in putrid black gunk and rotting matter, and his pulse was thumping like a machine gun with the exertion.

He figured there were two more shallow mudbanks that he couldn't navigate his way around; that he'd be forced to cross. No doubt about it, he was going to be utterly finished by the time they reached the far side.

If they reached the far side.

He waded in again, pulling the raft after him, then resumed the prone position behind it. As he kicked out and propelled the craft towards the centre of the river, the current tugged at it more powerfully. Jaeger was forced to struggle with all his might to keep it balanced, his legs pumping to make any headway.

Downstream the water was shallower, but faster moving near the bank. Jaeger could see the river getting turbulent as it coursed over rocks that created a stretch of white water. He needed to get across before they were swept into those rapids.

The raft neared the second of the mudbanks. As it did so, Jaeger felt an unexpected touch. Something had brushed against his right arm. He glanced up, only to find that it was Narov's hand. Her fingers reached out, curled around his, and she gave a faint squeeze.

He didn't know quite what she was trying to tell him; reading this woman was nigh-on impossible. But maybe, just maybe, the ice queen was starting to melt a little.

'I know what you are thinking.' Her voice barely reached him, reduced to a half-whisper as it was by all the toxins burning through her system. 'But I am not being intimate. I am trying to alert you. The first caiman – it is coming.'

Using his wrists to keep hold of the raft, Jaeger grabbed both weapons. He held them by their pistol grips, index fingers curled around the triggers, barrels menacing the water to left and right, his eyes scanning the surface.

'Where?' he hissed. 'Which side?'

'Eleven o'clock,' Narov whispered. 'More or less dead ahead. Forty feet. Closing fast.'

It was coming at them in his blind spot.

'Hold tight,' Jaeger yelled.

He released his grip on the weapon on his left, slipped free the knot that held the combat shotgun, grabbed it and dropped off the raft, diving beneath it, kicking hard with both legs. As he came up on the far side, he caught sight of a massive black snout knifing through the water towards him, a ribbed, scaly, armoured body snaking out behind it a good five metres or more.

It was a black caiman all right, and a real monster.

Jaeger levelled the weapon just as the caiman's jaws yawned wide before him. He was staring down its very throat. There was no time to aim. He pulled the trigger at close to point-blank range, his left hand jerking the pump action backwards and ratcheting in another round, and another.

The impact of the repeated shots blew the reptile's giant head clean out of the water, but it wasn't enough to halt its forward progress. It might have been killed instantly, a blasted funnel of lead shot tearing into its brain, but still its bloodied corpse slammed into Jaeger with all the force of a 400-kilogram beast.

Jaeger felt the air being crushed out of his lungs as he was driven deep down under the raft, the dark and turbid waters closing all around him.

Above, the bloodied mass of the caiman's front end came to rest with a sickening crunch, its dead eyes staring hungrily, its lacerated jaw slamming down into the forward arm of the raft.

The lightweight craft lurched alarmingly, the impact half breaking it in two. Moments later, the limp, lifeless weight of the caiman's corpse began to slip below the surface of the river.

The stricken craft keeled over still further, the muddy water beginning to lap around Narov's head and shoulders as it cannoned off rocks and was swept into the first of the rapids.

She sensed that it was going down. For a moment her muscles tensed as she tried to hold on.

But the effort was too much for her.

Finally Jaeger forced his way back to the surface, lungs choking out the fetid water of the Rio de los Dios. He'd been down deep and long fighting for his life and he felt half drowned. For a long moment he struggled for breath, his body screaming out for oxygen and desperate to drag the life-giving air into his system.

To either side of him were more caimans, closing in on the corpse of the monster he had just killed. They were drawn by the smell of blood. As Jaeger had been driven down towards the riverbed he'd lost his combat shotgun, and he was pretty much defenceless now, but the caimans weren't paying much attention to him.

Instead, they had one of their own to feast upon, and the taste of the blood thick in the water was driving them wild.

For a long moment Jaeger tried to orientate himself, and then he too was dragged into the rapids. He tried to protect his torso as he was swept against the rocks, keeping his feet downstream to push off any obstacles and his arms out to the sides to steady himself.

He pulled himself into the slower current at the edge of the white water and did a 360-degree sweep, scanning for the raft. But as he eyed the river all around him, he couldn't seem to locate it in any direction. The lightweight craft had completely disappeared, and its loss made his blood run cold.

He kept searching, growing ever more frantic, but still there was no sight of the makeshift craft.

And as for Irina Narov – there wasn't the slightest sign of her anywhere.

35

Jaeger hauled himself on to the riverbank.

He sank to his knees in a sodden, exhausted heap, his limbs burning, his lungs gasping for breath. To any watching eyes he would appear more like a mud-encrusted, semi-drowned rat than a human being – not that he expected many to be watching.

For hours on end he'd quartered the Rio de los Dios searching for Irina Narov. He'd scanned the river from bank to bank, searching everywhere and yelling out her name. But he'd been unable to find the slightest sign of her, or the raft. And then he'd discovered what he'd most feared to find: his pack and the canoe flotation bag, still lashed together, but torn and shredded by caiman tooth and claw marks.

The battered remains of the makeshift raft had drifted into the shallows a good distance downstream. On an adjacent mudbank Jaeger had discovered one unnerving sign of the woman he'd tried so desperately to safeguard: her sky-blue headband, now sodden and torn and stained with mud.

Still he'd continued to search the riverbanks as far as he could go, but even as he'd done so, he'd feared his efforts were futile. He figured Narov must have been thrown from the raft, even as the caiman's dead body had thrust him deep into the river's inky depths. The rapids and the caimans would have done the rest.

He'd fought for the best part of a minute to regain the surface, but it was still enough time for the raft to have been swept completely out of his sight. Had it still been intact and afloat, he'd have been able to see the makeshift craft. He'd have been able to catch it and draw it into land.

And had Irina Narov still been with it, he might have been able to save her.

As it was ... Well, he didn't like to contemplate Narov's exact fate, yet he didn't doubt for one moment that she was gone. Narov was dead – either drowned in the Rio de los Dios, or torn apart by ravening black caimans; and most likely a mixture of the two.

And he, Will Jaeger, had been unable to do anything to save her.

He struggled to his feet and stumbled further up the muddy riverbank. In the dark shock of the moment, his training began to kick in. He slipped into full-on survival mode; it was all he knew how to do. He'd lost Narov, but the rest of the expedition was still out there somewhere in the jungle. There were eight people presumably waiting at that distant sandbar; reliant upon him.

Right now they had no coordinates to make for; no way to head towards the air wreck. And without a way forward, there was no easy way out of this savage Lost World; no exit strategy. To withdraw from a place as remote and as seemingly damned as the Cordillera de los Dios took a great deal of planning and preparation, as Jaeger well knew.

If Narov's loss were to mean anything, he had to get himself reunited with his team and get them on the move. He had to lead them to the site of that wreck, and to do that he had to get himself to the sandbar – although the odds of him doing so were rapidly turning against him.

He proceeded to empty out the contents of his pockets, plus those of his belt pouches. After the chaos of the river crossing, he had no idea what if any of his kit remained. The rucksack had been rendered useless – shredded by the caimans and voided of its contents – but as he scanned his meagre possessions, Jaeger began to count his blessings.

His single most vital piece of kit – his compass, stuffed deep in a trouser pocket and zipped tight – was still there. With that one piece of equipment alone he stood a chance of making it through to the distant sandbar. He dragged out the map from his trouser side pocket. It was sodden and battered, but just about usable.

He had both map and compass; it was a start.

He checked his chest-mounted knife. It was still there, clipped firmly into its sheath; the knife Raff had given him; the one he'd put to such good use during the epic fight on Fernao beach – the fight in which Little Mo had been killed.

So much death; and now one more to contend with.

36

What Jaeger wouldn't have given to have Raff alongside him now. Had the big Maori been here, Narov might have lived. There were no guarantees, of course, but Raff would have helped him fight off the killer caiman, and one or other of them would have likely escaped unscathed from that first attack, and so been able to safeguard the raft and its precious cargo.

But Jaeger was alone, Irina Narov was gone, and he had to steel himself to the hard facts. He had no choice. He had to go on.

He continued with his kit check. He had two full bottles of water slung in his belt rig – although the Katadyn filter was gone. He had a little emergency food, the roll of paracord that he'd used to lower Narov and himself from the canopy, plus two dozen rounds for the shotgun.

He dumped the shotgun shells. They were a useless dead-weight without the weapon.

Amongst the few other bits and pieces that the kit check revealed, his gaze came to rest upon the shiny form of the C-130 pilot's coin. The Night Stalkers' motto glistened in the sunlight: *Death Waits in the Dark*. No doubt about it – death red in tooth and claw had lurked in the dark waters of the Rio de los Dios.

And it had found them; or at least, it had found Narov.

But that wasn't in any way the pilot's fault, of course.

The pilot of that C-130 had got them out of his aircraft at exactly the right release point. That was no mean feat. The disaster that had followed – it was none of his doing. The coin went with the rest of Jaeger's meagre possessions – deep into his pocket. Hope was what kept people alive, he reminded himself.

The last piece of equipment that he contemplated was also the most difficult: it was Irina Narov's knife.

After he'd used it to cut them free from the abseil line, Jaeger had slung it on his own belt. Amidst all the chaos, and with Narov so incapacitated from the spider bite, it had seemed like the right thing to do. Now it was all he had that linked him to her.

He held it in his hands for a long moment. His eyes traced the knife's name, stamped into the steel hilt. He knew all about the history of the blade, for he'd researched his grandfather's.

In the months following Hitler's spring 1940 blitzkrieg – his lightning war that had driven the Allied troops out of France – Winston Churchill had ordered the creation of a special force, to launch butcher-and-bolt terror raids against the enemy. Those special volunteers were taught to wage war in what was then a very un-British way – fast and dirty, with no holds barred.

At a top-secret school for mayhem and murder, they'd been shown how to hurt, maul, injure and kill with ease. Their instructors had been the legendary William Fairbairn and Eric 'Bill' Sykes, who over the years had perfected the means to terminate silently, at close quarters.

From Wilkinson Sword, Sykes and Fairbairn had commissioned a combat knife to be used by Churchill's special volunteers. It had a seven-inch blade, a heavy handle to give firm grip in the wet, plus razor edges and a sharp stabbing profile.

The knives had rolled off Wilkinson Sword's London production line. Etched on the square head of each were the words: 'The Fairbairn–Sykes Fighting Knife'. Fairbairn and Sykes had taught the special volunteers that there was no more deadly weapon at close quarters, and most importantly, 'It never runs out of ammunition.'

Jaeger had never got to see Narov use her blade in anger. But the fact that she'd chosen to carry such a knife – the same as his grandfather had used – had somehow drawn him to her, though he'd never got the chance to ask her where she had got it, or what exactly it might mean to her.

He wondered how she'd come by it: a Russian; a veteran of the Spetsnaz, with a British commando knife. And why that comment she'd made – *good for killing Germans?* During the war, every British commando and SAS soldier had been issued with one of those knives; doubtless the iconic blade had accounted for more than its fair share of the Nazi enemy.

But that was many decades and a whole world ago.

Jaeger replaced the knife on his belt.

For a brief moment he wondered if he'd been wrong; wrong to insist that Narov come with him. If he'd done as she'd asked and left her, she more than likely would still be alive. But it was in his DNA never to leave a man behind – or woman, for that matter – and anyway, how long would she have lasted?

No. The more he thought about it, the more he knew that he had done the right thing. The only thing. She'd have perished either way. If he'd left her, she'd just have died a longer, lingering death, and she'd have died alone.

Jaeger forced all thoughts of Narov to the back of his mind.

He took stock. A daunting journey lay ahead: twenty-plus kilometres through thick jungle with only two litres of clean water to sustain him. A human could survive without food for many days; not so water. He'd have to ration himself strictly: a gulp every hour; nine gulps per bottle; eighteen hours walking, max.

He checked his watch.

Last light was barely two hours away. If he was to get to that sandbar in time to make the emergency RV, he'd most likely have to keep marching through the night hours, which was a big no-no in the jungle. It was impossible to see in the pitch black beneath the night-dark canopy.

He had nothing with which to defend himself, apart from his bare hands and his knife. If he stumbled into serious trouble, the only thing to do would be to run. He had one advantage: with Narov gone, he no longer had her weight to slow him down.

He was equipped only with what he stood up in, which meant he could move fast. All things considered, he figured he stood a half-decent chance. But even so, he dreaded the coming journey.

He got to his feet, placed the compass in the palm of his hand and took a first bearing. The point he'd aim for was a fallen tree trunk lying more or less due south – the direction in which he needed to travel. He replaced the compass, bent down and picked up ten small pebbles, placing them in his pocket. Every ten paces he'd transfer one pebble to his other pocket. When all had been moved across he'd have completed a hundred paces.

From long experience Jaeger knew that it would take seventy left footfalls for him to cover 100 metres of terrain, on the flat and under a light load. With a full pack, plus weapon and ammo, it would take him eighty, for the legs made less of a stride under a heavy load. When going steeply uphill, it might take him one hundred left footfalls.

The passing of the pebbles was a simple system that had worked for him countless times during epic yomps across tough terrain. And moving them from pocket to pocket would keep his mind focused and busy.

He did one last thing before setting out: he grabbed a pen and marked his present position. Next to it he wrote: 'Last known location of Irina N.'

That way, if he ever got the chance, he could return to this spot and search methodically, with time and manpower, for her remains. At least that way they'd have something to return to her family – not that Jaeger had any idea who or where her family might be.

He set off walking; walking and counting.

He moved deeper into the forest, clicking a stone from one

pocket to the other with each ten paces. One hour in and it was time for his first quick gulp of water and a map check.

He marked his position on the map – two kilometres due south of the riverbank – took a bearing and pressed onwards. In theory, he could navigate his way the whole distance through the jungle to that sandbar using the simple process of pacing and bearing. Whether he'd make it or not, with two litres of water and no weaponry, was another matter entirely.

Even as his lone form was swallowed by the gloom of the dense jungle, Jaeger could sense that those mystery eyes were upon him still, watching from the shadows.

As he pushed ahead into the dark, brooding forest, his left hand gripped his pocket full of pebbles, his lips moving as they counted out his footfalls.

37

Far away, across several hundred miles of jungle, another voice was speaking.

'Grey Wolf, this is Grey Wolf Six,' the voice intoned. 'Grey Wolf, Grey Wolf Six. Do you copy?'

The speaker was hunched over a radio set in a camouflaged tent positioned at the edge of a rough and ready airstrip. To all sides lay a sagging fringe of trees, with hills in the distance rearing up against a ragged grey sky. A rank of black helicopters with drooping rotor blades lined the dirt runway.

Otherwise, it was empty.

The scenery was reminiscent of the Serra de los Dios, but somehow not the same.

Close, but not too close.

This was the South American jungle, but somewhere higher in the mountains; somewhere remote and undisturbed, hidden amongst the wild and lawless Andean foothills that rolled onwards into Bolivia and Peru. Somewhere perfect for the kind of black operation that was designed to make a Second World War aircraft disappear forever; to vanish off the face of the earth.

'Grey Wolf, Grey Wolf Six,' the radio operator repeated. 'Do you copy?'

'Grey Wolf Six, this is Grey Wolf,' a voice confirmed. 'Send, over.'

'Team inserted as planned,' the operator announced. 'Awaiting further orders.'

He listened for a few seconds to whatever was being said.

Whoever this man – this soldier – was, there wasn't a single mark of unit or rank, or even of nationality, to be seen on his plain, drab-green jungle fatigues. To either side of him, the tent was equally lacking in identifying features. Even the helicopters lined up on the airstrip were devoid of decals, flight numbers or national flags of any sort.

'Yes, sir,' the operator confirmed. 'I have sixty sets of boots on the ground. It wasn't easy, but we got them in there.'

He listened for a few seconds to his instructions, then repeated them back to confirm he'd understood them

'Use all means to secure the coordinates of the warplane. Spare no one in the search for its exact whereabouts. Understood.'

There was a further short burst of message before the operator gave his final response.

'Understood, sir. Their force is ten strong, of which all are to be eliminated. No survivors. Grey Wolf Six, out.'

That done, he killed the radio call.

38

Jaeger sank to his knees, grasping his agonised, throbbing head in his hands.

He could feel his brain spinning out of control, as if it was about to burst through his forehead with the stress of the exertion.

The gnarled and twisted vegetation swam before his eyes, transforming itself into a writhing horde of fearsome monsters. He figured he was close to losing it completely. The disorientation had set in hours ago, as the dehydration had reached critical levels, followed by the ever-worsening pain and the hallucinations.

Away from the river there was very little water, and it hadn't yet rained, which Jaeger had been banking on to revive him. His water bottles had long run dry, after which he'd been reduced to drinking his own urine. But an hour or so back he'd stopped peeing – and sweating – completely, a sure sign of imminent body collapse. Yet somehow he'd kept stumbling forward.

By force of will alone he dragged himself upright again, placing one foot in front of the other.

'It's Will Jaeger, coming in!' His voice rang out – hoarse, guttural and parched, the sound echoing through the confused mass of trees ranged all around him. 'Will Jaeger, coming through!'

He was calling out a warning to the expedition team, who should be gathered just ahead of him on that sandbar – terrain that he hoped and prayed he was now approaching, though the state that he'd been in these last few hours, he began to question if this was the right place. A small clearing in a massive expanse of jungle: his margin for error was tiny.

He pushed on with an erratic, exhausted, weaving gait, his mind screaming, but still somehow counting out the footfalls, passing the pebbles from pocket to pocket to mark his onward progress.

It was a given that no trans-jungle journey ever went strictly as the crow flies, and certainly not one undertaken by a man in his state, who'd been forced to keep moving through the night hours. Hence twenty-seven kilometres had become forty-five-plus on the ground. With barely any water, it had been a Herculean feat.

He tried the yell again: 'Will Jaeger, coming through!'

No answer. He stood, trying to keep still and to listen, but he was swaying with exhaustion and fatigue.

He tried again, louder. 'Will Jaeger, coming in!'

There was a moment's silence, before a response rang out. 'Hold your ground, or I fire!'

It was the unmistakable voice of Lewis Alonzo, the former Navy SEAL on his team, echoing through the trees.

Jaeger did as ordered, swaying once then collapsing to his knees.

A powerful, bulky form melted out of the bush sixty yards ahead of him. The Afro-American Alonzo combined Mike Tyson's physique with Will Smith's looks and humour – or at least that was how Jaeger had come to see him over the two short weeks he'd known him.

But right now, Jaeger was staring down the barrel of a Colt assault rifle, Alonzo's index finger bone-tense on the trigger.

'Step one and identify!' Alonzo yelled, his voice thick with aggression. 'Step one and identify!'

Jaeger forced himself to stand, taking one step forward. 'William Jaeger. It's Jaeger.'

Perhaps it wasn't surprising that Alonzo didn't recognise him.

Jaeger's voice was choked with fatigue, his throat so parched that he could barely croak out the words. His combats were ripped to shreds, his face swollen, red and bloodied from all the insect bites and scratch marks, and he was plastered in mud from head to toe.

'Arms above your head!' Alonzo snarled. 'Drop your weapon!'

Jaeger raised both hands. 'William Jaeger – unarmed, goddammit.'

'Kamishi! Cover me!' Alonzo yelled.

Jaeger saw a second figure step out from the bush. It was Hiro Kamishi, their Japanese special forces veteran, and he had Jaeger's form pinned in the sights of a second Colt assault rifle.

Alonzo moved forward, his gun at the ready. 'Hit the deck!' he yelled. 'And spread 'em.'

'Jesus, Alonzo, I'm on your side,' Jaeger objected.

The big American's only response was to move in closer and kick Jaeger forward into the mud. He went down hard, spread-eagled in the dirt.

Alonzo moved around to a position behind him. 'Answer these questions,' he barked. 'What are you and your team here for?'

'To find an air wreck, identify it and lift it out of the jungle.'

'Name of our local contact: Brazilian brigadier.'

'He's a colonel,' Jaeger corrected. 'Colonel Evandro. Rafael Evandro.'

'Names of all the members on your team.'

'Alonzo, Kamishi, James, Clermont, Dale, Kral, Krakow, Santos.'

Alonzo knelt down until he was staring into Jaeger's eyes. 'You missed one. We were ten.'

Jaeger shook his head. 'I didn't. Narov's dead. I lost her when we tried to cross the Rio de los Dios to get to you guys.'

'Jesus wept.' Alonzo ran a hand through his close-cropped hair. 'That makes five.'

Jaeger gazed around himself, confusedly. Surely, he hadn't heard Alonzo right. What did he mean – *that makes five*?

Alonzo unhooked a bottle from his belt and handed it across. 'Buddy, you would not begin to believe what we've been through these past two days. And for the record, you look like shit.'

'Say the same about you,' Jaeger gasped.

He took the proffered water bottle, opened his throat and drained it in one desperate glug. He waved the empty bottle at Alonzo, who signalled Kamishi over, and Jaeger proceeded to drain another and another, until his thirst was all but sated.

Alonzo called a third figure out of the shadows. 'Dale, Christmas just came early! You got a green light. Roll!'

Mike Dale stepped forward, his diminutive digital video camera clamped to his shoulder. Jaeger could see the light on the front of the microphone blinking red, meaning that he was filming.

He eyed Alonzo. The American shrugged apologetically. 'Sorry, buddy, but the guy's been bugging the shit out of me. *If Jaeger and Narov make it, I gotta be able to film their arrival . . . If Jaeger and Narov make it, I gotta be able to film their arrival.*'

Dale came to a halt a foot or so before them, sinking to his haunches, which put the camera at just about eye-level. He held the shot for a few seconds, then punched a button, the red film light blinking out.

'Man, you could not make this up,' Dale whispered. 'Awesome.' He peered at Jaeger from behind the camera. 'Hey, Mr Jaeger, you figure you could maybe take a step back into the bush for me, and kind of come back in like you just did? Just a bit of re-enactment, 'cause, you know, I missed that part.'

Jaeger stared at the cameraman in silence for a long second. Dale. Mid-twenties, long hair, good-looking in a manufactured kind of way – never without a three-day growth of designer stubble. There was something of the preening cockatoo about him that Jaeger didn't like.

Or maybe that was just his instinctive aversion to the man's camera. It was so intrusive and disrespectful of any privacy – which was Dale pretty much in a nutshell.

'Re-enact my arrival for the camera?' Jaeger rasped. 'I don't think so. And you know something else? You film one second more of this and I'll take that camera, smash it into pieces, and make you eat the lot.'

Dale held up his hands – one still dangling the camera – in mock surrender. 'Hey, I understand. You've been though one hell of an ordeal. I get that. But Mr Jaeger, that's exactly when the cameras need to be running; when things are rough as hell. That's what we need to capture. That's what makes for great TV.'

In spite of the water he'd drunk, Jaeger was still feeling like death, and he was in no mood for bullshit. 'Great TV? You still think this is about making great TV? Dale, there's something you need to grasp: this is about trying to stay alive now. Survival. Yours as much as anyone's. This is not a story any more. *You're living it.*'

'But if I can't film, there's no TV series,' Dale objected. 'And the people funding all of this – the TV execs – they're throwing good money after bad.'

'The TV execs aren't here,' Jaeger growled. 'We are.' A beat. 'You shoot one more frame on that thing without my say-so, your film is history. And so, my friend, are you.'

39

'So tell me – what the hell happened here?' Jaeger prompted. He was sitting in the makeshift camp that Alonzo and the rest had hacked out of the jungle, where the thick vegetation met the open sweep of the sandbar. Shaded by some overhanging trees, it was about as comfortable as you could get in such terrain.

He'd managed a quick wash in the river, which snaked past as sluggish and brooding as ever. He'd pulled a daysack out of one of the para-tubes, and grabbed the bare essentials to help him recover from his epic trans-jungle journey: food rations, bottled water, rehydration salts, plus some insect repellent. As a result, he was starting to feel vaguely human again.

The expedition team – or rather, those that remained – were gathered for a communal heads-up. But there was a weird, wired tension to the air, a sense that hostile forces were prowling the fringes of the camp and lurking just out of sight. Jaeger had retrieved a back-up combat shotgun from one of the para-tubes, and he wasn't alone in keeping one eye on the jungle and one hand on his weapon.

'Best I start at the beginning – when we lost you guys in the freefall.' Alonzo's reply was delivered in the deep, rumbling tones so typical of the big Afro-American.

As Jaeger had begun to realise, Alonzo was the kind of guy who tended to wear his heart very much on his sleeve. As he continued speaking, his words became thick with regret at what had happened.

'We lost you guys pretty quickly after the jump, so I led the stick in. We made it down good. All here, no injuries, firm and clear underfoot. We set camp, sorted our gear, agreed a sentry roster, and figured no big deal: we'd wait for you and Narov to come to us, this being the first RV.

'It was then we kind of broke into two camps,' Alonzo continued. 'There was my lot – let's say the Warrior Brigade – who wanted to send out probing patrols in the direction we figured you guys must've put down. See if we could help bring you in – that was if you were still alive . . . And then there was the Tree-hugger Brigade . . .

'So the Hugger Brigade – led by James and Santos – they wanted to go that way.' Alonzo jerked a thumb westwards. 'They figured they'd found a riverside path made by the Indians. Well, we all knew the tribe was out there somewhere. We could feel eyes in the jungle. The Hugger Brigade – they wanted to reach out and make peaceful contact.

'Peaceful contact!' Alonzo glanced at Jaeger. 'You know, I just spent a year doing peacekeeping ops in Sudan; the Nuba mountains. About as remote as you can get. Some of those Nuba tribes, they still wander around pretty much butt-naked. But you know something – man, I grew to love those people. And one lesson I learned from the get-go: they wanted peaceful contact, they'd let you know about it.'

Alonzo shrugged. 'Long story short, James and Santos set out around lunchtime on day one. Santos argued she knew what she was doing; she was Brazilian, and she'd spent years working with Amazonian tribes.' He shook his head. 'James: man, he's stir-crazy; a total loon. He'd scrawled some note to the Indians; scribbled some pictures.' He glanced at Dale. 'You got the footage?'

Dale grabbed his camera, flipped open the side screen and scrolled through the digital files stored on the camera's memory card. He pressed 'play'. An image appeared on the screen – a close-up of a scribbled note. The thick, Kiwi-accented voice of Joe James could be heard reading out the words in the background.

'Yo! Amazon dwellers! You like peace, we like peace. Let's make peace!' The shot panned out to reveal James's massive Bin Laden beard and his craggy biker features. 'We're coming into your domain to say hello and to make peaceful contact.'

Dale shook his head in disbelief. 'Can you believe this guy? "Yo! Amazon dwellers!" I mean – like the Indians read English! A genuine wacko – spent too long in his cabin in the woods. Perfect for the camera. Not perfect for the mission!'

Jaeger signalled that he'd seen enough. 'He is a little unusual. But who isn't? Anyone who's a hundred per cent sane wouldn't be here. A little crazy is okay.'

Alonzo scratched his stubble. 'Yeah, but man, that one – James – he's kinda off the scale. Anyhow, he and Santos set out. Twenty-four hours later there was no sign of them, but we'd had no sign of trouble either. So the second tier of the Hugger Brigade – the Frenchie, Clermont, and bizarrely, the German, Krakow; you'd never have him down as a natural-born hugger – they set out to link up with James and Santos.

'I shouldn't have let 'em go,' Alonzo growled. 'I had this bad feeling. But hell, with you and Narov gone, we had no expedition leader and no deputy. Around midday – an hour after Clermont and Krakow had left – we heard yelling and gunfire. Sounded like a two-way range; like an ambush, with return fire.'

Alonzo glanced at Jaeger. 'That was it: hugging declared over. We set out as a hunter force, tracking Clermont and Krakow's trail to a point maybe a half-mile out. There, we hit major disturbance of the undergrowth. Fresh blood. Plus there were several of these.'

He pulled something out of his pack and handed it to Jaeger. 'Careful. Figure that's some kind of poison.'

Jaeger studied what he'd been given. It was a thin piece of wood around six inches long. It was finely carved and sharpened at one end, the point being smeared in some kind of dark and viscous fluid.

'We pushed on,' Alonzo continued, 'and we picked up James and Santos's trail. We found their camp, but no sign of them. No sign of any struggle, either. No sign of a fight. No blood. No darts. Nothing. It was like they'd been teleported out of there by aliens.'

Alonzo paused. 'And then there was this.' He pulled a spent bullet casing from his pocket. 'Found it on the way back. Kind of stumbled across it.' He handed Jaeger the casing. 'It's a 7.62 mm. More than likely GPMG or AK-47. It ain't one of ours, that's for sure.'

Jaeger rolled the casing around in his hand for a couple of seconds.

Until a few decades back, 7.62 mm had been the calibre of round used by NATO forces. In the Vietnam War, the Americans had experimented with a smaller calibre: 5.56 mm. With lighter bullets a foot soldier could carry more rounds of ammo, which meant more sustained firepower – crucial when undertaking long missions on foot in the jungle. Since then, 5.56 mm had become a common NATO calibre, and none of those gathered on the sandbar were using a 7.62 mm weapon.

Jaeger eyed Alonzo. 'There's been no further sign of the four of them?'

Alonzo shook his head. 'None.'

'So what d'you make of it?' he prompted.

Alonzo's face darkened. 'Man, I dunno . . . There's a hostile force out there, that's for sure, but right now that force remains a mystery. If it is the Indians, how come we've got a 7.62 mm weapon in the mix? Since when does a lost tribe pack a punch like that?'

'Tell me,' Jaeger asked, 'what was the blood like?'

'At the ambush? Pretty much what you'd expect. Pools of it. Congealed.'

'Lot of blood?' Jaeger queried.

Alonzo shrugged. 'Enough.'

Jaeger held up the thin sliver of wood that he'd been given. 'Blow-dart, obviously. We know the Indians are armed with them. Supposedly poison-tipped. You know what they use to arm their darts? Curare – made from the sap of a forest vine. Curare kills by stopping the muscles of the diaphragm from working. In other words, you suffocate to death. Not a nice way to go.

'I learned a bit about it while out here training Colonel Evandro's B-SOB teams. The Indians use them for hunting monkeys in the treetops. Dart hits; monkey falls down; tribe collects monkey and retrieves dart. Each is hand-carved and they don't tend to leave them lying around. But most importantly, if you are shot by a curare-tipped dart, it sticks in you like a pin; you hardly bleed at all.

'Plus there's this.' Jaeger took the dart and put it to his mouth, tasting the black goo on the pointed end. Several of his team flinched.

'You can't get poisoned by ingesting curare,' Jaeger reassured them. 'Has to go direct into the bloodstream. But the thing is, it has an unmistakably bitter taste. This? My guess is it's a syrup made of burned sugar.' He gave a bleak smile. 'Put it all together and what've you got?'

He glanced around the faces of his remaining team members. Alonzo: square-jawed, open-faced, exuding a homely honesty – every inch a former Navy SEAL. Kamishi: quiet, expectant, body like a coiled spring. Dale and Kral: two rising stars in the media intent on shooting their slick, blockbuster movie.

'No one was shot by blow-darts.' Jaeger answered his own question. 'They were ambushed by gunmen; the blood alone proves that. So unless this lost tribe has somehow managed to get seriously tooled up, we've got a mystery force out there. The fact that they left this,' he held up the dart, 'and did their best to clear away their bullet cases suggests they're trying to fit up the Indians for the crime.'

He stared at the dart for a second. 'No one is supposed to be here apart from us and this lost tribe. At present, we have no idea who this mystery force of gunmen is, how they got here or why they're hostile.' He glanced up, darkly. 'But one thing is clear: the nature of this expedition has changed irreversibly.

'Five have been taken,' he announced slowly. There was a cold steeliness in his gaze now. 'We've barely set foot in the forest and already we've lost half of our number. We need to consider our options – carefully.'

He paused. His eyes were etched with a hardness few had seen before. He hadn't known any of the missing that well, yet still he felt personally responsible for their loss.

He'd been drawn to the openness and the lack of guile of the big crazy Kiwi, Joe James. And he was painfully aware that Leticia Santos was Colonel Evandro's presence on his team.

Santos was striking-looking, like a more streetwise – or maybe jungle-wise – version of the Brazilian actress Tais Araujo. Dark-eyed, dark-haired, impetuous and dangerously good fun, she had been pretty much the polar opposite of Irina Narov.

For Jaeger, losing one – Narov – had been a tragic disaster. Losing five within the first forty-eight hours of his expedition – it was unthinkable.

40

'Option one,' he announced, his voice tight with the tension of the moment. 'We decide the mission's no longer tenable and we call in an extraction team. We've got good comms, this is a usable landing zone; we could conceivably get pulled out of here. We'd remove ourselves from the threat, but we'd be leaving our friends behind – and right now we have no idea if they're dead or alive.

'Option two: we go searching for the missing team members. We work on the assumption that all are alive until proven otherwise. The upside: we do right by our fellows. We do not turn our backs on them at the first sign of trouble. The downside: we're a small, lightly armed force, facing one with potentially greater firepower, and we have zero idea of their numbers.'

Jaeger paused. 'And then there is the third option: we continue with the expedition as planned. I have a suspicion – and this is only instinct – that by doing so we'll discover what's happened to our missing friends. One way or another, whoever has attacked us, it makes sense that they've done so in order to stop us getting to our goal. By continuing, we'll force their hand.

'This is no military operation,' Jaeger continued. 'If it were, I'd give my men orders. We're a bunch of civvies and we need to make a collective decision. As I see it, those are the three options – and we need to vote. But before we do, any questions? Suggestions? And feel free to talk, 'cause the camera isn't running.'

He cast Dale a menacing look. 'The camera's not running, is it, Mr Dale?'

Dale brushed back his longish, lank hair. 'Hey, you vetoed this stuff, remember. No filming of this meeting.'

'I did.' Jaeger glanced around for questions.

'I am curious,' Hiro Kamishi remarked quietly, his English all but perfect, apart from the faint Japanese lilt. 'If this were a military operation, which option would you order your men to pursue?'

'Option three,' Jaeger replied, without a moment's hesitation.

'Would you mind explaining why?' Kamishi spoke in an odd, careful way, each word chosen seemingly with great precision.

'It's counter-intuitive,' Jaeger replied. 'The normal human re-action to stress and danger is fight or flight. Flight would be to pull out. Fight would be to go directly after the bad guys. Option three is the least expected, and I'd hope it would throw them: force them into revealing themselves; into making a mistake.'

Kamishi bowed slightly. 'Thank you. It is a good explanation. One I agree with.'

'You know, buddy, it's not five,' Alonzo growled. 'It's six. With Andy Smith, that makes six gone. Never thought Smith's death was an accident, and even less after what's happened.'

Jaeger nodded. 'With Smith it makes six.'

'So when do we get the coordinates?' a voice prompted. 'Those of the air wreck?'

It was Stefan Kral, the Slovakian cameraman on Jaeger's team – his English tinged with a strong, guttural accent. Jaeger eyed him. Short, stocky, with almost albino looks, Kral was the Beast to Dale's Beauty, with pitted, pockmarked skin. He was six years older than Dale, though he didn't look it, and by right of seniority alone he should have been directing the film.

But Carson had put Dale in charge, and Jaeger could pretty much figure out why. Dale and Carson were birds of a feather. Dale was slick, easy and cool, and a master at surviving in the media jungle. By contrast Kral was a clumsy, somewhat nerdy bag of nerves. He was one hell of an oddball to be trying to cut it in the TV industry.

'With Narov gone, I've made Alonzo my deputy,' Jaeger replied. 'I've shared the coordinates with him.'

'And so? The rest of us?' Kral pushed.

Whenever Kral spoke, an odd, lopsided half-smile played across his features, no matter how serious the topic at hand. Jaeger figured it was his nervousness shining through, but still he found it oddly unsettling.

He'd known enough guys like Kral in the army – the semi-introverted; those who found it tough relating to others. He had always made a point of nurturing any who made it into his unit. More often than not they'd proven to be loyal to a fault, and absolute demons when the red mist of combat came down.

'If we vote for option three – to continue – you'll get the coordinates once we're on the river,' Jaeger told him. 'That's the deal I cut with Colonel Evandro: once we start our journey down the Rio de los Dios.'

'So how did you manage to lose Narov?' Kral probed. 'What exactly happened?'

Jaeger stared. 'I've already explained how Narov died.'

'I'd like to hear it again,' Kral pressed, the lopsided smile creeping further across his features. 'Just, you know, to de-conflict things. Just so we're all clear.'

Jaeger was haunted by Narov's loss, and he wasn't about to relive it all again. 'It was a God-awful mess that went ugly fast. And trust me – there was nothing I could do to save her.'

'What makes you so convinced she's dead?' Kral continued mulishly. 'And not so with James, Santos and the others?'

Jaeger's eyes narrowed. 'You had to be there,' he remarked quietly.

'But surely there was *something* you could have done? It was day one, you were crossing the river . . .'

'You want me to shoot him now?' Alonzo cut in, his voice rumbling a warning. 'Or later, after we cut out his tongue?'

Jaeger stared at Kral. A distinct edge of menace crept into his tone. 'It's a funny thing, Mr Kral: I get the impression you're interviewing me here. You're not, are you? Interviewing me?'

Kral shook his head nervously. 'I'm just airing a few issues. Just trying to deconflict things.'

Jaeger glanced from Kral to Dale. The latter's camera was lying beside him on the ground. His hand crept towards it, furtively.

'You know what, guys,' Jaeger rasped, 'I got something myself that needs *deconflicting*.' He eyed the camera. 'You've taped over the red filming light with black gaffer tape. You've set it on the ground, lens facing my way, and I presume it was already filming before you put it down.'

He lifted his eyes to Dale, who seemed to quake visibly under his gaze. 'I'll say this one time. Once only. You pull a trick like this again, I'll ram that camera so far up your backside you'll be able to clean the lens as if it were your teeth. Are – we – clear?'

Dale shrugged. 'Yeah. I guess. Only—'

'Only nothing,' Jaeger cut him off. 'And when we're done here, you're going to wipe everything you've filmed from the tapes, with me watching.'

'But if I can't film key scenes like this, we've got no show,' Dale objected. 'The commissioners – the TV execs—'

Jaeger's look was enough to silence him. 'There's something you need to understand: right now, I do not give a damn about your TV execs. Right now, there's only one thing I care for – which is getting the maximum number of my team through this alive. And right now, we're five – six – down, so I'm on the back foot and sliding.

'And that makes me dangerous,' Jaeger continued. 'It makes me mad.' He stabbed a finger at the camera. 'And when I get mad, stuff tends to get broken. Now, Mr Dale: turn – it – the hell – off.'

Dale reached for the camera, hit a couple of buttons and powered down. He'd been caught red-handed, but from his sulky demeanour you'd have thought he was the one who had been wronged.

'You get me to ask a load of idiot questions,' Kral muttered at Dale, half under his breath. 'Another of your dumb-ass ideas.'

Jaeger had met guys like Dale and Kral before. A few of his elite forces mates had tried to make it in their world – the world of the out-there, reality-show TV media. They'd found out too late how ruthless it could be. It chewed people up and spat them out again, like dried husks. And honour and loyalty were a rare commodity.

It was a cut-throat business. Guys like Dale and Kral – not to mention their boss, Carson – had to be driven to make it, often to the detriment of all others. It was a world wherein you had to be prepared to film people making life-or-death decisions when you had promised not to – because it went with the territory; that was what it took to get the story.

You had to be ready to put the knife into your fellow camera-man's back, if that might advance your own fortunes a little. Jaeger hated the ethos, and that was in large part what had made him so unreceptive to the media team from the get-go.

He added Kral and Dale to the list of things he'd have to keep a close watch on here – along with toxic spiders, giant caimans, savage tribes, and now an unidentified force of gunmen seemingly intent on delivering bloody violence.

'Okay, so – with the camera turned well and truly off – let's move to a vote,' he announced. 'Option one: we pull out and abandon the expedition. All in favour?'

Every hand remained down.

That was a relief: at least they weren't about to turn tail and run from the Serra de los Dios any time soon.

41

'Mind if I film?' Dale gestured at Jaeger.

Jaeger was crouched by the water's edge doing his evening ablutions – his shotgun propped to one side, just in case of trouble.

He spat into the water. 'You're persistent, I'll give you that. Expedition leader cleans his teeth. Gripping stuff.'

'No, really. I need to capture some of this stuff. Background colour. Just to establish how life goes on amongst . . .' He waved a hand at the river and surrounding jungle. 'Amongst all of this.'

Jaeger shrugged. 'Be my guest. Highlight coming up: I'm about to wash my stinking face.'

Dale proceeded to take a few shots covering Jaeger's attempts to use the Rio de los Dios as his bathroom. At one point the cameraman had his boots in the water and his back to the river, filming a low-level shot, his lens thrust halfway down Jaeger's throat.

Jaeger half hoped a five-metre caiman would come grab Dale by the balls, but no such luck.

Apart from Alonzo, who'd typically wanted to go hunting for the bad guys directly, the vote had been unanimous. Option number three – to continue with the expedition as planned – had been everyone's choice. Jaeger had had to clear things with Carson, but a short call via a Thuraya satphone had got it sorted.

Carson had made his priorities very clear very quickly: nothing was to stand in the way of the expedition's progress. From the get-go, everyone had known and understood the dangers.

All team members had signed a legally binding disclaimer, recognising that they were going into harm's way. The five missing people were just that: *missing, until proven otherwise*.

Carson had a twelve-million-dollar global TV spectacular to keep on track, and Wild Dog Media's fortunes – not to mention those of Enduro Adventures – were very much dependent on its success. Come what may, Jaeger had to get his team to the site of that air wreck, uncover its secrets, and if possible pull the mystery warplane out of there.

If anyone got injured or died in the process, their misfortune would be overshadowed by the awesome nature of the discovery, or so Carson argued. This was, after all, the Last Great Mystery of the Second World War, he reminded Jaeger; *the plane that never was; the ghost flight*. Funny how rapidly Carson had made the archivist's, Simon Jenkinson's, phrases so completely his own.

Carson had even gone as far as trying to upbraid Jaeger for standing in the way of some of the filming – which meant that Dale must have called him to complain. Jaeger had given Carson short shrift: he was in charge of the expedition on the ground, and here in the jungle his word was law. If Carson didn't like it, he could fly out to the Serra de los Dios and take his place.

Call to Carson done, Jaeger had placed a second – this to the Airlander. The giant airship had taken a while to fly out from the UK, but it was now moving towards its point of orbit high above them. Jaeger knew the pilot, Steve McBride, from when their paths had crossed in the military. He was a good, safe pair of hands to have at the Airlander's controls.

Jaeger had another reason to trust the Airlander's crew absolutely. Before leaving London, he'd cut a deal with Carson: if he couldn't have Raff with him on the ground, he wanted him as his eyes in the sky. Carson had capitulated, and the big Maori had duly been appointed McBride's operations officer on the Airlander.

Jaeger had put a call through to the airship, getting a heads-up from Raff on all aspects of the expedition's bigger picture. There was no further update on Andy Smith's death, which didn't exactly surprise him. But the one thing that was a shocker was the news about Simon Jenkinson.

The archivist had had his London flat broken into. Three things had gone missing: his file on the Ju 390 ghost flight, the iPhone on which he'd taken the recent – surreptitious – photos of the Hans Kammler file, and his laptop. Jenkinson had been spooked by the robbery, and triply so once he'd checked with the National Archives.

The reference number for the Hans Kammler file had been AVIA 54/1403. The National Archive claimed there was no record of any such file ever having existed. Jenkinson had seen it with his own eyes. He'd sneaked some photos of it on to his phone. But with his flat being burgled, and the file having been expunged from the archives, it was as if AVIA 54/1403 had never even existed.

The ghost flight now had its own ghost file.

42

Jenkinson was scared, but he didn't seem to be running, Raff had explained. Quite the reverse. He'd vowed that he'd retrieve those photos, come what may. Fortunately, he'd stored them on a number of online cloud systems. Just as soon as he managed to get a replacement computer, he'd go about downloading them.

The news from Jenkinson could mean only one thing, Jaeger reasoned: whoever they were up against had the power and the influence to make an entire British government file disappear. The ramifications were deeply worrying, but there wasn't a great deal he could do about it from the heart of the Amazon.

Jaeger had urged Raff to keep a close watch, and to brief him whenever they could establish communications between the ground team and the Airlander.

He packed away his wash kit, rolling it into a tight bundle. Early the following morning they would set off downriver, and space in the boats was limited. Dale had clearly filmed enough, for he powered down the camera. But Jaeger could sense him lingering, as if he wanted to have words.

'Look, I know you're not comfortable with much of this,' he ventured. 'The filming. And I'm sorry about the incident earlier. I was bang out of order. But my neck is on the line here if I don't capture enough of this to make it work.'

Jaeger didn't reply. He didn't particularly like the man, and even less so after the underhand filming episode.

'You know, there's a quote about my industry,' Dale ventured. 'The TV industry. Hunter S Thompson. Mind hearing it?'

Jaeger shouldered his shotgun. 'I'm all ears.'

'"The TV business is a cruel and shallow money trench,"' Dale began, '"a long plastic hallway where thieves and pimps run free and good men die like dogs." Probably not word for word, but . . . *Good men die like dogs* sums up the industry perfectly.'

Jaeger eyed him. 'There's a similar saying in my business: "The pat on the back is only ever a recce for the knife going in."' He paused. 'Look, I don't have to like you to be able to work with you. But I'm not here to break your balls either. As long as we have some workable ground rules, we should be able to get through this without killing each other.'

'What kind of rules?'

'Reasonable ones. Ones that you guys adhere to. Like, one: you do not have to ask my permission to film. Film as you see fit. But if I ever tell you not to, you do as I say.'

Dale nodded. 'Fair enough.'

'Two: if any other team member asks you not to film, you do as requested. You can come to me to query it, but in the first instance you respect their wishes.'

'But that means everyone has a de facto right of veto,' Dale objected.

'It doesn't: only I have. This is my expedition, and that means you and Kral – you're on my team. If I think you should be allowed to film, I will come down on your side. You have a difficult and challenging job to do. I respect that, and I will be an honest arbitrator.'

Dale shrugged. 'Well, okay. I guess I don't have much choice.'

'You don't,' Jaeger confirmed. 'Rule three: you ever try a repeat performance of this morning – filming when you've agreed not to – your camera ends up at the bottom of the river. I'm not joking. I have lost five people. Don't push it.'

Dale spread his hands in a gesture of contrition. 'Like I said, I'm sorry.'

'The fourth and final rule.' Jaeger stared at Dale for a long second. 'Don't break the rules.'

'Got it,' Dale confirmed. He paused. 'There is maybe one thing you could do, though – to make things easier from our side. If I could interview you, say here by the riverside, I could get you to recap on all of today – the stuff we weren't allowed to film.'

Jaeger thought about it for a moment. 'If there are questions I don't want to answer?'

'You don't have to. But you are the expedition leader. You're the right and proper spokesperson for this thing.'

Jaeger shrugged. 'Okay. I'll do it. But remember: the rules are the rules.'

Dale smiled. 'I got it. I got it.'

Dale fetched Kral. They put the camera on a lightweight tripod, fixed Jaeger up with a throat microphone to get some decent sound, and with Kral behind camera framing the shot, Dale settled into interviewer mode. He sat himself beside the camera, asking Jaeger to speak to him direct and to try to ignore the lens that was staring him in the face, and to give a recap of the events of the last forty-eight hours.

As the interview progressed, there was a part of Jaeger that had to admit that Dale was good at his job. He had a way of teasing out information that made you feel as if you were just having a chat with a mate down the local pub.

Fifteen minutes into the interview, and Jaeger had almost forgotten the camera was there.

Almost.

'It was pretty obvious that you and Irina Narov prowled around each other like lions gearing up for a fight,' Dale ventured. 'So why risk everything for her at the river crossing?'

'She was on my team,' Jaeger answered. 'Enough said.'

'But you went into battle against a five-metre caiman,' Dale pressed. 'You almost lost your life. You went to war for someone who seemed to have it in for you. Why?'

Jaeger stared at Dale. 'It's an old rule in my profession that you never speak ill of the dead. Now, moving on . . .'

'Okay, moving on,' Dale confirmed. 'So, this mystery force of gunmen – any idea who they are or what they might be after?'

'I've almost zero idea,' Jaeger answered. 'This far into the Serra de los Dios there shouldn't be anyone else around other than us and the Indians. As to what they're after? I figure maybe they're trying to discover the location of that air wreck; maybe to stop us getting to it. Nothing else makes any sense. But it's just a gut feeling, no more.'

'That's quite a proposition – that a rival force might be out there searching for the wreck,' Dale pressed. 'Your suspicions must be based upon something?'

Before Jaeger could answer, Kral made an odd slurping sound. Jaeger had noticed that the Slovakian cameraman had an unfortunate habit of sucking his teeth.

Dale turned and gave him the daggers. 'Mate, I'm trying to interview here. Keep focused, and keep the bloody noise down.'

Kral glared back. 'I am focused. I'm behind the bloody camera pushing the bloody buttons, if you hadn't noticed.'

Great, thought Jaeger. They were just days in and already the camera crew were at each other's throats. What were they going to be like after weeks in the jungle?

Dale turned back to Jaeger. He rolled his eyes, as if to say, *look what I have to deal with*. 'This rival force – I was asking you about your suspicions.'

'Think about it,' Jaeger answered. 'Who knows the exact whereabouts of that warplane? Colonel Evandro. Myself. Alonzo. If there is another force out there trying to find it, they'd have to follow us. Or force someone on our team to talk. We had an unidentified aircraft tailing us when we flew in here. So maybe – just maybe – we've been followed and menaced pretty much all of the way.'

Dale smiled. 'Perfect. I'm done.' He gestured at Kral. 'Power down. That was sweet,' he remarked to Jaeger. 'You did a great job.'

Jaeger cradled his shotgun. 'A little less dirt-digging would be appreciated. But either way it's preferable to you guys sneaking about filming on the quiet.'

'Agreed.' Dale paused. 'Say – would you be up for filming something like this every day, kind of like a video diary?'

Jaeger set off across the sandbar towards camp. 'Maybe, time permitting . . .' He shrugged. 'Let's see how it goes.'

43

Night falls quickly in the jungle.

With the approach of darkness, Jaeger slapped on insect repellent and tucked his combat trousers well into his boots to stop any creepy-crawlies from sneaking in during the night hours. He'd sleep like that – fully clothed, boots on, and with his combat shotgun cradled in his arms.

That way, if they were attacked during the hours of darkness he'd be good to fight.

But none of this could entirely defeat one diehard adversary here in the Serra de los Dios – the mosquitoes. Jaeger had never seen such monsters. He could hear their fierce whine as they circled his body like mini vampire bats, intent on wreaking blood-sucking, disease-ridden mayhem. And sure enough, they could chomp through his combats; Jaeger could feel the odd one driving its tiny insect jaws in.

He climbed into his hammock, his limbs burning with exhaustion. After his fight to save Narov, and his solo trek across the jungle, he was utterly, utterly spent. He had barely rested at all the previous night. He didn't doubt that he would sleep the sleep of the dead, especially as Alonzo had promised to keep guard all through the hours of darkness.

The former SEAL had set a sentry routine, so that there would be eyes on the jungle all night long. If anyone needed to leave their sandbar camp for any reason – even to take a crap – they had to do so in pairs, buddy-buddy fashion. That way, everyone had back-up in case of trouble.

A thick and velvety darkness enveloped the sandbar, and with it came a cacophony of night-time sounds: the mindless rhythmic beat of the cicadas – *preeep-preeep-preeep-preeep* – which would continue until sunrise; the bumbling, fizzy thud of massive beetles and other flying things cannoning about; the all but inaudible high-pitched shrieks of giant bats swooping across the water, hunting on the wing. The air above the Rio de los Dios was thick with them, wings beating the darkness. Jaeger could see their fleeting forms silhouetted against the faint glow of the stars that filtered through the feathery treetops. Their ghostly shapes contrasted markedly with the eerie, pulsating glow of the fireflies.

Those fireflies peppered the silken night like bursts of falling stardust. All along the riverbank they formed a blur of fluorescent blue-green, dipping in and out of the trees. And every now and again one would disappear – *phffutt*; a light being snuffed out – as a bat swooped and plucked it from the air. Just as four of Jaeger's team had been plucked from the shadows of the forest by a dark and ghostly force.

Alone in the night hours, Jaeger found himself besieged by the doubts he'd kept hidden during the day. They were barely days into this and already he was five people down. Yet somehow he had to rescue his expedition's fortunes, and in truth, he didn't know how he was going to do that.

But this wasn't the first time he'd been so deeply in the shit, and he'd always managed to turn things around. He had an inner strength born of such situations, and a part of him thrived on the uncertainty and the overwhelming odds.

Of one thing he was certain: the answers to everything – every misfortune that had befallen them – lay deeper in the jungle, at the site of that mystery air wreck. That was the one thing that kept driving him onwards.

Jaeger kicked his feet higher in the hammock, and reached to unlace his left boot. He removed it, delved deep and pulled something out of the insole. He flashed a torch across it briefly, the light and his eyes lingering on the two faces that stared up at him – the green-eyed, raven-haired beauty of a mother, and the boy who was Jaeger's spitting image standing protectively at her side.

Some nights – many nights – he still said a prayer for them. He'd done so during the long and empty years in Bioko. He did so tonight, lying in a hammock slung between two trees on a sandbar on the Rio de los Dios. At that distant air wreck he knew there would be answers, and perhaps even the ones he most longed to learn – about what had happened to his wife and his boy.

Jaeger rested, cradling that photo.

As he drifted off to sleep, he sensed somehow that a truce had been declared in whatever war it was they were fighting here. For the first time since parachuting into the Serra de los Dios, he couldn't detect any watchers – any hostile eyes in the jungle shadows.

But he sensed also that this was a temporary lull. The first skirmishes had been fought. The first casualties suffered.

The war proper was only just beginning.

44

They'd been three days on the Rio de los Dios – three days during which Jaeger had brooded over the next stage of their journey until it had driven him almost to distraction. Three days travelling due west on a river flowing at an average speed of six kilometres an hour: via the water, they'd covered a good 120 kilometres.

Jaeger was pleased with their progress. That kind of distance would have taken many times as long and proven many times more exhausting – not to mention fraught with danger – had they attempted it overland.

It was approaching mid-afternoon on the third day when he spotted what he was looking for: the Meeting of the Ways. Here the Rio de Los Dios was joined by a slightly smaller water-course, the Rio Ouro – the Golden River. Whereas the Rio de los Dios was full of silty residues from the jungle, and dark brown – almost black – in colour, the Rio Ouro was golden-yellow, its waters being rich in sandy sediments swept down from the mountains.

Where the two converged, the colder, denser waters of the Rio Ouro proved reluctant to intermingle with those of its warmer, less dense cousin, hence what Jaeger could see ahead of him – a striking section of river where black and white ran side by side for a good kilometre or more, almost without mixing.

At the Meeting of the Ways, the smaller confluence – the Rio Ouro – would become subsumed into the Rio de los Dios. And at that moment, Jaeger and his team would be just three kilometres short of their must-stop position – for ahead lay an impassable barrier, the point where the river tumbled close to a thousand feet over the Devil's Falls.

The journey thus far had taken them across a high plateau cloaked in jungle. Where the Rio de los Dios thundered over the falls marked the point at which the plateau was torn in two by a jagged fault line. The land to the west of there lay a thousand feet lower, forming an endless carpet of lowland rainforest.

Their end point – the mystery air wreck – lay some thirty kilometres onwards from the Devil's Falls, in the midst of that lowland jungle.

Jaeger nosed his canoe ahead, his paddle dipping into the waters noiselessly and causing barely a ripple. As a former Royal Marines Commando, he was well at home on the water. He'd led the river leg, helping those behind navigate through the more treacherous shallows. He reflected upon their next move. Decisions now would prove critical.

The journey downriver had been relatively peaceful, at least compared to what had gone before. But he feared that with landfall approaching, this transitory period of stillness was about to come to an end.

He could detect a new threat resonating in the air now: a deep, throaty roar filled his ears, as if a hundred thousand wildebeest were thundering over an African plain in a massive stampede.

He glanced ahead.

On the horizon he could see a tower of rising mist – the spray thrown up by the Rio de los Dios as it cascaded over the edge of the rift, forming one of the world's tallest and most dramatic waterfalls.

There was no way over the Devil's Falls – that much had been obvious from studying the aerial photos. The only possible route ahead appeared to be a pathway of sorts leading down the escarpment, but that lay a good day's march north of here. Jaeger's plan was to leave the river shortly and to undertake the last stage of the journey – including the steep descent – on foot.

Skirting around the Devil's Falls would take them a good distance out of their way, but there was no alternative as far as he could determine. He'd studied the terrain from every angle, and the path down the escarpment was the only way to proceed. As to who or what exactly had made that path – it remained a mystery.

It could be wild animals.

It could be Indians.

Or it could be that mystery force that was out there somewhere – armed, hostile and dangerous.

45

The secondary problem that Jaeger was grappling with was the fact that they'd always envisaged making this final part of the journey as a ten-person team. Now they were reduced to five, and he was unsure what to do with the missing team members' kit. They'd packed their personal effects into the canoes, but there was no way to carry them onwards from here.

To leave such kit behind would be tantamount to telegraphing their acceptance that the missing team members were dead, but Jaeger couldn't see any way around it.

He glanced behind him.

His canoe was leading, the others in line astern. There were five vessels in all, each an Advanced Elements convertible kayak – a fifteen-foot semi-foldable inflatable expedition craft. The kayaks had been parachuted in by Kamishi and Krakow, packed in the para-tubes. Each twenty-five-kilo craft folded down to form a cube measuring around two square feet, but opened out into a boat capable of carrying 249 kilos of kit.

Back at the sandbar, they'd unpacked the kayaks, inflated them with stirrup pumps and launched them into the water loaded with gear. Each vessel boasted a triple-skin rip-stop hull, for extreme puncture resistance, built-in aluminium rods for added stability, plus adjustable padded seats, allowing for long-distance paddling without getting chafed raw.

With six inflatable chambers per canoe, plus flotation bags, they were pretty much unsinkable – as they had proven on the few sections of white water that they'd encountered.

Originally, Jaeger's plan had had five kayaks on the water, each crewed by two of his team. But with their numbers so depleted, the crafts had had the seating reconfigured so that each accommodated just one person. Dale and Kral had seemed the most relieved at not having to undergo a three-day river journey sharing the one cramped canoe.

Jaeger figured the film team's animosity was all down to one thing. Kral resented Dale's seniority. Dale was directing the filming, while Kral was only an assistant producer – and there were times when the Slovak's antipathy flashed through. As for Dale, Kral's unfortunate habit of sucking his teeth bugged him something rotten.

Jaeger had been on enough such expeditions to know how, in the crucible of the jungle, the best of friends could end up hating each other's guts. He knew he needed to get the problem sorted, for that kind of friction could endanger the entire expedition.

The rest of the team – Jaeger himself, Alonzo and Kamishi – had bonded pretty well. There was little that made alpha males pull together more than knowing they faced an enemy as unexpected as it was predatory. The three former elite forces soldiers were united in their adversity – it was just the film crew who were bitching behind each other's backs.

As the arrow-like prow of Jaeger's craft cleaved a furrow through the Meeting of the Ways – golden-white water on the one side, inky black on the other – he reflected on how he'd been almost happy on the river.

Almost. Of course, the loss of the five team members had cast a dark and continuous shadow over their progress.

But this had been the kind of thing that he had looked forward to back in London – a long paddle down a wild and remote river, in the heart of one of planet earth's greatest jungles. Here the rivers were corridors of both sunlight and life: wild animals flocked to their banks, and the air thrummed to the beat of a myriad bird wings.

213

Each kayak had elasticated deck lacing, providing quick access to vital gear. Jaeger had his combat shotgun meshed into that, just a hand's reach away. If a caiman tried to cause him any trouble, he could draw and fire within seconds if needed. As matters had transpired, most had chosen to keep their distance, for the kayaks were about the biggest thing moving on the river.

At one stage that morning Jaeger had allowed his kayak to drift silently downstream, as he watched a jaguar – a powerful male – stalk his prey. The big cat had padded along the riverside, taking great care not to raise a ripple or to make a sound. He'd got to the point where he was in a caiman's blind spot, and had swum across to the mudbank upon which the reptile was sunning itself. This was a yacare as opposed to a black caiman, so the smaller of the two species.

The big cat had stalked up the mudbank and pounced. The caiman had sensed danger at the last moment and tried to swing its jaws around to snap. But the cat was far quicker. Legs astride the caiman's front shoulders, claws sunk deep, he'd gripped the beast's head in his mouth, sinking his fangs into its brain.

It had been an instant kill, following which the jaguar had dragged the caiman into the water and swum back to shore. Having watched the entire hunt, Jaeger had felt like giving the big cat a round of applause. It was one–nil to the jaguar, and Jaeger for one was happy for it to remain that way.

After his earlier battle with one of the giant reptiles, and his loss of Irina Narov, he had developed a dislike of the caiman that went more than skin deep.

There had been one other joy to travelling by river: Dale and Kral's kayaks had been positioned at the rear of the flotilla. Jaeger had argued that they were the least experienced canoeists, and so they should be kept the furthest away from any likely trouble. As a bonus, putting them at the rear had kept him well away from Dale's camera lens.

But oddly, during the last day or so Jaeger had found himself almost missing the on-camera conversations. In a weird way the camera had been someone to talk to; to unburden himself to. Jaeger had never been on an expedition where he'd been so bereft of a soulmate; of company.

Alonzo was fine as a stand-in second-in-command. In fact, he reminded Jaeger of Raff in many ways, and with his massive physique the former SEAL would doubtless prove a superlative warrior. In time Jaeger figured Alonzo could become a good and loyal friend – but he was not his confidante; not yet, anyway.

And neither was Hiro Kamishi. Jaeger reckoned there was a lot he could share with the quiet Japanese – a man steeped in the mystic warrior creed of the East; of Bushido. But he needed to get to know Kamishi first. Both he and Alonzo were diehard elite forces types, and it took a while for such guys to drop their defences and open up.

In fact, the very same criticism could be levelled at Jaeger himself. After three years in Bioko, he was acutely aware of how comfortable he had become with his own company. He wasn't quite the archetypal loner – the trust-no-one ex-military type – but he had become adept at surviving alone. He'd grown used to his own company, and at times it was just easier that way.

For a moment Jaeger wondered how Irina Narov would have borne up. In time, would she have proven someone he could talk to? A soulmate? He just didn't know. Either way he'd lost her, and long before he'd been able to figure her out – if that would ever have been possible.

In her absence, the camera was an odd kind of a confidante. It came with another major downside: it had Dale attached, which meant it was hardly very trustworthy. But right now it was about all Jaeger had.

The previous evening, camped by the riverside, he'd filmed a second interview with Dale. Over the process of doing so, he'd found himself gradually warming to the man. Dale had a remarkable way of drawing out moments of real honesty from his interviewees with calmness and dignity.

His was a rare gift, and Jaeger for one was developing a grudging respect for him.

After the interview, it was Stefan Kral who'd lingered for a private chat. While he packed away the camera gear he'd proceeded to offer a mini confession about the forbidden filming episode back at the sandbar.

'I hope you don't think I'm telling tales, but I figured you needed to know,' he had begun, that odd lopsided smile twisting his features. 'That secret filming – it was Dale's idea. He primed me with the questions, while he kept an eye on the camera.'

He had glanced at Jaeger uneasily. 'I said it would never work. That you'd get wise to us. But Dale wouldn't listen. He's the big director and I'm only a lowly assistant producer, as he sees it – so he gets to call the shots.' Kral's words were thick with resentment. 'I'm years his senior, I've done many more jungle shoots, but somehow I'm the one under orders. And to be honest, I wouldn't put it past him to try the same trick again. Just flagging this up for you.'

'Thanks,' Jaeger told him. 'I'll be on the lookout.'

'I've got three kids, and you know their favourite movie?' Kral had continued, that crooked half-smile spreading further across his face. 'It's *Shrek*. And you know something else? Dale – he's Prince bloody Charming. And he uses it. The world of TV media is full of women – producers, executives, directors – and he's got them wrapped around his little finger.'

During his time in the military, Jaeger had acquired a reputation for nurturing zeros into heroes, which maybe went some way to explaining why he had a natural affinity for the underdog – and Kral was definitely the underdog in the expedition's film crew.

But at the same time he could well appreciate why Carson had put Dale in charge. In the military you often had younger officers commanding those with far more experience, simply because they had what it took to lead. And if he were Carson, he would have done the same thing.

Jaeger had done his best to reassure Kral. He'd told him that if ever he had serious concerns, he could bring them to him. But when all was said and done, it was up to the two of them to get it sorted. It was vital they did so.

That kind of tension – that seething resentment – it could tear an expedition apart.

Beneath the prow of Jaeger's kayak the white and the black river waters were mixing into dirty grey now, the roar of the Devil's Falls growing into an ominous, deafening thunder. It drew Jaeger's mind back to the relentless priorities of the present.

They needed to make landfall, and quickly.

Ahead and to his right he spotted a stretch of muddy riverbank, half hidden beneath overhanging branches.

He gave a hand signal and turned the prow of his kayak towards it, the other canoes swinging into line behind. As he thrust ahead with his paddle, he spotted a flash of movement beneath the canopy – no doubt some animal or other flitting along the shoreline. He studied the darkness beneath the trees, waiting to see if it might show itself.

The next moment a figure stepped out of the jungle.

A human figure.

Barefoot, naked except for a belt of woven bark strung around his waist, he stood in plain sight staring in Jaeger's direction.

A five-hundred-yard stretch of water separated Jaeger from the warrior of this hitherto uncontacted Amazonian Indian tribe.

46

Jaeger was in no doubt that the jungle warrior had chosen to show himself. The question was why. The Indian had melted out of the shadows, and doubtless he could have remained hidden had he so desired.

He held a gracefully arched bow and arrow in one hand. Jaeger was familiar with such weapons. Each of the long arrows was tipped with a twelve-inch length of flat bamboo honed to razor sharpness, and with vicious serrated edges.

One side of the bamboo arrowhead would be coated in the poison of the tiki uba tree, an anticoagulant, and the rear end would be hafted with a parrot's tail feathers, to ensure that it flew true. If you were pierced by the arrow tip, the anticoagulant would prevent your blood from clotting and you'd bleed to death.

The range of an Indian blowpipe was little more than a hundred feet – enough to reach the forest canopy. By contrast, the bow and arrow could fire four or five times that distance. It was these kind of weapons that the tribe would use when hunting large prey: caiman maybe, jaguar certainly, and without doubt any human adversaries who trespassed on their lands.

Jaeger used the flat of his paddle to beat out an alarm signal on the water – alerting those behind him, in case they hadn't noticed.

He lifted the paddle out of the river and laid it lengthwise on the kayak, resting his right hand on his shotgun. He drifted forward for several seconds, silently eyeing the Amazonian Indian, who in turn was staring right back at him.

The figure gave a signal: a single hand gesture, made to one side and then the other. Further figures stepped out to left and right, similarly dressed and armed.

Jaeger counted a dozen now, and more were very likely secreted in the shadows to their rear. As if to confirm his suspicions, the lead warrior – for leader he had to be – made a second hand gesture, as if cueing something.

A cry rang out across the river.

Animal, guttural, deep-throated, it rapidly grew into a chanted war cry, one that rolled across the water in challenge. It was punctuated by a series of incredibly powerful percussions, as if a massive drum were beating out a rhythm through the jungle: *kabooom-booom-booom, kabooom-booom-booom!*

The deep beats echoed across the water, and Jaeger recognised them for what they were. He'd heard something similar when working with Colonel Evandro's B-SOB teams. Somewhere just inside the treeline the Indians were beating their heavy battle clubs against a massive buttress root, the blows ringing out from the wall of wood like thunder.

Jaeger watched as the Indian leader lifted his bow and brandished it in his direction. The war cries rose in volume, the beating of the buttress-root drums punctuating every shake of the weapon. The gesture – the entire effect – needed no translating.

Come no further.

Trouble was, there was no way that Jaeger could turn back. Back lay only one-hundred-plus kilometres of river, upstream and in the wrong direction; and forward lay only the plunge over the Devil's Falls.

Either they made landfall here, or Jaeger and his team were in deep trouble.

It was hardly the most auspicious of ways to go about making first contact, but Jaeger didn't figure he had much choice. A few more seconds of this and he'd be within range of the tribe's arrows – and this time he didn't doubt that they were tipped with poison.

He lifted the shotgun from its mount, pointed it at the river just in front of his canoe, and opened fire. Six warning shots were pumped out in quick succession, cutting a swathe through the water and throwing a great spout of spray high into the air.

The reaction from the Indians was instantaneous.

Arrows were strung and the warriors let fly, their shots arcing high through the air bang on target but falling a little short of the prow of Jaeger's kayak. Cries of alarm echoed back and forth, and for a moment Jaeger was convinced that the tribe were determined to stand their ground and fight.

The last thing he had come here for was to do battle with this lost tribe. But if he had no choice, he would use all necessary means and defend his team to the last.

For a long moment he locked eyes with the tribe's warrior leader, as if a battle of wills had been joined across the water. And then the figure gestured again, his arm jerking backwards towards the jungle. On either side of him figures melted into the trees. The moment they did so, they were rendered invisible.

Jaeger had seen such forest tribes do this instantaneous disappearing act many times over, yet it never ceased to amaze him. He'd never seen anyone, not even Raff, who could equal it.

But the leader held his ground, unmoving – his face like thunder.

He stood alone facing Jaeger.

The kayak continued to drift inwards towards the riverbank. Jaeger saw the Indian raise something in his right hand, then, with a cry of rage, drive it deep into the mudbank. It looked like a spear with a battle flag or a pennant fluttering from its back end.

With that, the figure turned and was gone.

Jaeger took no chances making the landing. He pushed on alone, but with Alonzo and Kamishi to either flank and set slightly behind him, assault rifles at the ready. At the very rear he stationed Dale and Kral with their camera, for they were intent on filming every last move.

Jaeger knew that he was well covered, and he was banking that his show of force – the rounds unleashed from the shotgun – would prove a powerful deterrent against the tribe. With some powerful thrusts from his paddle he got the kayak drifting in the last few yards. He took the shotgun in hand and brought it to his shoulder, its wide, gaping muzzle menacing the dark line of trees.

Not a sign of movement anywhere.

The front of the kayak ground against the mud as it came to a halt. Jaeger was out in a flash, crouched low in the water behind his heavily laden craft, his weapon scanning the jungle in front of him.

For a good five minutes he didn't move.

He remained hunched over his shotgun, silently listening and watching.

He tuned his every sense to this new environment, filtering out any noises that he figured were entirely natural. If he could tune out all the normal pulses and rhythms of the forest – its heartbeat – he could tune in to anything that was abnormal, like a human footfall, or a warrior stringing an arrow to his bow.

But there was nothing of that nature that he could detect.

The tribe seemed to have melted away, just as swiftly as they had appeared. Yet Jaeger didn't believe for one moment that they were gone for good.

Keeping his weapon at the ready, he signalled Alonzo and Kamishi closer. When their canoes were almost level with his own, he stepped up from the crouch and waded through the shallows, shotgun held at the ready and primed to unleash hell.

Partway up the mudbank, he sank to one knee, weapon sweeping the dark terrain ahead of him. He signalled Alonzo and Kamishi in. Once they were alongside, he moved up further on to the sand, until he was able to take hold of the Indian warrior's spear and rip it out of the ground.

Leticia Santos, the missing Brazilian member of Jaeger's team, had worn a striking multicoloured silk scarf emblazoned with the word 'Carnivale!' Jaeger spoke decent Portuguese, having learned it during his time training the B-SOB teams, and he'd remarked on how the scarf complemented her warm Latino spirit. She'd told him it had been a gift from her sister during the previous February's Rio carnival, and that she wore it to bring her luck on the expedition.

It was Leticia Santos's scarf that was hanging from the end of the Indian warrior's spear.

47

Jaeger was busy stuffing kit into his backpack, talking fast and with a real edge of urgency. 'One: how did they get ahead of us so fast and without using the river? Two: why did they want to show us Santos's scarf? Three: why then simply disappear?'

'To warn us that it's only a matter of time before they take us all.' It was Kral, and Jaeger noticed that his signature smile was etched with worry now. 'This whole thing is turning bad fast.'

Jaeger ignored him. While he was all for a good dose of realism, Kral had a habit of being unrelentingly downbeat, and they had to keep positive and stay focused.

If they lost it here in the depths of the wilderness, they were finished.

They'd unloaded their canoes on to the riverbank to form a makeshift camp, and Jaeger continued repacking his gear as quickly as he could.

'Means they have a fix on our location,' he remarked. 'A point from where they can track us. Makes it all the more important that we get going, and we move light and fast.'

He glanced at a heap of equipment lying on a tarpaulin – kit that they were planning to leave behind. It included all their extraneous gear – their parachutes; their boating equipment; spare weaponry. 'Anything – I repeat anything – that you don't need, you leave it in the cache. Any extra weight – if you're in doubt, dump it.'

Jaeger eyed the kayaks, pulled up on the beach. 'We'll collapse the boats and cache those too. Where we're going, it's all going to be on foot from now on.'

Nods from the others.

Jaeger glanced at Dale. 'You guys take one Thuraya between the two of you. That's Wild Dog Media's satphone. I'll take another. Alonzo – you take a third. That's three between us, and the rest we leave in the cache.'

There was a series of grunts in the affirmative.

'And guys,' he eyed Dale and Kral, 'either of you know how to use a weapon?'

Dale shrugged. 'Nothing more than doing a shoot-'em-up on Xbox.'

Kral rolled his eyes in Dale's direction. 'I tell you – everyone learns to shoot in Slovakia. Where I come from, we all learn to hunt, especially in the mountains.'

Jaeger gave a thumbs-up. 'Go grab yourself an assault rifle, plus six full mags. That's one weapon for the two of you. You'd best shift the load between you as you go, 'cause I know you've got the extra weight of the camera gear.'

For an instant Jaeger weighed Narov's knife in his hand. It joined the pile of kit to be left behind. In theory, the cache was there to be picked up later – stored as best they could in a known location. In practice, he couldn't imagine who was ever going to get back here to retrieve what had been discarded.

In truth, he figured once it was gone it was gone.

He changed his mind, adding Narov's knife to the pile of kit that he was taking with him. He did the same with the C-130 pilot's Night Stalkers coin. Both were decisions driven by emotion: neither knife nor coin was crucial for what was coming. But Jaeger was like that: he was superstitious, saw portents, and didn't easily discard things that meant something to him personally.

'At least now we know who the enemy are,' he remarked, trying to buoy everyone's spirits. 'They couldn't have left a more direct message – not if they'd spelled it out in the sand.'

'What was that message, do you think?' Kamishi asked, his voice suffused with its signature quiet, measured calm. 'I think maybe it can be read in different ways.'

Jaeger glanced at Kamishi curiously. 'Santos's scarf, tied on a spear and planted in the sand? I'd say that's pretty clear: come no further, or meet the same fate.'

'There is perhaps another way to interpret it,' Kamishi ventured. 'It is not necessarily a direct threat.'

Alonzo snorted. 'Like hell it's not.'

Jaeger waved him into silence. 'What're you thinking?'

'It may help to try to see from their perspective,' Kamishi ventured. 'I think perhaps the Indians are scared. We must appear to them like aliens from another world. We drop from the sky into their isolated world. We glide across the water on these magical craft. We carry thunder sticks that explode the very river. If you had never seen any of this, would you also not be scared? And the overriding human reaction to fear – it is anger; aggression.'

Jaeger nodded. 'Keep going.'

Kamishi ran his eye around the others. They had stopped what they were doing to listen, or, in Dale's case, to film.

'We know this tribe have only ever suffered aggression from outsiders,' Kamishi continued. 'Their few contacts with the wider world have been with those who seek to do them harm: loggers, miners and others intent on stealing their lands. Why would they expect anything different from us?'

'Where's this going?' Jaeger pressed.

'I think perhaps we need a two-track approach,' Kamishi announced quietly. 'On the one hand, we put ourselves doubly on guard – especially once we are in the jungle, which is entirely their domain. On the other, we need to try to entice the Amahuaca in; we need to find ways to show them we have only friendly intentions.'

'Hearts and minds?' Jaeger queried.

'Hearts and minds,' Kamishi confirmed. 'There is one other

advantage we may gain by winning this tribe's hearts and minds. We have a long and difficult journey still ahead of us. The Indians – no one knows the jungle better than they do.'

'Come on, Kamishi, get real!' Alonzo challenged. 'They've taken one of our own, probably boiled and eaten her, and we're just gonna go and cosy up to them? I dunno what planet you come from, but in my world we fight fire with fire.'

Kamishi bowed slightly. 'Mr Alonzo, we should always be ready to fight fire with fire. Sometimes it is the only way. Yet we should also be ready to hold out the hand of friendship. Sometimes that is the better way.'

Alonzo scratched his head. 'Man, I dunno . . . Jaeger?'

'Let's be ready on both counts,' Jaeger announced. 'Ready to hold out the hand of fire or the hand of friendship. But no one takes any unnecessary risks to draw the Indians in. No repeats of what went down before.'

He indicated the cache of gear. 'Kamishi, choose some stuff from there you think they might like. Gifts. To take with us. To try to lure them in.'

Kamishi nodded. 'I will make a selection. Waterproofs, machetes, cooking pots – a remote tribe will always have use for such things.'

Jaeger checked his watch. 'Right, it's 1400 Zulu. It's a day and a half's trek to the start of the path – the one that descends the escarpment – less if we really push it. We set off now, we should reach it by nightfall tomorrow.'

He pulled out his compass, then collected up a few counting pebbles similar to those he'd used before. 'We'll be moving under the canopy, by pacing and bearing only. I figure some of you,' he eyed Kral and Dale, 'are unfamiliar with the technique, so stick close. But not too close.'

Jaeger glanced at the others. 'I don't want us bunched up so we present too much of an easy target.'

48

The trek through the jungle had gone as well as Jaeger could have hoped for. Their route lay along the rim of the fault line, and the ground had been rocky and drier underfoot, the forest slightly less dense. As a result, they'd made decent progress.

The first night they'd camped in the jungle and put into practice their dual strategy – to double their watch while at the same time trying to lure the Indians into making some kind of peaceful contact.

During his time in the military, Jaeger had done his fair share of hearts-and-minds operations – designed to befriend the native populace wherever they might be operating. The locals would have invaluable knowledge as to enemy movements, and they would also know the best routes to use to track and ambush them. It had made every sense to try to bring them onside.

With Hiro Kamishi's help, Jaeger had strung up gifts for the Indians, hanging them in the forest just out of visual range of their camp. A few knives, a couple of machetes, some cooking pots: it was the kind of equipment Jaeger would have appreciated were he a member of a remote tribe living in the midst of the world's largest jungle.

They didn't bother with the kind of note that Joe James had written for the Indians. Uncontacted tribes didn't tend to read. But the good news was that by morning, several of their offerings had been taken.

In their place, someone – the Indian warriors presumably

– had left gifts: some fresh fruit; a couple of animal-bone amulets; even a quiver made of jaguar skin for holding blow-darts.

Jaeger was heartened. The first signs of peaceful contact appeared to have been made. Even so, he was determined not to relax their vigilance. The Indians were definitely close. They were on the trail of Jaeger and his team, and that meant the threat remained very real.

Jaeger had led the way towards their second intended campsite, at the lip of the thousand-foot precipice, and the path leading to the lowlands far below. It was beginning to get dark by the time he had found a suitable spot to spend the night.

He signalled the team to a halt. They dropped their packs and settled themselves upon them, not a word being spoken. Jaeger had them spend ten long minutes doing a 'listening watch'; tuning into the forest and scanning for any threat.

All seemed quiet.

That done, he signalled that they should set camp.

They worked away in the gathering darkness by feel alone, so as not to show any lights and alert the Indians to their exact location. Once camp was set, Jaeger and Kamishi planned to hang out more offerings – but they'd site them a good distance away from the camp, to furnish an added layer of security.

Jaeger unrolled his poncho from his pack and tied it between four trees – forming a waterproof roof. That done, he changed out of his sweat-soaked trekking gear. Everyone on his team carried one set of dry clothing: combat shirt and trousers, plus socks. The night was dry-kit time – a precious few hours in which to allow the body to recover a little.

Having dry time was crucial. If it were left permanently wet, skin would quickly start to rot in the hot and humid conditions.

Once in his dry gear, Jaeger slung his hammock beneath the poncho. It had been hand-stitched from parachute silk, making it strong, lightweight and durable. There were two layers of para-silk – one to lie on, and the other to pull over the top, forming a cocoon. It helped keep the mozzies off and the heat in – for the jungle at night could prove surprisingly chilly.

On either end of the hammock's lines was threaded a squash ball cut in half, cup face towards the tree. It was there to prevent water running down the lines and soaking the hammock's head and foot ends. Jaeger sprayed the area directly behind the squash ball with a powerful insect repellent: it would soak into the hammock line and deter any insects from crawling in.

He placed his compass into his dry-kit pocket. If they did need to make a run for it during the night, he had to have such vital kit to hand. His wet kit was stuffed inside a poly bag and strapped beneath the flap of his backpack. The pack was laid beneath his hammock, with his weapon placed on top.

If he needed to reach for his shotgun in the night, it would come easily to hand.

They were six days into this expedition now, and with the constant exertion and the need for permanent vigilance, everyone was getting seriously fatigued. But keeping a strict wet-kit/dry-kit routine was vital. Jaeger knew from experience that the moment someone failed to get into their dry kit on a long expedition such as this one – *I'm too tired; I can't be bothered* – they were done for. Likewise if they allowed their dry kit to get wet. Trench foot and groin rot could come on fast and would slow the pace of a man almost as fast as any bullet.

Before retiring to his hammock, Jaeger would rub a dab of anti-fungal powder into his most vulnerable parts: between the toes, under armpits and in the groin. Those were the places where dirt, moisture and bacteria tended to collect, and they would be the first to start to rot and turn septic.

Come morning, he and his team would reverse the entire night-time routine, changing out of dry kit into wet, stowing their dry kit away, dosing socks and more with talcum powder, and preparing for the onward journey. It was laborious, but it was also the only way to keep the body functioning in these kinds of conditions.

Lastly, Jaeger checked the sticky plasters that he had taped over his nipples. The constant friction of wet gear tended to rub your chest raw. He cut off some fresh strips, applied them, and stuffed the old plasters into a side pocket of his pack. The less they left behind, the harder it would be to track them.

That done, he was ready to hang out tonight's presents to lure the Indians in. He and Kamishi did a repeat of the previous night – tying their few remaining gifts in the low-hanging branches amongst a distant patch of trees. Then they returned to camp, where they would be taking first watch. There would be two sets of eyes alert and watchful all night long, standing a rota of two-hour sentry duties.

Jaeger and Kamishi settled down, focusing intently on their senses – chiefly hearing and sight, their best early-warning systems. The key to survival in the deep jungle was watchfulness in every sense of the word.

It was like a form of meditation, this tuning in to the night-dark forest – and Jaeger could feel Kamishi doing the same at his side.

He opened his mind to changes in the setting, becoming hyper-alert to any hint of threat. If his ears caught the faintest sound – anything distinct from the deafening night-time beat of the insects pulsating out of the shadows – his eyes immediately swivelled around to focus on the threat.

Tension rippled back and forth as he and Kamishi sensed movement in the darkness. Every noise from the brooding bush sent Jaeger's pulse racing. Weird animal noises echoed through the jungle, ones that Jaeger figured he'd not heard before. And tonight he was convinced that some of them at least were human.

Odd, unnatural piercing shrieks and wails echoed back and forth through the trees. A lot of jungle animals did make similar calls – troops of monkeys in particular. But so too did the native Amazonian tribes as they signalled to each other.

'You hear that?' Jaeger whispered.

Kamishi's teeth showed white in the faint moonlight. 'Yes. I hear it.'

'Animals? Or Indians?'

Kamishi eyed Jaeger. 'I think Indian. Maybe they signal they are happy to find our new gifts?'

'Happy is good,' Jaeger muttered.

But those cries – they weren't like any shouts of joy that he had ever heard before.

49

Jaeger awoke.

It was sometime in the depths of the night. At first he was unsure what had disturbed him.

As his senses tuned in to his immediate surroundings, he detected a thick and ghostly tension about the camp. And then, from the corner of his eye, he spotted a wraith-like form melt out of the dark jungle. Almost at the same instant, he became aware that there were dozens more such figures emerging from the trees.

He saw all-but-naked forms detach themselves from the gloom, and flit noiselessly through the camp. Weapons held at the ready, they moved with a single-minded purpose. Jaeger reached down, his fingers feeling for the cold steel of his combat shotgun. He slipped his hand around it, drawing it into the hammock beside him.

Other than himself, he could see that only Alonzo was awake. An unspoken understanding was telegraphed across the darkness between them: somehow the team's watch must have fallen apart, and the Indians had stolen unnoticed into their camp.

They were outnumbered many times over, that much was clear, and Jaeger felt certain the Indians had further firepower secreted in the forest. It was also clear what the consequences would be if he and Alonzo opened fire. There would be a bloodbath, but by sheer force of numbers the Indians would end up slaughtering the lot of them.

Jaeger forced himself to hold his fire, signalling Alonzo to do likewise.

Moments later, three figures materialised at his side. Silent, dressed only in bark strips and bedecked in feather and bone amulets, each hefted a hollow wooden tube – a blowpipe – which was aimed at Jaeger's head. Jaeger didn't doubt that they were armed with darts tipped in curare.

All around him, Jaeger's fellow expeditioners were prodded into life, each coming awake to the frightening realisation of capture. Only Hiro Kamishi was absent from his hammock. They'd set staggered watches, with different changeover times, and Jaeger figured it was Kamishi who must have been on sentry and failed to spot their attackers.

But why had Kamishi been standing guard alone? It was supposed to be two on watch all night long. Either way, presumably he was a captive now, along with the rest of them.

Jaeger had precious little time to ponder that now. With hand gestures and harsh, guttural commands – the exact meaning was lost on Jaeger, but the sense was crystal clear – he was ordered down from his hammock. As two of the Indians covered him with their blow-darts, the third wrestled his shotgun out of his hands.

He was forced to collapse his camp, pack his hammock and poncho, and hoist his pack on to his shoulders. Then he was shoved powerfully in the back, leaving little room for doubt about what was required of him. Jaeger needed to march, and there would be no changing into wet gear for the coming journey, wherever it was taking them.

As he exited the camp, Jaeger spotted the leader of the Indian party – the same warrior commander he had confronted on the riverbank – issuing orders. Their eyes met and Jaeger found himself looking into pools of blank nothingness.

It reminded him of the gaze of the jaguar.

Flat, dark, unreadable.

Hunting.

Jaeger fell into step alongside Hiro Kamishi. The veteran of the Tokusha Sakusen Gun – Japan's elite military force – was unable to meet his gaze. Kamishi had to know that he had let the entire team down, perhaps with fatal consequences.

'I am so sorry,' he muttered, hanging his head in shame. 'It was my second sentry duty, I closed my eyes for just a second and—'

'We're all tired,' Jaeger whispered. 'Don't beat yourself up about it. But where was the other guy on watch?'

Kamishi flicked his eyes up to Jaeger. 'I was meant to wake you, but I let you sleep. I thought I was strong enough to last my watch alone. This,' he gestured at their Indian captors, 'is the result. I have failed in my duty as a warrior. My pride has shamed my Bushido heritage.'

'Listen, they took some of our gifts,' Jaeger reminded him. 'Proves they're capable of friendly contact. Seeking it even. And without you, we'd never have reached out to them. So no need for shame, my friend. I need you strong—'

Jaeger's words were cut short by an agonising blow to the head. One of the Indians had noticed him and Kamishi talking, and his reward was a crack with a club to the skull. Talk was clearly not what was expected of them; they were expected to march.

As they moved further away from their camp, more figures melted out of the shadows. In some inexplicable way the Indians seemed able to remain invisible even at close quarters – at least until they wished to show themselves.

Jaeger was well acquainted with elite forces camouflage techniques. He'd spent days in hidden jungle observation posts, remaining all but invisible to any passers-by. But it wasn't simply camouflage that the Indians were employing here; it was something far deeper and more profound. Somehow, they used a force – an intangible energy and skill – to render themselves at one with the jungle.

At a top-secret SAS training school Jaeger had been briefed

by a man who'd spent years living with the world's most remote tribes. The aim of the session had been to learn how to move and fight as well as the natives in such an environment. But no one among their number had ever kidded himself that he'd truly mastered it.

The way these tribes were able to use the force – it was incredible. And in spite of their dire predicament, Jaeger was fascinated to observe at close quarters how the Indians operated. They moved silently and without putting a foot wrong, even in the pitch darkness. By contrast, his team were stumbling over roots blindly or blundering into trees.

Jaeger knew that the best – sometimes the only – chance of escape lay immediately after capture. It was when captives still had the energy and spirit to make a break for it, and captors were least equipped to deal with handling prisoners. The captors were generally soldiers and not guards – and that was a big difference. Yet he had few doubts what would happen if anyone tried to make a run for it now: it would be a matter of moments before they were stuck full of poison darts, or arrows.

Yet as he walked, Jaeger silently counted out his footfalls. In one hand he held his compass, the faintly luminous dial just visible in the darkness, and in the other he clutched the pebbles.

It was crucial he kept track of where they were, for in doing so he might just give them all a chance of escape.

50

It was around first light when the Indians led Jaeger and his team into their village – not that much of it was visible.

There was a small clearing, at the very centre of which stood a single building – a large, doughnut-shaped communal-type meeting house. It was roofed over with reed thatch reaching almost to the ground, and a thin coil of grey cooking smoke snaked up from the open centre of the structure.

The entire building was shielded by trees, making it largely invisible from the air. For a moment Jaeger found himself wondering where the villagers actually lived, before he heard voices calling from above. He glanced up, only to discover the answer. This was a tribe who'd made their homes in the treetops.

Rectangular hut-like structures were perched sixty feet or more above the ground, shielded by the topmost branches. They were reached by ladders made of vines, and between some of the huts there were rickety-looking aerial walkways.

Jaeger had heard of tribes living like this. He'd been on an expedition to Papua New Guinea, where the native Korowai people were renowned for living in the treetops. Clearly they weren't alone in their predilection for a life spent high above the jungle floor.

The column of marchers came to a halt.

Everywhere, eyes stared at them.

The adult males held their ground, but the women seemed desperate to hurry away, youngsters clutched protectively to their chests. Children – dusty, naked; half-curious, half-petrified –

peered out from behind trees, eyes wide with wonder and fear.

An incredibly thin and gnarled old man came wandering over.

He straightened up and brought his face uncomfortably close to Jaeger's, staring into his eyes – almost as if he could see right inside his skull. He carried on peering around for several seconds, then broke away laughing. The experience was strangely unsettling; violating almost. Whatever that aged Indian had seen inside his head, it left Jaeger nonplussed and disturbed.

Warriors crowded in from either side now – heavily armed with spears and blowpipes – until Jaeger and his team were surrounded. A second figure stepped forward – an aged and grizzled village elder. As the old man began to speak, Jaeger sensed that this was a person of some gravitas and standing.

The old man's words sounded strange – the language echoing bird and animal cries, with its odd high-pitched chirps, clicks and yelps. To his immediate left stood a younger figure, who was clearly listening to the elder's words intently. Whatever was going on here, Jaeger had the unsettling impression that he and his team were being subjected to some sort of trial.

After a good two minutes the chief stopped talking. The younger man at his side turned to Jaeger and his team.

'You are welcome.' The words were spoken slowly, in broken but perfectly comprehensible English. 'The chief of our tribe says that if you come in peace – welcome. But if you come in anger, and you wish harm on us or our forest home, you will die.'

Jaeger did his best to try to recover from the shock. No tribe that had never had contact with the outside world had a young man in its number who could speak such English. Someone had either lied to them, or at the very least they had been badly misinformed.

'Please forgive us if we look surprised,' Jaeger began, 'but we were told that your tribe had had no contact with the world outside. Some four days' walk west of here lies an aircraft, something that we think crashed when the world was at war.

It's very likely seventy years old, maybe more. Our purpose is to find that aircraft, identify it and try to lift it out of here. We have entered your lands solely for this purpose, and we wish to pass entirely in peace.'

The young man translated, the village chief said a few words in reply, and he translated those back to Jaeger.

'You are the force that fell from the sky?'

'We are,' Jaeger confirmed.

'You were how many when you fell? And how many were lost along the way?'

'We were ten,' Jaeger answered. 'We lost one almost immediately, in the river. Two more were taken that day, two more the following day. We don't know how they were taken or their fates, but one of your men . . .' Jaeger's eyes searched the crowd, coming to rest on the warrior leader, 'left this.' He pulled Leticia Santos's scarf from his pack. 'Maybe you can tell us more?'

His question was ignored.

Words went back and forth between the chief and the young man, and then: 'You say you come in peace – why then do you carry such weapons as we have seen?'

'Self-defence,' Jaeger answered. 'There are dangerous animals in the forest. There appear to be dangerous people too – although we are unsure exactly who they are.'

The old man's eyes gleamed. 'If we offer to show you gold, will you take it?' he demanded, via the translator. 'We have little value for such things. We cannot eat gold. But the white man fights to get it.'

Jaeger knew that he was being tested here. 'We came for the aircraft. That's our only mission. Any gold – it should stay right here, in the forest. Otherwise it will only bring you trouble. And that is the last thing we would ever want to do.'

The old man laughed. 'Many of our people say this: only when the last tree is cut and the last animal hunted and the last fish caught, only then will the white man finally understand that he cannot eat money.'

Jaeger remained silent. There was a wisdom in those words with which he couldn't argue.

'And this aircraft that you seek: if you find it, will it also bring us trouble?' the old man queried. 'Like the gold, is it better for it to remain lost in the jungle – the white man failing to reclaim what was originally his?'

Jaeger shrugged. 'Perhaps. But I don't think so. I think if we fail, more will come. What was lost has been found. And in truth, I think we're the best you're going to get. We understand the aircraft has poisoned the forest that lies around it. And this,' Jaeger gestured at the jungle, 'this is your home. It's more than your home. It's your life. Your identity. If we remove that aircraft, we'll stop the forest from being poisoned.'

He let the silence hang between them.

The old man turned and gestured at the communal structure. 'You see that smoke is coming from the spirit house. A feast is being prepared. We were preparing it for one of two reasons: either to welcome you as friends, or to say goodbye to an enemy.' The old man laughed. 'So, let us celebrate friendship!'

Jaeger thanked the village chief. A part of him felt driven by a sense of urgency to get on with their mission. But he also knew that amongst such cultures there was a way in which things had to be done, a timing and a rhythm. He would respect that and trust to his destiny. He also knew he had little choice.

As he fell into step with the chief, his attention was drawn to a group of figures standing to one side. In the midst was the warrior leader he'd first encountered at the riverside. Not everyone seemed happy with the outcome of the chief's interrogations, it seemed. Jaeger figured that the warrior and his men had been sharpening their spears in preparation for ridding their forest of an enemy.

Distracted for a brief moment, he failed to spot Dale dragging out his video camera. By the time he'd noticed, Dale had it on his shoulder and had started to film.

'Stop!' hissed Jaeger. 'Lose the bloody camera!'

But it was too late: the damage had been done.

A shiver of electric tension tore through the gathering as the Indians noticed what was happening. Jaeger saw the chief turn on Dale, his face stony, his eyes wide with fear. He uttered a few strangled words of command, and instantly spears were levelled at the entire team.

Dale seemed frozen, the camera clamped to his shoulder, all colour drained from his features.

The chief walked up to him. He reached for the camera. Dale handed it over, his face aghast. The chief turned it the wrong way around, put his eye against the lens and stared inside. For a long moment his gaze roved around the camera's innards, as if trying to locate what exactly it had stolen from him.

Finally, he handed it to one of his warriors, then turned back without a word towards the spirit house. The spears were lowered.

The translator shuddered. 'Do not ever do that again. To do so – it could undo all the good that you have done.'

Jaeger fell back a step or two, until he was on Dale's shoulder. 'You pull that trick again, I'll make you boil and eat your own head. Or better still – I'll let the chief boil and eat it for you.'

Dale nodded. His pupils were wide with shock and fear. He knew how close they'd come to disaster, and for once the slick-tongued media operator was lost for words.

Jaeger followed the chief into the smoky interior of the spirit house. It had no walls as such, only posts supporting the roof, but with the thatch reaching almost to the ground, it was shaded and dark inside. It took a moment for Jaeger's eyes to adjust from the bright light to the gloom of the interior.

Even before they had done so, a voice rang out, one that sounded impossibly . . . familiar.

'So tell me – you do have my knife?'

Jaeger felt rooted to the spot. That voice was one he'd told himself he would never hear again; it seemed to be speaking to him from way beyond the grave.

As his eyesight adjusted, he caught sight of an unmistakable figure seated on the ground. Jaeger's mind reeled as he tried to figure out how she could have got there, not to mention how she could still be alive.

That figure was the woman he'd long presumed dead: Irina Narov.

51

Narov was seated with two others. One was Leticia Santos, their Brazilian team member, the other the giant figure of Joe James. Jaeger was rendered speechless, and his raw confusion wasn't lost on the Indian chief. In fact, he could feel the aged tribal leader watching him closely, and studying his every move.

He approached the three of them. 'But how . . .' He glanced from one to another, his face breaking into a slow smile. If anything, Joe James's Osama Bin Laden beard looked even bushier than ever.

Jaeger held out a hand. 'You big Kiwi bastard! Could have done without seeing you again.'

James ignored the proffered hand, enveloping Jaeger in a crushing bear hug. 'Dude, one thing you gotta learn: real men hug.'

Leticia Santos was next, throwing her arms around him in a typical show of unrestrained Latino warmth. 'So! Like I promised – you do get to meet my Indians!'

Narov was last.

She stood before Jaeger, an inch or so shorter than him, her eyes as expressionless as ever, her gaze avoiding his. Jaeger gave her the once-over. Whatever she had suffered since he'd lost her on the river – pain-racked from the *Phoneutria* bite and curled up on his makeshift raft – she didn't seem much the worse for wear.

She held out one hand. 'Knife.'

For an instant Jaeger checked that hand. It was her left, and the horrible swelling and bite marks seemed to have almost disappeared.

He bent slightly so that he could whisper in her ear. 'I gave it to the chief. Had to. It was the only thing I could do to bargain for our lives.'

'*Schwachkopf.*' Was there the barest hint of a smile? 'You have my knife. You'd better have my knife. Or the chief will be the least of your worries.'

The chief gestured at Jaeger. 'You have friends here. Spend time with them. Food and drink will come.'

'Thank you, I'm grateful.'

The chief nodded at the translator. 'Puruwehua will stay with you, at least until you feel at home.'

With that he was gone, wandering off amongst his people.

Jaeger took a seat with the others. James and Santos were the first to tell their story. They'd set camp in the forest maybe an hour's walk from the sandbar, on the same day they'd parachuted into the jungle. They'd hung offerings in the trees – a scattering of presents – and waited.

Sure enough, the Indians had come – but not quite in the way they had hoped. Overnight, both of them had been taken captive and marched to the village, the Indians knowing the forest's secret pathways and being able to move silent and fast. There they were questioned by the chief along similar lines to Jaeger's interrogation: whether they came in anger or in peace, and the nature of their mission.

When they had told the chief all they could, they felt as if they had passed some kind of unwritten test. It was then that the chief had allowed them to be reunited with Irina Narov. He'd kept them apart so as to ensure their stories matched.

And in Jaeger's questioning there lay a third layer of scrutiny. The chief had kept his missing team members hidden to check if their stories married up. Clearly he was no pushover.

In fact he'd played Jaeger – he'd played them all – like an old hand.

'So what about Krakow and Clermont?' Jaeger asked. He peered around the shadows of the spirit house. 'They somewhere here too?'

It was the translator, Puruwehua, who answered. 'There is much to talk about. But it is best you let the chief tell you about your two missing friends.'

Jaeger glanced at the others. James, Santos and Narov nodded solemnly. Whatever fate had befallen Krakow and Clermont, he didn't figure it could be good news.

'And you?' He eyed Narov. 'Tell me – how on earth did you make it back from the dead?'

Narov shrugged. 'Clearly you underestimated my capacity to survive. Wishful thinking on your part, maybe.'

Her words stung Jaeger. Maybe she was right. Maybe he could have done more to save her. But as he cast his mind back to his exhaustive efforts, and the subsequent search of that river, he couldn't for the life of him imagine how.

It was Puruwehua, the translator, who filled the silence. 'This one – this *ja-gwara* – we found her on the river clinging to some bamboo. At first we thought she had drowned; that she was *ahegwera* – a ghost. But then we saw she had been stung by the *kajavuria* – the spider that eats people's souls.

'We know what plant can cure this one,' he continued. 'So we nursed her. And we carried her through the jungle to here. There came a moment when we knew she would not die. It was the moment of her *ma'e-ma'e* – her awakening.'

Puruwehua turned his dark eyes on Jaeger. There was something in the translator's gaze that reminded him of the Indian warrior leader's look: a watching cat; the flat, blank eyes of the jaguar, scrutinising its prey. In fact there was something in his gaze that reminded Jaeger somehow of . . . of Narov.

'She seems angry at you,' Puruwehua continued. 'But we

believe she is one of the spirit children. She survived what no one should ever survive. She has a very strong *a'aga* – spirit.' He paused. 'Keep her close. You must cherish this one – this *ja-gwara*. This jaguar.'

Jaeger felt a flush of embarrassment. He'd come across this tendency before with remote peoples. With them, most thoughts and experiences were communal. They tended to rec-ognise few boundaries between the personal and the private; between what should be discussed publicly and what it was best to keep one-on-one.

'I'll do my best,' Jaeger remarked quietly. 'Not that my best seemed good enough ... But tell me something, Puruwehua, how does an "uncontacted" tribe come to include a young man who speaks English?'

'We are the Amahuaca – the cousins of a neighbouring tribe, the Uru-Eu-Wau-Wau,' Puruwehua replied. 'We and the Uru-Eu-Wau-Wau speak the same Tupi-Guarani language. Two decades ago the Uru-Eu-Wau-Wau decided to make contact with the outside. Over time, they told us what they had learned. They told us that we live in a country called Brazil. They said we needed to learn the language of the outsiders, for inevitably they would come.

'They told us we would need to learn Portuguese, and also English – one the language of Brazil; the other the language of the world. I am the chief's youngest son. His eldest – one of our prized warriors – you met on the riverbank. My father believed that my qualities lay in the strength of my head, not of my spear arm. I would be a warrior of the mind.

'With the Uru-Eu-Wau-Wau, he sent me to be educated,' Puruwehua rounded off his story. 'I spent ten years in the out-side, learning languages. And then I returned. And now I am my tribe's window on to the world.'

'I'm glad you are,' Jaeger told him. 'I think maybe today you saved our lives ...'

*

The eating and drinking lasted long into the evening. At intervals, both the men and the women of the tribe danced in the open centre of the spirit house, strings of moon-shaped seeds from a forest fruit – the *pequia* – worn around upper arms and legs. As they stamped their feet and swung their arms in unison, the seeds clashed together, beating out a rhythm that pulsated through the gathering darkness.

Jaeger found himself being offered a gourd full of a strange red paste. For a moment he didn't know what he was supposed to do with it. It was Leticia Santos who showed him. The paste was made from the bark of a certain tree, she explained. Smeared on the skin, it acted as a powerful insect repellent.

Jaeger figured he'd better have some. He allowed Santos to rub the paste on his face and hands, enjoying the flare of discomfort – *was it jealousy?* – that flashed through Narov's eyes. A larger bowl was passed around, full of a grey, frothy liquid with a pungent smell. It was *masata*, Santos explained – an alcoholic drink common amongst native Amazonian tribes. It would be seen as an insult to reject it.

It was only when Jaeger had taken a good few glugs of the thick, warm, chewy liquid that Santos revealed exactly how it was made. She was speaking Portuguese, which effectively froze out the others from the conversation – Narov included. It left her and Jaeger in a bubble of intimacy, as they laughed in disgust at what he'd just been drinking.

To make the brew, the women of the tribe took raw manioc – a potato-like starch-rich root – and chewed it up. They spat the resulting gunk into a bowl, added water, and left it to ferment for a few days. The resulting mixture was what Jaeger had just consumed.

Nice.

The highlight of the feasting was the roast, the rich smell of which filled the spirit house. Three large monkeys were being turned over a central fire pit, and Jaeger couldn't help but admit the smell was enticing, even if roast monkey wasn't high on his fantasy food list. After a week on dry rations, he felt hungry as hell.

A cry went up from the gathering. Jaeger didn't have a clue what it meant, but Narov for one seemed to understand.

She held out a hand to Jaeger. 'For the third and final time: *knife*.'

He threw up his arms in mock surrender, reached into his backpack and retrieved Narov's Fairbairn–Sykes fighting knife. 'More than my life's worth to lose this.'

Narov took it. She unsheathed the blade reverentially, spending a long moment checking it over.

'I lost the other in the Rio de los Dios,' she remarked quietly. 'And with it I lost a thousand memories.' She got to her feet. 'Thanks for returning it.' Her eyes were averted from Jaeger's, but the words sounded genuine. 'I consider it your first success of this expedition.'

She turned and moved into the centre of the spirit house, Jaeger kept his eyes on her. She bent over the fire pit, seven-inch blade clasped in hand, and began to cut off hunks of steaming flesh. For whatever reason the Amahuaca were giving this outsider, this woman, this *ja-gwara*, the right to cut the first of the meat.

Thick chunks were passed around, and soon Jaeger could feel the hot, greasy juices running down his chin. He lay back, resting on his pack, relishing the feeling of a full belly. But there was something else that he was enjoying here – something far more valuable and replenishing than any meal. It was the knowledge that for once he didn't have to be alert and watchful; for once he and his team weren't being menaced by a mystery enemy lurking in the shadows.

For a brief moment, Will Jaeger could allow himself to relax and feel contented.

52

The food and the sense of security must have lulled him to sleep. He awoke to find the fire pit glowing a dull red and the feasting long done. The odd star glinted in the heavens high above, and a warm stillness seemed to have settled over the hut, mixed with an undercurrent of expectancy; of anticipation.

Jaeger noticed that the same thin and gnarled old man who had stared deep into his eyes was now the centre of attention. He bent over something, busy with his hands. It looked like a shorter, thinner version of one of the Amahuaca's blowpipes, and Jaeger could see him stuffing something into one end.

He glanced at Puruwehua enquiringly.

'Our shaman,' Puruwehua explained. 'He prepares *nyak-wana*. You would call it I think "snuff". It is . . . I forget the exact word. It makes you see visions.'

'Hallucinogenic,' Jaeger volunteered.

'Hallucinogenic,' Puruwehua confirmed. 'It is made of the seed of the *cebil* tree, roasted and ground into a fine powder, and mixed with the dried shells of a giant forest snail. It sends the taker into a trance state, so he can visit the spirit world. When you take it, you can fly as high as the *topena* – the white hawk that is big enough to steal a chicken from the village. It can take you to far distant places, and maybe even out of this world.

'We sniff maybe half a gram at a time.' Puruwehua smiled. 'You – you should try no more than a fraction of that amount.'

Jaeger started. 'Me?'

'Yes, of course. When it reaches here, one of your party will need to accept the pipe. Not to do so – it would undo much of the good achieved tonight.'

'Me and drugs . . .' Jaeger tried a smile. 'I've got enough on my hands without a monged-out head. I'm good, thanks.'

'You are the leader of your group,' Puruwehua countered, quietly. 'You can let another take the honour. But it would be . . . unusual.'

Jaeger shrugged. 'I can do unusual. Unusual is okay.'

He watched the pipe do the rounds of the spirit house. With each stop, a figure placed one end to his nostril, while the shaman blew the snuff deep into his nose. Minutes later, the taker would get to his feet, chanting and dancing, his mind clearly far away in another world.

'Via the *nyakwana* we commune with our ancestors and our spirits,' Puruwehua explained. 'Those anchored in the world of the jungle – the animals, birds, trees, rivers, fish and mountains.'

He pointed out one of the entranced sniffers. 'So this man – he relates a spirit story. "Once there was an Amahuaca woman who turned into the moon. She had climbed a tree, but decided to stay in the sky, because her boyfriend had found a rival love, and so became the moon . . ."'

As Puruwehua talked, the pipe drew ever closer. Jaeger noticed that the chief was keeping a careful eye out for what would happen when it reached him. The shaman stopped. He crouched low, the snuff piled on a length of smooth wood, the long, ornately carved pipe clutched in his hand.

As the snuff was readied, Jaeger found himself remembering a different pipe, one offered to him long ago and a whole world away. Momentarily he was back in his grandfather's Wiltshire study, the familiar smell of Latakia oak and pinewood cured tobacco strong in his nostrils.

If his grandfather had felt able to offer a sixteen-year-old boy that pipe, maybe Jaeger could accept a different type of pipe, prepared by a different set of hands – a different elder – now.

For a moment he wavered.

The shaman looked at him enquiringly. Barely had he done so when Joe James practically knocked everyone out of the way in his rush to be first.

'Dude, I thought you'd never ask!' He sat before the shaman cross-legged, his massive beard reaching to the floor. He grasped the near end of the snuff pipe, placed it in his nose and took the shot. Moments later, the big Kiwi's mind had clearly gone into warp factor.

Good on James, Jaeger told himself. Cavalry arrived in the nick of time.

But the shaman didn't move. Instead he readied a second pinch of snuff and loaded it into the pipe.

'You are two groups,' Puruwehua explained. 'Those who came first – they have already opened their minds to the *nyak-wana*. It is not James's first time with the pipe. And then – the new arrivals. This second pipe, it is for you.'

The shaman glanced up.

His eyes – the same as had peered deep inside Jaeger's skull – fixed him with a look. A testing one. Jaeger felt himself compelled forward, drawn inexorably towards the proffered pipe. He found himself sitting before the Amahuaca shaman just as James had done before him.

Again his mind drifted to his grandfather's study. But he was no longer that sixteen-year-old boy. As his grandfather had been, Jaeger was now a leader, a figurehead – albeit in a very different place and time, but somehow still connected by a common enemy.

The men and women in his charge needed him to be strong, constant and lucid. Despite the Indians' customs and their hospitality, Jaeger was here to do a job, and he was determined to stick to it. He held his hands up in front of him, in a gesture signifying *stop*.

'As I think you know, I have many ghosts,' he remarked quietly. 'But right now I also have a mission to lead. So those ghosts have to remain caged, at least until I've pulled everyone through the jungle and back to their homes.' He paused. 'I can't take the pipe.'

Puruwehua translated, and the shaman searched Jaeger's gaze intently. Then he nodded, briefly, a look of respect flashing through his eyes.

He lowered the pipe.

It was some time before Jaeger came back to his senses.

He was lying against his rucksack, eyes closed. After being forgiven the snuff pipe, he'd clearly fallen asleep – his full belly and the warmth of the spirit house lulling him into a deep rest. His mind remained a complete blank – all except for one mesmerising image that seemed seared across the inside of his eyelids.

It was a scene he'd clearly dreamed, one no doubt provoked by the close encounter with the shaman. It was one that he'd begun to think was a total impossibility, but right now it seemed so utterly real.

It was of a beautiful green-eyed woman, a child standing protectively at her side. The woman had been speaking, her voice calling to him from across the missing years. And the child – he'd seemed so much taller. In fact he'd seemed the right height for an eleven-year-old boy.

And he was even more the spitting image of William Jaeger.

53

Jaeger didn't have long to ponder this extraordinarily haunting dream. By now the snuff pipe had done the full round of the spirit house, and the Amahuaca chief came to join him and his team. He began to talk, Puruwehua translating, and the gravity of what he was saying demanded all their attention.

'Many moons ago – too many for we Amahuaca to remember – the white men first came. Strangers with fearful weapons journeyed into our lands. They captured a party of our warriors and took them to a remote part of the jungle. There they were forced under pain of death to fell the forest, and to drag the trees to one side.'

At first Jaeger was unsure whether the chief was relating a tribal myth, or the story of his people, or a vision inspired by the *nyakwana*.

'They were made to clear all vegetation,' the chief continued, 'and to beat the ground as flat as if it were a river. All of this went against what we believe. If we do harm to the forest, we do harm to ourselves. We and the land are one: we share the same life force. Many sickened and died, but by then the strip of land had been cleared and the forest with it killed.'

The chief glanced at the open roof and the starlit sky above. 'One night there came a giant monster of the heavens. It was a huge eagle of smoke, thunder and darkness. It pounced on that dead stretch of land and made its nest there. From its insides the sky monster disgorged more strangers. Those of our warriors who had survived were made to unload heavy cargoes from the belly of the beast.

'There were metal drums,' the chief continued, 'and the air monster started to suck liquid from them, like a huge and hungry mosquito. Once it was done, it clawed into the sky again and was gone. Two more came, each like the last. Each landed in the clearing, sucked up more of the liquid, and took to the air, heading that way,' the chief indicated due south, 'into the mountains.'

He paused. 'And then a fourth air monster came snarling out of the darkness. But there was not enough blood to satisfy this last hungry mosquito. The drums ran dry. It sat there awaiting more; hoping that more would come. But none did. And the white men aboard that monster – they had misjudged the anger of the forest, and how unforgiving the spirits would be to those who had harmed her.

'Those white men – they floundered in death and ruin. Finally, the last two survivors closed up their metal sky monster, and left carrying what little they could. They too perished in the jungle.

'Over the years the forest reclaimed the clearing, the trees reaching high above the monster until it became forgotten by the outside world. But it never left the memory of the Ama-huaca, the story being passed from father to son. And then it brought more darkness. We had thought it was dead; a carcass of a dead thing brought here by the white man. But it – or rather something inside it – still lives; and still it has the capacity to do us harm.'

As the chief related the story, Jaeger had become aware that one amongst his team was absolutely riveted. She seemed glued to his every word; obsessed; an intensity burning in her eyes. It was the first time that Jaeger had seen Irina Narov looking truly engaged – yet at the same time her look struck him as bordering on a kind of madness.

'The animals were the first to suffer,' the chief continued.

'Some had made the shelter of the air beast's wings their home. Some fell ill and died. Others gave birth to offspring that were horribly deformed. Amahuaca warriors hunting in that area sickened after drinking from the rivers. The very water seemed cursed; poisoned. Then the plants of the forest all around started to die.'

The chief gestured at his youngest son. 'I was still young at the time – around Puruwehua's age. I remember it well. Finally, the trees themselves became the air monster's victims. All that remained were bare skeletons: dead wood, bleached white as bone in the sun. But still we knew that the story of this beast wasn't finished.'

He glanced at Jaeger. 'We knew that the white men would return. We knew that those who came would seek to drive the curse of the air monster from our lands once and for all. That is why I ordered my men not to attack you, but to bring you here. So I could test you. So I could be sure.

'But sadly, you are not alone. A second force has also trespassed into our lands. They came immediately after you, almost as if they had followed you here. I fear they have come with a far less benign purpose. I fear they have come to breathe new life into the evil the monster carried.'

Jaeger had a thousand questions burning through his mind, but he sensed that the chief wasn't yet done.

'I have men shadowing that force,' the chief continued. 'We call them the Dark Force, and with good reason. They are slashing a route through the jungle, one pointing direct to the air beast's lair. Two of my warriors were captured. Their bodies were left strung up in the trees, strange symbols carved into their backs, as a warning.

'It will be difficult to fight them,' the chief added. 'There are too many – perhaps as many as ten times your team. They carry many thunder sticks. I fear a massacre of my tribe should this descend into open warfare. In the deep forest perhaps we could be victorious. Perhaps. Even then it is uncertain. But in the open ground of the air monster's lair – my people would be wiped out.'

Jaeger tried to say something, but the chief waved him into silence.

'The only guarantee of success lies in reaching that air monster first.' He threw Jaeger a shrewd glance. 'There is no way that you can overtake this Dark Force. Not alone. Yet if you accept the help of the Amahuaca, you will make it. We know the forest's secret ways. We can move fast. Only those with brave hearts should join such an undertaking. The journey will involve making a short cut that only we Amahuaca know of.

'No outsider has ever attempted such a journey,' the chief continued. 'To do so, you must head direct to the Devil's Falls, and from there . . . Well, you must take your life in your hands. But it is the only way to stand a chance of beating the Dark Force to the site of the air beast, and to triumph.

'The forest will guide and guard,' the chief announced. 'At dawn, all who are ready will go. Puruwehua will be your guide, and you will have two dozen of my finest warriors. It remains to be seen if you will accept this offer, and who will go from your side.'

For a moment Jaeger was lost for a reply. It was all moving so fast, and he had a hundred questions clouding his mind. It was Joe James who was the first to respond.

'Give me another hit on your pipe, and I'll follow you guys anywhere,' he growled.

There was laughter, James's comment grounding everyone in the moment.

'One question,' Jaeger prompted. 'What about our missing two? What news of them?'

The chief shook his head. 'I am sorry. Your friends were captured by this same Dark Force and beaten to death. We retrieved their bodies and cremated them. In Amahuaca tradition, we mix the ash of the bones of our dead with water and we drink it, so that our loved ones are forever with us. We have kept the

remains of your friends, for you to do with them as you will . . .
I am sorry, Mr Jaeger.'

Jaeger stared into the fire. So much loss. More good men and
women. Ones under his command. He felt his stomach turn
with a raw mix of anger and frustration bordering on despair.
He vowed to himself that he'd account for whoever was doing
this. He'd find answers and justice. Even if it was justice on his
terms.

The conviction steadied him, readying him for whatever was
coming.

54

Jaeger glanced at the chief, trouble clouding his eyes. 'I think we'll go scatter their ashes among the trees,' he remarked quietly. He turned to his team. 'And you know something else – I think I'm better off going on alone, with the chief's warriors. I can move faster on my own, and I don't want you guys getting any deeper into this—'

'Typical,' a voice cut in. 'You may have the heart of a lion but you've got the brains of a monkey – like the one you just ate.' It was Irina Narov. 'You take it upon yourself to be tougher than everyone else. The loner. The lone hero. You'll do it on your own. Everyone else is a burden. A liability. You cannot see the value in others, and that amounts to a betrayal of all in your team.'

Jaeger felt stung by her words. The loss of his wife and child plus the subsequent years in Bioko had made him distrustful of others – he knew that. But right now, it wasn't that which was driving him to go it alone: it was the fear of losing more of his team, and being next to powerless to protect them.

'Two are dead already,' he countered. 'It's gone from being an expedition of discovery to something altogether shittier. It's not what you – any of you – signed up for when you agreed to do this thing.'

'*Schwachkopf*,' Narov's voice softened a little. 'It is as I said after we nearly died in the freefall: you need to learn to trust your team. And you know something: by your example, you have earned the right to lead. You have earned it. Prove that you are worthy of our belief; our *trust* in you.'

What was it about this woman? Jaeger wondered. How was it that with a few choice sentences she could get so deep beneath his skin? She had a way of speaking that went direct to the heart of the matter, and bugger the social niceties.

He glanced around his team. 'And the rest of you?'

'It's easy.' James shrugged. 'Hold a vote. Those who want to go get to go. Those who don't stay behind.'

'Yeah,' Alonzo added. 'Ask for volunteers. And let's make it clear: there's no dishonour – *none* – on those who opt to stay behind.'

'Okay,' Jaeger conceded. 'And chief – are you good safeguarding those who choose to remain? At least until this thing is done.'

'They are welcome,' the chief confirmed. 'Our home is their home, and for as long as they are in need of it.'

'Right, I'm asking for volunteers,' Jaeger announced. 'And you all know the dangers.'

'Count me in,' James declared, almost before Jaeger was done speaking.

'It's a shitty kind of a holiday,' Alonzo growled. 'But man, I'm in.'

Kamishi raised his gaze to Jaeger. 'I have already failed you once. I fear I may—' Jaeger placed a hand on Kamishi's shoulder to quieten him. Kamishi brightened. 'If you would accept—'

Alonzo slapped him on the back. 'What brother Kamishi's trying to say is – he's in!'

Dale glanced at the village chief, then at Jaeger. 'If I'm in, am I allowed to film? Or will they stick me full of spears as soon as I pull out my camera?'

Jaeger eyed Puruwehua. 'I am sure we can broker some kind of deal with the chief and his warriors.'

Puruwehua nodded. 'The elders – they believe your camera hurts their soul. With the younger men – the warriors – I'm sure I can persuade them otherwise.'

Dale hesitated for an instant, clearly torn between his desire to go and his fear of what lay ahead. He shrugged. 'Then I guess it'll be the film to die for.'

Jaeger turned to Santos. 'Leticia?'

Santos gave a faint shrug. 'I would like to very much. To come. But my conscience tells me I am better here, staying with my Indians. What do you think? No?'

'If you think you should stay, you should stay.' Jaeger pulled out her silk scarf. 'And here's your scarf – like you, a survivor.'

An emotional Santos took the length of material. 'But you must wear it, no? It is . . . good luck for the coming journey.'

She reached up and proceeded to knot it around Jaeger's neck, kissing him on the cheek once she'd done so.

Jaeger fancied he could see Narov burning with that same jealousy that he'd detected before. It made him all the more determined to wear the scarf through all that was coming. Anything to rattle Narov; to try and find a way to get to the hidden person that lay within.

'Four are in; one's staying,' Jaeger summed up. 'And the rest?'

'I've got three kids at home,' a voice volunteered. It was Stefan Kral. 'In London. Correction. Not London any more. We've just moved out to lovely Luton.' He threw a resentful look at Dale. 'Can't afford London, not on an assistant producer's wage. I'm staying alive and I'm getting home in one piece.' He glanced at Jaeger. 'I won't be coming.'

'Understood,' Jaeger told him. 'Get home safely, and be the father your kids need you to be. That matters more than any air wreck lying lost in the jungle.'

As he said those words, Jaeger felt a spit of bile rise from his stomach. He forced it back down. He'd spent a year searching for his own family after they disappeared. He'd travelled every highway; turned over every stone. He'd chased down every clue and pursued every lead, until all had turned cold. But had he really done everything he could to find them?

Had he given up on his family and given up on life – running to Bioko – just when he should have kept going? Jaeger kicked the thought away.

He glanced at Narov. 'You?'

She met his gaze. 'Do you need to ask?'

He shook his head. 'I guess not. Irina Narov's in.'

The Amahuaca chief glanced at the sky. 'And so, you have your team. You leave at sun-up, maybe three hours away. I will order my warriors to make ready.'

'One thing,' a voice cut in. It was Narov's, and she was directing her words at the chief. 'Have you ever been to the site of that air beast?'

The chief nodded. 'Yes, *ja-gwara*, I have.'

Ja-gwara – it was a uniquely fitting name for Narov, reflecting her incredible ability to adapt and survive.

'How well do you remember it?' Narov asked. 'And will you draw for me any marking that you saw there.'

The chief started sketching something in the sandy floor of the hut. After a few false starts, it gradually resolved itself into a darkly familiar image: an eagle in silhouette, wings outstretched, hooked beak thrown over its right shoulder, and with a bizarre circular symbol superimposed over its tail.

A *Reichsadler*.

This symbol was stamped on the rear of the aircraft, the chief explained, just forward of its tail. And it was the same symbol that had been carved into the skin of his warriors, he added – those who had been captured by the Dark Force and killed.

Jaeger stared at the image for a long second, his mind a whirl. He sensed that they were closing in, towards an end point; towards a reckoning. Yet at the same time he was gripped by an overwhelming feeling of dread, as if the fates were crowding in on him from all sides and he had no control . . .

'There are words stamped beside that eagle symbol,' Puruwehua volunteered. 'I made a note of them.' He scrawled something in the sand: *Kampfeswader 200* and *Geswaderkomodore A3*. 'I speak English, Portuguese and our native language,' he added. 'But this – I believe it is maybe German?'

It was Narov who responded, her voice low and burning with a barely suppressed loathing. 'Your spelling is a little off, but Kampfgeschwader 200 was the Luftwaffe's special forces flight. And Geschwaderkommodore A3 was one of the titles given to SS General Hans Kammler, the commander of that flight. After Hitler, Kammler was one of the most powerful men in the Nazi Reich.'

'He was Hitler's plenipotentiary,' Jaeger added, remembering the archivist's mystery email. 'Towards the end of the war – that's what Hitler made him.'

'He was,' Narov confirmed. 'But do you know what that confers – the status of plenipotentiary?'

Jaeger shrugged. 'Kind of a special representative?'

'So much more . . . A plenipotentiary is someone given full power to act on behalf of a regime, and with total impunity. After Hitler, Kammler was the most powerful and evil man in a uniquely evil group. By the end of the war he had the blood of many thousands on his hands. And he had also become one of the richest men in the world.'

'Priceless artworks, gold bullion, diamonds, cash,' Narov continued. 'Across all of conquered Europe the Nazis plundered everything of value they could lay their hands on. And you know what happened to SS Oberst-Gruppenführer Hans Kammler and his loot when the war was over?'

The bitter anger behind Narov's words was bleeding through now. 'Disappeared. Vanished off the face of the earth. It is one of the greatest mysteries – and scandals – of the Second World War: what happened to Hans Kammler and his ill-gotten fortune? Who protected him? Who hid his millions?'

She glanced around the faces, her burning gaze coming to rest on Jaeger's. 'This aircraft – it is very likely Kammler's personal warplane.'

55

They were ready to depart the Amahuaca village just after first light. Jaeger and his team were accompanied by twenty-four Indians, including the chief's youngest son, Puruwehua, and his eldest, the distinctive warrior-leader. His name was Gwaihutiga, which meant 'the biggest pig in the wild boar herd' in the Amahuaca's language.

It struck Jaeger as being peculiarly appropriate: the wild boar was one of the most prized and feared animals in the jungle. No Amahuaca male was ever truly a warrior until he had faced one down and killed it.

By now, Gwaihutiga appeared to have accepted that his father didn't want Jaeger and his team speared to death; indeed, he wanted them hastened to that air wreck, and safeguarded from all harm along the way.

But Jaeger was glad to see that the chief's eldest son was still in the mood for battle, if only against the right enemy. He carried spear, bow and arrow, blowpipe and club, and around his neck he wore a collar of short feathers. It was a *gwyrag'waja*, Puruwehua explained, each feather signifying an enemy killed in battle. He likened it to a white man carving notches on his gun – something that he had seen in the movies when he had lived in the outside.

At the eleventh hour there had been an unexpected change in the make-up of Jaeger's team. Leticia Santos had decided that she was coming after all. Impetuous, impulsive – a hot-blooded Latino through and through – she hadn't been able to bear seeing the others preparing to depart without her.

Earlier that morning, Jaeger had given Dale and Kral a short interview, to help capture all that had happened during the last twenty-four hours. It was also the final scene that Stefan Kral would be filming with them. After he'd packed away the camera and tripod, the Slovak asked for a few private words with Jaeger.

Kral had outlined his reasons for dropping out of the expedition. He should never have accepted the present contract, he explained. He was years Dale's senior and far more experienced in remote-area filming; he'd taken it purely because he needed the money.

'Just imagine it,' he had reasoned, 'serving under a guy like Dale and knowing you're better, more professional. Could you stand it?'

'Shit like that happens all the time in the military,' Jaeger told him. 'Rank rising above capability. Sometimes you've just got to roll with the punches.'

He didn't dislike Kral, but in truth he was relieved to be losing him. Their Slovakian cameraman seemed to have a chip on both shoulders, and Jaeger figured they'd be better off without him. Dale would doubtless have his hands full filming solo, but better a one-man crew than two guys who were permanently at each other's throats.

One of them had had to go – and for the film's sake, it was better that it was the Slovak.

'Whatever happens from here on in with the expedition,' Kral had explained, 'I guess you know my reasons. *Whatever happens*. Or at least, you know most of them.'

'Something you're trying to tell me?' Jaeger prompted. 'You're leaving us. You're free to say whatever you want.'

Kral shook his head. 'I'm done. Good luck with whatever path you're taking. You know the reasons why I'm not on it with you.'

The two men said an amicable enough goodbye, Jaeger promising to meet Kral for a beer in London when all was done.

Scores of Amahuaca turned out to see them off – seemingly the entire village. But as Jaeger led his team towards the fringe of dark jungle, he was struck powerfully by one thing: Kral had a decidedly troubling expression on his features.

He'd grown used to the Slovak's crooked half-smile, but for the briefest of moments he caught him staring at Dale with a look that could freeze the blood. His pale blue eyes seemed hooded, his gaze oddly triumphant.

Jaeger had little time to dwell upon that look, or what it might signify. A path opened before them – one that a casual observer would have missed – and they were quickly swallowed by the jungle. But one thought did linger in Jaeger's mind.

At several junctures – in particular back at the river, when Kral had reported on Dale's secret filming antics – something had struck Jaeger as being not quite right. It had only just become clear to him now. There was something in Kral's manner that had seemed too holier-than-thou; his see no evil, hear no evil, speak no evil routine. His righteous indignation had been overplayed, almost as if it was a cover.

But a cover for what, Jaeger didn't know.

He forced the thought – that nagging worry – to the back of his mind.

As soon as they'd entered the jungle, he'd realised what a murderous pace the Amahuaca warriors were going to set. They had begun to move at a slow run, singing out a deep, rhythmic, throaty chant as they went. It would take all Jaeger's concentration to press ahead at such a speed.

He glanced at Puruwehua, who'd taken up a position at his side. 'So, does your name have any meaning?'

Puruwehua grinned sheepishly. 'Puruwehua – it is a big, smooth reddish-brown frog, speckled black and white underneath. A very fat one came and sat on my mother's belly just prior to her giving birth.' He shrugged. 'We tend to name our children after such things.'

Jaeger smiled. 'So a wild boar came and sat on your mother just prior to your brother Gwaihutiga's birth?'

Puruwehua laughed. 'My mother – she was a fine hunter in her youth. She and a wild boar had a fierce battle. Finally, she speared it and killed it. She wanted her firstborn to have the spirit of that boar.' He glanced at his elder brother at the head of the column. 'Gwaihutiga – he has that spirit.'

'And the frog? The one you were named after? What happened to the frog?'

Puruwehua fixed Jaeger with a dark, blank-eyed stare. 'My mother was hungry. She killed it and ate it as well.'

They walked on in silence for several minutes, before Puruwehua pointed at something high in the treetops. 'That green parrot feeding off the fruit – it's a *tuitiguhu'ia*. People keep them as pets. The bird can learn to talk, and it will warn you when the jaguar is about to attack your village.'

'Very useful,' Jaeger remarked. 'How d'you go about taming it?'

'You must first find a *kary'ripohaga* bush. You cut a bunch of leaves and hit the parrot a few times around the face with them. Then it is tamed.'

Jaeger raised one eyebrow. 'That easy?'

Puruwehua laughed. 'Of course! Many things become easy when you know the ways of the forest.'

They moved on, passing by a rotten log. Puruwehua brushed his hand against a blackish-red fungus, then put his fingers to his nose. '*Gwaipeva*. It has a distinct smell.' He patted his stomach. 'Good to eat.'

He pulled it out by its roots, and stuffed it into a woven bag that he carried over his shoulder.

A few paces further on he pointed out a big black insect clinging to the trunk of a nearby tree. '*Tukuruvapa'ara*. The king of grasshoppers. It chews on the tree until it falls.'

As they passed the tree, Puruwehua warned Jaeger to step carefully on the path, for there was a twisted vine underfoot.

'*Gwakagwa'yva* – the water vine with thorns. We use the bark for making the cord from which we weave our hammocks. Its seed pods are shaped like bananas, and when they burst open the seeds float away on the wind.'

Jaeger was fascinated. He'd always viewed the jungle as entirely neutral: the more you learned of its secrets, the more you could make it your ally and your friend.

A short while later, Puruwehua cupped a hand to his ear. 'You hear? That *prrrikh-prrrikh-prrrikh-prrrikh-prrrikh*. It is the *gware'ia* – a big brown hummingbird with a white front and a long tail. It sings only when it sees a wild pig.' He reached for an arrow. 'Food for the village . . .'

As Jaeger's hand went to his shotgun, he saw Puruwehua transform himself from a translator into a hunter, stringing an arrow to a bow almost as tall as he was. Puruwehua was barely an inch shorter than his warrior brother, and just as broad and powerful in the shoulder.

When the moment came for battle, Jaeger figured Puruwehua was one frog that wouldn't allow himself to be eaten very easily.

56

A good way behind, the Amahuaca village square was largely silent and deserted now. But a lone figure lingered in the open.

He glanced at the dawn sky, moving a few paces to where there was practically zero tree cover and maximum privacy. He pulled something from his pocket – a Thuraya satphone – placed it on a tree stump and squatted down in the undergrowth to wait.

The phone bleeped once, twice, then three times: it had acquired enough satellites. The figure punched speed-dial, followed by a single digit.

The phone rang twice before a voice answered. 'Grey Wolf. Speak.'

Kral's teeth showed a thin smile. 'This is White Wolf. Seven have left with two dozen Indians, heading due south back towards the falls. From there, they take some route known only to the Indians, west towards the target. I couldn't speak before now, but I have managed to give them the slip. You can do your worst.'

'Understood.'

'I can confirm it is SS Oberst-Gruppenführer Kammler's warplane. Contents more or less intact. Or as good as can be expected after seventy-odd years.'

'Understood.'

'I have the exact coordinates of the warplane.' A pause. 'Have you made the third payment?'

'We have the coordinates already. Our surveillance drone found the plane.'

'Fine.' A shadow of irritation flitted across Kral's features. 'Those I was given are: 964864.'

'964864. They match.'

'And the third payment?'

'It will be in your Zurich account, as arranged. Spend it quickly, Mr White Wolf. You never know what tomorrow may bring.'

'*Wir sind die Zukunft,*' Kral whispered.

'*Wir sind die Zukunft,*' the voice confirmed.

Kral killed the call.

The figure on the other end cradled the receiver against his neck, letting it rest there for a long moment.

He glanced at a framed photo on his desk. It showed a middle-aged man in a grey pinstriped suit. The face was hawkish, the nose aquiline, the eyes arrogant yet rakish, speaking of untrammelled power and influence – something that had given him a casual confidence in his own abilities long into old age.

'At last,' the seated figure whispered. '*Wir sind die Zukunft.*'

He placed the receiver back to his ear, and punched '0'. 'Anna? Get me Grey Wolf Six. Yes – right now, please.'

He waited for a beat, before a voice came on the line. 'Grey Wolf Six.'

'I have the coordinates,' he announced. 'They match. Eliminate them all. There are to be no survivors – White Wolf included.'

'Sir, understood,' the voice confirmed.

'Keep it clean; at a distance. Use the Predator. Keep it *deniable*. You have the tracking unit. Use it. And trace their comms systems. Find them. Eliminate them all.'

'Understood. But sir, beneath the canopy, we'll have problems tracking them from the air.'

'Then do what you must. Unleash your dogs of war. But they are to get nowhere near that warplane.'

'Understood, sir.'

The seated figure killed the call. After a moment's thought, he leaned forward and tapped the keyboard of his laptop, bringing it out of sleep mode. He composed a short email.

> **Dear Ferdy,**
>   *Adlerflug IV* **found. Will soon be salvaged/dealt with.**
> **Clean-up operation under way. Grandpapa Bormann would**
> **have been proud of us.**
>   *Wir sind die Zukunft.*
> **HK**

He pressed 'send', then leaned back in his chair, fingers knitted behind his head. On the wall behind him was a framed picture showing a photo of his younger self, wearing the distinctive uniform of a colonel in the American military.

Under the guidance of the Amahuaca Indians, it took Jaeger and his team less than half the time to retrace their route to the Devil's Falls. They arrived at the bank of the Rio de los Dios just a kilometre or so downstream from where they had cached their expedition gear.

Puruwehua called a halt beneath the fringes of the forest canopy, where a permanent cloud of spray seemed to fog the air. He pointed into the river mist – a sharp precipice sliced through the rock before them, carved by the rushing waters over countless millennia. He had to shout to make himself heard above the deafening roar, as the Rio de los Dios tumbled nearly a thousand feet to the valley below.

'That way – there is a bridge to the first island,' he announced. 'From there we swing by rope. Two rope swings to two further *evi-gwa* – land islands – and we reach the far side. There, a rock-cut passage runs down the face of the falls, one carved long ago by our forefathers. One hour – maybe less – we will be at the base of the falls.'

'From there – how long to the air wreck?' Jaeger queried.

'At Amahuaca speed, one day.' Puruwehua shrugged. 'At white-man speed, a day and a half, no more.'

Jaeger moved to the lip of the precipice, eyes searching for the first crossing. For a while he failed to find it, so well was the bridge concealed. It took Puruwehua to point it out to him.

'There.' His arm stabbed downwards, indicating a tiny, rickety-looking structure. '*Pyhama* – a vine rope that we use for climbing the trees. But it makes for a fine river bridge also. It is covered over by the leaves of the *gwy'va* tree, from which we get the wood to make our arrow shafts. Like this, it is almost invisible.'

Jaeger and his team shouldered their packs and followed the Indians as they slithered down the cliff face to the start of the crossing. Before them lay a crazy-looking, precipitous rope bridge spanning the first mighty chasm. On the far side it was attached to a rock island, the first of three perched on the very lip of the falls.

The noise of the waterfall prevented any talk here. Jaeger followed Puruwehua, the first of his team to set foot on the perilous structure. He grabbed the vine-rope handrails on either side, forcing himself to step from woven cross rope to cross rope, which were spaced a man's stride apart.

For a brief moment he made the mistake of looking down.

Two hundred feet below, the brown and angry waters of the Rio de los Dios thundered past, before churning into a maelstrom of seething white and gushing into the abyss. Jaeger figured it was best to keep eyes front. With his gaze firmly fixed on Puruwehua's shoulders, he forced his feet to continue shuffling forward.

He was approaching the halfway point on the bridge, with most of his team bunched up behind him, when he sensed it.

With zero warning, an impossibly sleek projectile ripped

apart the river mists swirling above them, the howl of its passing clawing into his ears. It tore through the centre of the rope bridge, a millisecond later ploughing into the Rio de los Dios far below and exploding in a massive gout of blasted white water.

Jaeger stared transfixed as the plume of onrushing destruction tore upwards – the noise of its eruption pounding in his ears and echoing back and forth across the chasm.

It was all over in less than a second. The bridge was left swinging violently to and fro, as figures clung to it, eyes wide in terror. Jaeger had called in enough Hellfire missile strikes to recognise the high-pitched, tortured howl of the weapon – yet this was the very first time he had ever been the target of one.

'HELLFIRE!' He screamed out a warning. 'HELLFIRE! Get back! Back to the bank! Get under the trees!'

In the strange but signature way that time seemed to slow down in life-threatening combat, Jaeger felt as if he were living a hundred years for every second. His mind processed a thousand and one thoughts as he shovelled figures ahead of him, getting them to make for the cover of the jungle.

This far into the Brazilian Amazon – they were in the extreme west of the state of Acre, in the department of Assis Brazil, right on the Peruvian border – he figured it could only be one sort of warplane flying above them. It had to be a pilotless drone, for only that would have the range and the loiter time to orbit over the jungle for long enough to have found them.

Jaeger knew how long a Predator – the most common drone used by the world's more advanced militaries – would take to rearm and reacquire its target. The very act of firing a Hellfire tended to wobble the aircraft, breaking up the video link with the unmanned warplane's remote operator.

It would take around sixty seconds to stabilise and to re-establish firm video contact.

The next AGM-114 Hellfire – and most Predators carried a maximum of three – would be ready to fire any moment now. Depending on what altitude the Predator was orbiting at – most likely 25,000 feet – the missile might take as long as eighteen seconds to reach earth – which was the maximum time that Jaeger had remaining.

The first Hellfire had failed to detonate when it struck the rope structure, cutting through a strand of the bridge like a knife through butter.

But second time around they mightn't be so lucky.

The last figure – the chief's eldest son – came clambering back across, Jaeger shoving him towards the riverbank. He turned himself now, heading for the safety of the jungle, boots scrabbling at the rungs underfoot, the forest coming closer with every footfall.

'GET INTO THE TREES!' he screamed. 'GET UNDER THE TREES!'

The canopy wouldn't shield them from a Hellfire strike. There was little that could do that. But the Predator would find it next to impossible to see through the carpet of thick vegetation, which would prevent it from acquiring a target.

Jaeger kept running, rung to rung, the last man remaining on the bridge.

Then the second missile struck.

He felt the jolt of its impact an instant before the howl of its descent drilled into his ears – for the missile travelled at Mach 1.3, faster than the speed of sound. It exploded in the very centre of the bridge, the skeletal structure dissolving into a ball of boiling flame, razor-sharp shards of shrapnel ripping through the air all around him.

Moments later, he felt himself falling.

With his last reserves of strength Jaeger spun around, grabbing hold of the handrails, locking his arms around them and bracing for the impact. For a second or so his half of the bridge dropped vertically, before the end still attached to the wall of the chasm pulled up short, dragging what remained in a violent whiplash towards the rock face.

Jaeger tensed his body into a block of steel.

He struck the wall of rock, the crushing blow ripping the skin from his forearms, as his head was catapulted forward by the impact.

His forehead hit with a terrible crack.

A blinding burst of stars rocketed through Jaeger's brain, and an instant later his world turned dark.

57

J aeger came to.

His head was spinning. Bolts of burning pain tore through his temples. His vision swam. He felt like throwing up.

Slowly, he became aware of his surroundings. Above him there stretched a wide umbrella of dark green.

Jungle.

Canopy.

High above.

Like a protective blanket.

Shielding him from the Predator.

'Turn everything off!' Jaeger screamed. He fought to raise himself on to one elbow, but hands were trying to restrain him, to hold him down. 'Get everything the hell off! It's tracking something! GET EVERYTHING OFF!'

Jaeger's wild, bloodied eyes flashed around his team, as figures scrambled for pockets and belt pouches.

Jaeger gasped as another stab of agony tore through his head. 'PREDATOR!' he cried. 'Carries three Hellfire! Get everything off! TURN IT THE HELL OFF!'

As he screamed and raved, his eyes came to rest on one individual. Dale was crouched at the very lip of the river gorge, one knee supporting his camera, his eye bent to the viewfinder as he filmed the unfolding drama.

With a Herculean effort, Jaeger broke free from whoever was holding him down. He charged forward, eyes flashing dangerously, his face slick with blood, his visage that of a near-madman.

A yell issued forth from his throat like an animal howl. *'TURN IT – THE HELL – OFF!'*

Dale glanced up uncomprehendingly – his entire world had been focused through the camera lens.

The next moment, eighty kilos of William Jaeger slammed into him, the rugby tackle sending both men tumbling into the thick vegetation, the camera spinning off in the opposite direction. It rolled once, and disappeared over the lip into the chasm of the gorge.

The camera came to rest on a thin ledge of rock.

Seconds later, there was a howl like all the gates of hell had opened, and a third missile flashed earthwards. Hellfire number three tore through the mists, ripping into the narrow shelf where Dale's camera had landed. The detonation burned across the narrow ledge, pulverising what little vegetation there was, but the wall of rock above served to shield Jaeger's team from the worst of the blast.

The explosion was funnelled upwards, a storm of shrapnel tearing into the open sky, the deafening explosion roaring back and forth across the wide expanse of the Rio de los Dios.

As the echoes died away, a silence of sorts settled over the gorge. The scent of scorched rock and blasted vegetation hung heavy in the air, plus the choking, smoky firework smell of high explosives.

'Hellfire number three!' Jaeger cried, from where he and Dale had landed in the undergrowth. 'Should be all it's got! But search your gear – ALL OF IT – and get everything turned the hell off!'

Figures ran to it, grabbing Bergens and emptying them of their contents.

Jaeger turned to Dale. 'Your camera: it records date, time and location, right? It's got an embedded GPS?'

'Yeah, but I got Kral to disable it, on both units. No cameraman wants date and time burned across their film.'

Jaeger jerked a thumb towards the ledge where Dale's camera

had breathed its last. 'Whatever the hell Kral was doing – *that one wasn't disabled.*'

Dale's eyes swivelled to his backpack. 'I've got a second in there. Back-up.'

'Then get beneath the canopy and make sure it's turned off!'

Dale hurried to it.

Jaeger struggled to his feet. He felt like death – his head and forearms throbbing in agony – but he had bigger issues to deal with right now. He had his own pack to search and verify. He stumbled across to it and began turfing out the contents. He was certain everything had been switched off, but one mistake now could easily prove the death of all of them.

Five minutes later, the checking was complete.

No one had had a GPS unit running at the time of the Hellfire strikes, let alone a satphone. They'd been moving fast, following a route and a pace set by the Amahuaca Indians. No one on Jaeger's team had needed to navigate, plus they'd been under deep canopy, where there was zero satellite signal.

Jaeger gathered his team. 'Something triggered the Predator,' he announced, through teeth gritted with pain. 'We emerged from under the canopy at the edge of the falls, and *bleep!* A signal popped up on a Predator's screen. It takes a satphone, GPS or similar to do that: something instantly trackable.'

'It's got infrared,' Alonzo volunteered. 'Predator. Via IR it'll see us as heat sources.'

Jaeger shook his head. 'Not beneath a hundred feet of jungle it won't. And even if it could penetrate all of that – and trust me, it can't – what would it see? A bunch of indistinct heat blobs. We could just as easily be a herd of forest pigs as a bunch of humans. No, it was tracking something; something that threw up an instant, traceable signal.'

Jaeger eyed Dale. 'Were you filming when the first Hellfire hit? Was your camera powered up?'

Dale shook his head. 'Are you kidding? On that bridge? I was bloody shitting myself.'

'Okay, everyone: double-check your gear,' Jaeger announced grimly. 'Search the side pockets of your backpacks. Your trouser pockets. Shirt pockets. Hell, your underwear even. It was tracking something. We've got to find it.'

He proceeded to rifle through his own pack once more, before running his hands through his pockets. His fingers came to rest upon the smooth form of the Night Stalkers coin, stuffed deep into his trousers. Oddly, it seemed to have become bent – almost buckled – during the chaos and mayhem of the last few minutes.

He pulled it out. He figured the coin must have taken some serious punishment when the end of the broken bridge slammed him into the rock face. He studied it for a moment. There seemed to be a tiny crack running around the circumference. He forced a broken, bloodied nail into it and applied some pressure.

The coin pinged in two.

Inside, one half was hollow.

Jaeger couldn't believe the evidence before his eyes.

The hollowed-out interior of the coin held a miniaturised electrical circuit board.

58

'Death Waits in the Dark.' Jaeger spat out the words of the Night Stalkers' motto, stamped on one side of the so-called coin. 'It sure does – when you're carrying one of these.'

He placed it on a nearby rock, circuit board face up, then grabbed a second, smaller rock. He was going to smash the thing to smithereens, using the rocks like a hammer and anvil. He raised one fist, and was poised to bring the rock powering down-wards – all his pent-up rage and his burning sense of betrayal focused into the blow – when a hand reached out to stop him.

'Don't. There is a better way.' It was Irina Narov. 'All track-ing units have a battery. They also have an on–off button.' She reached for the device and flicked a tiny switch. 'It is now off. No more signal.' She glanced at him. 'The question is, where did you get it?'

Jaeger's fingers curled around the coin, as if he could crush it in his grip. 'The C-130 pilot. We got chatting. He said he was a SOAR veteran. A Night Stalker. I know the SOAR well. There's no better unit. I told him as much.' He paused, darkly. 'He of-fered me his coin.'

'Then let me posit a scenario,' Narov suggested, her voice as cold and empty as a frozen Arctic wasteland. 'The C-130 pilot slipped you a tracking device. That now is clear. We – you and I in tandem – were snagged when we made our jump. His crew – his PDs – deliberately did that to us, to send us into the spin. And they loosened your weapon, to destabilise us still further.'

Narov paused. 'The C-130 crew was charged either to kill us

or to enable someone to follow us. And whoever it was is now tracking us using that coin, they are also trying to kill us.'

Jaeger nodded, acknowledging that Narov's scenario was the only one that seemed to make any sense.

'So who is trying to kill us?' Narov continued. 'It is a rhetorical question. I do not expect you to answer. But right now it is the million-dollar question.'

There was something about Narov's tone that set Jaeger's teeth on edge. At times she was so cold and robotic, like an automaton. It was hugely disconcerting.

'I'm glad you're not expecting an answer,' he rasped. ''Cause you know something? If the pilot of that C-130 could slip me a tracking device, I don't have the slightest damn clue who is friend or foe any more.'

He jerked a thumb in the direction of the Indians. 'About the only people I know I can trust right now is that lot – a supposedly uncontacted Amazon Indian tribe. As to who the enemy are, all I know is they've got some serious hardware to hand – like a Predator, tracking devices, and God only knows what else.'

'Carson hired the C-130 and crew?' Narov queried.

'He did.'

'Then Carson is a suspect. I never liked him anyway. He is an arrogant *Schwachkopf*.' She glanced at Jaeger. 'There are two kinds. The nice *Schwachkopfs*, and those I utterly despise. You – you are one of the nicer ones.'

Jaeger glared. He couldn't get his head around Narov. Was she flirting with him now, or playing with him like a cat did a mouse? Either way, he figured he might as well take the backhanded compliment.

Alonzo appeared beside them. 'I figure you gotta call the HAV,' the big Afro-American suggested. 'The Airlander. They're doing P-WAS, right? Persistent wide-area surveillance – they should have it up and running by now. Ask them what they've seen.'

'You're forgetting something,' Jaeger objected. 'I make a call, we get a Hellfire up our ass.'

'Send data,' Alonzo suggested. 'Data-burst mode. Predator takes a good ninety seconds to trace, track and acquire a target. Data-burst – it's gone in the blink of an eyelid.'

Jaeger thought about it for a second. 'Yeah. I guess it should work.' He glanced at the edge of the chasm. 'But I do this out there. Myself. Alone.'

Jaeger powered up his Thuraya. He typed a quick message, secure in the knowledge that he'd only acquire the satellites to send it when out in the open.

The message read: *Grid 964864. Comms being intercepted. Team targeted: Hellfire. Query drone? Comms now only encrypted data-burst. What has Airlander seen? Out.*

Jaeger stepped to the brink of the river gorge.

He emerged from under the canopy and held the Thuraya at arm's length, watching as the satellite icons bleeped on to the screen. The instant he had a usable signal, the message was gone, and he powered down, hurrying back beneath the jungle.

Jaeger and the team waited in the shadows, the tension thick as they counted out the seconds. A minute passed: no Hellfire. Two minutes passed: still no missile strike.

'That's three minutes, buddy,' Alonzo growled at last, 'and still no Hellfire. Data-burst – looks like it's gonna do the business.'

'It does,' Jaeger confirmed. 'So, what next?'

'First, you need to let me tend to that head of yours.' It was Leticia Santos. 'It is too handsome to get so hurt and damaged.'

Jaeger acquiesced, letting Santos do her stuff. She cleaned the abrasions to his arms, rubbing some iodine – a steriliser – into them, after which she wrapped a thick gauze around his forehead.

'Thanks,' he told her, once she was done. 'And you know what – as far as medics go, you're a big improvement on the hairy commandos I'm used to.'

He moved across to Puruwehua, spending a minute or two explaining what had happened. Few of the Indians had had the slightest idea what the Hellfires might be. Death from the skies like that – it might as well have been a bolt of lightning sent by their gods. Only Puruwehua – who'd watched a bunch of war movies – seemed to have any sense of an understanding.

'Brief your guys on what it means,' Jaeger told him. 'I want them to fully understand what we're up against. Against Predator, blowpipes and arrows are utterly useless. They decide they want to turn back, I can't say I'd blame them.'

'You saved us on the bridge,' Puruwehua replied. 'There is a debt of life to be repaid. Our women send us out with a saying whenever we go to fight. It would translate something like "Return victorious, or dead". It would be a deep dishonour to return to the village having achieved neither death nor glory. There is no question: we are with you.'

59

Jaeger's eyes glowed with relief. It would have been one hell of a blow to lose the Indians right now. 'So, I'm curious. Tell me – how the hell did *I* survive the fall on the bridge?'

'You were unconscious, but your arms remained locked around the *pyhama*.' Puruwehua glanced at his brother. 'Gwaihutiga and me – we climbed down to fetch you. But it was my brother who finally prised you free and lifted you to safety.'

Jaeger shook his head in amazement. The simple understatement embodied in the Indian's words masked what must have been a moment of sheer death-defying terror.

He eyed the young Amahuaca warrior – for Puruwehua was far more than just a translator in Jaeger's eyes now. 'So what you're telling me, Puruwehua – the bravest damn frog in the entire jungle – is that the debt of life is owed both ways.'

'It is,' he confirmed simply.

'But why Gwaihutiga?' Jaeger asked. 'I mean, he's the guy who most wanted us killed.'

'My father decreed otherwise, Koty'ar.'

'Koty'ar?'

'Koty'ar: it is what my father named you. It means "the permanent companion"; the friend who is always at your side.'

Jaeger shook his head. 'More like you're the *koty'ar* to us lot.'

'True friendship – it goes both ways. And as far as Gwaihutiga sees it, you are now of our tribe.' Puruwehua eyed Narov for an instant. 'As is the *ja'gwara*, and the small man from Japan, plus the big bearded one on your team.'

Jaeger felt humbled. He stepped across the short distance to Gwaihutiga. The Amahuaca warrior rose to his feet at his approach. They came up against each other, face to face, each about the same height and breadth. Jaeger extended his hand for Gwaihutiga to shake in a gesture of heartfelt gratitude.

The Indian stared at it for an instant, then brought his eyes up to Jaeger's face – his gaze a dark pool of nothingness. Unreadable. Again.

For a long moment Jaeger feared that the gesture had been rejected. But then Gwaihutiga reached out, gathered both Jaeger's hands and cupped them within his.

'*Epenhan, koty'ar,*' Gwaihutiga announced. '*Epenhan.*'

'It means welcome,' Puruwehua explained. 'Welcome to the friend who is always at our side.'

Jaeger felt emotion well up in his stomach. Moments like this, he knew, were rare. He was face to face with the warrior leader of a largely uncontacted people – one who had risked his life to save a complete stranger and an outsider. He grabbed Gwaihutiga in a momentary embrace, then pulled away.

'So, tell me, guys, any idea how we get down from here?' Jaeger asked, not knowing quite what else to say. 'Now the rope bridge has been blown in two.'

'This is what we have been discussing,' Puruwehua volunteered. 'We have no way to cross the river, and from there to take the route down. The only alternative is the path you originally planned to use. But it is a three-day detour, maybe more. We will reach the target long after those we are trying to beat—'

'Then there's no time to waste,' Alonzo cut in. 'Man, we'll run the entire way if we have to. Let's get goin'.'

Jaeger held up a hand for silence. 'One second. Just the one.'

He glanced around the faces ranged before him, a wild smile playing across his features. It had been a given in special forces that they'd always endeavour to do the unorthodox and the unexpected, to outfox the enemy. Well Jaeger was about to do the unexpected big time – right here and now.

'We've got the parachutes back at the cache, right?' he declared. 'Eight of them – double that number if we separate out the reserve chutes.' A beat. 'Anyone here ever done a base jump?'

'Done a few,' Joe James volunteered. 'Almost as wild as taking a hit on an Amahuaca snuff pipe.'

'I too have base-jumped,' Leticia Santos confirmed. 'It is good, but never as exciting as dancing at *carnivale*. Why?'

'Base-jumping is basically the shortened version of HAHO-ing from 30,000 feet – only you're jumping off a cliff face or a tower block, as opposed to a C-130's open ramp, and you've got a fraction of the distance in which to pull your chute.'

The raw excitement was burning in Jaeger's eyes now. 'That's what we're going to do: we're going to grab our chutes from the cache and jump the Devil's Falls.'

It took a few moments for his words to sink in. It was Hiro Kamishi who raised the first – wholly sensible – objection.

'What about the Amahuaca? Puruwehua, Gwaihutiga and their warrior brothers? It would not be . . . wise to leave them behind.'

'We're seven – so that leaves nine spare chutes. Plus we can tandem a good number of 'em down.' Jaeger glanced at Puruwehua. 'You ever wanted to fly? Like that eagle you told me about – the *topena*, wasn't it? The white hawk that can steal a chicken from the village?'

'The *topena*,' Puruwehua confirmed. 'I have flown as high as the *topena*, when taking *nyakwana* snuff. I have flown over wide oceans and to distant mountains – but these are the mountains of my mind.'

'I'm sure you have,' Jaeger enthused. 'But today, right now, you're going to learn to fly for real.'

Puruwehua's gaze remained expressionless, devoid of even the slightest hint of fear. 'If it is the only way down and the quickest, we will jump.'

'We can get seven of you down for certain, maybe more if

some fly solo,' Jaeger explained. 'And at least this way we can be first to that wreck.'

'We will jump,' Puruwehua announced simply. 'Those who cannot will descend via the long route – the path – and from there they will chase after and harass this Dark Force. In this way, we hit them from two sides.'

Gwaihutiga volunteered a few words, punctuated by the brandishing of a weapon. 'My elder brother says that after today, we will follow you anywhere, even over the falls,' Puruwehua translated. 'And he used a new name for you: Kahuhara'ga. It means "the hunter".'

Jaeger shook his head. 'Thanks, but here in the jungle it's you guys who are the true hunters.'

'No – I think Gwaihutiga is right,' Narov cut in. 'After all, Jaeger means "hunter" in German too. And today, here in the jungle, you have been given that name for a second time, and by an Amahuaca warrior who could not know the meaning of the original. That has to signify something.'

Jaeger shrugged. 'Fine. But right now I feel more like the hunted. Right now I'd rather avoid a fight with whoever we're up against. That means getting to that air wreck first, and there's only one way to do that.' He glanced towards the falls. 'Let's get moving.'

'There is perhaps one problem,' Narov ventured. 'The flying bit I am happy with, not so the landing. I have no desire to end up dangling from the canopy again, getting eaten alive by *Phoneutria*. Where do you intend that we land?'

In answer, Jaeger led the way to the very lip of the Devil's Falls.

He glanced over, his arm jabbing downwards. 'See that? That pool carved out of the jungle at the base of the falls? When we were planning the expedition, we considered that as an alternative touchdown point. We discounted it, for any number of reasons. But right now, we've got zero options: that's where we'll land.

'One of the reasons we discounted it,' he continued, 'was we figured it would be full of caimans. Are there, Puruwehua? Caimans? In that pool at the base of the falls?'

Puruwehua shook his head. 'No. No caimans.'

Jaeger eyed him. 'There's something else, though, isn't there?'

'There are *piraihunuhua*. How do you call it? A black fish that eats bigger fish. Sometime even large animals?'

'Piranha?'

'Piranha,' Puruwehua confirmed. He laughed. 'There are no caimans because of the piranhas.'

'Man, I hate freakin' fish,' Alonzo growled. 'Hate 'em. We're gonna jump off a cliff, fly down a waterfall, land in a river and get munched alive by the world's most deadly fish. A Jaeger classic.'

Jaeger's eyes glowed. 'Oh no we're not. You follow me in close and land in the same patch of water that I do – we're going to be just fine. All of us. Don't linger. It still isn't a great time to take a bath. But trust me, we can do this.'

He flashed a look at each of his team. The faces that stared back at him were streaked with sweat and grime, pockmarked from insect bites and furrowed deep with stress and exhaustion. His eyes came to rest upon their cameraman. The only one who wasn't ex-military, Dale seemed to possess hidden reserves of strength, not to mention sheer guts and determination.

Incredibly, nothing yet seemed to have beaten him.

'That spare camera,' Jaeger announced. 'Let's double-check that the date, time and location function is disabled. When we do this, I *want* the camera rolling. *I want you to film.* And I want you to shoot everything you can from now on. I want a record of everything, just in case of the worst.'

Dale shrugged. 'I take it you're going first. I'll set the camera running when you jump the Devil's Falls.'

60

Jaeger stood on the very edge.

Behind him, his team was bunched up close. To his left and below, a massive volume of water seethed over the lip of the falls, and beneath his feet the rock was slippery. Glancing across the wall of falling water, it seemed as if the very earth were moving.

As he turned to face the emptiness, there was only a whirling mass of mist and swirling water vapour, along with a powerful upwelling of warm tropical air.

Plus, there was Puruwehua, lashed tight to Jaeger in the tandem.

Every one of Jaeger's team bar one was leaping tandem, with an Amahuaca warrior strapped to his or her person.

Joe James – one of the strongest of the lot of them, and the most experienced base-jumper – would also be making the short flight with the extra weight of a folded-up kayak roped to him. Narov had had a novel idea of how they could make use of that canoe, once they'd jumped the Devil's Falls.

Because he was filming it all, Dale would be the last over. Being non-military, he was their least experienced parachutist, and he had a challenging enough task as it was filming all the jumps. To try to make it a little easier on him, Jaeger had suggested that he alone should jump solo.

Jaeger leaned further into the void, nudging Puruwehua forward. A final pause, a deep breath and then he shifted them past the point of no return, and together they took the plunge.

As he had anticipated, there was no need to leap a great distance from the pinnacle of rock on which they were standing. The overhang was significant and Jaeger had kept them stable as they dived. But even so, it was to Puruwehua's credit that he didn't panic and flounder, which might have sent them into a spin. It was his calm warrior mentality coming to the fore.

As they accelerated, the upwelling of warm, wet air caught them, and propelled them away from the cliff face into the swirling mass of opaque whiteness.

Two thousand, three thousand . . . Jaeger counted inside his head. 'And PULL!'

He'd packed the BT80 himself, which was hardly ideal, and for a moment he feared the chute had failed to deploy, in which case he and Puruwehua were going to end up very wet and very dead, very fast. But then he felt the familiar billowing jerk as a vast expanse of silk caught the air above them, the individual panels of the parachute dragging at the hot, steamy atmosphere.

The thunder of the tumbling water was thick in his ears as Jaeger felt himself and Puruwehua dragged upwards by the shoulders, until they were left floating in the sticky, damp whiteness five hundred feet below the lip of the falls.

For the briefest of moments, Jaeger found himself staring into a wall of rainbow colours, the plume of spray from the falling water caught in the intense sunlight. And then the moment was past, and he was turning away from the falls towards the open jungle.

He steered right with the toggles, bringing the chute into a series of gentle loops, but taking special care to avoid the thick spray from the mass of white water cascading through the air beside them.

If he blundered into that, it would collapse their chute, and he and Puruwehua would be finished.

He corkscrewed towards the pool below. *Piranhas.* There wasn't much that scared Will Jaeger, but getting chomped to death by scores of jet-black gnarly fish jaws was one of them. Relative to its size, the piranha had a bite more powerful than a *Tyrannosaurus rex*, and three times that of a caiman.

For an instant he checked the sky above. He counted four chutes already in the air, and a fifth pair of figures tumbling off the rock face. His team was coming in good and tight, which was just as he wanted it.

He glanced down.

The water was maybe four hundred feet below and coming up fast.

He unzipped his chest pouch, and his fingers curled around the cold steel of the grenade.

During the three lost years he'd spent on Bioko, Jaeger had learned to perfect the little-appreciated skill of killing time. One way he'd found to do so was by researching the fate of the *Duchessa* – that mystery Second World War cargo ship that Britain had seemingly risked all to capture.

Another way had been to try his hand at fishing.

Invariably, he'd done so in the company of the Fernao village boatmen – only they hadn't used traditional nets or lines very often. The villagers' favoured means of catching fish was by using dynamite. It was bad for wildlife and for conservation, but undeniably effective in terms of netting their catch – or rather, blowing them out of the water.

Jaeger removed the grenade from the pouch and ripped the retaining clip out with his teeth whilst holding the release lever flush with the metal casing. He had Colonel Evandro to thank for the few grenades he was carrying, though he'd never once envisaged using one in the way that he was intending to right now.

When he judged the timing and distance was just right, he let the grenade fall, the clip springing free.

It was now armed and plummeting towards the base of the waterfall. It would explode in six seconds, by which time Jaeger reckoned it would be six feet or more under the water.

He saw the grenade hit, the ripples from the impact pulsing out across the pool. A second or two later it exploded, throwing up a plume of white water before the eruption crashed back to the boiling surface below.

As Jaeger steered for the heart of the explosion, he just had time to release a second grenade. His demolitions instructor had once told him that PE – plastic explosives – actually stood for 'plenty everywhere' if they were ever in any doubt how much was needed for a job.

The second grenade detonated; this time the plume of spray blasted almost as high as Jaeger's feet. Already he could see stunned fish floating to the surface, belly to the sky. He prayed like hell that this was going to work.

His boots hit, and the instant they did so, Jaeger tugged at the release straps that allowed him to ditch his parachute harness, freeing Puruwehua at the same time. To his left he saw Irina Narov hit the water; to his right, Leticia Santos. Alonzo followed a moment later to his front, with Kamishi to his rear – each of them with an Amahuaca warrior likewise strapped in the tandem.

Five down – ten with the Indians included.

It was time to make for shore.

After studying the waters intently from their vantage point high above, Puruwehua had advised Jaeger exactly where to make splashdown. He'd chosen a point adjacent to an *evi-gwa* – a place where a tongue of land jutted into the river, ending in a sharp drop to deep water.

A few powerful strokes with arms and legs, and Jaeger made dry land. He hauled himself out and turned to check behind him. More and more stunned fish were bobbing to the surface, and his team – Indians included – were striking out for land.

Above him, the unmistakable form of Joe James spiralled in to make the last but one splashdown. James had Gwaihutiga strapped to his person, plus the folded kayak hanging on a line below him. The kayak hit first, James and the Indian followed, and they too unclipped themselves and struck out for land, James towing the kayak in his wake.

Last down would be Dale.

He'd remained on the high point filming the jumps, until the final man was gone. Then he'd powered down his camera, stuffed it into a canoe bag so as to keep it safe and dry, and shoved that deep into his backpack.

Jaeger watched him jump and pull his chute, floating towards the surface of the pool.

Suddenly, there was a yell of alarm: '*Purug!* The fish! They are jumping!'

It was Puruwehua. Jaeger looked where he was pointing. Sure enough, a gleaming black form broke the surface and leaped high. In amongst the flash of glistening water Jaeger caught sight of its gaping mouth, lined with two rows of fearsome serrated teeth, below eyes that were staring wide and black as death.

It was like a miniature, and intensely evil-looking, bullet-headed shark, all powerful body and cruelly armed jaws. An instant later, the patch of water where Jaeger and his team had landed began to seethe and boil.

'*Piraihunuhua!*' the Indians yelled.

Jaeger didn't need the warning. He could see the black piranhas tearing into the dead and dying fish thrown up by his grenade blast. There were hundreds of them, and Dale was headed right for their very midst.

For a split second Jaeger was about to hurl a third grenade, but Dale was too low and he would be caught in the explosion.

'Piranha!' Jaeger yelled at him. 'PIRANHA!' He jabbed his hands at the water at his feet. 'Land here! Here! We'll drag you in!'

For a horrible moment he feared that Dale had failed to hear him, and that he was about to plunge into the centre of the feeding frenzy, where his body would be stripped of its flesh in seconds.

At the last moment Dale made a tight left turn – too tight

– and came whooshing in towards where Jaeger and his team were standing. He approached too fast and at the wrong angle, his chute striking the treetops where they reached out over the water.

The topmost branches splintered under the impact, and Dale became stuck fast, dangling over the water, swinging to and fro.

61

'Let's get him down!' Jaeger cried.

His words were drowned out by an explosive crack from above, as the main branch holding Dale snapped in two. He plummeted downwards, his chute ripping as he fell, and moments later he hit the water.

'Drag him in!' Jaeger yelled. 'GET HIM IN!'

All around Dale he could see powerful black shadows darting to and fro just below the surface. All it would take was one bite and the taste of blood, and the piranha would realise that Dale was prey. It would send a signal pulsing through the water to the entire shoal: *come and eat, come and eat.*

Alonzo and Kamishi were nearest. They dived in.

Even as they hit the water, Dale let out a fearful scream. 'Shit! Shit! Shit! *Get me out! Get me out!'*

A stroke or two across the pool, and the two men grabbed Dale by his harness and hauled him towards the bank. His eyes wide with terror – and pain – they dragged the screaming cameraman out of the water.

Jaeger bent to inspect him. Dale had been bitten in several places. He'd gone as white as a sheet, mostly with the shock. Jaeger could hardly blame him: a few seconds more and he would have been terminally chewed. He asked Leticia Santos to do her stuff with the medical kit as Alonzo and Kamishi issued their own damage reports.

'Man! Freakin' fish bit me on the ass!' Alonzo complained. 'I mean, what kind of fish does that?'

Joe James stroked his massive beard. 'Piranha, dude. Don't ever get back in the water. They got a taste for you now. They'll smell you coming.'

Kamishi glanced up from where he was inspecting a wound to his thigh. 'I would like to know if this fish tastes as good as it clearly thinks I tasted.' He eyed Jaeger. 'I would like to catch one and eat it, preferably with some wasabi sauce.'

Jaeger couldn't help but smile. In spite of everything, morale still seemed high among his team. Despite being hunted by Predator and piranhas, they were on message and sparking.

He turned to the next task in hand. 'Narov, James – let's ready the boat.'

Together the three of them unfolded the Advanced Elements kayak, inflated it and got it into the water. They loaded it with a few rocks for ballast, and added some of the bundled-up parachutes for bulk. Finally, Narov threw in her backpack plus weapon and climbed aboard.

She was about to paddle off, heading for the point where the Rio de los Dios snaked off into the wall of thick jungle, when she turned to Jaeger. She eyed the scarf he had knotted around his neck; Santos's *carnivale* scarf.

'I need something to wrap it in,' she remarked. 'The tracker device – to shield it from any impacts. It is delicate; it needs cushioning.' She held out a hand for the scarf. 'That – it is a useless piece of decoration, but it is perfect for my needs.'

Jaeger shook his head. 'No can do, I'm afraid. Leticia told me it's a lucky charm. "Lose my scarf, darling, and it brings bad luck on you all." She was speaking Portuguese, so you probably missed it.'

Narov scowled. The scowl became a sulk.

Jaeger was heartened. He was needling her. Getting right beneath her skin – which was about the only way he figured he would ever start to unpick the enigma that was Irina Narov.

There was so much about her that didn't add up: her bizarre attachment to her knife; her fluent German; her seemingly encyclopedic knowledge of all things Nazi; her burning hatred of Hitler's legacy; not to mention her seeming lack of emotional literacy or empathy with others. One way or another Jaeger was determined to discover what made Irina Narov tick.

Without another word, she turned moodily and dipped her paddle into the piranha-infested waters.

Once Narov was a good distance away – the current starting to pull and tug fiercely at her kayak – she headed into shore. She climbed out of the craft, took the Night Stalkers coin from her pocket, switched the tracking device to the 'on' position, and taped the two halves together with black gaffer tape.

Then she popped the coin into a waterproof Ziploc bag, dropped it into one of the kayak's secure stowage compartments, and went to shove the craft out into midstream.

For an instant, she hesitated.

An idea – a spur-of-the-moment flash of inspiration – blazed through her eyes. She rifled in her pack and retrieved one of the small pay-as-you-go cell phones she kept in her grab bag. She carried a few for emergency communications if she were ever forced to go on the run.

She switched the phone on and threw it into the Ziploc bag alongside the tracking device. She doubted if there was a cell phone tower anywhere within a thousand kilometres of where they were now. But perhaps it didn't matter. Maybe the simple act of calling for a signal would be enough to get it detected, traced and tracked.

That done, she shoved the kayak away from the shore.

The current caught it, and within moments the boat was whisked away. With its triple-skin hull, six inflatable chambers, plus flotation bags, it should remain afloat no matter what it ran into downstream. It could capsize, get holed on rocks and still keep going, which meant the tracker unit would keep on bleeping out its signal.

Narov shouldered her pack, grabbed her weapon and began

to make her way back to the main body of the team, being careful to keep well away from the water and sticking to the cover
of the jungle.

Ten minutes later she was back with Jaeger.

'It is done,' she announced. 'From here the Rio de los Dios
veers northwards. Our route – it lies almost due south. By sending the tracking device that way, it will help spread confusion
amongst our enemies.'

Jaeger stared at her. 'Whoever they may be.'

'Yes,' Narov echoed, 'whoever they may be.' She paused. 'I
added a final touch of my own. A cell phone – I sent it onwards
with the canoe. I understand that even without being able to
acquire a signal, it can be tracked.'

Jaeger cracked a smile. 'Nice one. Let's hope so.'

'Grey Wolf, this is Grey Wolf Six,' a voice intoned. 'Grey Wolf,
Grey Wolf Six.'

The speaker was hunched over the same radio set as before,
in the same camouflaged tent positioned at the edge of the
same rough and ready airstrip. To all sides lay the jagged fringe
of jungle, the rank of unmarked black helicopters lining the dirt
runway, mountains rising dark and lowering on all sides.

'Grey Wolf Six, this is Grey Wolf,' a voice confirmed.

'Sir, we lost them for a good hour there. The tracker went off
air.' The radio operator eyed a laptop. It showed a computer-
generated map of the Serra de los Dios, with various icons
dotted across the screen. 'They've popped up again at the base
of the Devil's Falls, heading downriver into the jungle.'

'Which means?'

'They managed to descend the falls. They're moving on the
water, so presumably by canoe, but they're heading northwards. The warplane – it lies more or less due south of their
position.'

'Which means?'

The figure shrugged. 'Sir, they're headed the wrong way. I've no idea why. I've got a Predator vectored into their position, and just as soon as we have visual with their craft we'll send the video feed. If it is them, that's where we'll finish them.'

'What d'you mean – *if it is them*? Who else could it possibly be?'

'Sir, there's no one else moving on that stretch of water. Once we have the video feed, we'll make doubly certain and execute the kill.'

'About time. Now, patch me into the images of the last strike. The hit on the bridge.'

'Sir.' Hands punched the laptop's keyboard, and a new image appeared on the screen.

Footage played of a grainy video feed – showing what the Predator had filmed of the recent Hellfire strikes. The first missile hit the vine-rope bridge. The image was lost, pixelating badly, before it stabilised once more, and for an instant the face of the lone figure remaining on the bridge was clear.

'Rewind,' the voice demanded. 'That figure: freeze-frame it. Let's see who we're up against here.'

'Sir.' The operator did as requested, freezing the image and zooming in on the features.

'Grab several video frames from around that exact point.' The voice had hardened, growing in intensity. 'Send them to me via secure means. In the next minute, please.'

'Sir,' the operator confirmed.

'And Grey Wolf Six, I'd like your next communication to be "mission complete". You understand? I don't like to be kept waiting or repeatedly disappointed.'

'Understood, sir. Next time, the Predator won't miss.'

'And remember – that aircraft: that warplane – it never flew. It never even existed. You are to obliterate every trace of it – after, of course, we've retrieved what we're looking for.'

'Understood, sir.'

The operator killed the call.

*

The figure on the other end – code name Grey Wolf – leaned back in his chair, his mind lost in thought. He eyed the framed photo on his desk. He and the middle-aged man in the grey pin-striped suit – eyes arrogant, confident, exuding absolute power – bore more than a striking resemblance.

It wasn't hard to imagine them as father and son.

'They are proving remarkably difficult to kill,' the figure muttered, almost as if he were speaking to the man in the photo.

A message dropped into his computer's inbox. It was the secure email from Grey Wolf Six. He leaned forward and tapped at his keyboard. He clicked on the attachment, and the frozen video frame of the figure on the bridge appeared on the screen.

He stared at it for a long moment, studying the grainy image intently. His face darkened.

'It *is* him,' he muttered. 'It has to be.'

His fingers punched the keyboard, pulling up a private email account. He began typing with a fierce intensity.

Ferdy,

    Something troubles me. Will email you images. Face of one of the targets in the vicinity of *Adlerflug IV*. It looks unpleasantly familiar. I fear it is William Jaeger.

    You said he was hit by your people working out of London. You said you left him alive 'to torture him over the loss of his family'. I am all for vengeance, Herr Kamerade. Indeed, with those like Jaeger, revenge is long overdue.

    However, he now seems to be in the Amazon searching for our warplane. Let's hope he's not taken up the mantle from his grandfather.

    Jaeger Senior, as you know, caused us no end of trouble.

    Experience has taught me not to believe in coincidences.

I will send the pictures.

    Wir sind die Zukunft.

    HK

He punched send.

His gaze returned to the image on his screen. His eyes were focused inwards; brooding pools of inky darkness that sucked all energy – all life – into them.

62

The forest dripped and glistened.

All around there was the noise of trickling, dribbling, oozing water. With the clouds low and glowering above the canopy, and the rain falling thick and fast, even less light made it through to ground level.

The first belt of storms sweeping down from the mountains had put a real chill in the air; after several hours of torrential rain it was dark, damp and sodden underfoot, not to mention surprisingly cold.

Jaeger was soaked to the skin, but in truth he welcomed the conditions. As water oozed from the rim of his jungle hat, he said a few quiet words of thanks. Puruwehua had warned him that this was *kyrapo'a* – heavy rain that wouldn't clear for days on end – as opposed to the many other types of rain they had here.

There was *kyrahi'vi*, a light rain that would pass quickly; *ypyi*, driving, wind-blown rain; *kyma'e*, rain that lasted no more than a day, after which it quickly became hot; *kypokaguhu*, drizzly, intermittent rain that was little more than mist; *japa*, rain and sun together, forming a permanent rainbow; and so many more.

Anyone who passed British special forces selection became a rain connoisseur. The southern Welsh mountains – the Brecon Beacons – were a bleak, glowering, windswept mass, where it seemed to rain 364 days of the year. In fact, from Jaeger's experience those forbidding hills seemed to have as many types of rain as the Amazon jungle. It had made him glad that human skin was waterproof.

But this, Puruwehua had concluded, this was definitely *kyrapo'a*: rain without a break for days and days on end. And Jaeger was glad of it.

It wouldn't do much for Dale, Alonzo and Kamishi's piranha bites. Wet, dirty clothing rubbing against wet, dirty bandages didn't tend to help wounds heal. But right now that was the least of Jaeger's worries.

Prior to departing the piranha-infested pool at the base of the Devil's Falls, Jaeger had risked taking receipt of a data-burst message from the Airlander. Raff had kept it short and sweet, and entirely to the point.

Confirm your grid: 964864. Moving into overwatch. Predator detected 10 klicks north of your location. Watch Kral; Narov. Listening watch. Out.

Decoded a little, the message meant that the Airlander was moving into orbit over their location. Sure enough, they had at least one Predator drone in the skies above them – although the fact that it was ten kilometres north suggested it was very likely tracking their decoy, the unoccupied kayak moving downriver.

'Listening watch' meant that Raff would maintain a 24/7 watch for any data-burst message from Jaeger. Plus he had alerted Jaeger to who was suspect amongst his team: Kral and Narov.

Before leaving the UK, Jaeger had had precious little opportunity to check out the team's backgrounds. After Andy Smith's death he'd figured he had every right to do so, but time had run out on him. He'd left it up to Raff to do some digging, and clearly those two – Kral and Narov – had come up suspect.

Over time, Jaeger had found himself warming to Dale, but there was also a part of him that had sympathised with the Slovakian cameraman, who was undeniably Wild Dog Media's little guy. Yet clearly there was something in Kral's background that had thrown up a red flag.

And in the back of Jaeger's mind there was the niggling worry that Kral had failed to disable the GPS units on Dale's cameras. Had he done so deliberately? Jaeger had no way of knowing, and Kral wasn't exactly around to ask.

As to Narov, she was proving to be as much of a riddle wrapped in a mystery inside an enigma as that air wreck ever was. Jaeger figured she'd have stumped even Winston Churchill himself. He felt as if he knew her less now that when they'd first met. One way or another he was determined to crack her seemingly granite exterior, and get to the kernel of whatever truth lay within.

But back to the rain.

Rain was good because it needed clouds to fall from, and clouds blanketed the forest from whatever might be sitting high above. With hostile eyes watching from the skies, Jaeger felt that much more secure because of the rain clouds. As long as he and his team kept all use of communications and navigation kit to zero, they should remain unseen and undetected.

For a moment, Jaeger put himself into the mind of the enemy commander, whoever he might be. The last definite trace he had had of his prey – Jaeger and his team – would have been at the lip of the Devil's Falls. There, he'd have picked up both the coin's tracker trace and the video camera's GPS signal.

After that, an hour's silence, and then a tracker trace and maybe a cell phone roaming signal moving downriver on the Rio de los Dios.

The enemy commander would have to work on the assumption that Jaeger and his team were on the water; he would have no other intelligence to go on. And it was upon that deception – one that had been masterminded by Irina Narov – that Jaeger was gambling much of their future.

He figured that any smart commander – and Jaeger never liked to underestimate his enemy – would have a belt-and-braces approach. He'd track the kayak, waiting for a break in the cloud cover to verify who and what it might be carrying, in preparation for launching a final Hellfire strike.

But at the same time he'd get his ground force in to that air wreck double quick, to get boots on the ground at the target.

The race was on. And right now, by Puruwehua's calculations, Jaeger and his team were a good day's march or more in the lead. The air wreck lay less than eighteen hours away. All being well, they would reach it the following morning. But Jaeger wasn't kidding himself that the journey from here on was going to be easy.

The rain brought out the worst of the jungle.

As they trekked ever onwards, Puruwehua pointed out the changes wrought by the downpour. Some were obvious: at times Jaeger and his team found themselves wading through patches of jungle that were flooded up to waist height. Unidentified creatures plopped, slopped and slithered through the shallows, and iridescent water snakes roped through the shadows.

Puruwehua indicated one particularly evil-looking serpent: it was striped black, blue and two shades of red. 'This one – no need to worry so much,' he explained. '*Mbojovyuhua*; it eats frogs and small fish. It bites, but the bite doesn't kill.'

He turned to Jaeger. 'It is the big *mbojuhua* you need to be wary of. That one is as long as five people laid end to end, and as thick as any caiman. It is black and white spotted, and it will grab you in its jaws, wrap you tight, then squeeze. The pressure will break every bone in your body, and it won't stop squeezing until it cannot feel your heartbeat any more. Then it swallows you whole.'

'Nice,' Jaeger muttered. 'A constrictor with a real bad attitude. My next favourite after piranhas.'

Puruwehua smiled. Jaeger could tell that the Indian got something of a kick out of putting the shits up the team.

'Even worse is the *tenhukikiuhũa*,' Puruwehua warned. 'You know this one? It is a grey lizard about the size of a forest pig, with black squares all down its back. It has feet like hands, with suckers. Its bite is very poisonous. We say it is worse than any snake.'

'Don't tell me,' Jaeger snorted. 'It comes out only when it rains?'

'Worse: it lives only in the flooded forest. It is a fine swimmer; an excellent climber of trees. It has white eyes like a ghost, and if you try to grab it by the tail, the tail breaks free. That is the *tenhukikīuhūa's* means of escape.'

'Why would you ever want to *grab* it?' a voice interjected. It was Alonzo's; the big American seemed about as disgusted at this lizard thing as Jaeger was.

'To eat, of course,' Puruwehua replied. 'As long as you can avoid getting bitten, *tenhukikīuhūa* tastes very good – like a cross between fish and chicken.'

Alonzo snorted. 'Kentucky Fried! Somehow I don't think so.'

It was something of a cliché to describe survival food as tasting like chicken. As both Jaeger and Alonzo knew, it rarely if ever did.

Other changes brought by the rain were less obvious, and known only to the Indians. Puruwehua showed them a narrow hole in the forest floor. Jaeger presumed it was a rodent's burrow. In fact, Puruwehua explained, it was home to the *tairyvuhua*, a fish that lived underground, hibernating in the mud and only coming to life when it rained.

An hour before dusk, they stopped to eat. Jaeger had placed his team on 'hard routine': no fires or cooking allowed – meaning fewer traces for an enemy to track. But hard routine was never much fun. It meant boil-in-the-bag military rations eaten cold and cheerless from the pouch.

It might cure your hunger, but it did little for morale.

63

Jaeger sat on a fallen log and munched on a bag of what was supposedly chicken and pasta but which tasted like congealed glue. His mind drifted to memories of hippy Annie's carrot cake, back on her barge in London. Probably raining there too, he reflected ruefully.

He finished off with a handful of dry biscuits, but still he could feel the pangs of hunger gnawing at his stomach.

Alonzo dropped his backpack and plonked himself down beside Jaeger. 'Ouch!' He rubbed his backside, where the piranha had bitten him.

'How does it feel to be bested by a fish?' Jaeger needled him.

'Freakin' piranha,' Alonzo growled. 'Can't take a goddam crap without thinking about goddam fish bites.'

Jaeger glanced around at the dripping vegetation. 'So, the fates seemed to have smiled on us at last.'

'You mean the rain? Damn rainforest livin' up to its name. Let's just hope it holds right through.'

'Puruwehua says it's rain that lasts for days and days.'

'Puruwehua should know.' Alonzo clutched at his stomach. 'Man, I could murder a McDonald's. Double Quarter Pounder with cheese, fries, and a Triple Thick chocolate shake.'

Jaeger smiled. 'We get through this, I'm buying.'

'Deal.' Alonzo paused. 'You know, I've been thinking. Doesn't happen much, so pay special attention. We got us a Predator on the hunt. Only a few governments in the world operate that kind of hardware.'

Jaeger nodded. 'Can't be the Brazilians. Even if they do have Predator, which I doubt, Colonel Evandro's watching our backs.' He cast a sideways glance at Alonzo. 'Most likely scenario – it's your fellow Americans.'

Alonzo grimaced. 'Man, don't I know it. South America: it's our backyard. Always has been. But you know how it is: lot of agencies out there – lot of 'em are borderline rogue.' He paused. 'Whoever it is operatin' that Predator, what're they gonna make of the Airlander? You thought about that?'

'It's got good cover,' Jaeger replied. 'Colonel Evandro's assigned it B-SOB special mission status. It's terra incognita out there, and the Brazilians have had flights out surveying the borders for months now. The Airlander's flying the Brazilian flag, plus B-SOB colours, like it's on a bona fide survey mission.'

'You figure it'll work? Bad guys won't smell a rat when it's sat right above us?'

'The Airlander cruises at ten thousand feet. Predator orbits at around twice that. Airlander will be sitting there clear for all to see, hiding in plain sight. Plus it doesn't need to be anywhere near us. With its surveillance technologies – with PWAS – it can keep watch from several miles away.'

'Goddam better be right, Jaeger, or we're toast.'

Jaeger glanced at Alonzo, who was likewise tucking into a cold boil-in-the-bag. 'So, you got anyone you could call?' he ventured. 'Like in spec ops? Try to get a fix on who the hell it is hunting us? See if whoever's unleashed their dogs of war can be persuaded to call them off again?'

Alonzo shrugged. 'I'm a SEAL reservist, rank of master sergeant. I do know folks in that world. But post 9/11, you know how many spec ops agencies there are out there?'

'Hundreds?' Jaeger ventured.

Alonzo snorted. 'Right now, there are eight hundred and fifty thousand Americans with top-secret clearance. There are twelve hundred government agencies working on secret projects

– largely counter-terrorism – plus two thousand privately contracted companies.'

'That's . . . hard to believe.' Jaeger shook his head. 'It's messed up.'

'No, man, it's not. That alone isn't. It's what comes next that is truly unbelievable.' He glanced at Jaeger. 'In 2003, the President was persuaded to sign an EXORD: a presidential executive order. It gave his blessing for those eight hundred and fifty thousand guys to do pretty much as they please; to mount operations without any need for clearance. In other words, to act with zero presidential oversight.'

'So whoever's deployed that Predator, it could be one of a thousand different outfits?'

'Pretty much, yeah,' Alonzo confirmed. 'And whatever son-of-a-bitch is trying to take us out, that's how they'll be operating – deep in the black. Trust me – no one knows what anyone is doing out there. And with an EXORD like that, no one thinks they have the right to challenge anything, or even to ask.'

'Crazy.'

'You got it.' Alonzo glanced at Jaeger. 'So, yeah, I could call a couple of people. But honestly, I'd be pissing in the wind.' He paused. 'Can you run through our exfil strategy one last time?'

'Think of the Airlander as a massive lozenge-shaped airship,' Jaeger began. 'It's got four propulsors, one at each corner, via which it can make a direct thrust and lift in any direction: up, down, back, front, sideways. The flight deck is situated in the centre of the underside, between twin air-cushion landing systems – basically a pair of mini hovercrafts situated to either side of the hull.'

He grabbed one of his uneaten biscuits to represent the airship. 'It can move or hover at any altitude, in any direction. It's fitted with internal winches and cranes, to enable loading and unloading. Plus the main cabin holds up to fifty passengers. Best-case scenario, we confirm on the ground that the Airlander's safe to come in. She drops to low altitude, hovers over the jungle, we throw some airlift slings around the warplane, and she lifts it out of there – us with it.

'That's the plan if we get there well ahead of the bad guys,' Jaeger continued. 'And if the toxic threat proves manageable on the ground. The Airlander's slow. She cruises at around two hundred kph. But she's got a three and a half thousand kilometre range. That's more than enough to get us back to Cachimbo, and a rendezvous with Colonel Evandro.'

Jaeger shrugged. 'Worst-case scenario is the toxic threat's a killer, the Airlander can't do the lift and we're left running for our lives.'

Alonzo rubbed his chin pensively. 'I sure hope we ain't headin' for scenario number two.'

'*Evo'ipeva*,' a voice called over. It was Puruwehua, and he had something dark and bloody gripped between his fingers. 'I do not know the English word. Rain brings them out; they suck the blood.'

'Leeches,' Jaeger muttered. 'Bloody leeches.'

Alonzo shuddered. 'Yeah, and monsters by the looks of 'em.'

Puruwehua indicated his legs and groin area. 'We Amahuaca wear no trousers, so we can see them to pull them off. But you . . . you will need to check.'

Jaeger and Alonzo glanced at each other.

'Rank before beauty,' Alonzo announced. 'Schlong the size of mine, they got the whole nine yards to feast upon.'

Jaeger got to his feet reluctantly. He undid his trousers and his belt, and dropped his pants. Even in the dim light he could see that his legs and groin were a mass of writhing, glistening bodies like short, stubby tentacles. Tiger leeches. God, how he hated them. Black body, slashed with stripes of violent yellow, each by now engorged to five times its normal size.

When the first leech had slithered up Jaeger's trouser leg, searching for somewhere warm and moist to attach itself, it had been the size of a small pen lid, no bigger. Now, after a few hours' feeding, each was the size of a thick marker pen and swollen fat with Jaeger's blood.

'Lighter?' Alonzo offered.

The most satisfying way to get rid of them was to burn the bastards off. The second most satisfying method was to dose them in insect repellent and watch them twist and worm.

Jaeger held out his hand for the lighter. 'Thanks.'

He knew he really shouldn't. Leeches secreted an anaesthetic in their saliva, so the victim didn't feel their bite. Once attached, they pumped hirudin, a powerful enzyme, into the victim's veins, to stop the blood from clotting – enabling them to feed and feed and feed.

If you put a naked flame to one, it immediately contracted, withdrew its teeth and dropped off – but in the process it voided much of its stomach contents back into your bloodstream. In other words, it vomited all the blood back into your veins, including any diseases it might be carrying.

But Jaeger hated tiger leeches with a vengeance, and he couldn't resist the urge to get even. He flicked the lighter, lowered the flame and watched the first of the swollen black tentacles hiss, writhe and burn.

'We've got Hellfire missiles trying to blow us to shit . . . I'll happily risk burning a few of these bastards off.'

Alonzo laughed. 'Yeah – that's one battle we can win.'

After a few seconds, the leech dropped, leaving a stream of blood pouring down Jaeger's leg. The wound would bleed for some time, but he figured it was worth it.

He had tortured the leech in two ways: one, it had lost its precious meal of blood; and two, it would never recover from the burns.

64

By the time they'd finished burning off the leeches, it was last light. Jaeger figured they'd set camp where they were. He sent word round his team. But as hammocks and ponchos were slung between dark trees slick with rain, he noticed that one amongst their number was in trouble.

He moved across to Dale, who'd yet to change out of his wet gear. The cameraman had swung his legs into his hammock, and was lying back seemingly ready for sleep. He had his film kit clutched to his chest, and was using a can of compressed air to blow-brush the worst of the gunk and the moisture out of his camera.

It had to be tough keeping such equipment functioning in these kind of conditions. Dale was religious about his evening kit-cleaning ritual, and many were the nights when he'd fallen into an exhausted sleep holding his camera like a kid would a teddy bear.

'Dale, you don't look too good,' Jaeger prompted.

A head appeared over the side of the hammock. The cameraman's face looked horribly pale and drawn. Jaeger didn't doubt that Dale had yet to discover his load of leeches, for only by changing out of his wet gear would he do so.

'Just so totally knackered,' Dale muttered. 'Gotta clean my gear and sleep.'

Nine days in the jungle had taken a heavy toll. Doubly so on Dale, who was tasked to film the entire expedition in addition to being a part of it. Whereas the others found a little time for basic body hygiene, Dale seemed to spend every spare moment cleaning his gear, changing batteries and backing up whatever he'd filmed on to a spare drive.

Plus he had all the extra weight of the film equipment to carry. On several occasions Jaeger had offered to share the burden, but Dale had demurred. His excuse had been that he needed his kit close at hand, but in truth Jaeger figured that he was just a proud and determined operator – and he respected that.

'You've got to change into dry gear,' Jaeger told him. 'If you don't, you're finished.'

Dale stared, a crushing fatigue etched in his eyes. 'I've hit the wall. Truly hit the wall.'

Jaeger delved into one of his pouches, pulling out a high-energy bar – part of his emergency rations. 'Here – get that down you. Plus there's one other thing you've got to deal with right now. No way to break this to you gently: leeches.'

It was Dale's first close encounter with the revolting parasites, and it would prove a particularly traumatic one. Due to his habit of stopping regularly to film, and often crouching on the wet forest floor to get a low-angle shot, he'd presented the easiest of targets. As a result, he had a bumper harvest.

Jaeger offered him the lighter. As a horrified Dale went about burning off the leeches, Jaeger struck up a conversation to help get his mind off the task at hand.

'So, how's it been without Kral?'

Dale glanced at him. 'Truthfully?'

'Truthfully.'

'The downside – I've got more weight to carry, 'cause Kral and me spread it across the two of us. The upside – I don't have that ugly leech carping on the whole time, bitter, angry and self-centred. So on balance, I'm better off.' He smiled, exhausted. 'But I could do without *these* leeches.'

'One thing's for sure – the two of you were on shaky ground from the very start. What was it with you guys?'

'Tell you a story,' Dale muttered, as he put the flame to another fat leech. 'I'm an Aussie by birth, but my dad sent me to a fine English boarding school – a place where they beat any residual Aussieness out of me along with my accent.

'The school was renowned for its sport. Trouble was, I hated the staples – rugby, hockey and cricket. Was crap at them too. In short, I was a resounding disappointment to my father. There were only two things that I excelled at. One was rock-climbing; the other was using a camera.'

'A fellow rock jock; that was my thing at school too. It's a good skill to have in this kind of game.'

'My dad's a high-flying Sydney lawyer,' Dale continued. 'When I refused to follow him into the law and opted for a media career, he reacted like I'd been caught dealing drugs or something. Cut me off. So I threw myself into the shark pool of the London media, to doubly mess him up.

'I had no option but to sink, swim or get eaten. I chose to specialise in remote-area and high-risk filming. But it's a hand-to-mouth existence. Totally. Kral could afford to run at the first sign of trouble. I can't. Not if I want to prove the naysayers – *my father* – wrong.

'High-risk adventure filming – it's what I do. If I quit when it gets too lively, what do I have? Nothing.' Dale fixed Jaeger with a very direct look. 'So screw Kral, with his resentment and his envy. But truth be told – I'm shitting myself out here'

De-leeching done, Jaeger volunteered to cover Dale's watch duties so he could get a full night's rest. For once, the Australian agreed to the offer of help. Somehow it seemed to signal that the most unlikely of friendships was being forged between the two of them.

As he sat his first sentry, staring into the night-dark forest, Jaeger found himself wondering if he'd misjudged the man. Dale had an independent, maverick streak and a think-outside-the-box mentality – the kind of qualities that Jaeger had valued in his men when in the military.

Had they travelled different life paths, it was just conceivable that Jaeger might have ended up as the war cameraman, and Dale the elite forces warrior.

More than most, Jaeger knew how a man's destiny could turn on a dime.

65

When Jaeger was relieved of his watch duty, he found that someone else around the camp was still awake – Leticia Santos.

He wandered over, figuring he'd remind her to check for leeches. Santos was already on top of the problem, and she found his obvious discomfort – especially when he suggested she might want to check her female parts – highly amusing.

'Eight years with B-SOB, five with FUNAI,' she reminded him. 'I've grown used to checking around those areas!'

Jaeger smiled. 'That's a relief. So why the move?' he asked, crouching down beside her. 'From hunting bad guys to saving Indians?'

'Two reasons,' Santos replied. 'First, I realised we can't stop the narco gangs unless we protect the jungle. It's where they run their drugs and where they hide. And to do that we need the help of the Amazonian tribes. Brazilian law says that their lands – their forest home – have to be protected. So, if we can contact and safeguard the Indians, it's also the key to saving the Amazon.'

She eyed Jaeger. 'If this was your country and you possessed this great wonder – the Amazon rainforest – would you not also want to safeguard it?'

'Of course. And the second reason?' Jaeger prompted.

'I lost my marriage due to my work with B-SOB,' Santos answered quietly. 'A career in special ops is never a recipe for a long and happy marriage, no? Always on call. So many secrets.

Never able to plan anything. So many cancelled holidays, birthdays, anniversaries. My husband complained I was never there for him.' She paused. 'I don't want my daughter to grow up and level the same accusation at me.'

Jaeger nodded. 'I get that. I left the military shortly after I started a family. But it's a tough one, for sure.'

Santos glanced at Jaeger's left hand; the only adornment was a single gold band. 'You are married, yes? And with children?'

'I am. One son. Though . . . Well, it's a long story.' Jaeger stared off into the brooding jungle. 'Put it this way – they're lost to me . . .' His words petered out to nothing.

Santos reached out and placed a hand on his arm. Her eyes searched his face with undisguised warmth. 'To be alone is hard. If you ever need a friendly ear – you know you can count on me.'

Jaeger thanked her. He got to his feet. 'We need to get some rest. *Dorme bem*, Leticia. Sweet dreams.'

Jaeger awoke hours later, a sweaty bundle of screaming.

His hammock was swinging wildly to and fro, from where he'd been thrashing about, fighting the monsters that so often seemed to assail him in his dreams.

It had been a repeat of the nightmare – the one he'd last had in his Wardour Castle apartment. Again it had taken him up to the very moment of his wife and child being snatched away from him – and then an impenetrable wall had crashed down.

He gazed around: the darkness was so complete that he could barely see his hand in front of his face. Then he heard it: movement. Someone – or something – was creeping through the thick bush.

His hand slipped out of the hammock and felt for his combat shotgun.

A voice came to him from the darkness. 'It is Puruwehua. I heard you screaming.'

Jaeger relaxed.

In a way, he wasn't surprised that his cries had woken the Indian. Puruwehua had slung his hammock adjacent to his own. And far better him than some of the others – for Jaeger trusted the Amahuaca warrior just about as much as he trusted anyone right now.

Puruwehua squatted beside him. 'The lost memories – they are in there, Koty'ar,' he remarked quietly. 'You just need to allow yourself to unlock them; to go there.'

Jaeger stared into the darkness. 'Every returning soldier and failed father has nightmares.'

'Still, you carry much darkness,' Puruwehua told him. 'Much pain.'

Silence for a long second.

'You have light?' Puruwehua prompted.

Jaeger switched on his head torch, keeping it shielded inside the hammock so that it cast a faint greenish glow. Puruwehua handed him a cup, brimful with liquid. 'Drink this. A jungle remedy. It will help you.'

Jaeger took the cup and thanked him. 'I'm sorry to have woken you, my warrior friend. Let's rest, and be ready for tomorrow.'

With that he drained the contents dry. But the calm he was expecting never came.

Instead, he felt an immediate burst of pain to the inside of his skull, as though someone had kicked him hard in the eye socket. Moments later, his senses started to fail. He felt hands holding him down, and Puruwehua's distinctive voice murmuring soothing words in his Amahuaca dialect.

Then, quite suddenly, the insides of Jaeger's eyelids seemed to explode into a kaleidoscope of colours, fading gradually into a bright yellow canvas.

The image intensified and became clearer. Jaeger was lying on his back in a tent, two sleeping bags zipped together, warm and cosy with his wife and child beside him. But something had woken him, pulling him out of a deep sleep into the cold reality of a Welsh winter.

His head torch played across the yellow canvas above as he tried to zero in on the disturbance and the threat. All of a sudden, a long blade came thrusting through the tent's thin side. As Jaeger went to react, fighting his way out of the constrictions of the sleeping bag, there was a hiss from a nozzle thrust through the opening.

Thick gas filled the tent, knocking Jaeger backwards and freezing his limbs. He saw hands reach in, dark faces clad in respirators above them, and moments later his wife and child were dragged out of the warmth and into the darkness.

They couldn't even scream, for the gas had incapacitated them as much as it had Jaeger. He was helpless; helpless to defend himself, or, more importantly, his wife and child.

He heard the snarl of a powerful engine; the cry of voices, the slamming of doors, as something – someone – was dragged towards a vehicle. With a superhuman force of will he made himself crawl towards the knife slash in the tent. He thrust his head outside.

He caught barely a glimpse, but it was enough. In the glare of headlights reflecting off a dusting of frost and snow he saw two figures – one slight and boyish; the other lithe and female – bundled into the rear of a 4x4.

The next moment, Jaeger was grabbed by the roots of his hair. His head was forced upwards, so that he was staring through the glass eyelets of a gas mask into hate-filled eyes. A gloved fist hammered out of the darkness with massive force, slamming into Jaeger's face once, twice, three times, blood from his broken nose spattering across the snow.

'Take a good long look,' the face behind the mask hissed, as he twisted Jaeger savagely towards the 4x4. The words were muffled, but still he caught their meaning, the voice somehow sounding chillingly familiar. 'Get this moment burned into your brain. Your wife and child – they're ours.'

The mask bent lower, so the front of the respirator was pressing into Jaeger's bloodied features. 'Don't ever forget – you failed to protect your wife and child. *Wir sind die Zukunft!*'

The eyes were wide behind the glass eyelets, pumped with adrenalin, and it struck Jaeger that he knew the face behind that manic gaze. He knew it, yet at the same time he didn't know it, for he couldn't put a name to those hate-twisted features. Moments later the horrific scene – the unspeakable memories – faded, but not before one image had lodged in Jaeger's mind irrevocably . . .

When finally he came back to his senses in his hammock, Jaeger was feeling utterly drained. The most abiding image of the attack hadn't exactly surprised him. In his heart he'd been expecting it; dreading it. He'd feared it was there, embedded in the darkness of that snow-washed Welsh hillside.

Etched into the hilt of the knife that had sliced through the tent was a dark iconic image: a *Reichsadler*.

66

Puruwehua kept a vigil besides Jaeger's hammock all through the lonely night hours. He alone understood what Jaeger was going through. The drink he'd given him was laced with *nyakwana*, the key to unlocking so many powerful images buried deep in the mind. He knew the white man would be shaken to his very core.

At dawn, neither spoke about what had happened. Somehow it didn't need words.

But the whole of that morning Jaeger was moody and withdrawn, trapped inside the shell of the memories that had resurfaced. Physically, he set one foot in front of the other as he trekked through the damp and dripping jungle, but mentally he was in an entirely different place, his mind entombed within a shredded tent on an icy Welsh mountainside.

His team couldn't help but notice his change of mood, though few could fathom the reason. This close to the air wreck – its discovery now within their grasp – they had expected Jaeger to be utterly energised; to be leading the charge. But quite the contrary: he seemed locked in a dark and lonely place that excluded all others.

It was pushing four years ago now when his wife and child had disappeared. Jaeger had been training for the Pen y Fan Challenge – a twenty-four-kilometre race over the Welsh mountains. It was Christmas, and he, Ruth and Luke had decided to spend it in a novel way, camped out in the Welsh foothills. It had been the perfect excuse to be together in the mountains – something that little Luke loved – and for Jaeger to get in some extra training. It was their family adventure combo, as he'd jokingly told Ruth.

They'd set camp near the start of the race. The Pen y Fan Challenge was inspired by British special forces selection. In one of the toughest stages, candidates had to ascend the almost sheer face of the Fan, descend Jacob's Ladder, then push onwards along the undulating old Roman road, at the end of which they'd hit the turnaround point and do it all again in reverse.

It had become known as 'the Fan Dance', and was a brutal test of speed, stamina and fitness – things that Jaeger found came naturally to him. Though retired from the military, he still liked to remind himself every now and then what he was capable of.

They'd gone to sleep that night with Jaeger's body aching from a hard day's training, and his wife and son likewise exhausted from mountain-biking across the snowy lowlands. Jaeger's next conscious memory had been of coming to his senses a week later in intensive care – only to learn that Ruth and Luke were missing.

The gas used against them had been identified as Kolokol-1, a little-known Russian knockout agent that took effect in between one and three seconds. It was generally non-fatal – unless the victim suffered prolonged exposure in a closed environment – but even so it had taken Jaeger months to fully recover.

The police had discovered the boot of Jaeger's car stuffed full of Christmas presents for his family – ones that would now never be opened. Apart from the 4x4's tyre tracks, no trace of his missing wife and child had been found. It had appeared to be a motiveless abduction, not to mention possible murder.

While Jaeger wasn't exactly the prime suspect, at times the line of questioning had left him wondering. The more any motive or leads had evaded the police, the more they had seemed to want to dig for reasons in Jaeger's past as to why he might have wanted to make his wife and child disappear.

They'd trawled his military records, highlighting any history of extreme trauma that might have triggered post-traumatic stress disorder. Anything that might account for such apparently unaccountable behaviour. They'd questioned his closest friends. Plus they'd grilled his family relentlessly – his parents in particular – about whether there were any problems in his marriage.

That had in part precipitated his mother and father's move to Bermuda – to escape the unwarranted intrusions. They'd stuck around to help him through the worst, but when he'd gone AWOL and fled to Bioko, they'd likewise seized the chance for a clean start. By then the trail had gone utterly cold anyway. Ruth and Luke had been missing almost a year, presumed dead, and in the relentless search Jaeger had come close to tearing himself apart.

It had taken days, months – and now years – for the hidden recollections of that dark night to start bleeding back to the surface. And now this: he'd reclaimed some of the very last of the memories, those most deeply buried, at the hands of an Amahuaca warrior and a good dose of a *nyakwana*-infused drink.

Of course, it wasn't any old *Reichsadler* that he'd seen on that knife hilt. It was the same design that his great uncle Joe had found so utterly terrifying in a cabin deep in the Scottish hills. His words flashed into Jaeger's mind now, as he trudged through the sodden jungle, along with the look of sheer terror that had flitted across his gaze.

And then this precious boy comes here with that. Ein Reichsadler! That damn cursed damnation! It seems as if the evil has returned . . .

According to the Amahuaca Indian chief, it was a similar *Reichsadler* that had been carved into the bodies of his two captured warriors – and by the same force with which Jaeger and his team were locked in a life-and-death struggle.

But what confounded Jaeger most was that he seemed to

have recognised the voice spitting at him from behind the gas mask. Yet as much as he might rack his brains, no name or image came into his mind.

If he did somehow know his chief tormentor, the man's identity remained utterly lost to him.

67

It was approaching midday on their tenth day in the jungle by the time Jaeger had started to shake free of his malaise. It was their impending arrival at the air wreck that had dragged him out of the dark and troubling past.

In spite of that morning's disquiet, Jaeger still had his pebbles and compass gripped in hand. He figured they were maybe 3,000 yards short of the line at which the forest would start to die. Beyond that it would be only the bleached bones of toxic dead wood leading up to the wreck itself.

They entered a particularly sodden patch of jungle.

'*Yaporuamuhũa*,' Puruwehua announced, as they began to wade deeper. 'Flooded forest. When the water becomes this big, the piranhas tend to swim in from the rivers. They feed on anything they can find.'

The dark water was swirling around Jaeger's waist. 'Thanks for the warning,' he muttered.

'They are only aggressive when driven by hunger,' Puruwehua tried to reassure him. 'After such rains, there should be plenty for them to eat.'

'And if they *are* feeling hungry?' Jaeger queried.

Puruwehua glanced at the nearest tree. 'You must get out of the water. Quickly.'

Jaeger spotted something sleek and silvery streaking through the shallows beside him. Another and another darted past, one or two brushing against his legs. The bodies looked silky-green on the dorsal surface, with large yellow eyes turned upwards, and two rows of massive teeth likes spines.

'They're all around us,' Jaeger hissed.

'Not to worry – this is good. This is very good. *Andyrapepo-tiguhūa*. Vampire fish. It eats piranhas. It spears them with its long teeth.'

'Right, let's keep 'em close – at least until we reach that warplane.'

The water deepened. It was almost at chest height now. 'Soon time to swim like the *pirau'ndia*,' Puruwehua remarked. 'It is a fish that holds itself vertical, with its head out of the water.'

Jaeger didn't reply.

He'd had enough of fetid water, mosquitoes, leeches, caimans and fish jaws to last him a lifetime. He wanted to get hooked up to that aircraft, lift himself and his team out of there, and start searching for his missing family.

It was time to finish the expedition and start afresh. At the end of this crazed road he felt certain he'd know his wife and son's fate one way or the other. Or if not, he'd have died in the attempt to discover it. Living in the half-light as he had been was not living at all. This was what his awakening had shown him.

Jaeger could feel Puruwehua's eyes upon him as they walked onwards in silence.

'You have a clearer mind now, my friend?'

Jaeger nodded. 'Time to wrest back control from those who seek to destroy your world, Puruwehua, and mine.'

'We call it *hama*,' Puruwehua remarked knowingly. 'Fate or destiny.'

For a while they waded on in companionable silence.

Jaeger felt a presence in the water beside him. It was Irina Narov. Like the rest of his team she was moving ahead holding her main weapon – a Dragunov sniper rifle – high out of the water, in an effort to keep it dirt free and dry. It was backbreaking work, but with the air wreck so close, she seemed driven by a relentless energy.

The Dragunov was an odd choice of weapon for the jungle, where combat was invariably at close quarters, but Narov had insisted it was the weapon for her. Sensibly, she'd opted for an SVDS – the compact, lightweight variant of the gun.

But it hadn't escaped Jaeger's notice that her two chosen weapons – the knife and the sniper rifle – were so often the tools of the assassin. The assassin; the loner. There was something about Narov that set her apart, that was for certain, but there was also a part of Jaeger that found those traits oddly familiar.

His son's best friend at school, a boy called Daniel, had exhibited some of Narov's characteristics: his speech had been oddly matter-of-fact and direct, sometimes seemingly bordering on the rude. He'd often failed to pick up on the social cues that came naturally to most kids. And he'd found it painfully difficult making and holding eye contact – not until he really knew and trusted someone.

It had taken Daniel a good while to learn to trust Luke, but once he'd done so, he'd proved the most loyal and constant of friends. They'd competed over everything: rugby, air hockey, even at the local paintball facility. But it had only ever been the healthy competition between best friends, and they'd stuck up for each other against all outsiders.

When Luke had disappeared, Daniel had been devastated. He'd lost his one true companion – his battle buddy. Just as Jaeger had.

Over time, Jaeger and Ruth had become friendly with Daniel's parents. They'd confided in them that Daniel had been diagnosed with Asperger's, or high-functioning autism – the experts didn't appear sure which exactly. As with many such kids, Daniel proved to be obsessed by and brilliant at one thing: mathematics. That, plus he had a magical way with animals.

Jaeger cast his mind back to the close encounter they'd had with the *Phoneutria*. Something had struck him then, although he hadn't quite realised what it was. Narov had acted almost as if she had a relationship with the venomous spiders – like she understood them. She'd been reluctant to kill even one of them, not until there was no other option.

And if there was one thing that Narov would obsess over and excel at, Jaeger had a good idea what it might be: the hunt and the kill.

'How far?' she demanded, her voice cutting through his thoughts.

'How far to what?'

'The air wreck. What else is there?'

Jaeger pointed ahead. 'Around eight hundred metres. You see where the light breaks through the canopy – that's where the forest starts to die.'

'So close,' she whispered.

'*Wir sind die Zukunft.*' Jaeger repeated the line that he'd heard in the closing stages of his *nyakwana*-induced vision. 'You speak German. *Wir sind die Zukunft*. What does it mean?'

Narov stopped dead. She stared at him for a long second, her eyes frozen. 'Where did you hear that?'

'An echo from my past.' Why did this woman always have to answer a question with a question? 'So, what does it mean?'

'*Wir sind die Zukunft,*' Narov repeated, slowly and very deliberately. 'We are the future. It was the rallying cry of the *Herrenrasse* – the Nazi master race. Whenever Hitler tired of *Denn heute gehort uns Deutschland, und morgen die ganze Welt*, he'd try a bit of *Wir sind die Zukunft*. The people lapped it up.'

'How come you know so much about it?' Jaeger demanded.

'Know your enemy,' Narov replied cryptically. 'I make it my business to know.' She threw Jaeger a look that struck him as being almost accusatory. 'The question is – how do you know so little?' She paused. 'So little about your own past.'

68

Before Jaeger could answer, there was a terrified scream from behind. He turned to see a blaze of fear flash across Leticia Santos's features as she was dragged beneath the water. She broke the surface, arms flailing desperately, her face a mask of terror, before she was ripped under once more.

Jaeger had caught the briefest glimpse of what had hold of her. It was one of the massive waterborne snakes that Puruwehua had warned him about: a constrictor. He charged through the shallows, diving for the deadly serpent and grappling with its tail as he frantically tried to wrest the coils free from her body.

He couldn't use his shotgun. If he opened fire he'd blast Santos at the same time as hitting the snake. The water thrashed and boiled, Santos and the serpent entwined in a blur of snakeskin and limbs as she fought a battle that she could never win alone. The more that Jaeger fought it, the more the monster constrictor seemed to tighten its murderous grip around her.

Then from behind him Jaeger heard a sudden crack. It was the distinctive sound of a sniper rifle. At the same moment, somewhere in amongst the blur of snake and human, something erupted in a burst of blood and pulverised flesh as a high-velocity round hit home.

A second or so later the struggle was over, the snake's head hanging limp and lifeless. Jaeger could see where most of its skull had been blown away, the high-velocity sniper round leaving a telltale exit wound. One by one Jaeger started to unwind the dead coils, and along with Alonzo and Kamishi he hauled Santos free.

As the three of them tried to pump the water out of her lungs, Jaeger glanced at Narov. She was standing in the swamp, the Dragunov still at her shoulder in case she needed to take a second shot.

Santos spluttered back into life, coughing frantically, her chest heaving up and down. Jaeger made sure they'd got her stabilised, but she was badly traumatised, and still shaking with terror at the attack. Alonzo and Kamishi agreed to carry her the final stretch to the warplane, leaving Jaeger free to rejoin Narov at the head of the party.

'Nice shooting,' he remarked icily, once they were on the move again. 'But how could you be sure you were going to blow the snake's head off, and not Leticia's?'

Narov eyed him coldly. 'If someone hadn't taken the shot she would now be dead. Even with your help it was a losing battle. With this,' she patted the Dragunov, 'at least I stood chance. A fifty-fifty chance, but still better than none. Sometimes a bullet saves a life. They are not always fired to take one.'

'So you flipped the coin and pulled the trigger . . .' Jaeger lapsed into silence.

It didn't escape him that Narov's bullet could just as easily have hit him as Santos, yet she had barely hesitated before taking such a shot – such a gamble. He didn't know if that made her the ultimate professional or a psychopath.

Narov looked over her shoulder towards where the snake had been killed. 'It is a pity about the constrictor. It was only doing what comes naturally to it – trying to get a meal. The *mbojuhua*. *Boa constrictor imperator.* It is a CITES Appendix II listed species, which means it is in high danger of extinction.'

Jaeger glanced at her out of the corner of his eye. She seemed more concerned for the dead snake than she was for Leticia Santos. He figured if she was an assassin it made it far easier if all she really cared about was animals.

The ground rose as they neared the dead zone.

Ahead, Jaeger could see where the vegetation fell away on all sides. It was replaced by ranks of bare tree trunks bleached white in the sun, like endless rows of gravestones. Above lay a skeletal latticework of dead wood – what remained of the once verdant canopy – and above that again, a bank of low grey cloud.

They gathered on the brink of the zone wherein all life had died.

From ahead of him, Jaeger could hear the rain drumming deafeningly, instead of dripping from the leaf cover high above. It sounded unnatural somehow, the area of the dead zone seeming horribly empty and exposed.

He sensed Puruwehua shiver. 'The forest – it should never die,' the Indian remarked simply. 'When the forest dies, we Amahuaca die with it.'

'Don't go dying on us now, Puruwehua,' Jaeger muttered. 'You're our *koty'ar*, remember? We need you.'

They stared into the dead zone. Far ahead, Jaeger could just make out something dark and massive, half obscured among the bony fingers reaching towards the clouds. His pulse quickened. It was the barely discernible silhouette of a warplane. In spite of the previous night's vision – or maybe because of it – he longed to get inside it and uncover its secrets.

He eyed Puruwehua. 'Your people would warn us if the enemy were anywhere close? You've got men shadowing that Dark Force, right?'

Puruwehua nodded. 'We have. And we move faster than they do. Long before they get near we will know.'

'So how long d'you think we've got?' Jaeger asked.

'My people will try to give us one day's warning. One sunrise and one sunset before our work here must be done.'

69

'Okay, heads-up,' Jaeger announced, calling his team together.

They'd gathered in the cover of the last few yards of the still living forest. They were on higher ground, and it didn't look as if the flood waters ever reached this far.

'First, no one goes any nearer without full NBC gear. We need to ID the threat, at which stage we'll know the severity of what we're dealing with. Once we know the toxicity, we can work out a regime to better safeguard against it. We have three full NBC suits. I'd like to be first aboard, to take samples of water and air and whatever else we find. We can then rotate protective kit around the team, but we've got to keep the risk of cross-contamination to a minimum.

'We'll set a base camp here,' he continued. 'Sling hammocks well away from the dead ground. And understand the urgency: Puruwehua reckons we have twenty-four hours before we get a visit from the bad guys. We should get early warning from his people, but I'd like a cordon of security thrown around the site as well. Alonzo – that's something I'd like you to get sorted.'

'You got it,' Alonzo confirmed. He nodded towards the distant warplane. 'That thing – man, it gives me the creeps. Don't mind if I'm the last to see inside.'

'You okay to stand security?' Jaeger asked Leticia Santos. 'Or you need us to sling you a poncho and hammock? That was one hell of a snake you picked a fight with back there.'

'As long as I can keep out of the water,' Santos replied bravely.

She eyed Narov. 'And as long as the crazy Cossack keeps her sniper rifle pointed in someone else's direction.'

Narov's attention was elsewhere. She seemed utterly transfixed; unable to tear her eyes away from the distant silhouette of the warplane.

Jaeger turned to Dale. 'I presume you want to film this – and make no mistake, I want it filmed. The first opening of this aircraft after seven decades – this needs to be recorded. You take the second NBC suit so you can follow me in.'

Dale shrugged. 'How bad can it get? Can't be worse than facing down a shoal of piranhas, or a crotch full of leeches.'

It was the kind of response Jaeger had come to expect from the guy. Dale wore his fear on his sleeve, but it wasn't about to stop him from doing what was necessary.

Jaeger eyed Narov. 'I get a sense you know more about this warplane than anyone: you take the third suit. You can help guide us around whatever we find in there.'

Narov nodded, but her gaze was still fixed on the distant plane.

'Puruwehua, I'd like you to get your guys out deep into the forest, forming an early-warning screen in case of trouble. The rest of you – you're on Alonzo's security cordon. And remember, zero use of comms or GPS. Last thing we want is to send a warning signal to whoever's keeping watch.'

That agreed, Jaeger broke out the nuclear, biological, chemical protective gear. The threat from whatever toxic material was leaking from that aircraft was twofold: one, breathing it in; two, ingesting it via a living porous membrane like the skin.

With the need to carry all their kit on their person, they'd only been able to bring three full NBC suits. They were a lightweight design, made by the British company Avon, and would protect the body from any droplets or vapour that might remain in the air.

With the suit went the Avon C50 mask – which with its single eyepiece, high protection and close-fitting design was a superlative piece of kit. It was the mask – the respirator – that shielded the face and eyes and prevented the lungs from breathing in any toxic material.

Once fully suited up, they'd be shielded from just about any chemical, biological, nuclear or radiological threat, plus toxic industrial chemicals – which should encompass every conceivable hazard lurking on that warplane.

As a bonus, each Avon mask carried an embedded transmitter-receiver, which meant that those wearing them could speak to each other via a short-range radio intercom.

Having fought his way into the cumbersome suit, Jaeger paused. He figured he'd power up the Thuraya and check for any data-burst messages. Once he pulled on the bulky mask and gloves, there would be no easy way to use such equipment.

Jaeger held the satphone in the open, and a message icon appeared on the screen. He stepped back beneath the cover of the jungle to read Raff's missive.

0800 Zulu – called all satphones. One + 882 16 7865 4378 answered, then immediately killed call. Gave a call-sign (?) sounded like White Wolf (?). Voice Eastern European accent. KRAL?? Come up comms – urgent confirm locstat.

Jaeger read the message three times over as he tried to fathom its import. Clearly Raff was worried as to their location and status (military speak: 'locstat'), or he wouldn't have risked making a voice call. Jaeger would have to send a quick data-burst response to let him know all were present and correct at the site of the air wreck.

Or rather, all bar one – Stefan Kral.

And in light of the message, Jaeger sensed that a dark cloud had fallen over their absent Slovakian cameraman.

He scrolled through the numbers held in speed-dial on his Thuraya, checking those of the other members of his team. In theory, they only had three satphones with them – his own, Alonzo's and Dale's – the rest having been left in the cache above the Devil's Falls.

Sure enough, number + 882 16 7865 4378 was a Thuraya that supposedly had been left behind.

Jaeger cast his mind back to 0800 Zulu that morning. They'd just broken camp and recommenced their trek. None of his team would have been able to receive Raff's call. But if Kral had hidden a Thuraya in his kit, he was quite capable of taking a call at the Amahuaca village clearing.

Not to mention making calls as well.

The question was – why would he have hidden a satphone? And why the code name – if Raff had caught it right – White Wolf? And why had he immediately killed the call upon realising that it was from Raff in the Airlander?

Jaeger felt a horrible suspicion taking hold of him. Viewed in conjunction with Kral's failure to disable the GPS units on Dale's cameras, the only possible conclusion seemed to be that the Slovakian was the enemy within. If he was indeed a traitor, Jaeger felt doubly betrayed. He had been suckered right in by Kral's hard-done-by family-man act.

He called Puruwehua over. As quickly as he could, he explained what had happened.

'Can one of your men head back to the village and warn the chief? Tell him to hold Kral until we can get to him to question him. I'm not saying he's definitely guilty – but all evidence points that way. And remove all but his bare essentials, to prevent him making a break for it.'

'I will send one,' Puruwehua confirmed. 'One who can move fast. If he is an enemy to you, he is also an enemy to my people.'

Jaeger thanked the Indian. He sent Raff a brief update by data-burst, then returned to the task at hand.

He threw his shoulders forward, pulled apart the rear of the Avon gas mask and dragged the thing over his head, making sure that the rubber formed an airtight seal with the skin of his neck. He tightened the retaining straps, and felt it pull closer around the contours of his face.

He placed his hand over the respirator's filter, his palm making an airtight seal. He breathed in hard, sucking the mask tighter on to his face, so making doubly sure the seal was good. That done, he dragged in a few gasps of air through the filter, hearing the rasp and suck of his own breathing roaring in his ears.

He pulled the hood of the suit over his head, the elastic sealing around the edge of the mask. He dragged the bulky rubber over-boots on so they encased his jungle boots completely, then laced them up tight around his ankles. Last but not least, he pulled on the thin white cotton under-gloves, plus the heavy rubber over-mitts.

His world was now reduced to whatever he could see through the eyepiece of the gas mask. The dual filter sat to the front and the left, in an effort to prevent it from impeding the view, but already Jaeger was feeling claustrophobic, and he could sense the heat and the stuffiness starting to build.

Suited up, the three figures stepped out of the living jungle and into the wasteland.

70

After the chattering of birdlife and the buzz of insects in the green and leafy jungle, their entry into the dead zone seemed eerily quiet. The steady patter of the rain against Jaeger's hood beat out a regular rhythm to accompany the suck and rasp of his breathing, and all around, the terrain appeared devoid of life.

Rotten branches and bark squelched underfoot.

Where Jaeger's over-boots kicked aside such debris, he could see that insects had started to recolonise the dead zone. Swarms of ants with iron-clad skin scuttled about angrily beneath his footfalls. Plus there were his old friends from Black Beach Prison – cockroaches.

Ants and roaches: if there were ever a cataclysmic world war using nuclear or chemical weapons, it would be insects that would very likely inherit the earth. They were largely immune to man-made toxic threats, very likely including whatever might be leaking from that warplane.

The three figures pressed onwards in silence.

Jaeger could feel the tension emanating from Narov at his side. A step or two behind came Dale, filming. But he was struggling to keep the picture properly framed, with his hands encumbered by the thick gloves, and the gas mask restricting his vision.

They came to a halt fifty feet short – from where they could try to take in the enormity of what lay before them. It remained half shielded by cadaverous tree trunks – denuded of leaves and bark, and dead to the core – but still there was no mistaking the sleek, elegant lines of the gigantic aircraft that had lain hidden in the jungle for seven decades or more.

After the epic journey to get here, they were left gazing at it in silent wonder.

Even Dale had stopped filming to stare.

Everything had been building to this moment: so much research; so much planning; so many briefings; so much speculation as to what the aircraft might actually be; and, after the last few days, so much death and suffering along the way, as well as the cold steel of betrayal.

As he gazed upon it in wonder, Jaeger marvelled at how intact the aircraft appeared to be. He almost felt as if it simply needed that vital refuelling it had missed all those years ago, and it could fire up the engines and be ready to take to the skies once more.

He could quite understand why Hitler had trumpeted this aircraft as his Amerika Bomber. As Jenkinson, the archivist, had declared, it looked custom-made for dropping sarin nerve gas on New York.

Jaeger stood entranced.

What in God's name was it doing here? he wondered. What had its mission been? And if it was the last of four such flights, as the Amahuaca chief had told them, what was it – *what were they all* – carrying?

Jaeger had only ever seen one photo of a Junkers Ju 390.

It was an old black-and-white shot that Jenkinson had emailed to him – one of the very few images that existed of the warplane. It had shown a dark and sleek six-engined aircraft – one so massive that it dwarfed the soldiers and airmen who were busy all around it, like so many worker ants.

It had a nose cone shaped like a cruel eagle's head in side profile, and a raked, streamlined cockpit, with a score of porthole-like windows running along its sides. The only major differences between the aircraft shown in that photo and the one now lying before them were the location and the markings.

That photo had shown a Ju 390 at its last known destination – a frozen, snowbound airstrip in Prague, in occupied Czechoslovakia, on a bitter February morning in 1945. Painted on each of the aircraft's massive wings was the distinctive form of a black cross set against a white background – the insignia of the German Luftwaffe – with similar markings on the aft section of the fuselage.

By contrast, the aircraft now lying before Jaeger displayed an equally distinctive roundel – a five-pointed white star overlying red-and-white stripes – the unmistakable markings of the United States Air Force. Those roundels were sun-bleached and weathered almost to the point of having disappeared, but to Jaeger and his team they were still clearly recognisable.

The giant tyres on the warplane's eight massive wheels had perished and part-deflated, but even so each reached to around Jaeger's shoulder height. As to the cockpit, he figured it reared a good third of the way to what had once been the jungle canopy, but was now a web of dead branches high above them.

As Carson had promised, back in Wild Dog Media's London office, the aircraft dwarfed a modern-day C-130 Hercules – the aircraft that Jaeger and his team had flown in on. And apart from the wilted vines and creepers that trailed around the fuselage, and the fallen dead wood lying on the 165-foot span of her wings, she seemed incredibly intact – proof indeed that she had landed here.

Sure, she showed the effects of seven decades secreted in the jungle. Jaeger could see that some of the rivets holding her skin together had corroded, and here and there a cowling or cover had fallen off an engine. The wings and fuselage were covered in a sodden carpet of mildew, and the remains of dead tree ferns and epiphytes littered the aircraft's dorsal surfaces.

But the deterioration was mostly cosmetic.

Structurally the aircraft looked sound. A quick spruce-up and Jaeger figured she would be almost good enough to fly.

There was a loud squawking from above, as a flock of

iridescent green parrots flitted through the skeleton forest. It served to break Jaeger's trance-like state.

He turned to Narov. 'Only one way in.' His words were muffled by the gas mask, but via the inbuilt radio intercom they were audible. He traced a line with his gloved hand from the aircraft's tail, along the length of her fuselage and onwards to the cockpit.

Narov eyed him through her mask. 'I will go first.'

71

With the tail wheel having deflated, the aircraft's tailplane lay just within Narov's grasp, but only if she used a dead tree to get a leg-up. She reached for the warplane's upper surface and hauled herself up until she was standing on the flat of the tailplane.

Jaeger followed. He waited for Dale, taking the camera that he passed up, and helping him on to the flat surface. Narov hurried ahead, scuttling along the dorsal surface of the warplane and disappearing from view.

The undersurface of the Ju 390's fuselage was flattish, the upper surface tapering to a dull ridge. Jaeger climbed on to that, and followed Narov up the aircraft's spine, clambering around the astrodome set just aft of the cockpit, where the navigator would have sat, surrounded on all sides by a series of glass panels. It was from there that he would have taken measurements of the stars, so as to steer the aircraft across thousands of miles of trackless ocean and jungle. Jaeger noticed that some of the rubber seals around the astrodome's windows had perished, and one or two of the panels had fallen in.

He reached the cockpit, slithered down and joined Narov perched on the very nose of the aircraft. It was a precarious position: the ground lay some forty feet below them, straight down. The nose of the warplane was smooth and aerodynamic, yet smeared in seventy years of jungle debris. Jaeger did his best to boot the worst of it away, so he had a half-decent footing.

Dale appeared above, camera in hand, and settled down to film.

Jaeger pulled out a length of paracord from a pouch in his NBC suit, tossed it up to Dale, and had him sling it around the radio mast that protruded from the top rear of the cockpit. Dale dropped it back, and Jaeger fashioned two loops, so that he and Narov had something to hang on to.

Narov was staring through one of the two front window panels. Jaeger could see the smeary marks where she'd used her gloves to try to clear away the worst of the grime, dirt and mildew.

For the briefest of moments, she glanced his way. 'The side window – I think it has been left unlocked. That is our way in.'

She reached around to the side, her distinctive knife grasped in one hand. Deftly, she inserted the blade into the semi-rotten rubber that formed the seal, and applied pressure. Most such aircraft had sliding windows, so the pilots could speak to the aircrew on the runway below.

Narov was trying to lever this one open.

Inch by inch she prised it back, until there was a gap wide enough to lower herself through. Taking one loop of Jaeger's paracord, she swung herself around the side of the cockpit, walking her feet along the aircraft's flank, and kicked her legs inside. Lithe as a cat, she wriggled her hips and torso through the open window, and with barely a glance at Jaeger she was gone.

Gripping the paracord, Jaeger swung himself around and followed after Narov, his boots landing with a harsh clang on the cockpit's bare metal floor.

It took a few seconds for his eyes to adjust to the gloom.

The first thing that struck him was that he had entered some kind of time capsule. There was no smell, of course, for the respirator filtered everything out, but he could just imagine the fusty, musty aroma of the leather seats, mixed in with the acrid scent of corroded aluminium from the scores of dials that lined the massive flight panel.

Behind him lay what had to be the flight assistant's seat, tucked into its own cramped alcove and facing towards the rear, with a mass of dials and levers before it. Behind that again lay the navigator's seat, thrust high into the astrodome, and beyond that in the shadows lurked the bulkhead separating the cockpit from the cargo hold.

The interior of the warplane appeared spookily untouched – as if the aircrew had only abandoned it a few hours previously. There was a tin flask tucked beside the pilot's seat; next to that, a mug with what Jaeger figured had to be encrusted coffee caked to the bottom.

A pair of Aviator-type shades lay on the pilot's seat, as if he'd thrown them there while stepping aft to have a chat with the crew manning the hold. The entire impression was somehow so ghostly; yet what had Jaeger been expecting?

There was something bolted above the pilot's seat that caught his eye. It was an odd – almost alien-looking – contraption, mounted on a swivel, as if it could be dropped over the pilot's eyes. He glanced at the co-pilot's seat; a similar device was set above that position as well.

He sensed Narov staring.

'Is that what I think it is?' Jaeger queried.

'Zielgerät 1229 – the Vampir,' Narov confirmed. 'Infrared night vision sight, as we would call it today. For making landings and taking off in complete darkness.'

Seeing that Vampir sight clearly came as no surprise to her. But for most of Jaeger's adult life he had believed night vision to be something invented by the American military, and only a few decades ago. Seeing a working set of such equipment here in this Second World War German plane was mind-blowing.

On the navigator's desk behind him, Jaeger discovered the remains of a mildewed chart, with pencil and dividers lying to one side. The navigator had clearly been a heavy smoker. A heap of semi-decomposed cigarette butts lay in a flick-out ashtray, beside a Luftwaffe-issue packet of rip-off matches.

Tucked into what had to be the navigator's file was an old and yellowing image. Jaeger reached for it. It was an aerial photo, and he realised almost instantly that it showed the airstrip as it must have looked when it had first been hacked out of the jungle, some seven decades ago.

It was labelled with various German words, one of which, *Treibstofflager*, had the symbol of a fuel drum drawn beside it. It was the *Treibstofflager* that had run dry, of course, so trapping this warplane here seemingly for ever.

Jaeger turned to show Narov, but she had her back to him, and there was something furtive about her posture. She was bent over a leather flight satchel, her hands feverishly leafing through a sheaf of documents. From her body language alone, Jaeger figured she'd got whatever she'd come here for, and that no one was about to part her from whatever was in that satchel.

She must have sensed his eyes upon her. Without a word, she shrugged off her backpack, stuffed the satchel deep inside it, and turned towards the aircraft's hold. She glanced Jaeger's way. From what he could see of her face behind the mask, it appeared flushed with excitement. But there was also an evasiveness – a defensive, self-protective look – in her eyes.

'Found what you're looking for?' he queried pointedly.

Narov ignored the question. Instead, she gestured towards the warplane's rear. 'That way – if you really want to see what secrets this aircraft holds.'

Jaeger made a mental note to tackle her over that satchel-load of documents once they were done getting the warplane lifted out of there. Time was too pressing for any such confrontation now.

72

Narov indicated the bulkhead. There was an oblong hatch-way set into it, which had been sealed shut by a handle locked into the vertical position. An arrow pointed downwards, with the German words stamped beside it: *ZU OFFNEN*.

It needed no translating.

Jaeger reached for the handle. For a brief moment he hesitated, before slipping his hand inside his chest pouch and pulling out a Petzl head torch. He loosened its straps and pulled it on over his hood and mask. Then he reached for the lever again and wrenched it down into the horizontal position, before swinging the heavy door wide.

All was darkness inside the Ju 390's cavernous rear.

Jaeger felt about with his gloved hand and twisted the glass of his head torch, switching it on. A burning blue light stabbed out from the Petzl's pair of xenon bulbs. The twin rays pierced the gloom, playing like a laser show across the interior, catching in layers of what resembled mist lying thick across the hold.

The mist reached out towards Jaeger, trailing ghostly tendrils all around him.

He peered deeper inside. This far forward, the Ju 390's hold was at least the height of two fully grown men, and even wider at its base. And as far as Jaeger could tell, the entire length of the fuselage was stacked high with cargo crates. Each was lashed to steel lugs set into the aircraft's floor, to prevent the load from shifting about during flight.

Jaeger took a first cautious step inside. He had every confidence in their Avon NBC kit, but stepping into an unknown hazard like this was still daunting. There was no known toxic agent that could defeat such protective suits and masks, but what if the warplane's hold had somehow been booby-trapped?

The fuselage sloped away from him, the aircraft sitting lower to the ground at its rear. As he gazed about, he noticed the beam of his torch catching on long filaments of silver, strung from one side of the hold to the other. At first he thought he'd discovered the hidden trip wires left behind by those who had abandoned this warplane – perhaps tethered to explosive charges.

But then he noticed that each of the threads formed part of a larger complex of geometric patterns, spiralling in towards a dark mass crouched at the very centre.

Spiders.

Why were there always spiders?

'The *Phoneutria* is also called "the wandering spider",' Narov's voice cut in via the radio intercom. 'They get everywhere. Be watchful.'

She moved ahead of him with her knife drawn.

Bitten once by a *Phoneutria*, she seemed to show no fear, slashing expertly at the webs, collapsing them before her to clear a path through. As she pirouetted from side to side, slicing at the silken threads and flicking the bodies of the spiders away, she moved with the slender grace of a ballet dancer.

It was captivating. Jaeger traced her progress, noting her raw courage. She really was as unique – as dangerous? – as the *Phoneutria* she was so expertly outmanoeuvring.

He followed the path she cut, feeling for any trip wires set at just above floor level. His eye was drawn to a massive crate lying to his immediate front. It was so large, he'd have to squeeze past so as to continue down the warplane. For a moment he wondered how they'd manhandled it onto the aircraft. He could only imagine they had used heavy vehicles to do so, driving the crate up the warplane's rear ramp.

As he studied it, Jaeger's torch caught the lettering stamped on its side.

> *Kriegsentscheidend: Aktion Adlerflug*
> *SS Standortwechsel Kommando*
> *Kaiser-Wilhelm-Gesellschaft*
> *Uranprojekt – Uranmaschine*

Below that was the unmistakably dark form of . . . a *Reichsadler*.

Some of the words – plus the symbol – were instantly recognisable to Jaeger, but it was Narov who would add the missing links. She knelt before the crate, tracing the words in the light thrown by her own head torch.

'So, this is hardly surprising . . .' she began.

Jaeger crouched beside her. 'Some of the words I know,' he remarked. '*Kriegsentscheidend*: beyond top secret. SS *Standortwechsel Kommando*: the Relocation Commando of the SS. What about the others?'

Narov read and interpreted the words, Jaeger's head torch glinting off the glass lens of her mask. '*Aktion Adlerflug* – Operation Eagle Flight. *Kaiser-Wilhelm-Gesellschaft* – the Kaiser Wilhelm Society, the Nazis' top nuclear research facility. *Uranprojekt* – the nuclear weapons project of the Reich. *Uranmaschine* – nuclear reactor.'

She turned to Jaeger. 'Components of their nuclear programme. The Nazis had experimented with nuclear power and how it could be harnessed for weaponry in ways that we had never even imagined.'

Narov moved across to a second crate, tracing similar lines of lettering, plus a second *Reichsadler*.

> *Kriegsentscheidend: Aktion Adlerflug*
> *SS Standortwechsel Kommando*
> *Mittelwerk Kohnstein*
> *A9 Amerika Rakete*

'So the top two lines are the same. Below that: Mittelwerk was an underground complex tunnelled into the Kohnstein mountains, right in the very heart of Germany. It was where Hitler tasked Hans Kammler to relocate the Nazi's top rocketry and missiles, after their Peenemunde research centre was bombed by the Allies.

'During winter 1944 and spring 1945, twenty thousand forced labourers from the nearby Mittelbau-Dora concentration camp died building Mittelwerk – from exhaustion, starvation and disease. They were worked to death, or were executed when they were too weak to serve any further useful purpose.'

Narov gestured at the crate. 'As you can see, not all of the evil from Mittelwerk perished with the end of the war.'

Jaeger traced the last line of lettering. 'What's the A9?'

'Sequel to the V-2. The Amerika Rakete – the America Sky-rocket; designed to fly at over three thousand mph and to hit the American mainland. By war's end they had working wind-tunnel versions and they had even had successful test flights. Obviously they did not want the A9 to die with the Reich.'

Jaeger could tell that Narov knew so much more than she was letting on. It had been like this from the very start of the expedition. And now they'd made a series of mind-blowing discoveries – a secret German warplane decked out in American colours, lost for decades in the Amazon and stuffed full of what, by anyone's reckoning, was a cargo of Nazi horrors.

Yet nothing seemed to come as the least shock or surprise to Irina Narov.

73

They probed further into the darkness.

The heat inside the fuselage was stifling, the discomfort tripled by the cumbersome suit and mask, but Jaeger didn't doubt that the NBC kit was proving an absolute lifesaver. Whatever toxic fumes filled the aircraft, should either he, Narov or Dale have tried to enter without such protection, they would be in a whole world of hurt right now, of that he felt certain.

For an instant, he turned to check on Dale.

He found the cameraman attaching a portable battery-operated lamp to the top of his camera. He flicked it on – light by which to film – and the interior of the warplane was cast into stark, knife-cut light and shadow.

From every corner stared horrible, glowing twin pinpricks of light: *Phoneutria* eyes.

Jaeger was half expecting the ghosts of whoever had crewed this warplane to be woken by the glaring light and to step from the shadows, Luger pistols raised to defend their darkest mysteries to the last.

It seemed almost inconceivable that the aircraft could have been so utterly abandoned, complete with all its hidden secrets.

Narov crouched before a third crate, and almost instantly Jaeger sensed the change in her demeanour. As she traced the lettering, she let out a strangled gasp, and Jaeger figured that here at least was an element even she hadn't quite been expecting.

He bent to read the words stamped on the crate's side.

Kriegsentscheidend: Aktion Adlerflug
SS *Standortwechsel Kommando*
Plasmaphysik – Dresden
Röntgen Kanone

'This we did not expect,' Narov muttered. She glanced at Jaeger. 'Every line is obvious, but the last? You understand line three?'

Jaeger nodded. 'Plasma Physics – Dresden.'

'Exactly,' Narov confirmed. 'As to the *Röntgen Kanone*, there is no direct translation into English. You might call it a death-ray or direct energy weapon. It fires a particle beam, or electromagnetic radiation, or even sound waves. It sounds like the stuff of science fiction, but the Nazis were long rumoured to have had such a weapon, and to have used it to down Allied aircraft.'

Narov's gaze met Jaeger's through the eyepiece of her mask. 'It seems as if it is true, and that they held on to their *Röntgen Kanone* until the very last.'

Jaeger could feel the sweat pouring down his face. The heat was building to intolerable levels, and the perspiration was starting to condense inside his mask, blurring his vision. He figured they should head for the rear and try to open one of the side doors, which lay just aft of the tailplane.

As they fought their way through, Narov pointed out further crates packed with an array of staggeringly advanced weaponry. 'The BV 246 gliding bomb. It had a two-hundred-kilometre range, and it would home on to the target's radar signal . . . The Fritz-X guided bomb, with a heat-seeking or radar/radio homing warhead. Basically, these are the forerunners of our modern-day smart bombs.'

She bent beside a row of long, low crates. 'The Rheintochter R1 – a surface-to-air guided missile for shooting down Allied bombers . . . The X4 – an air-to-air missile, guided to the target by the pilot. The Feuerlilie – the Fire Lily – a guided anti-aircraft rocket . . .'

She paused before a group of smaller packing cases. 'A

Seehund active night-vision unit – used in conjunction with an infrared searchlight, it had unlimited range ... And here, stealth materials made by IG Farben, for their Schwarzes Flugzeug – Black Aircraft – programme. It was the precursor to our modern-day stealth warplanes.

'Plus, here – materials for coating their XXI submarine. The coating absorbed radar and sonar, making the XXI all but immune to detection.' She glanced at Jaeger. 'It was so revolutionary that the Chinese navy's copy – the Ming class submarine – is still in operation *today*. Plus the Russians' Project 633 – their Romeo class submarine – was a direct copy of the XXI, which lasted through the entirety of the Cold War.'

She rubbed the dust off another crate, revealing the words stamped thereon. 'Sarin, tabun and soman. The Nazis' cutting-edge nerve agents – ones still stockpiled by the world's major powers. We had no effective defences against them in 1945. None – and largely because we didn't even know they existed.'

Narov gave a sharp intake of breath. 'And next to it – a crate of bio-agents. Hitler code-named their biological weapon programme Blitzableiter: Lightning Rod. It was Nazi scientist Kurt Blome's brainchild. They always denied its existence, disguising it as a cancer research programme, yet here we have the absolute proof that Blitzableiter existed: plague, typhoid, cholera, anthrax and nephritis-based agents. Clearly, they wished to continue after war's end.'

By the time they'd reached the tail section of the warplane, Jaeger's head was spinning – both from the suffocating heat, and from all that they had discovered. Hitler's absolute belief in technology – that against all odds it would win the war for the Reich – had borne fruit, and in ways that Jaeger had barely imagined.

Both at school and at the Combat Training Centre Royal Marines, where he'd completed his officer training, Jaeger had been taught that the Allies had outfought the Nazi enemy both militarily and technologically. But if the contents of this warplane were anything to go by, that lesson seemed to be anything but true.

Guided rocketry and missiles; smart bombs; stealth aircraft; stealth submarines; night-vision kit; chemical and biological weapons; *death rays* even – the Nazis' stunning advancement was evidenced by the crates packed into this warplane's cavernous hold.

74

The Ju 390's rear cargo hatches turned out to be typical pieces of solid German engineering. On either side were double doors around six feet in height, which opened outwards. They were fastened by twin metal bars that ran the length of their centre, slotting into holes in the floor and ceiling.

The hinges and locking mechanism looked well greased, and Jaeger figured they should move easily. He applied force to one of the levers, and it barely creaked as he pulled it upwards, freeing the doors. He put his weight against them, and the next moment they swung wide. The instant they did so, the thick sludge of mist that clung to the aircraft's interior began to leak into the open.

Jaeger was surprised to see that it appeared to be heavier than air. It poured out of the aircraft, snaking to the ground and pooling like a dense toxic soup. When a shaft of sunlight hit the gas cloud, it appeared to glow from the inside with a strange metallic shimmer.

It reminded Jaeger that he had been also tasked to carry out some tests, to establish the source of the toxicity emanating from the warplane. He had been so caught up in the search it had almost slipped his mind.

But time enough for that later.

Right now he was burning up, and he needed a few minutes' breather and some air. He took a seat on one side of the open doorway, Narov taking up a position opposite him. From the corner of his eye he could see Dale filming away, as he tried to suck every last frame of this awesome discovery into his camera lens.

By the light streaming in through the open hatch Jaeger noticed what looked like a picture of a MANPAD stencilled along one side of a nearby crate. He bent to inspect it. Sure enough, it showed what appeared to be a shoulder-launched surface-to-air missile.

Narov traced the lettering running along the crate's side. 'Fliegerfaust. It means literally "pilot fist". The world's first shoulder-launched surface-to-air missile, to shoot down Allied warplanes. Again, thankfully, it came too late to make much of a difference to the outcome of the war.'

'Surreal . . .' Jaeger muttered. 'So many firsts . . . It'll take an age to catalogue all the secrets lying around in here.'

'What exactly is so surprising?' Narov asked, as she stared out into the white bones of the dead jungle. 'That the Nazis had such technology? They had this and so much more. Search that warplane fully, and who knows what else it may reveal.'

She paused. 'Or is your surprise that this aircraft is in American markings? The Allies supported the Nazis' efforts to relocate their weaponry – their *Wunderwaffe* – to the far-flung corners of the earth. By war's end we were facing a new enemy: Soviet Russia. It was a case of the enemy of my enemy is my friend. The Allies gave their blessing at the highest level to those Nazi relocations – hence why this aircraft is in USAF colours. The Allies – the Americans – owned the skies by then, and none would have made it through otherwise.

'By war's end it was a race against the Russians,' Narov continued. 'By seizing for ourselves the Nazis' secrets – their technology and their foremost scientists – we were able to win the Cold War, not to mention the space race. Back then, that was how we justified it all.'

'*We?*' Jaeger interjected. 'But you're Russian. You said it yourself – by the end of the war you were the enemy.'

'Of me you know nothing,' Narov muttered. She was silent

for a long moment. 'I may sound Russian, but my blood is British. I was born in your country. Before that, my distant heritage is German. And now I live in New York. I am a citizen of the free world. Does that make me the enemy?'

Jaeger shrugged, half apologetically. 'How was I to know? You've told me zero about yourself or—'

'Now is hardly the time,' Narov interjected, gesturing at the Ju 390's cargo hold.

'Fair enough. Anyway, keep talking – about the warplane.'

'Take for example the Mittelwerk underground facility,' Narov began again, picking up her thread. 'In early May 1945, American forces overran it, and the first V-2 rocket systems were shipped out to the US. Just days later, Soviet army officers arrived to take over the complex: it lay within the Soviet zone of occupation. The American Apollo moon landings were built upon those V-2 technologies.

'Or take Kurt Blome, the director of the Blitzableiter. One reason the Nazis' biological weapons programme was so advanced was that they had thousands of concentration camp victims to test them on. At war's end, Blome was captured and put on trial in Nuremberg. Somehow he was acquitted, after which the Americans hired him to work for their Army Chemical Corps, on a top-secret weapons programme.

'We cut deals,' Narov announced, unable to keep the bitterness out of her voice. 'And yes, we cut deals with those who were unspeakable – the very worst of the Nazis.' She eyed Jaeger. 'You have never heard of Operation Paperclip?'

Jaeger shook his head.

'It was the Americans' code name for a project to relocate thousands of Nazi scientists to the US. There they were given new names, new identities, plus positions of power and influence – as long as they would work for their new masters. You had a similar programme, only with typical British irony you named it Operation Darwin: survival of the fittest.

'Both projects were completely deniable,' Narov continued.

'Operation Paperclip was denied even to the level of the US president.' She paused. 'But there were layers of deniability that went even deeper. *Aktion Adlerflug* – Operation Eagle Flight – it is stamped on every one of the packing crates in this aircraft's hold. *Aktion Adlerflug* was the codename for Hitler's plan to relocate Nazi technology to places where it could be used to re-build the Reich. It was a project that we – the Allies – endorsed, as long as they worked with us against the Soviets.

'In short, you are sitting aboard a warplane that lies at the heart of the world's darkest ever conspiracy. Such was – *is* – the secrecy involved that most of the British and American files related to this activity – not to mention the Russian files – remain closed. And I doubt they will ever be opened.'

Narov shrugged. 'If all of this surprises you, it really should not. The supposed good guys cut a deal with the devil. They did so out of what they believed was necessity – for the greater good of the free world.'

75

Jaeger waved a hand at the crates lining the Ju 390's hold. 'It only makes this all the more incredible. This warplane – it's got to be the greatest collection of Nazi war secrets ever assembled. All the more vital that we get it lifted out of here, back to somewhere where we can—'

'Where we can what?' Narov cut in, turning her cold eyes upon him. 'Tell the world? Much of this technology we have now perfected. Take the *Röntgen Kanone;* the death ray. Recently, the Americans perfected just such a thing. It is code-named MARAUDER. It stands for Magnetically Accelerated Ring to Achieve Ultra-high Directed Energy and Radiation. Basically, it fires doughnut-shaped spheres of magnetically cemented plasma. Think balls of lightning.

'It is a classified deniable access programme,' Narov continued. 'In other words, the holy grail of secrets. As is MARAUDER's direct antecedent – the Nazi *Röntgen Kanone.* So no, Mr William Edward Michael Jaeger, we won't be presenting this discovery to the world any time soon. But that doesn't mean we shouldn't do everything in our power to save it, and for all the right reasons.'

Jaeger stared at Narov for a long second: *William Edward Michael Jaeger* – what was with the use of his full name?

'You know something, I've got a million questions.' Jaeger's voice rose above the suck and blow of his gas mask. 'And most of them seem to concern *you.* Mind telling me how you know so much? Mind telling me everything you know? Mind telling me who you are, even? Where you come from? Who you work for? Oh yeah, and mind telling me what's with the commando knife?'

When Narov answered, her gaze remained fixed on the dead forest. 'I might tell you some of these things, once we are safely out of this. Once we are truly safe. But right now—'

'Plus the satchel of documents,' Jaeger cut in. 'The one you retrieved from the aircraft's cockpit. Mind telling me what's in that? The flight manifest? Air charts? The intended destination of this and the other warplanes?'

Narov ignored the question. 'Right now, William Edward Michael Jaeger, I think you need to know only this: I knew Edward Michael Jaeger, your grandfather. Grandfather Ted, as all we who knew him called him. He was an inspiration and a guide to us all.

'I worked with your grandfather, or rather I worked in his memory; I worked with his inheritance.' Narov pulled out her knife. 'And it was your grandfather who bequeathed me this. I was curious to meet his living legacy: *you*. I remain curious. I do not know if he is everything – or even anything – that I had hoped he would be.'

Jaeger was speechless. Before he could think of a suitable response, Narov spoke again.

'He was the grandfather I never had. *That I couldn't have.*' For the first time since Jaeger had met her, Narov fixed him with a very direct, piercing look, one that held. 'And you know something else? I have always resented the relationship you had with him . . . and that you were left free to follow your dreams.'

Jaeger held up his hands. 'Whoa . . . Where did that come from?'

Narov turned away. 'It is a long story. I do not know if I am ready. If you are ready . . . And now—'

Her words were cut short by a fearful cry that rang out over the radio intercom. 'Arggghhh! Get it off! Get it off!'

Jaeger spun around, only to find that Dale had blundered into a place where the spiders' webs seemed at their thickest. The cameraman had been so focused on his lens that he'd not kept a proper watch on where he was going. Tough, sticky filaments wrapped around him, as he fought to retain hold of his camera and sweep the suffocating silken threads – and their arachnid hordes – away.

Jaeger dashed to his aid.

He figured there was little chance that even a *Phoneutria*'s fangs could pierce Dale's gloves or mask, and presumably the NBC suit was tough enough to resist a bite. But Dale was unlikely to know that, and his terror sounded all too real.

Jaeger used his thick rubber mitts to swipe the writhing mass of spiders aside, punching their squishy, hissing forms into the darkness. With Narov's help he dragged Dale free, still desperately clutching at his camera. But as they pulled him out of the tangle of webs, Jaeger caught sight of the real cause of Dale's fear.

Lying in the crushed mass of silken threads was a ghostly skeleton, its fleshless face a rictus of horror, the bones of its body still clad in a half-decayed SS officer's uniform. As Jaeger stared at the dead man – doubtless one of the Ju 390's original passengers – he heard a voice over the radio intercom.

'It wasn't the bloody spiders that got me!' Dale gasped. 'It was being in the clutches of some long-dead Nazi general!'

'I see him,' Jaeger confirmed. 'And you know something? He makes you look almost handsome. Come on – let's hustle.'

Jaeger was all too aware that they'd been in the suffocating confines of this aircraft for approaching an hour now. It was time to get moving. But as he led Dale and Narov back towards the cockpit, he was struck by a shocking realisation: he'd yet to spare a thought for how this warplane might hold the key to discovering the fate of his wife and child.

Luke and Ruth: their disappearance was tied up inextricably with whatever they had discovered here. The *Reichsadler* – the stamp of evil – was all over both this warplane and Jaeger's family's abduction.

And somehow he had to start searching for the answers.

76

Jaeger stood in the fringes of the jungle speaking to his team – Lewis Alonzo, Hiro Kamishi, Leticia Santos, Joe James, Irina Narov, and Mike Dale – who was still filming – plus Puruwehua, Gwaihutiga and their fellow Indians. He'd removed his gas mask so he could talk, though he was still wearing the rest of the cumbersome NBC suit.

'Right, you all know the score,' he announced, his voice thick with tension and exhaustion. 'We're about to start the lift. The Airlander crew figure they may need an hour to work the warplane free. That's the time I'm asking you to buy us. Do all you can to hold off the bad guys, but no heroics. Mission one: let's all stay alive. And remember – just as soon as we're gone, break contact and get the hell out of here.'

Jaeger glanced at the giant airship, which seemed to fill the sky above them. The Airlander was an awe-inspiring sight. It hovered less than one hundred feet above the broken bone ends of the dead canopy, like the belly of some huge white whale suspended in the clouds.

It was four times the length of the Ju 390's fuselage, and ten times its width – the airship's bulbous hull being filled with some three and a half million cubic feet of helium gas.

It simply dwarfed the warplane that lay beneath it.

The Airlander's pilot could risk bringing her no lower, for the topmost branches of the dead forest thrust skywards like jagged spear tips. The airship had an intelligent skin that could heal itself if holed, but multiple wounds would cause her real trouble.

Plus, there was that unknown toxin leaking out of the Ju 390, and no one aboard the Airlander fancied getting danger-close to that.

As per Raff's last data-burst message earlier that morning, there were no drones in the immediate vicinity. Their decoy – the kayak carrying the tracking device and cell phone – seemed to have drawn the surveillance a good distance north of here. It put the Predator out of video range of the Airlander, which in any case was hidden from view by 8,000 feet of cloud cover.

But an electronic intercept of the airship's radar signature was still possible, as was an infrared trace of her hotspots – not least her four propulsors. All it would take was one such pick-up and the Predator would be on to them. Time was of the essence, more than it had been since the very start of the expedition.

It was the morning of day eleven, and if all went to plan, it was to be their last before arriving back in comparative civilisation. Or at least it was for Jaeger, Narov and Dale. Over the preceding hours, he and his team had been immersed in a race against time, not to mention their unknown enemy.

The previous evening, a lone Amahuaca Indian runner had reached their location with worrying news: the Dark Force was less than eighteen hours away. If they continued marching overnight, they would arrive even sooner. That force consisted of sixty-odd operators, and they were heavily armed.

The Indians shadowing them had tried to frustrate their progress, but blowpipes and arrows had proven no match for machine guns and grenade launchers. The main force of Indians would keep tracking and harassing them, but there was only so much they could do to slow their progress.

Since then, Jaeger and his crew had worked feverishly, during which time several things had become clear. First, whatever toxic cocktail was leaking out of the warplane, it appeared to be some form of irradiated mercury plasma. But it was nothing that Jaeger could identify any more specifically, for it appeared to be a threat unknown to his detection kit.

That kit worked by comparing a detected chemical signature with a known index of agents. Whatever this was, it appeared to be completely off the scale. And that meant that no one could risk going anywhere near without wearing a full set of protective gear.

Second, while the Airlander had been able to lower a pair of lifting harnesses – Jaeger and team getting them slung beneath the points where the Ju 390's wings met the fuselage – there was no way she could lift the team out of the jungle as well.

The Airlander had the means to winch each person up the two-hundred-odd feet to the airship, but there simply weren't enough NBC suits – or the time – to enable them to do so. The Indians had sent out a series of runners all through the night. The last had arrived just after first light, with the warning that the enemy force was two hours away, and closing fast.

Jaeger had been forced to accept the inevitable: his team would have to split up. The main body – Alonzo, Kamishi, Santos and Joe James, plus Puruwehua, Gwaihutiga, and half a dozen Amahuaca warriors – would take up blocking positions between the warplane and the bad guys.

Gwaihutiga volunteered to lead the charge. He would depart with most of the Indian warriors, to set up the first ambush. Puruwehua, Alonzo and the rest would form a second blocking group, nearer to the wreck. In that way they hoped to buy those doing the lift-out some much-needed time.

As to Jaeger, Narov and Dale – they were going to ride in the Ju 390, as the Airlander dragged her free from the jungle. Or at least that was the plan.

Dale had been an obvious choice, as someone needed to film the raising of the aircraft. Jaeger had been chosen because the expedition leader needed to stick with its objective – the warplane. Leticia Santos had argued that she should be the third person to ride in the aircraft, for she was a Brazilian, and – arguably – the aircraft had been found on Brazilian soil.

For a while Narov had fronted up to Santos, making it clear

that no one was about to part her from her precious warplane. Jaeger had ended things by pointing out that Santos should probably stick with her foremost mission, which was safeguarding the Indian tribe.

He'd also made the salient point that the three of them – Jaeger, Dale and Narov – were already suited up, and that shifting about the NBC masks, gloves and suits would risk contaminating whoever was changing into and out of them. The threat was real, and it made sense for those already in the suits to be those to ride the warplane.

At that, Santos had reluctantly agreed.

'Alonzo, I'm leaving you in charge.' Jaeger continued with his briefing. 'Puruwehua has promised to do all he can to get you guys out safely. You'll return to the Amahuaca village and trek into the land of the neighbouring tribe. That tribe has contact with the outside world; they'll send you on your way home.'

'Got it,' Alonzo confirmed. 'Puruwehua, we're in your hands.'

'We will get you home,' Puruwehua replied simply.

'All being well, we three will ride the warplane all the way to Cachimbo,' Jaeger announced. 'En route I'll warn Colonel Evandro to prepare a cordoned-off landing area, where the Ju 390 can be set down and kept in isolation, at least until her cargo can be made safe.

'It's a fourteen-hundred-kilometre journey, so it should take the Airlander a minimum of seven hours, especially with that thing in tow.' Jaeger jerked a thumb in the direction of the Ju 390. 'As long as SS General Hans Kammler and his cronies didn't overload her, the lift should be doable, in which case we'll be at Cachimbo by this evening.

'I'll send a one-word message in data-burst once we get there: "SUCCESS". Hopefully you'll have enough of a signal somewhere en route to receive it. No message means something's gone wrong, but at that point your sole priority has to be to get yourselves safely out of here and on your way home.'

Jaeger glanced at his watch. 'Right, let's get moving.'

It was an emotional parting, but time kept the goodbyes short and sweet.

Gwaihutiga paused briefly before Jaeger.

'Pombogwav, eki'yra. Pombogwav, kahuhara'ga.'

With that he turned and was gone, leading his men off at a fast jog, a war chant rumbling from his throat and being taken up by his fellow warriors, reverberating powerfully through the trees.

Jaeger glanced at Puruwehua questioningly.

'Pombogwav – it means "farewell",' Puruwehua explained. 'You have I think no direct word for *eki'yra*. It means "my father's son", or "my older brother". So, "farewell, my older brother". And *kahuhara'ga* you know: so, "farewell, the hunter".'

Not for the first time since he'd met this tribe, Jaeger felt truly humbled.

Puruwehua proceeded to force upon Jaeger a magnificent parting gift: his blow-dart pipe. Jaeger was hard pressed to think of anything suitable in return. Finally, he settled on his Gerber knife – the one with which he'd fought on Bioko's Fernao beach.

'This knife and I have history,' he explained, as he strapped it around the Amahuaca Indian's chest. 'I once fought with it far away in Africa. It saved my life and that of one of my closest friends. You I now count among my closest friends – you and all your people.'

Puruwehua drew the knife and tested the keenness of the blade. 'In my language – *kyhe'ia*. Sharp, like a spear cut lengthways.' He glanced at Jaeger. 'This *kyhe'ia* – it has drawn the blood of the enemy. It will do so again, Koty'ar.'

'Puruwehua, thank you – for everything,' Jaeger told him. 'I promise one day I'll return. I'll come back to your village and share the mother of all monkey roasts in the spirit house – but only if you spare me the *nyakwana*!'

Puruwehua laughed and agreed that he would. No more shots of psychotropic snuff for William Jaeger any time soon.

Jaeger turned to each of his team in turn. He saved an

extra-warm smile for Leticia Santos. She in turn grinned at him and blew him a big Brazilian kiss.

'Be careful, no?' she whispered close to his ear. 'And especially of that . . . that *ja'gwara*, Narov. And promise – come pay me a visit next time we have the Rio *carnivale*! We'll get drunk together and go dancing!'

Jaeger smiled. 'It's a date.'

With that, the team, commanded by Lewis Alonzo but led by the Amahuaca Indians, hoisted their packs and weapons and disappeared into the jungle.

77

Raff's data-burst message was typically short and to the point: *Airlander good to go. Secure yourselves. Commencing lift three minutes, 0800 Zulu.*

It had come not a moment too soon as far as Jaeger was concerned. During the last few minutes he'd heard gunfire erupt from the jungle to the north – the approach route of the Dark Force.

There had been the sudden fierce crackle of assault rifles, which Jaeger figured was his team springing their ambush, but the return fire had sounded horribly intense, the signature rapid reports of SAW – squad automatic weapon – light machine guns mixing with heavier bursts of what sounded like GPMG fire, plus the hollow crump of grenades.

Such weaponry would cut a murderous swathe through the jungle.

Whoever this Dark Force might be, they were heavily armed, not to mention ready and willing to wage deadly battle. And in spite of the team's best efforts, they were closing in on Jaeger and the warplane with worrying speed.

Time was running out: the Airlander would commence her lift in 180 seconds, and Jaeger for one couldn't wait to get airborne.

He hurried down the Ju 390's dark hold and reached for the rear cargo doors, tugging them closed and securing them with their handle. He moved forward again, skirting around the shadowy ranks of crates, and slammed shut the bulkhead door, locking it firmly behind him.

Dale and Narov had forced open the cockpit's side windows: once the aircraft got moving, the through-flow of air should help clear it of any toxic fumes. Jaeger took up position in the co-pilot's seat, and buckled himself into the restraining flight belt and chest harness. Dale was in the pilot's seat next to him – a position he'd commandeered so he could best film the warplane as she was dragged free from the jungle.

As for Narov, she was hunched over the navigator's table, and Jaeger had a good idea what she was up to. She was studying one of the documents from the satchel that she'd retrieved from the Ju 390's cockpit. Jaeger had got a passing glance at it. The writing on the yellowing pages was in German, which meant it was mostly Double Dutch as far as he was concerned.

But he'd half recognised a word or two on the title page. There were the usual TOP SECRET stamps, plus the words *Aktion Feuerland*. From distantly remembered schoolboy German, Jaeger knew that *Feuer* meant 'fire', and *land* was obvious. Operation Fire Land. And typed below it was: *Liste von Personen*.

That needed little translation: 'List of personnel'.

As far as Jaeger had seen, every last crate lying in the Ju 390's hold was stamped *Aktion Adlerflug*: Operation Eagle Flight. So what was *Aktion Feuerland* – Operation Fire Land? And why Narov's fascination with it, almost to the exclusion of all else?

There was little time to ponder such matters now.

The lift that the Airlander was about to attempt – that of a Ju 390 packed full of cargo – would be accomplished by a combination of factors. One, aerostatic force – due to the simple fact that the airship's helium-filled hull was lighter than air.

Two, thrust – the use of the airship's four huge propulsors, each powered by a 2,350-horsepower gas turbine driving a giant set of propellers. That alone was akin to having four heavy-lift helicopters roped to the corners of the warplane, giving their all.

And three, aerodynamic lift – provided by the Airlander's laminated fabric hull. It was shaped like a cross section of a conventional aircraft wing, with a flatter underside and a curved upper. That shape alone would provide forty per cent of the lift, but only once the Airlander got moving in a forwards direction.

For the first few hundred feet, she'd be lifting vertically – during which time it was all up to the helium gas and the propulsors.

Jaeger heard the noise from the Airlander shift from a barely audible purr to a hollow roar, as she prepared for the lift. Right now, the four massive sets of rotor blades were set in the horizontal position, to provide maximum vertical thrust as the Airlander went about dragging the warplane free.

The downdraught increased to approaching storm force, blowing a blinding whirlwind of broken branches all around the warplane. It felt to Jaeger as though he was standing behind a monster combine harvester while the machine chewed its way through a field of giant wheat, spitting out the unwanted chaff into his face.

He slammed his side window closed, and gestured for Dale to do likewise, as blasts of rotten wood blew inside. Arguably, they were approaching the single most risk-laden moment of the whole crazy enterprise.

The Ju 390's standard loaded weight was 53,000 kilos. With a 60,000-kilogram lift capacity, the Airlander should be able to manage the carry – as long as Hans Kammler and his cronies hadn't overloaded the warplane.

Jaeger had every confidence in the strength of the slings looped beneath the Ju 390's wings. He had similar confidence in the Airlander's pilot, Steve McBride. It was whether they'd break free from the dead wood that was the million-dollar question. That, and the trust they were placing in German aeronautical engineering standing up to seven decades of rot and corrosion in the heart of the jungle.

Any error on either count could prove catastrophic. The Ju 390 – and maybe the Airlander with her – would plummet like a stone into the jungle.

Overnight, Jaeger and his team had felled some of the

largest trees, using shaped ring-charges of plastic explosives slung around their trunks to blast them down. But they'd been limited both by time and the number of charges they had to hand. As much as fifty per cent of the canopy of dead wood remained intact.

They'd blasted down the largest and least decayed tree trunks – those most likely to put up greatest resistance. They were banking on the fact that the surviving dead wood was rotten, and would break apart as the Airlander dragged the warplane free.

The roar of the propulsors rose to an ear-splitting howl, the downdraught approaching hurricane force. Jaeger could tell that the Airlander was nearing its maximum thrust. He sensed something falling from above, as a dark linear shadow slashed across the cockpit.

A massive tree limb smashed into the apex of the Ju 390's windscreen, where the front window panels met. The vertical steel strut linking the panels buckled under the blow, the thick Perspex warping under the crushing impact. As the branch broke in two and fell away, a jagged fault line streaked across the windscreen like a burst of forked lightning.

But, for now at least, the windshield had held.

Jaeger's head was filled with a tidal wave of sound. Heavy, wind-blasted debris rained down on the Ju 390's metal skin. He felt as if he were strapped inside a giant steel drum.

A long humming vibration rippled through the fuselage, as the turbulence from the propulsors set up some kind of resonance with the thick lifting straps wrapped around the plane. Jaeger could sense that every fibre of the airship was straining to make the lift, and that the aircraft herself was somehow fighting to be free.

Suddenly there was a violent lurch as the cockpit seemed to plunge towards the ground and the Ju 390's tail wheel flipped up and broke free. The rear of the fuselage rose, throwing off whatever fallen debris and tree limbs still lay across her.

Four double wheels – eight colossal tyres – held the warplane to the ground now. The massive aircraft seemed to twist and shake, as if she were a monstrous bird trying to drag her claws free of a cloying swamp and take to the skies.

Moments later, there was a sound like a giant Velcro strip being ripped apart, and the Ju 390 lurched into the air.

The force of her breaking free thrust Jaeger downwards into his seat, and threw him forward against the restraining straps. For several seconds the giant warplane rose into the air as if the force of gravity had suddenly been suspended, moving steadily closer to the jagged crown of the skeletal canopy.

With the dead wood casting a cobweb of shadows across the cockpit, the warplane's upper fuselage ploughed into the lowest branches. There was a tearing crash, the sudden impact throwing Jaeger off his seat, the straps of his harness ripping into his shoulders.

All around him, bony tree limbs clutched at the cockpit, as if a giant hand was trying to break its way in and pluck Jaeger, Dale and Narov out and hurl them to the ground. As the warplane tore a path upwards, an extra thick finger of wood punched through the Perspex side window, half knocking Dale's camera from his grasp and spearing towards Jaeger on the far side.

He ducked, the jagged branch jabbing into his seat where his head had been moments earlier. The impact snapped it in two, leaving the broken limb hanging out of the warplane's window.

Jaeger sensed the upward momentum of the aircraft slowing. He chanced a momentary glance to his left. He could see the giant propellers on the Ju 390's port wing – each twice the height of a fully grown man – ensnared in the branches. Moments later, the grasp of the skeleton canopy tightened around the aircraft and she came to a juddering halt.

They were suspended ninety feet above the ground, and stuck fast.

78

For several seconds the Ju 390 seemed to hang there in her nest of wooden bones.

From above, Jaeger heard the howl of the propulsors changing pitch, the downdraught dropping off to a faint breeze. For an instant he feared the pilot was giving up; that he'd been forced to admit that the dead wood had defeated him – in which case Jaeger, Narov and Dale would be facing a sixty-strong enemy force pretty damn quickly.

He risked flicking on his Thuraya, and instantly there was a data-burst message from Raff.

Pilot will reverse to make a forward run, using hull's lift to break you free. STAND BY.

Jaeger flicked the satphone off again.

The Airlander's hull provided almost half of her lift: by reversing and taking a run-up she could double her pulling power.

Jaeger shouted a warning to Narov and Dale to hold on tight for the ride. No sooner had he done so than there was an abrupt change in the direction of the force being exerted on the Ju 390, as the airship accelerated into forward motion at full power.

The cutting edges of the Ju 390's wings were driven into the dead wood, the sharp nose cone drilling forward. Jaeger and Dale ducked below the flight panel as the cockpit speared its way through a tangled wall of tree limbs bleached white by the tropical sun.

Moments later, the canopy appeared to thin noticeably, light flooding into the cockpit. With a tearing of deafening proportions, the mighty warplane broke free, and was catapulted into thin air. To left and right a cloud of rotten wood and debris tumbled from her wings and upper surfaces, spinning towards the forest below.

With the canopy sudden letting go of her, the warplane swung ponderously forward, sailing past the point where she was directly below the Airlander, then rocked back again until she came to rest suspended right below the airship's flight deck. No sooner had the oscillation slowed to manageable proportions than the Airlander began to reel her in.

Powerful hydraulic winches lifted her upwards, until she fell under the Airlander's shadow. Her wings came to rest on the underside of the air cushion landing system – the airship's hovercraft-like skids. The Ju 390 was now effectively attached to the bottom of the Airlander.

With the warplane locked into position, the Airlander's pilot set the propulsors to full speed ahead, and swung her around to the correct bearing, starting the long climb to cruise altitude. They were Cachimbo-bound, with barely seven hours' flight time ahead of them.

Jaeger reached triumphantly for the co-pilot's seventy-year-old flask, jammed into the side of his seat. He waved it at Dale and Narov. 'Coffee, anyone?'

Even Narov couldn't help but crack a smile.

'Sir, the aircraft just isn't there,' the operator known as Grey Wolf Six repeated.

He was speaking into his radio sat at the same remote and nameless jungle airstrip, the rank of helicopters with sagging rotor blades lined up awaiting orders; awaiting a mission.

The operator's English seemed fluent enough, but it was clearly accented, at times having the harsh, guttural inflexion so typical of an Eastern European.

'How can it not be there?' the voice on the other end exploded.

'Sir, our team is on the grid as given. They are in that patch of dead jungle. They have found the imprints of something heavy. They have found smashed-apart dead wood. Sir, the impression is that the aircraft has been ripped out of the jungle.'

'Ripped out by what?' Grey Wolf demanded, incredulously.

'Sir, we have absolutely no idea.'

'You have the Predator over that area. You have eyes-on. How could you miss an aircraft the size of a Boeing 727 getting lifted out of the jungle?'

'Sir, our Predator was on orbit north of there, awaiting a clear visual on the tracking device location. There is cloud cover up to ten thousand feet. There is nothing that can effectively see through that. Whoever has done the lift has done so observing complete communications silence, and under cover of the overcast.' A pause. 'I know it sounds incredible, but trust me – the aircraft is gone.'

'Right, this is what we're going to do.' Grey Wolf's voice was icy calm now. 'You've got a flight of Black Hawks at your disposal. Get them airborne and scour that airspace. You will – repeat *will* – find that warplane. You will retrieve what needs to be retrieved. And then you will destroy that aircraft. Are we clear?'

'Understood, sir.'

'I presume this is Jaeger and his team's doing?'

'I can only assume so, sir. We Hellfired their river position, targeting the tracker device and cell phone. But—'

'It's Jaeger,' the voice cut in. 'It has to be. Terminate them all. No one who is a witness to this gets out alive. You understand? And rig that warplane with so much explosive that not a shred of it will ever be found. I want it gone. For good. Don't mess up this time, *Kamerad*. Clean up. Every single person. Kill them all.'

'Understood, sir.'

'Right, get your Black Hawks airborne. And one more thing: I myself am flying out to your location. This is too important to leave to . . . amateurs. I'll take one of the Agency's jets. I'll be with you in under five hours.'

The operator known as Grey Wolf Six curled his lip. *Amateurs*. How he despised his American paymaster. Still, the money was good, as were the chances of wreaking bloody mayhem and murder.

And in the coming hours he, Vladimir Ustanov, would show Grey Wolf just what he and his so-called amateurs were capable of.

79

Jaeger powered down his satphone. The data-burst message he'd just received read: *Col. Evandro confirms preparing sanitised LZ. ETA at LZ 1630 Zulu. CE sending air escort to cover remainder of journey.*

He checked his watch. It was 0945 Zulu. They had six hours and forty-five minutes' flight time ahead of them before they put down on whatever part of Cachimbo airport Brazil's Director of Special Forces had prepared for them. By 'sanitised', Evandro meant an area where Jaeger and crew would be free to fully decontaminate themselves, and, in due course, the warplane. He was even sending some kind of an airborne escort to shepherd them in – most likely a pair of fast jets.

It was all working out beautifully.

For the next hour or so they steadily gained altitude, as the Airlander climbed to her 10,000-foot cruise ceiling. The higher they got, the thinner the atmosphere, and the more fuel-efficient the airship became – which was crucial for ensuring she had the range to reach Cachimbo.

Finally, they broke free of the cloud cover, sunlight streaming in through the cockpit windows. It was now that Jaeger could get a proper look at what an awesome spectacle they made – a space-age airship and the sleek Second World War aircraft clamped beneath her, flying as one.

With the rounded shape of the Airlander's undersurface, the Ju 390's wingtips stuck out a good fifty feet to either side, tapering off to narrow knife-edge points. Jaeger figured the wings would be producing their own aerodynamic lift as the Airlander pushed ahead at approaching 200 kph, helping the airship to speed them to their destination.

With Narov deep in her documents, and Dale filming for all he was worth, Jaeger found himself with little to do but admire the view. A blanket of fluffy white cloud stretched below them as far as the horizon, the blue heavens opening wide above. For the first time in what felt like an age, he had a moment to reflect on all that had happened, and on what might lie ahead.

Narov and her shock revelations – that she had known and worked with his grandfather; that she'd been treated as family almost – needed some serious investigating. It opened up a whole world of uncertainties. Once they had boots on the ground at Cachimbo – and were truly safe, as she had put it – he needed to have a long chat with Irina Narov. But at 20,000 feet and through radios and respirators was hardly a very private or fitting way to do so.

Jaeger's priority number one had to be to work out how exactly to deal with the Ju 390 and her cargo. They were riding on a Nazi warplane stuffed full of Hitler's war secrets, painted in US Air Force markings, discovered within what was arguably Brazilian territory, but could equally be Bolivian or Peruvian, and retrieved by an international expedition team.

The question was – who had the foremost claim upon her?

Jaeger figured the likeliest scenario was that a whole alphabet soup of intelligence agencies would descend upon Cachimbo once the discovery became known to them. Colonel Evandro was a smart operator, and he was sure to have chosen a part of the vast air complex set well away from watching eyes – the public and the press.

In all likelihood, those intelligence agencies would demand – and get – a media blackout, until they had assessed what version of the story to release to the world's public. In Jaeger's experience, that was generally how these things were done.

The American government would want to completely sanitise

its role in sponsoring such a flight, as would those of her allies – most notably Great Britain – who doubtless had been party to it.

As Narov had intimated, at least some of the technology held in the Ju 390's hold was very likely still classified, and it would doubtless need to remain so. It would have to be written out of whatever statement was released to the world's public.

But Jaeger could well foresee the kind of story that would eventually hit the press.

> After seventy years lying forgotten in the Amazon jungle, the markings on the Second World War aircraft were barely legible – but only a few such mighty warplanes ever flew. To those intrepid explorers who discovered her, she was instantly recognisable as a Junkers Ju 390, although few could have imagined what a breathtaking cargo she would contain, or what it might tell us about the final death throes of Hitler's Nazi regime . . .

Kammler and his cronies would be portrayed as trying to save the best of their technology from the ashes of the Third Reich, acting independently of the Allies. Something like that anyway. As for Wild Dog Media's TV extravaganza – Dale was filming away like a madman, aware that he had the story of his life.

As a gripping adventure-mystery yarn that would out-box-office *Indiana Jones*, Jaeger figured this was about as good as it got. He didn't much fancy playing the Harrison Ford character, but Dale did have a serious quantity of interview material with him in the can.

What had been filmed had been filmed, and Jaeger could see a sanitised version of the TV series – one glossing over at least some of the aircraft's contents, not to mention those US Air Force markings – going out on the air. Indeed, he figured it would make for gripping viewing.

The one other thing that would doubtless need to be edited

out of Dale's film was the Dark Force that had been hunting them. There had been enough drama with 'lost tribes' and the Lost World of the jungle to contend with – both of which were far more palatable to a family TV audience.

Jaeger figured that the Dark Force would have to call off the hunt now – the prize having fallen out of their grasp. But given that they had at least one Predator and a heavily armed ground unit at their disposal, he didn't doubt that the force was some US-generated black agency, one that had gone rogue.

When you sanctioned that many clandestine agencies, giving them total power and zero accountability, you had to expect 'blowback', as they called it in the trade.

At some point, somewhere, you would lose all control, and one of those agencies would step right over the line.

80

Even if the Dark Force commander had called off the hunt, Jaeger could hardly do likewise. His instinct had proven unerringly right: at the end of the expedition trail he figured he'd nailed Andy Smith's killers. Jaeger felt certain that Smith had been tortured and thrown to his death in an effort to get the Dark Force to that warplane first.

Jaeger had lost two other members of his team – Clermont and Krakow – to that same Dark Force. He had a score to settle – at the very least with whoever had ordered the torture and execution of his best friend, and thereafter two members of his expedition. As he had pledged to Dulce – back in what had once been her and Andy's Wiltshire family home – he didn't leave his friends hanging.

But first he had to get the remainder of his team – those led by Lewis Alonzo – safely out of the Serra de los Dios, which meant he had something of a logistical nightmare on his hands. And amongst all of that, he somehow had to find the time to search for the answers he most wanted – *needed* – those that might lead him to his missing wife and child.

He felt a nagging certainty that Ruth and Luke were alive. He had no absolute proof – just the memories awakened by a draught of psychotropic liquid – but still he felt convinced that the clues to their fate lay somewhere on this warplane.

A tap on his shoulder broke his reverie. It was Dale.

The cameraman gave an exhausted smile. 'Figure you could give me a few words? Kind of summing up what it feels like to be sat here right now, in the cockpit of this aircraft, flying out to show it to the world?'

'Okay, but let's keep it short.'

Dale was framing up the shot when Jaeger noticed Narov's head rise abruptly from the navigator's desk. The rearmost windows of the swept-back cockpit looked out over the sides of the aircraft, and she was staring out of hers intently.

'We have company,' she announced. 'Three Black Hawk helicopters.'

'Colonel Evandro's escort,' Dale remarked. 'Got to be.' He glanced at Jaeger. 'Just a second. Hold the interview while I grab some shots.'

Dale moved across to that side of the aircraft and began filming. Jaeger followed.

Sure enough, three squat black helicopters were keeping pace with the Airlander, set maybe five hundred feet off the airship's starboard side. As Jaeger eyed them, something struck him as being amiss. The helos were painted in some kind of a matt-black stealth material, and none of them were showing any markings.

The Brazilian air force did operate Black Hawks. Maybe they did have a fleet of unmarked stealth variants, but this was far from what Jaeger had been expecting. It made sense for Colonel Evandro to have scrambled some fast jets out of Cachimbo – most likely F16s – to see them safely home in a blaze of glory.

Unmarked Black Hawks – in Jaeger's mind it just didn't compute.

While the Black Hawk came heavily armed, it was mostly a troop transport, and it wouldn't have anything like the range to make Cachimbo airbase. The helo's combat reach was less than 600 kilometres, under half of what was required.

No way did Jaeger believe this was Colonel Evandro's escort. He turned to Narov. Their eyes met.

Jaeger shook his head worriedly. *This isn't right.*

Narov reciprocated.

He flicked the Thuraya satphone to the 'on' position and dial-led Raff. Keeping off-comms was an irrelevance now. Either this was a friendly escort, in which case they were safe, or they had been found by that hostile force. Whichever it was, there was little point in trying to remain hidden.

The moment the satphone acquired a signal, Jaeger heard the ringtone, followed by an instant answer. But it wasn't Raff's voice that came on the line. Instead he could hear what sounded like incoming radio communications from whoever was com-manding the mystery flight of Black Hawks. Raff was using the Thuraya link to relay the message to Jaeger and his team.

'This is unmarked Black Hawk calling Airlander on open means,' the voice intoned. 'Confirm you are receiving me. This is unmarked Black Hawk calling Airlander: acknowledge.'

'Open means' referred to the non-encrypted general traffic radio frequency that all aircraft monitored. Oddly, the pilot's voice sounded as if it had a slightly Eastern European – Rus-sian – timbre, the flat, guttural accent for an instant reminding Jaeger of . . . Narov's way of speaking.

Narov was glued to the voice blaring out of the satphone, but just for an second she flicked her eyes up to meet Jaeger's. And in them he detected a look that he had never once expected to see.

Fear.

81

Jaeger punched out a quick data-burst message: *I am live to your comms.*

The moment he'd sent it, he heard the gravelly tones of the big Maori come up on the air. 'Black Hawk, this is Airlander. Affirmative we hear you.'

'To whom am I speaking?' the Black Hawk commander asked.

'Takavesi Raffara, ops officer, Airlander. To whom am I speaking?'

'Mr Raffara, I ask the questions. I hold all the cards. Put Mr Jaeger on the air.'

'Negative. I am the ops officer of this aircraft. All comms go via me.'

'I repeat, put Mr Jaeger on the air.'

'Negative. All comms go via me,' Raff repeated.

Jaeger saw the foremost Black Hawk open fire, using its GAU-19, a fearsome six-barrelled 50-calibre Gatling gun. During the three-second burst, the air beneath the helicopter turned black with spent shell casings. In those three short seconds it had pumped out over a hundred armour-piercing rounds, each the size of a small child's wrist.

The burst of fire had gone a good three hundred yards to the front of the Airlander's flight deck, but the message it sent was crystal clear. *We have the ability to rip you to shreds one hundred times over.*

'The next burst will be bang into your gondola,' the Black Hawk commander threatened. 'Put Jaeger on.'

'Negative. I do not have Jaeger on board my aircraft.'

Raff was choosing his words very carefully. Technically speaking, it was true: Jaeger was not aboard the Airlander.

'Listen very carefully, Mr Raffara. My navigator has identified a cleared area of land 150 kilometres due east, at grid 497865. You are to put down on that grid. And make no mistake: when you do so, I will need every member of your team accounted for. Confirm you understand my instructions.'

'Wait out.'

Jaeger heard the bleep of an incoming message on his satphone: *Response?*

He punched out a reply: *They get us down we're dead. All of us. Resist.*

Raff's voice came up on the air again. 'Black Hawk, this is Airlander. Negative. We are proceeding to our destination as planned. We are an international team embarked upon a civilian expedition. Do not – repeat, do not – interfere with this flight.'

'In that case, take a good look at the open door of our lead aircraft,' the Black Hawk commander countered. 'You see that figure in the doorway: it is one of your beloved Indians. And as a bonus, we have some of your team members with us too.'

Jaeger's mind was racing. The enemy must have overrun one of his ambush parties and captured at least some of them alive. From there it would have been easy enough to load them aboard the helicopter, using the Ju 390's former resting place as a convenient landing zone.

'I believe some of you may know this savage,' the Black Hawk commander sneered. 'His name means "the big pig". Highly appropriate. Now, watch him fly.'

Moments later a stick-like figure tumbled out of the lead Black Hawk.

Even from such a distance, Jaeger could tell that it was an Amahuaca warrior, silently screaming as he fell. He was quickly swallowed by the cloud mass, but not before Jaeger figured he'd recognised the collar of short feathers strung around his neck – the *gwyrag'waja* – each feather signifying an enemy killed in battle.

He felt a blinding blaze of rage sweep over him, as the body of what appeared to be Puruwehua's brother plummeted out of sight. Gwaihutiga had saved Jaeger's life on the rope bridge, and now he'd very likely been hurled to his death as a result of Jaeger and his team trying to save their own skins. Jaeger smashed his fist into the wall of the aircraft, his mind a whirl of sickening anger and frustration.

'I have several more of these savages,' the Black Hawk commander continued. 'For every minute you do not agree to alter course and bearing to grid 497865, another will be thrown to his death. Oh, and your expedition team – they will also follow. Do as ordered. Alter course. One minute and counting.'

'Wait out.'

Again Jaeger's phone bleeped with a message: *Response?*

Jaeger glanced at Dale and Narov: what the hell was he supposed to say? As if in answer, Narov waved the satchel full of documents at him.

'There's something they want on this warplane,' she declared. 'Something they need. They cannot shoot us down.'

Jaeger's hand hovered over the Thuraya's keypad as he willed himself to type what he knew he had to. With a wave of bitter nausea rising from the base of his guts he punched out the message: *They need warplane intact. Will not shoot us down. Do not comply. Resist.*

'We are proceeding to destination as planned.' Raff's voice came up on the airwaves. 'And be warned: we are filming your every action and beaming it live to a server, where it's being uploaded to the internet.' It wasn't entirely true, of course, but it was a classic bit of Raff improvisation and bluff. 'You are being filmed, and you will be arraigned and charged for your crimes—'

'Bullshit,' the enemy commander cut in. 'We are a flight

of unmarked Black Hawks. Don't you get it, asshole? We are beyond deniable. We – don't – exist. You think you can try ghosts for war crimes? Asshole. Change course as ordered, or face the consequences. The blood is on your hands . . .'

Another stick figure plunged from the helicopter.

As it tumbled through the blinding blue, Jaeger tried to blank from his mind the thought of Puruwehua slamming into the jungle far below. It was impossible to identify exactly which Indian the Black Hawk crew had tossed into thin air, but death was death; murder was murder.

How much blood would lie on his hands?

'So far so good,' the Black Hawk commander continued. 'We have used up two of our quota of savages. We have one remaining. Will you comply with my orders, Mr Raffara, or does this last one have to learn to fly as well?'

There was no response from Raff. If they changed course and put the Airlander – and the Ju 390 – down on the grid as given, they were finished. They both knew that. During Krav Maga training, Raff and Jaeger had been taught the two orders never to comply with: one was being relocated; the other being tied up. Both spelled disaster. To obey such an order now would not end well for anyone.

Jaeger averted his eyes as a third figure spun through the sunlit skies, arms flailing helplessly as they tried to grab at the thin atmosphere. A memory flashed through Jaeger's mind: it was of Puruwehua telling him how often he had flown like the *topena*, the big white hawk that soared over the mountains.

I have flown high as the topena, Puruwehua had told him. *I have flown over wide oceans and to distant mountains.*

The memory tortured Jaeger almost beyond his capacity to withstand.

'So now, Mr Raffara – now we move on to the really interesting part. Act Two – your fellow team members. First up, look at the figure in our open doorway. He does not look very keen to learn to fly. Alter course towards the grid as given, or he is going to take a one-way journey to splattergeddon.' The Black Hawk commander laughed at his own joke. 'One minute and counting . . .'

Jaeger's satphone bleeped. *Response?*

Jaeger could see the shock of white-blond hair glistening in the sun as a figure was forced towards the Black Hawk's doorway. Though Jaeger believed Stefan Kral to be the traitor in their midst, he couldn't be absolutely certain, and the thought of Kral's young family at home in Luton further twisted and cramped his guts.

He forced himself to punch out a reply. *Warn them that CE has fast jets on the way. Keep him talking.*

'We are proceeding to destination as planned.' Raff's voice came up on the air. 'And be warned – we have an escort of Brazilian air force fast jets inbound—'

'We know all about your B-SOB friends,' the Black Hawk commander cut in. 'You think you have friends in high places!' He laughed. 'You would not believe where *we* have friends. In any case, the colonel's aircraft are a good ninety minutes away. Comply with my orders, or more will die.'

'Negative,' Raff repeated. 'We are proceeding to our destination as planned.'

'So, I bring my aircraft a little nearer,' the Black Hawk commander announced. 'That way, you can wish your friend a pleasant ride.'

The three helicopters closed in, sticking to their tight formation, until they were no more than 250 yards away from both the Airlander and the Ju 390. When they were in position, the distinctive figure of the Slovakian cameraman was forced to the very brink of the Black Hawk's open doorway.

'Last chance,' the Black Hawk commander rasped. 'Alter course as ordered.'

'Negative,' Raff repeated. 'We are proceeding to our destination.'

Moments later, Stefan Kral was forced out.

As his body tumbled earthwards, cartwheeling through the blinding blue, Jaeger could hear Dale vomiting on to the floor behind him. Jaeger himself felt ripped apart.

Traitor or not, this was no way for anyone's life – let alone that of a young father – to end.

82

'Congratulations, Mr Raffara,' the Black Hawk commander announced. 'You have been happy to see four of your friends die. So, the last candidate for the death ride – it is Ms Leticia Santos! Oh yeah – and we all know how those Brazilian ladies love to ride. Alter course, Mr Raffara. Obey my orders. Or the death of the delightful Ms Santos will haunt you for the rest of your days.'

The satphone bleeped: *Response?*

Jaeger stared at the screen, his mind whirling at breakneck speed. Whatever way he looked at it, he was all out of options. The killing had to stop. He would not let Leticia be thrown to the wolves. But what alternative was there?

Involuntarily his free hand went to the *carnivale* scarf that he had knotted around his neck. A sudden idea flashed briefly through his eyes, coming back to centre itself more solidly in his consciousness. It was a crazy, warped idea, but right now he figured it was about the best they'd got.

He punched out a message on the Thuraya's keypad. *Act as if complying. Alter course. Standby.*

Raff's voice came up on the air. 'Affirmative, we are complying with your orders. Altering course to bearing 0845 degrees. ETA at your grid as given in fifteen – repeat one-five – minutes.'

'Excellent, Mr Raffara. I am glad to see you are finally learning how to keep your people alive . . .'

Jaeger didn't wait to catch the last words. He grabbed Narov, unbolted the door leading into the Ju 390's hold, and sprinted

for a cargo crate lying in the far reaches of the aircraft's shadowed rear.

He bent over the long packing crate that held the *Fliegerfaust*
shoulder-launched missiles. For a moment he reached for his
knife, before remembering that he'd given it to Puruwehua. An
instant later Narov was beside him, hacking at the crate with
her seven-inch Fairbairn–Sykes blade.

The tough rope fastenings fell away, and – having prised
the nails out with the blade – the two of them wrenched the
wooden lid aside.

They reached in and lifted out the first of the two crated
rocket launchers. It was surprisingly light, but it wasn't the
weight that concerned Jaeger right now. It was the weapon's
mechanism. Most modern shoulder-launched missiles used a
battery-operated electronic firing system. If the *Fliegerfaust* employed something similar, the batteries would have long gone
flat and they were done for.

Jaeger was banking on the launcher working on a simple mechanical system, in which case it should still be usable. He ran
his eye over the forward handgrip and the trigger mechanism to
the rear. He placed the launcher on his shoulder and laid his eye
against the cold steel of the sight: it consisted of a basic metal rail
running the length of the dorsal surface, to look along and aim.

Just as he'd hoped, the *Fliegerfaust*'s operating apparatus
appeared to be one hundred per cent mechanical. The rocket
launchers had been left well oiled and there didn't appear to be
a speck of rust upon them. Even the multiple barrels seemed
smooth and crystal clear. After seven decades in a box, there
was no reason why they shouldn't work just fine.

Narov reached into the crate and fished out the nine-round
missile set – each a 20 mm projectile measuring about eight
inches long. As Jaeger held the weapon steady, she slotted the
rounds into the launcher's tubes; they gave a resounding *thunk*
as they slid home.

'You pull the trigger, it fires two salvoes,' Narov explained, her voice tight with urgency. 'One of four, followed by one of five – the second a split second after the first.'

Jaeger nodded. 'We need both launchers locked and loaded. You good to operate the second?'

Narov's eyes blazed with a killer smile. 'With pleasure. They were right to nickname you the Hunter.'

They readied the second launcher, then moved across to the cargo door set in the Ju 390's hold. Only an hour or so earlier, Jaeger had closed it in preparation for their lift out of the jungle. Little had he imagined that he'd need to throw it open again any time soon, and for the kind of action that he now had in mind.

He grabbed his Thuraya and typed a message. *Engaging Black Hawks from rear of Ju 390. Will not hit Santos aircraft. Stand by.*

His phone beeped once. *Affirmative.*

Jaeger eyed Narov. 'You ready?'

'Ready,' Narov confirmed.

'I'll go for the one at nine o'clock, you go for the one at three. Do not hit Santos's aircraft.'

Narov nodded curtly.

'Soon as we kick the doors open,' Jaeger added, 'let rip.'

He reached out and unlatched the cargo door, then sat back on the floor of the warplane and braced his boots against his side. Narov did the same. Jaeger didn't believe for one moment that the Black Hawk commander knew there was a force manning the Ju 390.

He was about to learn otherwise.

'NOW!'

Jaeger booted hard, and Narov did likewise. The doors flew open and Jaeger raised himself on one knee, the *Fliegerfaust* braced on his shoulder. The nearest Black Hawk was no more than two hundred yards away. He lined the simple iron sight up with the cockpit, said a brief prayer that the launcher would work, and pulled the trigger.

Four missiles streaked away, the backblast from their eruption punching a fiery cloud of choking fumes into the Ju 390's hold. Jaeger held his aim, and a split second later the five remaining projectiles blazed towards their target. Beside him, Narov unleashed with her weapon, nine missiles blasting through the heavens towards the second Black Hawk.

Armour-piercing and high-explosive, each rocket was stabilised by a set of small holes drilled around its tail. A tiny amount of the rocket's exhaust fumes voided through those holes, spinning the projectile along its axis. It was the spin that ensured the rockets would fly true to their target – in the same way that a bullet fired from a gun was set to spin via the barrel's rifling.

Jaeger saw five of his veer wide of the mark, but four struck home. The 20 mm projectiles sparked grey puffs of smoke along the Black Hawk's flank as the armour-piercing tips sliced through the metal skin. A split second later, the high-explosive charges detonated, raking the inside of the aircraft with a storm of burning-hot jagged shrapnel.

The blast punched out the windshield of the cockpit and shattered the side windows, shrapnel lacerating the bodies of those riding inside. Moments later, the helo veered off course and fell into a steep dive, trailing a column of angry grey smoke in its wake.

To its rear, target number two had fared even worse. In the moment of maximum need, the sniper – *the assassin?* – within Narov had come to the fore. Eight of her missiles had struck home, just one lone projectile veering wide of the target.

At least one of the 20 mm rockets must have pierced the Black Hawk's fuel tank. Full enough to complete a 600-kilometre combat sortie, there was fuel in there to burn and burn. A gout of angry orange flame erupted from the helicopter, and a moment later it disintegrated in a massive, blinding fireball.

Jaeger felt the heat of the blast wave wash over him, as fingers of burning shrapnel reached out from the epicentre of the explosion. For a moment, the fiery conflagration seemed to menace the Airlander above, before the plumes of burning debris tumbled towards the cloud bank far below and were lost from view.

The blasted carcass of the second Black Hawk plummeted to earth like a stone. All that remained of the two aircraft was a dark cloud of smoke drifting on the hot tropical air.

They were down to one Black Hawk versus an Airlander/Ju 390, thundering through the open skies.

The surviving Black Hawk had veered off sharply, putting a safe distance between it and any further rocket salvoes. Not that Jaeger and Narov could unleash any: they were all out of *Fliegerfausts*. In any case, Leticia Santos was aboard that helicopter, and Jaeger for one was not willing to see her life sacrificed too.

'Mr Raffara, you will wish you hadn't done that!' screamed a voice wild with rage. 'Now I start shooting out your engines!'

'You do that, we're going down,' Raff countered, 'and with us your precious aircraft. It'll smash into the jungle—'

A burst of deadly-accurate fire from the surviving Black Hawk's GAU-19 drowned out Raff's words. Rounds tore into the Airlander's front starboard propulsor. The instant they did so, Jaeger felt the Ju 390 lurch horribly to the right, as one of the airship's four giant rotors was torn to pieces.

Inside the Airlander, the crew would be struggling to keep her airborne on three propulsors, adjusting thrust direction and power to try to even up the stricken aircraft's load, and pumping helium back and forth between the airship's three giant hulls.

'Airlander to Black Hawk.' Raff's voice came up on the air. 'You shoot out another propulsor, we are no longer airworthy with this load, and we will be forced to jettison the Ju 390. Ten thousand feet straight down. Back the hell off.'

'I don't think so,' the Black Hawk commander countered. 'You have a team aboard that aircraft, and I really don't think you'll let them fall. Comply with my instructions, or I will shoot out a second engine.'

A message bleeped on Jaeger's Thuraya: *Response?*
Jaeger didn't know how to respond.
Now they really were all out of options.
Stalemate.

83

For a third time the Black Hawk's GAU-19 spat fire.

A vicious burst tore into the Airlander's rear port propulsor. Jaeger and Narov were back in the cockpit by now, and they felt the Ju 390 give a sickening jolt to the left as a second set of rotors was put out of action.

For a few frantic seconds the giant airship fought to right herself, the two surviving propulsors set at opposite ends and sides of the craft struggling to even out the impossible load. But when the Airlander finally reached some kind of new equilibrium, it was clear that she no longer had the grunt to manage the weight she was carrying.

Almost instantly, the airship's speed started dropping dramatically, deprived as she was of half her forward propulsion. Added to that, she was losing altitude. With the Ju 390 slung beneath her, she was slipping towards disaster.

The Black Hawk shifted position, dropping behind and moving out of sight of those in the Ju 390's cockpit. Jaeger didn't think for one moment that the commander had called off the attack: what the hell was he up to now?

A message pinged through on the Thuraya. *BH moving around to your rear. Closing in towards your port wingtip. About to board your aircraft???*

Jaeger stared at the message for an instant: the Black Hawk was doing what?

He glanced out of the port window.

Sure enough, the helicopter pilot was inching his aircraft's side door towards the Ju 390's port wingtip. Jaeger could see a dozen heavily armed operators clustered at the doorway, clad in black NBC suits and respirators.

He felt Narov appear beside him. 'Just let them try!' she snarled, as she caught sight of the black-clad figures.

A split second later, she'd grabbed her Dragunov sniper rifle, ready to nail anyone who tried to board the Ju 390.

'Don't!' Jaeger forced the barrel of her weapon down. 'Right now, they don't have a clue where we are. You open fire, they'll mallet the cockpit. They'll chew us to pieces.'

'Then let me take out the Black Hawk's pilot!' Narov protested. 'At least that!'

'You take out the pilot, the co-pilot takes control, and they still mallet us with fire. Plus Santos – she's aboard that aircraft.'

'Sometimes you have to take a life to save a life,' Narov responded coldly. 'Or as in this case, you take a life to save *many lives*.'

'No!' Jaeger shook his head violently. 'No! There has to be a better way.'

He cast his eyes around the warplane's cockpit in desperation. They came to rest upon a heap of dusty bundles stowed below the navigator's seat. Each was labeled *Fallschirm*. While he didn't understand the German, he figured he knew what they had to be. He reached across and grabbed one.

Do the unexpected.

He waved it at Narov. 'Parachute, right?'

'Parachute,' Narov confirmed. 'But . . . ?'

Jaeger glanced out of the window. The Ju 390's speed had dropped dramatically, and he saw the first black-clad figure leap from the Black Hawk's open doorway and spring on to the plane's giant wingtip, landing in a crouch. Moments later, a second figure joined him, and they started moving along in a steady crouching shuffle.

Jaeger thrust the parachute bundle into Narov's arms and threw a second at Dale, grabbing a third for himself.

'Get 'em on,' he yelled. 'And let's hope that like most things German they're bloody built to last!'

As they struggled into the parachute rigs, a message pinged in on the Thuraya. *Enemy gathered at your fuselage. Setting explosive charges.*

The black-clad operators were poised to blast a hole through the Ju 390's central fuselage to gain entry to the hold.

Jaeger messaged back: *When all bad guys are aboard, cut us loose. Let us fall. And Raff, don't bloody argue. I know what I'm doing.*

A message bleeped back. *Affirmative. See you in Paradise.*

Thank God Jaeger had Raff aboard the Airlander. No one else would have complied with such an order so unquestioningly. That was the unique bond the two men shared, one forged over many years at the extreme end of soldiering.

From the rear of the warplane Jaeger detected a muffled explosion. The Ju 390 shuddered for an instant, as the cutting charge blasted a man-sized hole in her skin. In his mind's eye he could see the black-clad operators piling into the dark, smoke-filled hold, their weapons at the ready.

It would take them several seconds to orientate themselves, and to search the aircraft's rear for Jaeger and his fellows. That done, they'd advance towards the bulkhead and set a second set of charges. The bulkhead door, once locked, could only be opened from the inside – the cockpit side – so they'd have to blast a way through that too.

But even so, Jaeger, Narov and Dale had only a matter of seconds remaining to them.

'Okay, here's the plan,' Jaeger yelled. 'Any moment now, the Airlander's cutting us free. Like any fine aircraft released with a little forward momentum, she'll pick up speed as she falls, then start to glide. As soon as we're cut loose, we hurl out the rest of those,' he jabbed a hand at the remaining parachutes, 'and then we jump.

'Do not pull your chute until you're well into the clouds,' he continued, 'or the Black Hawk will be able to follow. Try to stick together and link up in the fall. Order of jump: Dale, Narov, myself. Ready?'

Narov nodded. There was a glow of battle lust and adrenalin burning in her eyes.

As for Dale, he looked as white as a sheet, and as if he were about to vomit his guts up for a second time. But still he gave a half-hearted thumbs-up. Jaeger was amazed at the guy: he'd been through enough to faze the most battle-hardened of soldiers, and yet he'd stood the test pretty damn well.

'Don't forget your camera, or at least the memory cards,' Jaeger yelled at him. 'Whatever happens now, we're not losing the film!'

He pulled out the remaining parachutes and stacked them by the cockpit's side, then threw open both windows so they had maximum room to make their exits.

He turned to Narov. 'Don't forget your documents, whatever they are. Get that satchel strapped on tight, and don't let it out of your . . .'

He was forced to swallow the rest of his words as the Ju 390 gave a sudden sickening lurch and plunged into the fall. The Airlander had released her, and for a few horrible seconds the Ju 390 seemed to shoot vertically downwards plummeting like a stone, before her wings caught the air and the drop bottomed out into a steep but breathtaking glide.

'Go! Go! Go!' Jaeger yelled, as he started stuffing the parachutes out of the window.

One after another he hurled the spare *Fallschirms* into the howling void.

Dale reached for the window, thrust the top half of his body through, and then promptly froze. The slipstream was tearing at his torso, but his feet seemed glued to the aircraft's metal floor.

Unmoving.

Jaeger didn't hesitate. He dropped his powerful shoulders,

grabbed Dale's legs, and lifted him with all his might, forcing him – screaming – into thin air.

He could hear voices yelling from the far side of the bulkhead now. The black-clad operators were preparing to blast their way through. Narov jumped on to the pilot's chair, grabbed the cockpit roof, and swung her legs through the window.

She glanced back at him. 'You are coming, yes?'

She must have read the indecision that flashed through Jaeger's eyes. For an instant his mind was back on that dark mountain side as his wife and child were stolen away from him. He hadn't done all he could – *hell, he hadn't done anything* – to search the warplane for clues as to who had taken them, and why.

For an agonising second that voice from behind the gas mask – the voice that Jaeger had half recognised – seared through his mind: 'Don't ever forget – you failed to protect your wife and child. *Wir sind die Zukunft!'*

Jaeger felt riveted to the spot; unable to move.

Deep in his heart, he was desperate for answers.

And if he abandoned the warplane, he'd maybe lost them for ever.

'Get to the window!' Narov screamed. 'NOW!'

Jaeger found himself staring down the barrel of a gun. Narov had whipped out a short-barrelled, compact Beretta pistol and had it levelled at his head.

'I know all about it!' she yelled. 'They killed your grandfather. They came for you and your family. Something you did triggered them to do that. That's how we'll find the answers. But if you go down now, with this plane, they've won!'

Jaeger tried to force his limbs to move.

'JUMP!' Narov screamed at him, her finger bone-white on the trigger. 'I AM NOT HAVING YOUR LIFE WASTED!'

Suddenly there was an ear-splitting roar from behind. The bulkhead blew, the cockpit filling with a blinding cloud of choking smoke. The force of the blast threw Jaeger against the side window, and it served to bring him to his senses. As he reached for the exit, Narov opened fire with the Beretta, pumping shots into the mass of black-clad figures that were surging through the opening.

Moments later, Jaeger hurled himself out, plunging into the thin and howling blue.

84

An instant after he had jumped, Jaeger found himself tumbling over and over in the freefall, just as he'd done during the near-death plunge from the C-130. He forced his arms out wide and arched his body to stabilise himself. That done, he adopted the delta-track profile – arms tight by his sides, legs stretched out behind him – to get into the cloud bank as quickly as possible.

But as the speed of his fall increased, he cursed himself for having been such a bloody fool. Narov had been right. If he'd died on that warplane, what good would it have done anyone, least of all his wife and son? He'd been an idiot to hesitate, and he'd put Narov's life in danger. Hell, he didn't even know if she'd made it out of the warplane alive, and there was no way he could check now – not in the crazed maelstrom of the freefall.

The Ju 390 had been accelerating ever since the Airlander had released her. She would be speeding into the skies ahead at pushing 300 kph, like a massive ghostly dart – and he just had to hope and pray that Narov had made it out alive.

Seconds later, he was swallowed by the clouds. As the thick water vapour enveloped him, he reached for the chute's deployment handle, tugged hard . . . and prayed. If ever he hoped that the Nazis had built something to last, it was now.

Nothing happened.

Jaeger glanced around to check he was pulling the right handle. Nothing was easy in the half-light of this swirling white-out, especially when being thrown around like a rag doll. But as far as he could tell, the main chute seemed to be stuck fast.

A phrase flashed through his head as the ground rushed up to meet him: *look-locate-peel-punch-pull-arch*. It was the drill he'd been taught years earlier, for emergency procedures in the free-fall when your main chute failed.

Same principles, different system, he told himself.

He grabbed for what he figured was the reserve. It was an old-fashioned system, but there was no reason why it wouldn't work just fine. It was now or never, for the ground was fast approaching. He pulled extra hard, and the reserve parachute – an expanse of German silk; silk that had been folded away for seven decades awaiting the chance to fly again – billowed into the air above him.

Like most things German, this *Fallschirm* had been built with quality in mind, and it opened like a dream. In fact, it was a joy to fly under. Had Jaeger not been in such a world of turmoil right now, he might have found himself enjoying the ride.

The Germans had used a chute design similar to that employed by British airborne units in the Second World War. It had a high-domed mushroom-shaped profile, and was stable and solid in the air – as opposed to the flatter, faster, more manoeuvrable design of modern-day military parachutes.

At around five hundred feet of altitude, Jaeger emerged from the clouds. His first thoughts were for Dale and Narov. He glanced west and figured he could just make out the distinctive scar of a parachute at ground level, marking where Dale appeared to have made it down.

He glanced east just as a flash of white popped out of the base of the cloud.

Narov. It had to be. Somehow she must have made it out of the Ju 390's cockpit, and by the look of the body slung beneath the chute, she was still alive.

He fixed both positions in his head, then checked the ground below.

Dense jungle, with nowhere obvious to land.

Again.

As he drifted towards the canopy, Jaeger spared a momentary thought for the Ju 390. From 10,000 feet, the speeding warplane could glide for scores of kilometres, but he knew she was doomed. With every second after the Airlander had released her, she'd been gaining in airspeed but losing altitude.

Sooner or later she'd smash into the jungle at more than 300 kph. The upside was that she'd take with her those black-clad operators, for no way would the surviving Black Hawk be able to lift them off that careering warplane. And Jaeger, of course, had hurled all the spare chutes out the cockpit window.

The downside was that she'd be lost for ever, together with the secrets she'd been carrying – not to mention her toxic cargo being strewn across the rainforest.

But there was little Jaeger could do about that now.

The lone unmarked Black Hawk touched down on the isolated jungle airstrip.

The operator code-named Grey Wolf Six – real name Vladimir Ustanov – stepped down from the aircraft, satphone glued to his ear. His face was grey and drawn, the experiences of the last few hours sitting heavy upon him.

'Sir, understand the situation.' He spoke into the satphone, his voice tight with exhaustion. 'I have myself and four others remaining from my airborne force. We are incapable of mounting any form of meaningful operation.'

'And the warplane?' Grey Wolf demanded incredulously.

'A smoking ruin. Spread across several dozen miles of jungle. We overflew her until the moment she went down.'

'And her cargo? The *documents*?'

'Smashed into smoking wreckage, along with a dozen of my finest men.'

'If we couldn't get our hands on them, better they are destroyed.' A beat. 'So finally, Vladimir, you have achieved something.'

'Sir, I've lost two Black Hawks, plus three dozen men—'

'Worth the cost,' Grey Wolf cut in, mercilessly. 'They were paid to do a job, and paid well, so don't expect any sympathy from me. Tell me, did anyone get out of that warplane alive?'

'We saw three figures bale out. We lost them in the clouds. Whether any survived is doubtful. We don't know if they had chutes, and even if they did, it's uncharted jungle down there.'

'But they might have?' Grey Wolf hissed.

'They might,' Vladimir Ustanov conceded.

'They might have survived, which means they might well have retrieved from that warplane some of the very things we were after?'

'They might.'

'I am turning my aircraft around,' Grey Wolf snapped. 'With no force remaining operational, there is no point my flying into theatre. I want you and your fellow survivors to take a holiday somewhere suitably remote and obscure. But don't disappear. Keep in communication.'

'Understood.'

'Those who survived – if there are any – will need to be found. That which we sought – if they have it – will need to be returned to us.'

'Understood, sir.'

'I'll be in touch in the normal way. In the meantime, Vladimir, you may want to recruit some new foot soldiers, to replace those you have so carelessly lost. Same terms; same mission.'

'Understood.'

'One final thing: you still have the Brazilian?'

Vladimir glanced at a figure lying on the floor of the Black Hawk. 'We have her.'

'Keep her. We may be able to use her. In the meantime, interrogate her in your own special way. Find out all she knows. With luck, she may lead us to the others.'

Vladimir smiled. 'With pleasure, sir.'

*

From a Learjet 85 flying high over the Gulf of Mexico, the commander known as Grey Wolf made a second call. It was routed to an obscure grey office lying within a grey-walled complex of buildings, positioned deep within a swathe of grey forest in remote rural Virginia, on the eastern coast of the USA.

The call went through to a building stuffed full of the world's most advanced signals intercept and tracking systems. Next to the entryway to that building was a small brass plaque. It read: *CIA – Division of Asymmetric Threat Analysis (DATA)*.

A figure dressed in smart–casual civilian clothes answered. 'DATA. Harry Peterson.'

'It's me,' Grey Wolf announced. 'I'm inbound on the Learjet and I need you to find that individual I sent you the file on. Jaeger. William Jaeger. Use all possible means: internet, email, mobile phones, flight bookings, passport details – *anything*. Last known location, western Brazil, near the Bolivia–Peru border.'

'Understood, sir.'

Grey Wolf killed the call.

He settled back into his seat. Things certainly hadn't gone so well in the Amazon, but this was just a skirmish, he told himself. One of many such battles fought in a far longer war; a war that he and his forefathers had been fighting since the spring of 1945.

A setback, certainly, but a manageable one, and nothing compared to some they had suffered in the past.

He reached for a sleek-looking tablet computer lying on the table before him. He powered it up and opened a file, revealing a list of names in alphabetical order. He ran the cursor down the list and typed a few words beside one of them: *Missing in action. If alive, terminate. PRIORITY*.

That done, he picked up an attaché case lying beside him, laid it on the table and slipped the tablet inside. He closed the lid with a resounding click, flicking the combination lock so it was securely fastened.

On the lid of the attaché case in small gold lettering were the words: *Hank Kammler, Deputy Director, CIA.*

Hank Kammler – AKA Grey Wolf – ran his fingertips gently, reverentially, over the embossing. At the end of the war his father had been forced to change his name. SS Oberst-Gruppenführer Hans Kammler had become Horace Kramer – the better to ease his recruitment into the Office for Strategic Services, the forerunner of the CIA. As he'd worked his way up through the CIA into its highest ranks, Horace Kramer had never lost sight of his true mission: to hide in plain sight, to regroup and to rebuild the Reich.

By the time his father's life was cut prematurely short, Hank Kammler had decided to take up the mantle and follow him into the CIA. Kammler smiled to himself thinly, an edge of mockery creeping into his eyes. As if he would ever have been content quietly serving as a CIA man, forgetting the glory of his Nazi forefathers.

Recently, he'd opted to recover what was rightfully his. Born Hank Kramer, he'd changed his surname formally to Kammler – thus reclaiming the legacy of his father, and what he saw as his birthright.

And as far as he was concerned, that reclamation was only just beginning.

85

Jaeger settled into his seat for the short connecting flight to Bioko airport.

The flight from London to Nigeria had been all that he'd expected – fast, direct and comfortable, although this time his budget hadn't quite stretched to first class. At Lagos he'd boarded some clapped-out regional airliner for the short jump across the Gulf of Guinea to the island capital of Equatorial Guinea.

The contact that he'd had from Pieter Boerke had been as unexpected as it had been intriguing. Some two weeks after bailing out of that doomed warplane as it plunged towards the jungle, Jaeger had made it out to a place of relative safety – Cachimbo airbase. And it was at Cachimbo that Boerke had managed to get a call through to him.

'I have your papers,' the South African had announced. 'The seventh page of the manifest, just like you asked for.'

Jaeger hadn't had the heart to tell Boerke that the last thing on his mind right then was an obscure Second World War cargo ship that had docked in Bioko's harbour towards the end of the war. He'd asked the coup leader to scan the papers and email them over. He hadn't quite got the answer he'd been expecting.

'No, man; no can do,' Boerke had told him. 'You have to come see, in person. Because, my friend, this isn't just papers. There's something physical. Something I can't email or post. Trust me, man – you have to come see.'

'You got a hint?' Jaeger had asked. 'It's a long way to fly. Plus, after the last few weeks—'

'Put it this way,' Boerke had cut in. 'I am not a Nazi. In fact, I hate bloody Nazis. I am not the grandson of one, either. But if I were, I'd go a very long way – in fact I'd go to the ends of the earth, and maybe even have a lot of people killed – to make sure this never saw the light of day. That's all I am willing to say. Trust me, Jaeger, you need to be here.'

Jaeger had considered his options. He was working on the assumption that Alonzo, Kamishi and Joe James were still alive, and being guided by the surviving Indians to a place where they could rejoin the outside world. He felt pretty certain that Gwaihutiga was dead, thrown from the Black Hawk along with Stefan Kral, their seemingly traitorous cameraman.

As for Leticia Santos, she was still missing, fate unknown. Colonel Evandro had promised to do all he could to find her, and Jaeger reckoned he and his B-SOB teams would leave no stone unturned.

Jaeger's ruse with getting the Airlander to jettison the Ju 390 had doubtless saved the lives of the airship's crew, Raff included. The Black Hawk had been forced to chase after the warplane as it had accelerated into its gliding dive, leaving the Airlander to limp in to Cachimbo.

Dale had managed to injure himself when his parachute had ploughed into the jungle canopy, and Narov had taken a shrapnel wound to the arm as the Dark Force had blasted their way into the Ju 390 cockpit. But Jaeger had managed to link up with them both on the ground and help get them moving – although it had been touch and go whether they would make it out of there.

Typically, both Dale and Narov had claimed that they'd suffered only flesh wounds and were quite capable of surviving the onward journey. Jaeger had worried that in the hot and humid jungle, and with little chance of rest, proper nutrition or medical treatment, their injuries were at risk of turning septic.

Still, he'd realised there was little chance of either Narov or Dale listening to his concerns – and in any case, there was precious little he could do to help right now. Either they made it out of the jungle under their own steam, or they would die.

Jaeger had located a small stream, and they'd followed that for two days, moving only as fast as their condition allowed. Eventually the stream had led to a tributary, leading in turn to a larger river, one that turned out to be navigable. As luck would have it, Jaeger had managed to flag down a passing timber barge – one used to shunt tree trunks downriver towards the sawmills.

A three-day river trip had followed, during which the greatest danger seemed to be Narov falling out with the drunken Brazilian captain. But only for so long.

Once Narov and Dale were aboard ship, the infections that Jaeger had feared might take hold did, and with a vengeance. By the time their journey was over – Jaeger delivering them to Cachimbo airbase and its state-of-the-art high-security hospital via a local taxi cab – they both had raging fevers.

They were diagnosed with septicaemia: their wounds had become infected and turned the entire circulatory system septic. In Dale's case at least, the situation was exacerbated by acute exhaustion. They'd been rushed into intensive care, and were now getting treatment under Colonel Evandro's careful watch and guard.

Having got those he could out of the worst of the danger – and with little else he could do to help Leticia Santos – Jaeger had figured he could risk booking himself a flight from Brazil to Bioko. He'd made sure the colonel kept him briefed every step of the way.

He'd promised to be back in time to bring Dale and Narov home, once they were well enough to travel. He'd got Raff to sit permanent guard outside their hospital door, as an added layer of security.

Before leaving, Jaeger had grabbed a few moments with Narov, only recently released from the intensive care unit.

He'd taken a look at the papers she'd retrieved from the Ju 390. The German was still mostly lost on him, and much of the *Aktion Feuerland* document proved to be written in a sequence of apparently random numbers, which Narov figured had to be code.

Without breaking that code, there wasn't a great deal more that she – or Jaeger – could glean from the document.

At one point she had asked Jaeger to wheel her into the hospital garden, so she could feel the sun on her face and get some fresh air. Once they were positioned somewhere reasonably private, she had gone a little way to explaining some of what had happened over the past few days. Predictably, in order to do so she'd had to start with the Second World War.

'You saw the kind of technology that was on that warplane,' she had begun weakly. 'By the spring of 1945, the Nazis had test-fired intercontinental ballistic missiles. They had fitted warheads with sarin nerve gas, not to mention plague and botulinum toxins. With just a handful of such weapons – one each to hit London, New York, Washington, Toronto and Moscow – the fortunes of the war might have turned completely.

'Against that we had the atom bomb, but we hadn't yet perfected that. And remember, it could only be delivered by a lumbering bomber, not by a guided missile travelling at many times the speed of sound. We had zero defence against their missiles.

'The Nazis had the ultimate threat, and they offered the Allies a deal – one that would allow the Reich to relocate to chosen safe havens, complete with their highest-tech weaponry. But the Allies made a counter-offer. They said: "Okay, relocate. Take all your *Wunderwaffe* with you. But on one condition: you join us in the real struggle – the coming global fight against communism."

'The Allies cut a deal to sponsor the most secret relocations. They couldn't of course have the top Nazis turning up in mainland Britain or the USA. The public wouldn't have stood for it.

They sent them instead into their own backyards – the Americans to South America; the British to the colonies – to India, Australia and South Africa, places where it was easy enough to hide them.

'So a new pact was forged. An unspeakable one. The Allied–Nazi pact.' Narov had paused, digging deep to find the strength to continue. '*Aktion Adlerflug* – Operation Eagle Flight – was Hitler's code name for the plan to relocate the Nazis' top technology and weaponry; hence those stamps on the crates in the Ju 390's hold. *Aktion Feuerland* – Operation Fire Land – was the code name for the relocation of their top people.'

She glanced at Jaeger with pained eyes. 'We have never had a list of exactly who those people were. Never, in spite of all the years searching. The documents retrieved from that warplane – that's what I hope they may yield. That, and a sense of where exactly the technology and the individuals went.'

Jaeger had been tempted to ask why it mattered. It was seven decades ago. It was old news. But Narov must have guessed as much.

'There is an old saying.' She'd motioned him closer, her voice weakening with the exhaustion. 'The child of a snake is still a snake. The Allies had forged a pact with the devil. The longer it was kept hidden, the more powerful and controlling it became, until it was all but unassailable. We believe it persists at all levels of the military, banking and world government – even today.'

She must have seen the doubt clouding Jaeger's eyes.

'You think this is far-fetched?' she had whispered defiantly. 'Ask yourself for how long the Knights Templar legacy lasted. Nazism is less than a hundred years old; the Knights Templar legacy has lasted two thousand years, and it is still with us today. You think the Nazis just faded away overnight? You think those who were relocated to the safe havens would have allowed the Reich to die? You think their children would have abandoned what they saw as their birthright?

'The *Reichsadler* with the strange circular symbol beneath the tail – we believe that is their symbol, their stamp. And as you well know, it has started to rear its head again.'

For a moment Jaeger had thought she was done, the exhaustion silencing her. But then from somewhere she'd found the strength for a final few words.

'William Edward Michael Jaeger, if you still have doubts, there is one thing that should prove this for you. Think about the people who tried to stop us. They killed three of your team, and many more Indians. They had Predator, Black Hawks and God only knows what else. They were deep black and ultra-deniable. Imagine who might wield that kind of power, or act with such impunity.

'The sons of the snakes are rising. They have a global network and their power grows. And as *they* have a network, so there is a network that aims to stop them.' She paused, her face drained of all colour. 'Before his death, your grandfather was the head of it. Those invited to join each get given a knife – a symbol of resistance – similar to the one that I carry.

'But who wants this poisoned chalice thrust upon them? Who? The power of the enemy is on the rise, while ours – it is waning. *Wir Sind die Zukunft*. You have heard their motto: *we are the future*.'

Her eyes had flickered across to Jaeger. 'Those of us who hunt them – we do not normally get to live for long.'

86

'Sir, hello. Sir, a drink before we land?' the air hostess repeated for the third time.

Jaeger had been miles away, reliving that conversation with Narov. She hadn't said a great deal more. The exhaustion and pain had got the better of her, and Jaeger had wheeled her back to her hospital bed.

He flashed the hostess a smile. 'A Bloody Mary, please. Lots of Worcestershire sauce.'

Bioko airport hadn't changed a great deal since Jaeger's last visit. A new force of security and customs officers had replaced President Honore Chambara's corrupt and venal guard, but otherwise, it looked pretty much the same. The familiar figure of Pieter Boerke was waiting at Arrivals, complete with a couple of hulking great guys Jaeger recognised as his security detail.

Boerke had just overrun a despotic dictator, and he wasn't one for discreet, low-level close protection. The South African held out a hand of welcome, before turning to his bodyguards. 'Right, boys, bloody grab him! Let's get him back into Black Beach!'

For a moment, Jaeger tensed himself for battle, then Boerke burst into laughter. 'Calm down, man, calm down! We South Africans have a bloody nasty sense of humour. It's good to see you again, my friend.'

On the drive to Malabo, the island's capital, Boerke filled Jaeger in on how well the coup had gone. The intelligence that Major Mojo – Jaeger's former Black Beach jailer – had provided had proven crucial to its success, another reason why Boerke had been keen to deliver on the favour he'd promised.

They reached Malabo's Santa Isabel harbour and headed along the waterfront, pulling up in front of a grand colonial-era building overlooking the water. During his three years on the island, Jaeger had done his best to keep a low profile, and he'd rarely had cause to visit the government offices.

Boerke led him to the vaults, wherein successive regimes had stowed away the nation's most sensitive documents – not that there were many to be had in a place like Equatorial Guinea. Boerke got the doors to the vault firmly closed and bolted, with his bodyguards standing watch outside. Just he and Jaeger remained in the cool, dark, musty interior.

Boerke pulled a faded cardboard file off a nearby shelf. It was stuffed full of a thick wad of documents. He placed it on the table before them.

'This,' he tapped the file, 'trust me, man, it was worth flying halfway around the world for.'

He waved one hand at the shelves that lined the room. 'Not much of this is even worth keeping: Equatorial Guinea hardly has a wealth of state secrets. But it seems the island did play a role during the war . . . and towards the end, let me tell you, it was something close to mind-blowing.'

Boerke paused. 'Okay, some history, most of which I presume you know, but without which the contents of this file will not make a great deal of sense. Back then Bioko was a Spanish colony called Fernando Po. Spain was, in theory, neutral during the war, and so was Fernando Po. In practice, the Spanish government was basically fascist and an ally of the Nazis.

'The harbour here dominates the Gulf of Guinea,' Boerke continued. 'Control of this stretch of ocean was key to winning the war in North Africa, 'cause all the resupply convoys came via this route. German U-boats prowled these waters, and they came very close to shutting down Allied shipping. Santa Isabel harbour – it was their secret U-boat rearming and refuelling centre, one sanctioned by the island's Spanish governor, who hated the British.

'In early March 1945, things really started to get interesting.' Boerke's eyes glistened. 'An Italian cargo ship, the SS *Michelangelo*, docked at the harbour, and duly attracted the attention of the British spies based here. There were three, stationed at the British consulate under cover of being diplomats. Each was a serving agent with the Special Operations Executive.'

He glanced at Jaeger. 'I take it you know of the SOE? Ian Fleming is said to have based his James Bond character on a real-life SOE agent.'

He flipped open the file and pulled out an old black-and-white photograph. It showed a large steamship, one massive funnel set vertically amidships. 'That's the *Michelangelo*. But notice – she's painted in the colours of Compania Naviera Levantina, a Spanish shipping company.

'Compania Naviera Levantina was set up by one Martin Bormann,' Boerke continued, 'a man better known as Hitler's banker. It had one purpose only – to ship the Nazis' loot to the four corners of the earth, under the flag of a neutral country, Spain. Bormann vanished at the end of the war. Utterly. He was never found.

'Bormann's key role was to oversee the plunder of Europe. The Nazis carted back to Germany all the gold, cash and artwork they could rob and steal. By the end of the war, Hitler had become the wealthiest man in all of Europe – possibly even the world. And he had amassed the greatest art collection ever known.

'Bormann's job was to ensure that all that wealth didn't die with the Reich.' Boerke slapped a hand on the file. 'And apparently, Fernando Po became the transit point for much of the Nazis' loot. Between January and March 1945, five further shipments came through Santa Isabel harbour, each stuffed full of booty. It was transferred on to U-boats for onwards transportation, and there the trail seems to go cold.

'That trail was documented by the SOE agents in great detail,' Boerke continued. 'But you know the weirdest thing: the Allies seem to have done nothing to stop the Nazis. Publicly, they made out they were about to raid those ships. Privately, they did zero to stop them.

'The SOE agents – they were low on the feeding chain. They couldn't understand why those shipments were never stopped. And it didn't seem to make a great deal of sense to me, either – not until you get to the last few pages of the file. It's then that we come to the *Duchessa*.'

Boerke produced another photo from the file. 'There she is – the *Duchessa*. But notice the difference between her and the previous vessels. She's decked out in Compania Naviera Levantina colours again, but she's actually a cargo liner. She's designed to carry people as well as goods. Why send a passenger liner if your cargo consists mostly of priceless artwork and gold looted from across Europe?'

Boerke eyed Jaeger. 'I tell you why: because mostly she was carrying passengers.' He flipped a sheet of paper across the table. 'The seventh page of the *Duchessa*'s shipping manifest. It contains a list of two dozen passengers, but each is identified only by a series of numbers. No names. Which is not enough to have made you fly all the way out to Bioko for, eh, my friend?

'Luckily, your SOE agents were very resourceful.' He pulled out a final photo and slipped it across to Jaeger. 'I don't know how familiar you are with the top-flight Nazis from the spring of 1945. This was taken on a long lens, presumably from the window of the British consulate, which overlooks the harbour.

'Don't you just love those uniforms?' Boerke demanded sarcastically. 'The long leather coats? The thigh-length leather boots? The death's heads?' He ran his hand through his thick beard. 'Trouble is, dressed like that, they all look the bloody same. But these guys – they're top-tier Nazis for sure. Got to be. And if you can crack whatever code the names are listed in, that will prove it.'

'So where the hell did they go from here?' Jaeger asked incredulously.

In answer, Boerke flipped the photos over. 'It's date-stamped on the reverse: the ninth of May 1945 – two days after the Nazis signed their unconditional surrender with the Allies. But that's when the trail goes cold. Or maybe that's also detailed somewhere in the code. Man, I spent a month of Sundays studying this file. By the time I'd realised what it was – piecing together all it meant – it had scared the living daylights out of me.'

He shook his head. 'If it's all true – and no way is a file sat in this vault a fake – it rewrites everything we ever thought we knew. The entirety of post-war history. It is literally mind-blowing. I have been trying not to think about it. You know why? Because it scares the shit out of me. People like that don't tend to go quietly and start farming.'

Jaeger stared at the photo for a long second. 'But if it is an SOE file, how come it ended up in the hands of the Spanish governor of Fernando Po?'

Boerke laughed. 'Now that's the funny part. The governor figured out the so-called British diplomats were actually spies. So he decided – what the hell? He staged a break-in at the consulate and stole all their files. Not exactly cricket, but putting spies on his island posing as diplomats wasn't exactly cricket either.

'You know that old saying: beware of what you wish for?' Boerke pushed the entire file across to Jaeger.

'My friend – you asked for it. It's all yours.'

87

B oerke wasn't one for overdramatising things.

The file from the Bioko Government House archive was as shocking as it was revelatory. And as Jaeger packed it into his carry-on flight luggage, he was reminded of a phrase that Narov had used recently: 'poisoned chalice'.

The bag with the file in it seemed to weigh so heavily in his hands. It was another clue to the puzzle, and doubtless one the Dark Force would kill for.

Jaeger rejoined Boerke with his luggage. The South African had offered him a tour of the island before he was scheduled to catch a return flight to London. He'd promised further extra-ordinary revelations, not that Jaeger could imagine what would possibly top the Government House file.

They drove east out of Malabo, heading into the thick tropical bush. By the time Boerke had turned on to the tiny dirt track threading towards the coast, Jaeger knew where they were going. They were making for Fernao, the place where he had spent three long years teaching English to the children of a fishing village.

Jaeger was trying desperately to think what he would say to the village chief, whose son, Little Mo, had died during the battle on the beach. It was less than two months back, but to Jaeger it felt like a whole lifetime and a world away.

Boerke must have noticed the worry etched on his features. He laughed. 'Jaeger, man, I tell you – you look more scared now than when I ordered my guys to throw you into Black Beach. Relax. Next big surprise coming up.'

As they rounded the final bend in the road, Jaeger was surprised to see some kind of a reception party up ahead.

They drew closer, and it seemed as if most of the village had turned out . . . but for what? To welcome him? After what had happened, he really did not deserve that.

Jaeger noticed a home-made banner had been strung from one palm tree to another, stretching across the dirt road.

It read: *WELCOME HOME WILLIAM JAEGER.*

As Boerke pulled to a halt and Jaeger's former pupils mobbed the vehicle, he could feel a lump forming in his throat. Boerke and his guards left him to it, as little hands dragged him out and propelled him towards the chief's house. Jaeger steeled himself for what he knew was going to be a bittersweet reunion.

He stepped inside. After the harsh sunlight, the dark interior momentarily blinded him. The familiar sound of the surf from the nearby beach echoed through the thin mud walls of the hut. A hand was thrust forward in greeting, but the chief's welcome turned rapidly into a powerful bear hug.

'William Jaeger . . . William Jaeger, welcome. Fernao village – it will always be your home.'

The chief seemed close to tears. Jaeger fought back the emotion.

'Insh'Allah, you have travelled well?' the chief asked. 'After your escape, we did not know if you had made it across the waters – you and your friend.'

'Insh'Allah,' Jaeger replied. 'Raff and I – we made it through that and many more adventures.'

The chief smiled. He gestured into a dark corner of the hut. 'Come,' he commanded. 'We have kept Mr Jaeger waiting long enough.'

A figure leapt out of the shadows, throwing himself into Jaeger's arms. 'Sir! Sir! Welcome back! Welcome home! And look!' The small boy gestured at the sunglasses perched on his forehead. 'I still have these! Your sunglasses! Your Oakleys!'

Jaeger laughed. He could barely believe it. Little Mo still

had a thick bandage wrapped around his head, but he was very much alive!

Jaeger hugged him close, savouring the sweet miracle of the boy's survival. But at the same moment he felt the pang of an irreplaceable loss deep inside his heart. His own son would be around Little Mo's age now. That was if he was still alive . . .

With perfect timing, Boerke joined them, and the chief proceeded to relate the story of Little Mo's miraculous survival.

'We have God – and you, Mr Jaeger – to thank for this . . . this miracle. Plus Mr Boerke, of course. The bullet fired on the night of your escape hit my son a glancing blow. He was left for dead and we feared he would indeed die. And of course, there was no money to send him to the kind of hospital where they might save him.

'Then came the coup, and this man turned up,' the chief gestured at Boerke, 'with a piece of paper and some numbers. And that gave access to a bank account, in which you had left . . . money. With that money and Mr Boerke's help, I sent Little Mo to the best hospital in all of Africa, in Cape Town, and there they were able to save him.

'But it was a very large amount of money, and much was left over.' The chief smiled. 'So first I bought some new boats, to replace the ones that were taken or shot up. And then we decided to build a new school. A proper one, so teaching does not have to be done under a palm tree any more. And finally – if Mrs Topeka can show herself – we hired a permanent teacher.'

A young, smartly dressed local woman stepped forward, giving Jaeger a shy smile. 'All the children speak very fondly of you, Mr Jaeger. I am trying to carry on the good work that you began.'

'Of course, there is still a place for a teacher of your talents,' the chief added. 'And Little Mo misses your skills at beach soccer very much! But I sense that maybe you have business that has taken you back into the wider world, and that maybe this is a good thing.' He paused. 'Insh'Allah, William, you have found your path.'

Had he? Had he found his path?

Jaeger thought about that dark warplane, the debris of which now lay scattered across the jungle; he thought of Irina Narov and her precious dagger; he thought of Ruth and Luke, his missing wife and child. There seemed to be many paths before him now, but maybe, somehow, they were all converging.

'Insh'Allah,' he agreed. He ruffled Little Mo's hair. 'But do one thing for me, will you – keep that teaching post open, just in case!'

The chief promised he would.

'So, now the time has come,' he announced. 'You must come and see the site we have chosen for the school. It overlooks the beach where you made your escape, and we would like you to lay the foundation stone. We are thinking of calling it the William Jaeger and Pieter Boerke School, for without you there would not be one.'

Boerke shook his head in amazement. 'I'm honoured. But no, just the William Jaeger School is enough. Me – I was simply the messenger.'

The visit to the school site was a special moment. Jaeger laid the first stone, upon which the walls would be built, and he and Boerke stayed for the obligatory feast. But eventually they had to say their goodbyes.

Boerke had one more destination scheduled on their island tour, and Jaeger had a flight to catch.

88

From Fernao, Boerke drove west, heading back towards Malabo. By the time he hit the coast road, Jaeger was fairly certain where they were going. Sure enough, they pulled into the compound of Black Beach Prison, through gates swung wide by a new and much more efficient and capable-looking guard force.

Boerke pulled up in the shadow of a high wall.

He turned to Jaeger. 'A home from home, eh? It's still used as a prison, but there's a whole new bunch of inmates. Plus the torture cells are empty now, and the sharks are going crazy with hunger.' He paused. 'There's one thing I want to show you, and a few things you need to have returned.'

They stepped down from the vehicle and into the prison's dark interior. Jaeger couldn't deny that he felt uneasy heading back into the place wherein the proverbial shit had been kicked out of him endlessly, and the cockroaches had all but feasted on his brains. But hell, maybe this was the way to slay the demons.

Almost immediately, he knew where Boerke was leading him: to his former cell. The South African rapped on the bars, calling a figure to some form of attention.

'So, Mojo, time to meet your new jailer.' He gestured at Jaeger. 'My, how the tables have turned.'

The new inmate of Jaeger's former cell stared at him, a look of horror spreading across his features.

'Now, if you do not behave yourself very, very nicely,' Boerke continued, 'I am going to let Mr Jaeger here set up a new torture reserved for you exclusively.' He flashed a look at Jaeger. 'Are you good with that?'

Jaeger shrugged. 'Sure. I figure I can remember some of the nastier ones, from when the boot was on the other foot.'

'You hear that, Mojo?' Boerke demanded. 'And I tell you something else, man: the sharks – I am told they are very, very hungry right now. Be careful, my friend. Be very, very careful.'

They left Jaeger's former jailer and headed for the prison office. En route, Boerke paused before a side corridor leading to the isolation block. He glanced at Jaeger.

'You know who we have in there?' He nodded towards the corridor. 'Chambara. Caught him at the airport as he tried to flee. You want to go say hello? He's the bastard who ordered your arrest in the first place, isn't it?'

'He is. But let's leave him to his isolation. I'd take one of his yachts, though,' Jaeger added with a smile.

Boerke laughed. 'I'll add you to the list. No, man. We are not here to loot and pillage. We are here to rebuild this country.'

They made their way upstairs to the prison office, the place where Jaeger had first been processed into Black Beach. Boerke said something to the guard on reception, who handed over a small bundle of possessions – mostly clothes – tied up in the belt that Jaeger had been wearing at the time.

Boerke passed it to Jaeger. 'These I believe are yours. Mojo's lot robbed all the valuables, but there are a few personal effects in there I think you'd want to have.'

He led the way into a side room, and then excused himself so Jaeger could go through his possessions in some kind of privacy.

Apart from the clothes, there was Jaeger's old wallet. It had been stripped of all money and credit cards, but he was glad to have it back. It had been a gift from his wife. It was made of bottle-green leather and had the SAS motto – 'Who Dares Wins' – inscribed discreetly on the underside of the interior flap.

Jaeger flipped it open and checked the secret compartment lying deep inside the wallet's lining. Thankfully, the Black Beach guards hadn't thought to look in there. He pulled out a tiny photo. It showed a young and beautiful green-eyed woman cradling a fresh-faced baby: Ruth and Luke, shortly after Luke had been born.

There was a scrap of paper stuffed behind the photo. It was a record of the pin numbers for his credit cards, but written in such a way that no one should be able to work them out. Jaeger had employed a simple form of encoding: to each of the four numbers he'd added his date of birth – 1979.

In that way 2345 became 3.12.11.14.

Simple.

Coding.

For a moment Jaeger's mind flashed back to the old war chest lying in his Wardour Castle apartment, and to the book lying therein – a rare copy of a richly illustrated medieval text written entirely in a long-forgotten language. From there his mind flipped to a conversation with Simon Jenkinson, the archivist, at Wild Dog Media's Soho offices over stale and rubbery sushi.

There is something called the book code. The beauty is its absolute pure simplicity; that, and the fact that it's totally unbreakable – unless, of course, you happen to know which book each person is referring to.

After which the archivist had scribbled down an apparently random sequence of numbers . . .

Jaeger reached for his flight bag, pulled out the Malabo Government House file, and opened the sheet of paper from the *Duchessa's* manifest. He ran his eyes down the list of seemingly random numbers, feeling a surge of excitement kicking his guts as he did so.

Irina Narov had confirmed that Grandfather Ted had been a leading Nazi hunter. From the little that Great Uncle Joe had felt able to tell him, Jaeger knew that he had also played a role in Grandfather Ted's work. Both men had kept copies of the same rare and ancient book – the Voynich manuscript – to hand.

Maybe there was method to the apparent madness.

Maybe the Voynich manuscript unlocked the code.

Maybe Grandpa Ted and Great Uncle Joe had got their hands on some of the Nazi's end-of-war documents, and had been unravelling the coded language as part of the hunt.

In which case, Jaeger had the answer to breaking the codes in his possession. If he could get himself, Narov and maybe Jenkinson together with the relevant books and documents, it might all start to make some kind of sense.

Jaeger smiled to himself. Boerke had been right: it had been worth making this trip out to Bioko many times over.

The South African knocked and entered the room. 'So, man, you're looking pleased with yourself. I guess you've enjoyed coming here after all?'

Jaeger nodded. 'I'm in your debt, Pieter, a thousand times over.'

'Not a bit of it, man. It is a debt repaid, that's all.'

Jaeger pulled his iPhone from his flight bag. 'Two quick emails I need to send.'

'Go right ahead – as long as you can get a signal,' Boerke told him. 'Cell coverage around Malabo – it can be pretty bad.'

Jaeger powered up the phone and pulled up his email account, typing in the first message:

Simon,

I am transiting back through London, arriving tomorrow morning. Would you have the time for a meeting, just for an hour or so? I'll come to you, wherever's convenient. It's urgent. I think you'll like what we may have discovered. Let me know as soon as.

Jaeger

The message sat in his outbox 'awaiting signal' while he set about typing the second.

Irina (if I may),

I trust you are well and recovery is progressing. I'm en route back to Cachimbo shortly. Good news: I think I may have cracked the code. More when I see you.

Yours,

Will

He clicked 'send', and almost at the same time his phone beeped to indicate that it had acquired a signal, via some local network called Safaricom. The sending symbol twirled around and around for a few seconds, before the phone seemed to drop the connection.

He was about to power down, power up and try again when the iPhone appeared to fade to black of its own accord before coming back to life. A message seemed to type itself across the screen.

Question: how did we find you?
Answer: your friend told us where to look.

An instant later the screen went black again, before fading up on an image that had become sickeningly familiar: a *Reichsadler*.

But this *Reichsadler* was displayed on a Nazi-style flag pinned to a wall. Below it, Andy Smith, tied at the wrists and ankles, lay on his back on a tiled floor. By the looks of the cloth they threw over his face and the bucket of water being tipped over it, he was being waterboarded.

Jaeger stared at the horrifying image, transfixed.

He could only presume it had been taken in Smithy's Loch Iver hotel room, before they had marched him up on to the storm-lashed hills, forced a bottle of whisky down his throat and hurled him into the dark abyss. Most likely Stefan Kral had been the one who'd tricked Smithy into opening his hotel door to his torturers.

There would have been precious little Smithy could have told his captors before he died, apart from the general location of the air wreck, for Colonel Evandro hadn't yet released its exact coordinates.

More words typed themselves below the image:

Return to us what is ours.
Wir sind die Zukunft.

Return to us what is ours. Jaeger could only imagine they meant the documents from the Ju 390 cockpit. But how did they know Narov had retrieved them, and that they hadn't gone down with the warplane? Jaeger just didn't know . . . And then something hit him: *Leticia Santos.*

They'd clearly forced their Brazilian captive to talk. Like everyone else on the team, Leticia had been aware that something of crucial importance had been discovered in that cockpit. No doubt about it – under duress she must have revealed what she knew.

Jaeger heard a voice from behind him. 'Man, who in God's name sent you that? And why?' It was Boerke, and he was staring at the image on Jaeger's phone.

His words served to break Jaeger's trance, and with it a burning jolt of realisation seared through his mind. He raised his arm and hurled the smartphone through the open window, propelling it as far as it would go into the bush outside.

Then he grabbed his flight bag and took to his heels, yelling at Boerke to follow.

'RUN! Get everyone out! NOW!'

They sprinted out of the office block, screaming at the guards. Barely had they reached the former torture cells in the basement when the Hellfire struck. It tore into the ground where Jaeger's phone lay, ripping a massive hole in the perimeter wall of the prison and collapsing the adjacent office building – the place where Jaeger and Boerke had just been sitting.

Down in the basement, both men were uninjured, as were most of the guards. But Jaeger wasn't kidding himself any more: in the prison that had once almost been the death of him, the Dark Force had nearly killed him again.

And once again he, William Jaeger, was very much the hunted.

89

Fortunately, Malabo had a handful of internet cafés. Under Boerke's guidance, Jaeger chose one and managed to send the briefest of messages.

> **Close all open comms. Travel as arranged. Revert as agreed.**
> **WJ**

Even in civilian life, Jaeger tended to live by the old soldier's adage: 'Fail to plan, plan to fail.'

Before leaving Cachimbo, he'd set up alternative travel and communications arrangements, just in case of such an eventuality – the hunt being resumed. He figured the enemy would be working to a dual agenda now: either to have the documents returned, or to kill all those who knew of their existence. Ideally, they'd want to achieve both ends.

Via an address to which his core team – Narov, Raff and Dale – had access, he proceeded to post a draft email. They would know to read the draft without it ever having been sent – hence making it all but untraceable.

The email detailed the time of a proposed meeting a couple of days hence, at a prearranged location. If the draft box received no message saying otherwise, the meeting would be on. And under the 'travel as arranged' instruction, Narov, Raff and Dale would know to fly back to the UK using passports provided courtesy of Colonel Evandro's partners in Brazilian intelligence.

If necessary, they'd move under Brazilian diplomatic cover, so determined was the colonel to get them home safely and get the riddle of the Ju 390 solved.

Jaeger caught his flights from Bioko to London as planned.

There had been zero point in changing them, especially as they had been booked under the 'clean' passport that Colonel Evandro had provided him with, one that should be untraceable.

Upon arrival in London, he caught the Heathrow Express to Paddington and jumped in a black cab. He got the cabbie to drop him a good half-mile distant from Springfield Marina, so he could walk the last leg to his London home. It was one more precaution to ensure he hadn't been followed.

Living on a boat had several advantages, one of which was the lack of a traceable footprint. Jaeger paid no council tax, he wasn't on the electoral roll or the property register, and he'd chosen not to have a mailing address at the marina.

The boat itself was registered to an anonymous offshore company, likewise the mooring. In short, his Thames barge was as good a place as any to schedule the meeting.

En route to the marina, he called in at a grotty-looking internet café. He ordered a black coffee, logged on and checked the draft box. There were two messages. One was from Raff, postponing the meeting by a few hours, just to give them time enough to get there.

The other message was blank, but it had a link embedded in it. Jaeger clicked through and it took him to Dropbox, an online data storage system.

The Dropbox file contained one image – a JPEG file.

Jaeger clicked on it.

The internet connection was slow, and as the image downloaded it hit him like a series of savage punches to the guts. It showed the figure of Leticia Santos – kneeling naked and with her hands and feet tied, her eyes staring wide into the camera and red with terror.

Behind her was what looked like a torn and bloodstained bed sheet, on which were scrawled the now familiar words:

Return to us what is ours.
Wir sind die Zukunft.

They were crudely written in what appeared to be human blood.

Jaeger didn't bother to log off. He sprinted from the café, leaving his coffee untouched.

Somehow, even their draft email communications system had been penetrated. That being the case, who knew how quickly a drone unleashing a Hellfire might arrive overhead? Jaeger doubted the enemy had the wherewithal to deploy one over east London, but presumption was the mother of all screw-ups.

Instinctively he knew what the enemy was about here.

They were deliberately taunting him. It was a tried and tested means of waging battle, one that the Nazis had named *Nervenkrieg* – mind warfare. They were torturing him by careful design, in the hope that they could provoke him into remaining at a traceable location for long enough for them to find and kill him.

Or failing that, in the hope that he might be provoked into going hunting, solo.

And in truth, the *Nervenkrieg* was working.

Having watched that sickening image download, it was all Jaeger could do to resist the temptation to go seeking out Leticia Santos's tormentors right here and now. And alone.

There were any number of leads he could follow. The C-130 pilot, for a start. Carson would have his details on file, and that would be enough for Jaeger to start tracking him down. Plus Colonel Evandro had promised a whole caseload of new leads from his own investigations.

But Jaeger needed to hold off.

He needed to regroup his forces, learn from whatever it was they had discovered, study the ground, the enemy and the threat, and strategise and act accordingly. Somehow he had to reclaim the initiative – to make proactive decisions, not reactive heat-of-the-moment ones.

It was the old adage again: *fail to plan, plan to fail.*

90

First to arrive for that evening's meeting was the archivist, Simon Jenkinson.

Jaeger had spent most of the day on his Triumph Explorer, paying a furtive visit to his Wardour Castle apartment. There, he'd retrieved his edition of the Voynich manuscript – the one that Grandfather Ted had bequeathed to him.

He'd laid the thick tome on his desk in the barge with some degree of reverence, awaiting Simon Jenkinson's entry.

The archivist was a good half an hour early, and he looked only marginally less like a hibernating honey bear than when Jaeger had last seen him. At Jaeger's request, he'd managed to track down a copy of the Voynich manuscript translation. He'd brought it with him, tucked firmly under his arm.

Jaeger was barely able to offer him a cup of tea before Jenkinson sat himself down with the Voynich manuscript and the Bioko file, placing the translation beside them. And that was it: thick glasses perched on the end of his nose, Jenkinson got to work on the *Duchessa*'s list of apparently random numbers – code-breaking, or so Jaeger presumed.

An hour later, the archivist raised his head from his task, his eyes burning with excitement.

'Gotcha!' he exclaimed. 'At last! I've done two, just to make sure the first wasn't a fluke. So . . . number one: Adolf Eichmann.'

'I know the name,' Jaeger confirmed. 'But remind me of the details.'

Jenkinson already had his head bent over the books and

papers once more. 'Eichmann – truly a nasty piece of work. One of the chief architects of the Holocaust. He escaped Nazi Germany at war's end, only to be tracked down to Argentina in the 1960s.

'Next one: Ludolf von Alvensleben,' Jenkinson declared.

Jaeger shook his head: the name wasn't familiar at all.

'*SS Gruppenführer* and mass murderer par excellence. Ran the Valley of Death in northern Poland, which became a grave for thousands.' Jenkinson flashed Jaeger a look. 'Also disappeared to Argentina, where he lived to a ripe old age.

Jenkinson bent over his books again, flipping back and forth through the pages, until the third was decoded.

'Aribert Heim,' the archivist announced. 'Him you must have heard of. He's been at the centre of one of the longest man-hunts of all time. His nickname during the war was Dr Death. He earned it in the concentration camps, by experimenting on inmates.' Jenkinson shuddered. 'Also thought to be hiding out in Argentina, though rumour has it he may have died of old age.'

'There seems to be a theme developing,' Jaeger remarked. 'A Latin American theme.'

Jenkinson smiled. 'Indeed.'

Before he could reveal any more of the names, the rest of the party arrived. Raff led Irina Narov and Mike Dale into the barge, the latter two looking tired from their travels but also remarkably recovered, and noticeably better fed than when Jaeger had last seen them.

He greeted each in turn, and did the necessary introductions with Jenkinson. Raff, Narov and Dale had flown into London direct from Rio, with a connecting flight from Cachimbo prior to that. They'd been on the go for approaching eighteen hours, and it promised to be a long night.

Jaeger brewed some strong coffee, then gave them the good news: the book code seemed to be working – at least for the Bioko documents.

Five figures gathered around the Voynich manuscript and its translation, as Narov produced the satchel of papers retrieved from the Ju 390's cockpit. The atmosphere aboard the barge was electric with anticipation. Would seventy years of a dark and secret history finally be brought to life?

Narov took out the first set of papers.

Dale produced his camera. He waved it at Jaeger. 'You good with this? In here?'

'What's got into you?' Jaeger needled him. 'It's film first, ask later, isn't it?'

Dale shrugged. 'This is your home. Makes it a bit different from filming out in the wilds.'

Jaeger sensed a change in the man – an air of maturity and genuine concern, as though the trials and tribulations of the last few weeks had somehow been the making of him.

'Go ahead,' he told him. 'Let's get it documented – all of it.'

Under Jenkinson's initial tutelage, Narov set about the *Aktion Feuerland* document, while Dale framed up his shots, and Raff and Jaeger stood an informal guard. The archivist seemed remarkably talented at multi-tasking: it wasn't long before he was able to thrust a list under Jaeger's nose – the seventh page of the *Duchessa*'s manifest, fully decoded. He proceeded to point out some of the most notorious individuals.

'Gustav Wagner, better known as "the Beast". Wagner founded the T4 programme – to kill off the disabled – then went on to run one of the foremost extermination camps. Escaped to South America, where he lived to a grand old age.'

His finger stabbed at another name on the list. 'Klaus Barbie – "the Butcher of Lyons". A mass murderer who tortured and killed his way across France. At the end of the war—'

Jenkinson broke off as Jaeger's boatie neighbour, Annie, ducked through the barge's entranceway. Jaeger did the introductions.

'Annie's from the nextdoor barge. She's a . . . good friend.'

Narov spoke from where she was bent over her documents.

'Aren't they all? Women and Will Jaeger – they seem drawn like the moth to the candle flame. Isn't that how you say it in English?'

'Anyone who can make carrot cake like Annie – they'll win my heart, for sure,' Jaeger answered, doing his best to rescue an awkward situation.

Realising that he and his friends were busy, and sensing the tension in the air, Annie handed Jaeger the cake she'd brought and backed out quickly. 'Don't work too hard, fellas,' she called with a wave.

Narov hunched closer over her documents. Jaeger eyed her, irritated by what she'd just done. What right did she have to be rude to his friends?

'Thanks for helping the neighbourly relations,' he remarked, sarcastically.

Narov didn't even raise her head from her task. 'It is simple. No one outside of these four walls should be trusted with what these documents will reveal – that's if we can crack them. No one, no matter how good a friend.'

'So, Klaus Barbie,' Jenkinson volunteered.

'Yeah, tell me about the Butcher of Lyons.'

'At war's end Klaus Barbie was protected by British and American intelligence. He was posted to Argentina as a CIA agent, code-named Adler.'

Jaeger raised one eyebrow. 'Adler: eagle?'

'Eagle,' Jenkinson confirmed. 'Believe it or not, the Butcher of Lyon became a life-long CIA agent code-named The Eagle.' He moved his finger down the list. 'And this one. Heinrich Müller, former head of the Gestapo – the most senior Nazi whose fate remains an utter mystery. Believed by most to have fled to . . . well, you guessed it: Argentina.

'Below him, Walter Rauff, a top SS commander. The inventor of the mobile vehicles in which the Nazis gassed people. Fled to South America. Lived to a grand old age, and his funeral was reportedly a major celebration of all things Nazi.

'And finally,' Jenkinson announced, 'the Angel of Death himself, Joseph Mengele. Carried out unspeakable experiments on thousands in Auschwitz. At war's end he fled to – need I say it? – Argentina, where he is reported to have continued his experiments. A true monster of a human – that's if you can even call him human.

'Oh, and lest we forget, Bormann's also on the list. Martin Bormann – Hitler's right-hand man—'

'Hitler's banker,' Jaeger interjected.

'Indeed.' Jenkinson eyed him. 'In short, it's a Nazi rogues' gallery if ever there was one. Though the foremost rogue of all is missing: Uncle Adolf. They say he died in his Berlin bunker. I've never really believed it myself.'

Jenkinson shrugged. 'I've spent most of my adult life in the archives researching the Second World War. You'd be amazed what an industry has grown up around it. But I've never come across anything that even remotely rivals all this.' He waved a hand at the pile of documents on the table. 'And I must say, I'm rather enjoying myself. Mind if I have a crack at another?'

'Go right ahead,' Jaeger confirmed. 'There's too much for Ms Narov to deal with in the one night. But I'm curious, what happened to that Hans Kammler file that you found in the National Archives? The one you emailed me a couple of pages from?'

Jenkinson seemed to jump slightly, a hint of worry creeping into his eyes. 'Gone. Vanished. Kaput. Even when I checked the online cloud storage systems – not a page remains anywhere. It's the file that never was.'

'Someone went to great lengths to make it disappear,' Jaeger probed.

'They did,' Jenkinson confirmed uneasily.

'One more thing,' Jaeger added. 'Why use something so basic as a book code? I mean, the Nazis had their state-of-the-art Enigma cipher machines, didn't they?'

Jenkinson nodded. 'They did. But thanks to Bletchley Park,

we broke Enigma, and by the end of the war, the Nazi leadership knew that.' He smiled. 'A book code may be simple, but it's also utterly unbreakable, unless you have the exact same book – or, in this case, books plural – that the code is based upon.'

With that he joined Narov, turning his fine mind to cracking another of the documents.

91

Number crunching wasn't really Raff and Jaeger's strength. They busied themselves making brews, and keeping vigil on the deck outside. Jaeger wasn't exactly expecting any trouble here at the marina, but both he and Raff were still alive and in the game because they'd been trained to expect the unexpected – training they still lived by.

After an hour or so Dale came and joined them. He took a long pull on his coffee. 'Only so much reading documents a sane man can film.'

'Talking of film, how's it going?' Jaeger asked. 'Carson happy, or are you about to be shot at dawn?'

Dale shrugged. 'Oddly enough, he seems pretty sanguine about it all. We got to the aircraft and lifted it out of the jungle, just as we'd promised. Fact that we lost it along the way – it just means there won't be any sequel. But once I'm done here, I'm supposed to head to an edit suite, so I can start cutting the series.'

'How're you going to make me look?' Jaeger queried. 'You editing out my ums and ahs?'

'I'm going to make you look like an idiot,' Dale replied, deadpan.

'Do that and you *will* get shot at dawn.'

'Do that and there's no film.'

They laughed.

There was a certain camaraderie between them now – one that Jaeger would have never imagined possible upon their first meeting.

It was pushing midnight by the time Narov had her first document cracked. Sure enough, the Voynich manuscript was proving the key to unlocking its meaning, but even so it was slow and painstaking work. She came and joined Raff, Dale and Jaeger on the barge's open rear.

'I am maybe fifty per cent done,' she announced. 'And already it is incredible.' She glanced at Jaeger. 'We now know exactly where the first three Ju 390s – *Adlerflug I, II* and *III* – were headed, as would our warplane, *Adlerflug IV*, have been, had she not run out of gas. Which means we know exactly where the Nazis had their safe havens.

'*Aktion Feuerland*,' she continued. 'You know why they called it that? They named it after Tierra del Fuego – the land of fire. Where is that? It is the sliver of land where the extreme southern tip of Argentina slips into the Atlantic . . . For me, Argentina is no massive surprise. It always was the key suspect for sheltering the foremost Nazis.

'But there are several other locations that the document reveals. Other safe havens. And they do come as a real shock.' Narov paused, struggling to control her elation. 'You know, we have never had the wherewithal – the intelligence or expertise – to finish this. To end it. But with breaking these codes, maybe we do now.'

Before Narov could continue, there was a triumphant yell from inside. The voice was that of Jenkinson, and they figured it had to be something utterly extraordinary, for it wasn't in the archivist's nature to get needlessly overexcited.

They hurried inside.

Jenkinson held up a sheet of paper. 'This – is – it,' he stammered, breathlessly. 'This changes everything. It would have been so easy to overlook – one seemingly unremarkable sheet of numbers . . . But finally it all starts to make sense. Horrible, chilling sense.'

He gazed at the four of them, his lower lip trembling with . . . what? Excitement; trepidation; or was it dread?

'There is little point in shipping your loot, your top people and your *Wunderwaffe* – your wonder weapons – to the four corners of the earth, unless you have a reason. A schedule. A *master plan*.'

'This,' he waved the paper. 'This is it. *Aktion Werewolf*. Operation Werewolf: blueprint for the Fourth Reich.'

He glanced at them, fear etched in his eyes. 'Note: Fourth Reich. Not Third Reich. *Fourth Reich*.'

They gathered in stunned silence as Jenkinson began to read.

'It begins: "At the orders of the Führer, from the ashes of the Third Reich the Ubermensch" – that's the master race – "will work to ensure that we rise again . . ."'

Jenkinson proceeded to read through the entirety of the document. It outlined a plan to use the Allies' greatest weakness – their paranoia over the rise of the Eastern Bloc and Soviet communism – against them. Even at the Allies' hour of victory, the Nazis would use that paranoia as their Trojan Horse – one through which they would survive, and rise again to conquer.

'Using the stupendous wealth they had accumulated during the war years, they would infiltrate all sections of society with 'true believers'. They would appear to harness their technology for the benefit of their new masters, while in truth subverting them. The most promising *Wunderwaffe* technologies would continue to be developed, but in absolute secret, and for the benefit of a Nazism reborn under the Fourth Reich.

'"No one should underestimate the task now lying before us",' Jenkinson read from the last paragraph of the document. '"Operation Werewolf will not be accomplished overnight. We will need to be patient. We will need to rebuild our power and marshal our forces. The Führer, assisted by the greatest minds in the Reich, will work away in secret for this end. And when the Reich rises like a phoenix from the ashes, this time it will be global and unstoppable.

'"Many of us may not live to see this day",' he continued, '"but our children certainly will. They will seize their birthright.

The destiny of the *Ubermensch* will be fulfilled. And revenge – revenge will be finally bestowed upon us."'

Jenkinson flipped over the sheet of paper, turning to a second. 'They mention getting their people installed in the Office of Strategic Services – the forerunner to the CIA – the American government, the British Secret Intelligence Service, top corporations . . . the list goes on and on. And they give themselves seventy years to do so – seventy years from the date of their ultimate ignominy: their May 1945 unconditional surrender to the Allies.'

Jenkinson glanced up, fearfully. 'Which means that any time around about now, the new Reich is due to rise, Phoenix-like from the ashes.'

He turned the document around so that it faced Jaeger and the others. At the bottom of the second page was stamped a familiar form – a *Reichsadler*.

'That,' he indicated, 'is their mark. It is the emblem of the Fourth Reich. That circular symbol below the eagle's tail – the writing around it is also in code. In fact, it's triply encoded, but I've managed to break it.

'Decoded it reads: "*Die Ubermensch des Reich – Wir sind die Zukunft*. The master race of the Fourth Reich – we are the future."'

92

J aeger glanced across the warm aquamarine waters at Irina Narov. 'Your wave,' he challenged. 'If you think you're man enough.'

Behind them a massive swell was rolling towards the shimmering white sands, growing taller and more powerful as it neared the beach.

'*Schwachkopf*! Race you!' Narov threw back the challenge.

They turned and began to paddle furiously in the direction of the shoreline. For an instant Jaeger felt the roar of the surf fill his ears and then the powerful thrust of it lifted up the rear of his board. He paddled faster, trying to catch the wave and become a part of it, as it thundered towards the thin sliver of silver that was the beach.

He accelerated, the surfboard tearing down the face of the water, and in one smooth move sprang to his feet, his legs bent at the knees to better cushion the ride. As his speed increased, Jaeger felt the familiar adrenalin rush, and he figured he'd execute a quick roller turn, just to ensure he beat Narov in style.

He swivelled his shoulders towards the wave, his board riding up the twelve-foot wall of water. He reached the foaming white crest and went to flip himself around so he could come tearing down again. But he'd underestimated just how much five weeks in Black Beach Prison followed by almost as long again in the Amazon had affected him.

As he tried to shift his weight to his front foot, Jaeger realised how stiff his legs still were. He lost his balance, and an instant later he wiped out. The big wave swallowed him, sucking him under and thrashing him around and around within its roaring, throaty depths.

He felt the raw power of the ocean take hold of him and surrendered himself to it. It was the only way to survive such a massive wipeout. As Jaeger had told his son when he'd first taken him surfing: 'Take your time. Imagine you have ten seconds to save the world; always spend five of them having milk and cookies.' It was his way of teaching Luke to stay calm in the storm.

When the wave was done with him, Jaeger knew it would spit him out the far side.

Sure enough, several seconds later he surfaced.

He took a massive gulp of air and felt around for the leash of his board. He found it, pulled the board towards him, climbed on and paddled towards land. Narov was waiting on the sands, victory blazing in her eyes.

It was a week since the epic code-breaking session on Jaeger's barge, and the Operation Werewolf discovery. The idea of the Bermuda visit had been his. The intention: to spend a few days recharging batteries and making plans, courtesy of Jaeger's parents.

A rest before the coming fight.

Being a tiny British overseas territory set smack bang in the midst of the Atlantic Ocean, Bermuda was about as far away from any prying eyes as it was possible to get. Jaeger's parents didn't even live in the largest settlement, Main Island. They'd made their home in Horseshoe Bay, on the breathtaking territory of Morgan's Point.

Perfectly isolated. Perfectly beautiful.

And a long way from the hell of the Serra de los Dios . . .

Oddly enough for one so driven by the mission – by the hunt – Narov had seemed to jump at the chance of paying a visit to this tiny island paradise. Jaeger figured that once they were away from it all, she would be willing to talk at last about her hidden past, and not least her connection to his grandfather.

He'd tried to broach the subject a couple of times in London – but even there Narov had appeared to be stalked by demons.

The Bermuda trip also offered Jaeger the chance to talk to his parents about how Grandpa Ted had died, something that was long overdue. Sure enough, foul play had been suspected, though Jaeger had been too young to pick up on it at the time.

As the police had failed to uncover any evidence, the family had been forced to accept the suicide verdict pretty much at face value. But their suspicions had endured.

Predictably enough, his mother and father had interpreted Jaeger's arrival with Narov as being something other than what it was. His father had even gone as far as taking Jaeger into his study for a private chat.

He'd remarked upon how Narov – though at times somewhat odd in her mannerisms – was quite beautiful, and how refreshing it was to see Jaeger taking up with a . . . lady friend once more. Jaeger had pointed out that his father was ignoring one seminal fact – he and Narov were sleeping in separate rooms.

His father had made it clear that he didn't believe a bit of it. As far as he was concerned, the separate bedrooms act was just that – an act. It was all for show. And with Jaeger's wife and child absent pushing four years now, his father had made it clear that he and his mother believed it was time.

Time for Jaeger to move on.

Jaeger loved his parents to death. His father in particular had bequeathed to him his joy of all things wild – the sea, mountains, forests. Jaeger hadn't quite managed to tell him that he'd never felt more convinced that Ruth and Luke were alive. Most probably he'd held off doing so to save his parents any more uncertainty and anguish.

He didn't really know how to explain his new-found conviction. How could he tell his father that a psychotropic cocktail administered by an Amazon Indian – a brother warrior – had given him back his memories, and with them, his hope?

93

Surfing done for the morning, he and Narov wandered back towards the house. His parents were out, and Narov went to take a shower, to wash the salt off her skin and hair. Jaeger headed for his bedroom and grabbed his iPad. He needed to check for news of the rest of his team.

Until they were all safely out of the Amazon, he felt uneasy planning the next steps. Of course, simply uncovering the master plan for the return of the Reich – a global Nazi power-grab – didn't necessarily mean that plan was actually being put into action. But the evidence was all too compelling, and Jaeger feared the worst.

First Andy Smith had been killed, and then Jaeger and his team had been hunted across the Amazon. The Dark Force had done its damnedest to finish them and bury for ever the secrets of the Ju 390 ghost flight. They clearly had a global reach, and some serious technological and military prowess at their disposal. Plus, an official British government file had been snuffed out of existence, disappearing from the archives.

Any which way Jaeger looked at it, the sons of the Reich did indeed appear to be rising. And no one seemed to be aware of it or doing anything much to stop it – apart from him and his small, war-weary team.

When Jenkinson had cracked the Operation Werewolf papers, Jaeger had been tempted to reveal the presence in his grandfather's war chest of a document with the same title. But something instinctive had held him back. That was a card he'd keep close to his chest until the time was right to play it.

With Colonel Evandro's help, he had managed to set up a system of secure encrypted email, so that all the surviving team members could communicate in some degree of safety. Or rather, all bar Leticia Santos. Colonel Evandro had his best men, supported by his kidnap, ransom and extortion specialists, out scouring the country, searching for her whereabouts, but so far all leads had come to naught.

Jaeger fired up the iPad and logged on to ProtonMail – the end-to-end email encryption system they were now using. He had one message waiting, from Raff, with good news. In the last twenty-four hours, Lewis Alonzo, Hiro Kamishi and Joe James had surfaced. They had made it out of the Serra de los Dios under the guidance of Puruwehua and some of the neighbouring tribe, the Uru-Eu-Wau-Wau.

All three were as well as could be expected, and Raff was now working with Colonel Evandro to ensure they were brought home as quickly and safely as possible. Jaeger emailed him back, asking for an update on the search for Leticia Santos.

While he knew there was little he could do to help, a part of him wanted to return to Brazil forthwith to support Colonel Evandro in the hunt. Once he was done in Bermuda, that was what he intended to do, as long as Santos hadn't been rescued in the interim. He'd vowed to himself that she would be found and brought home safely.

There was a second message waiting in his inbox, this one from Pieter Boerke. He was about to click on it when there was a knock at his door.

It was Narov. 'I am going out for a run.'

'Okay,' Jaeger replied, keeping his eyes on the screen. 'And when you're back, maybe we can have that long-overdue chat about how you knew my grandfather. And why you resent me so much.'

Narov paused. 'Resent you? Maybe not so much now. But yes, in this place, maybe we can talk.'

The door closed and Jaeger opened the message.

First off, download the attached photograph. It's one I missed in the vaults. Once you've got it, dial me on my Skype link. It'll go through to my cell phone even if I'm out on the move, so you'll always get me. Do it immediately. Don't speak to anyone else.

Jaeger did as instructed. The photo was a grainy black-and-white image taken with a long lens. Once again, it was clearly of the *Duchessa*, and it showed a group of senior Nazi commanders clustered along the ship's rail. Nothing leaped out at him, so with the image on screen, he pulled up his Skype link and dialled Boerke.

The South African answered, his voice thick with tension. 'Look at the guy fourth from the left, in the very centre of the photo. You got him? That guy. That scowl; the appalling hairstyle; the frown marks. Remind you of anyone? Now imagine that face with a small and very bloody stupid-looking Charlie Chaplin moustache . . .'

Suddenly it was as if Jaeger couldn't breathe. 'No way,' he gasped. 'Can't be. We cracked the code, and he wasn't on the list. The top Nazis were, but not him.'

'Well double-check,' Boerke countered. ''Cause if that's not Adolf bloody Hitler, then I'm a bloody Chinaman! One more thing. The photo's date-stamped on the reverse. The date: the seventh of May 1945. And I guess I don't need to point out the significance of that.'

Once Boerke had signed off the call, Jaeger double-clicked his cursor, zooming closer on the image. He stared at the figure's features, hardly daring to believe the evidence before his eyes. No doubt about it: the face was the spitting image of the Führer's – suggesting that he had been standing on a ship's deck in Santa Isabel harbour fully a week after he had supposedly shot himself in his Berlin bunker.

It was a good while before Jaeger felt able to return to the task in hand. Boerke's revelation – presumably the last of the *Duchessa*'s dark secrets – had totally numbed him. It was one thing to discover that many of the Führer's deputies – the chief architects of the evil – had survived the war's end.

It was quite another to discover evidence that the Führer himself might have done so.

Using the ProtonMail search engine, Jaeger logged into their draft email account – the one that had been compromised. He couldn't resist the urge to take a look, and he knew that via ProtonMail his location should be pretty much untraceable. ProtonMail boasted that even the US National Security Agency – the world's most powerful electronic surveillance outfit – couldn't crack traffic going via their servers, which were based in Switzerland.

There was one new message sitting in the draft folder.

It had been there for several days.

Jaeger's unease deepened.

As before, it was blank, providing only a link to a Drop-box folder. Jaeger didn't figure it would be from any of his team. With a growing sense of dread, he opened Dropbox and clicked on the first JPEG file, fully expecting it to be another horrific photo of Leticia Santos – part of the enemy's ongoing *Nervenkrieg*.

He told himself that he had to look, for in one of those sickening images the enemy might inadvertently have left a clue as to their whereabouts – a lead from which Jaeger and the others could start to hunt them down.

The first image appeared: six lines of lettering only.

Holidaying in Paradise . . .
While your loved ones burn.

Question: how do we know so much?
Answer: little Lukie keeps telling us.

Supplementary question: where is little Lukie now?

Answer: *Nacht und Nebel.*

Nacht und Nebel – the night and fog.

With his heart pounding like a machine gun, Jaeger clicked on the second JPEG. The image that opened was of a once-beautiful green-eyed woman and an adolescent boy, their faces cadaverous, their gazes haunted, with dark rings around their sunken eyes.

Mother and child were kneeling in chains before some kind of Nazi flag dominated by a *Reichsadler*. They were clutching a copy of the *International Herald Tribune*. With shaking hands, he zoomed in on the newspaper's banner: the date revealed it to be not yet a week old. It was proof positive that as of five days ago, they were both still very much alive

Two lines of lettering were typed below the image:

Return to us what is ours.
Wir sind die Zukunft.

94

Jaeger turned and dry-retched. He found himself shaking and hurting in a way he'd never experienced before, not even during the worst of the torture he'd endured at Black Beach. He dropped off the chair, his body folding in on itself, but even as he lay on the floor, he couldn't drag his eyes away from that earth-shattering image.

Visions kept crashing through his head, ones so tormented and dark he felt as if his skull were about to explode. It was a long time that he lay there beside the desk, curled into a ball. Tears rolled silently down his cheeks, but they barely registered.

He lost track of time.

He felt spent. Totally void.

The noise that finally brought him back to his senses was that of the door to the bedroom opening.

Somehow he'd made it back into his chair, and was slumped before the desk and the screen.

He turned.

Irina Narov was standing behind him. She had a small towel wrapped around her midriff, the top of which was fastened just above her breasts. She must have been for a shower after her run, and beneath the towel Jaeger didn't doubt that she was naked.

He didn't care.

'Once, when trapped in the jungle treetops, I explained the reasons why two people may get intimate,' Narov remarked, in that odd, flat, matter-of-fact way of hers. 'Such close proximity can be necessary for three reasons,' she repeated. 'One: practical necessity. Two: to share body warmth. Three: sex.' She smiled. 'Right now, I should like it to happen for reason number three.'

Jaeger didn't reply. He wasn't particularly surprised. He'd realised by now that Narov had a near-total lack of ability to read other people's emotions. Even facial expressions and body language seemed strangely lost on her.

Jaeger moved the iPad to where she could see the image on the screen.

Narov's hand went to her mouth in shock. 'Oh, sweet Jesus—'

'The date on the newspaper,' Jaeger cut in, his voice sounding as if it were coming from the end of a very long and very dark tunnel. 'It's five days old.'

'Oh my God,' Narov gasped. *'They're alive.'*

Their eyes locked across the space between them.

'I will get dressed,' Narov continued, without the vaguest hint of any awkwardness or embarrassment. 'There is work to be done.'

She turned towards the door, but paused, flicking a troubled glance back at Jaeger. 'I confess – I did not just go for a run. I also had a rendezvous to make . . . I met with someone who believes he knows where Leticia Santos is being held.'

'You did what?' Jaeger asked, trying to shake the confusion out of his head. 'Where? And with who, for Christ's sake? And why didn't you warn—'

'You would not have wanted to meet with them,' Narov cut in. 'Not if you knew who they are.'

'Bloody try me!' Jaeger snarled. He jabbed a finger at the image on the screen. 'A lead to Leticia – that could take me back to them!'

'I know. I know that now,' Narov protested. 'But an hour ago – I had no idea they were alive.'

Jaeger rose to his feet. There was real menace in his stance now. 'So tell me – who the hell was at your secret meeting, and what did they tell you?'

Narov took a step back. She was clearly on her guard, but for once she was bereft of her knife. 'One of the nearest landfalls to Bermuda is Cuba. Cuba is still Russian territory, as far as the Kremlin is concerned. I met with one of my contacts—'

'You met with a bloody SVR agent? You shared news of what we're doing with *them*?'

Narov shook her head. 'A Russian mafiosa. A drug-runner, or rather one of the drug-running kingpins. They have their network spread right across the Caribbean. They know everything and everybody. They have to, to be able to run their cocaine through these islands.' She glared at Jaeger resentfully. 'But if you wish to find a devil, sometimes you have to do a deal with the devil himself.'

'So – what did he tell you?' Jaeger rasped.

'Two weeks ago, a group of Eastern Europeans turned up in Cuba. They started throwing money around and partying like crazy. Nothing so unusual. But two things came to the notice of my contact. One, they were mercenaries. Two, they had a woman they were holding captive.' Defiance blazed in Narov's eyes. 'That woman – she is Brazilian. And her last name – it is Santos.'

Jaeger's eyes searched Narov's features for a long moment. Oddly, as part of her complex psychological make-up, she seemed incapable of telling a lie. She could play a part to perfection, but with someone she trusted the truth would invariably out.

'Okay,' he growled, 'screw how you found them.' His gaze went back to the image on his iPad screen. 'First we find Leticia, and then . . .'

A look had come into Jaeger's eyes – one of ice-cold, steely calm. He had his team, he had a lead – and more importantly, he had the world and his family to save.

He turned back to Narov. 'Pack your bags. We're going on a journey.'

'We are,' Narov confirmed. 'You: Will Jaeger. And me. It's time we went hunting.'

Bear Grylls has become known as one of the most recognised faces of survival and outdoor adventure. His journey to this acclaim started with his three years in the British Special Forces, where he served with 21 SAS. It was here that he perfected many of the skills his fans all over the world enjoy watching him pit against mother-nature.

His TV Emmy-nominated show *Man Vs Wild / Born Survivor* became one of the most watched programmes on the planet with an estimated audience of 1.2 billion. He then progressed to US Network TV with *Running Wild* on NBC, where he takes some of the world's best known movie stars on incredible adventures, including the likes of President Barack Obama, Ben Stiller, Kate Winslet, Zac Efron and Channing Tatum. He also co-owns and hosts the BAFTA award winning *The Island with Bear Grylls* on Channel 4, which has sold as a format all around the world.

Bear is currently the youngest ever Chief Scout to the UK Scout Association and is an honorary Colonel to the Royal Marines Commandos.

He has authored over forty books, including the number one best-selling autobiography *Mud, Sweat & Tears*, which was voted the most influential book in China in 2012.

Find out more at www.beargrylls.com or follow Bear on Twitter @BearGrylls or instagram @beargrylls

THE
HUNT

BEAR GRYLLS

A secret Nazi horde of uranium is missing.
It's up to Will Jaeger to track it down.
And the clock is ticking . . .

1

Austria, 24 April 1945

They had been partying for hours.

The Allied guns might be pounding the German positions not twenty miles to the west, but these men in their smart Hitler Youth uniforms were drinking as if there was no tomorrow.

Patriotic songs echoed around the damp rock-hewn walls – the 'SS Marschiert in Feindsland' – 'The Devil's Song' – being tonight's favourite. The verses had been belted out time and time again.

> The SS marches into enemy land,
> And sings a devil's song . . .
> We fight for Germany,
> We fight for Hitler . . .

The beer steins had long run dry, but the schnapps had kept flowing, glass after glass being slammed down onto the bare wooden tables, the noise echoing like gunshots off the rough walls.

Though feigning high spirits, SS General Hans Kammler – hawk-faced, sunken-eyed, blonde hair swept back from his high forehead – had barely touched a drop.

He ran a gimlet eye around the vast space, lit by a dozen lanterns. The beast of a weapons system that was secreted within the bowels of this mountain had feasted upon electricity, but forty-eight hours ago, the power had been cut and the machine shut down – hence tonight's flickering illumination, casting grotesque shadows upon the curving walls.

Toast after toast had been drunk to the young men gathered here. Fired up with Nazism and a skinful of schnapps, they would hardly baulk at what was coming. There should be no eleventh-hour objections or last-minute nerves. And for sure, Kammler couldn't afford there to be any, for further back in the shadows of this tunnel complex was hidden the Reich's greatest ever secret.

It represented the fruit of the labours of Nazi Germany's foremost scientists – the Uranverein. Together they had produced a *Wunderwaffe* – a wonder weapon – without equal.

Kammler's grand plan – and arguably the SS high command's most Machiavellian operation – relied upon the Uranverein's work remaining hidden from the advancing Allies. Hence the coming sacrifice – an entirely necessary one as far as the general was concerned.

He glanced upwards momentarily. A narrow shaft rose almost vertically to the starlit heavens: a ventilation duct. These sixty young men would awaken to the dawn light filtering through with the mother of all hangovers. But that would be the least of their worries, he reflected grimly.

The tall, lean SS general rose to his feet. He took his ceremonial sword, its heavy hilt decorated with the distinctive skull-like SS death's head, and rapped it on the table. Gradually the din subsided, and a new cry was taken up in its place.

'*Das Werwolf! Das Werwolf! Das Werwolf!*'

Over and over the chant was repeated, growing in frenzied volume.

This army of fanatical young Nazis believed that they were readying themselves to wage a diehard war of resistance against the Allies. They had been given the name the Werewolves, and their supposed leader was SS General Kammler himself – *Das Werwolf* – the key orchestrator of tonight's gathering.

'*Kameraden!*' Kammler cried, still trying to silence the din. '*Kameraden!*'

Gradually the chanting subsided.

'*Kameraden*, you have drunk well! Toasts fit for heroes of the Reich! But now the time for celebration is over. The moment for launching the Great Resistance is upon us. Today, this hour, you will strike a glorious and momentous blow. What you safeguard here will win us the ultimate victory. With your heroic efforts, we will rise up in the enemy's rear! With your efforts, we will wield a weapon that renders us invincible! With your efforts, the enemies of the Reich will be vanquished!'

Wild cheers broke out afresh, the noise rebounding off the walls.

The general raised his shot glass: a final toast. 'To seizing victory from the jaws of defeat! To the Thousand Year Reich! To the Führer . . . Heil Hitler!'

'Heil Hitler!'

Kammler slammed down his glass. He'd allowed that one shot of schnapps to burn down his throat: Dutch courage for what was coming, for the one part in tonight's proceedings that he really did not relish.

But that would come later.

'To your stations!' he called. 'To your positions! It is 0500 hours and we blow the charges shortly.' He ran his gaze around the gathered throng. 'I will return. *We* will return. And when we come to free you from this place, we will do so with unassailable strength.' He paused. 'The darkest hour is just before the dawn – and this will prove the dawn of a glorious new Nazi ascendancy!'

More wild cheering.

Kammler thumped his free hand on the table with a fierce finality. 'To action! To victory!'

The last of the drinks were downed, and figures began hurrying hither and thither. Kammler followed their movements with his cold gaze. Everywhere seemed to be a hive of activity, which was just as he wanted it. He couldn't afford for any soldier to have second thoughts or attempt to slip away.

Having made one last check deep in the guts of the cave to ensure that the massive steel blast doors were firmly closed and bolted, Kammler made his way towards the shadowed entrance-way, where men were bent over spools of wire and detonation boxes, busy with last-minute preparations.

With a final word of encouragement, the general strode out of the entrance to Tunnel 88, as the vast edifice was known. In truth, Kammler had no idea how many tunnels made up this gargantuan complex. Certainly, hundreds of thousands of concentration camp inmates had died here, excavating the honeycomb of passageways that bored into the bowels of the mountain.

Not that he gave a damn. He was the architect of much of the mass murder. The genius behind it. Those who had perished here – Jews, Slavs, Gypsies, Poles; the *Untermenschen*, sub-humans – had got what they deserved. As far as he was concerned this was their birthright.

No, this was called Tunnel 88 for entirely different reasons. H being the eighth letter of the alphabet, 88 was thus SS code for 'HH' – or Heil Hitler. It had been named at the personal request of Der Oberste Führer der Schutzstaffel – the supreme commander of the SS, Hitler himself. In this place would be preserved the greatest achievement of Nazi Germany, something that might breathe life once more into the Thousand Year Reich.

For a moment Kammler paused to adjust his cap. It seemed to have fallen a little awry during the partying. As he did so, his fingers brushed against the SS *Totenkopft* – the death's head – emblazoned on its front: blank, empty eye sockets staring into the distance, lipless mouth fixed in a maniacal grin.

It was a more than fitting emblem for what was coming.

2

Cap straightened, Kammler turned to speak to the figure at his side, who was dressed in the uniform of a staff sergeant in the SS. This man too had barely touched a drop of alcohol.

'Konrad, my car, if you will. As soon as the charges blow, we will be on our way.'

Scharführer Konrad Weber gave a smart heel-click and hurried away. Old for his rank – not much younger than Kammler himself – Weber had never married and had no children. The Reich, and the SS in particular, was everything to him. His surrogate family.

Kammler turned back to face the mountainside that towered before him. Already the first bluish hints of dawn were streaking across the heavens, reminding him of the need to get this done. At this hour – this witching hour – few should notice the explosions, not that there were likely to be any witnesses. For days now Kammler had had his troops scouring the terrain to all sides, clearing it of hapless civilians.

From behind he heard the crunch of tyres on the single dirt track that led into this remote region. Hooded headlamps, partially blacked out to hide them from any marauding Allied night fighters, pierced the gloom.

Kammler smiled. Excellent: the ever-loyal Konrad at the wheel of his staff car.

The headlamps illuminated the scene before him, casting it into dull light and shadow. Thick pine forest clung to the lower slopes, making the yawning entrance to Tunnel 88 – and the series of similar openings to either side – all but invisible. From each sprouted a tangle of wires, set all along the rock face.

Kammler waited for his driver to park the vehicle, noting that he left the engine running just as he'd been ordered. Scharführer Weber was a good man, and he had proved an utterly loyal servant. An unspoken understanding – an instinctive empathy – had developed between them.

A pity, in view of what was coming.

A hand emerged from the darkness: it was Scharführer Weber's, holding out the handset of the field telephone.

'Sir.'

Kammler took it. 'Thank you. Wait in the vehicle. Just as soon as I have finished, we will be off – the same route as we came in.'

'Yes, Herr General.'

The car door slammed.

Kammler spoke into the handset. 'Herr Obersturmführer, you are ready?'

'Yes, Herr General.'

'Very good. Proceed when you see my staff car stop at the edge of the clearing. But give me time to dismount, so that I can personally witness this glorious spectacle.'

'Yes, Herr General. Understood. Heil Hitler.'

'Heil Hitler.'

Kammler opened the passenger door of the car and slid onto the polished black leather seat, signalling for Scharführer Weber to drive. The smooth Horch V8 engine rumbled throatily as the vehicle pulled away. A minute later, where the sandy track snaked off into the thick cover of the fir trees, Kammler signalled a halt.

'Just here will be fine.'

He swung his polished leather boots out of the vehicle and stood, facing the direction of the escarpment. As the early rays of dawn peeked over the mountains to the east, they burnished the rock face before him a golden bronze.

Kammler leant on the passenger door, bracing himself for what was coming. As he did so, his thick leather coat fell open a little, revealing the compact Walther PPK pistol he had strapped in a holster at his hip.

He brushed his hand against it, just as he had done with his death's-head cap, checking that it was within easy reach.

Soon now.

Kammler forced his mouth wide open, signalling to his driver to do likewise, and the two SS men faced the mountain, gaping like fish. Even this far away, they needed to take precautions, for a blast this powerful could blow their eardrums.

The explosion, when it came, was all Kammler had hoped it would be.

A series of blasts flashed outwards from the trigger point – Tunnel 88 – the detonation cords igniting with such speed that they appeared indistinguishable from each other. All along a four-hundred-yard front the rock face seemed to dissolve as one, transforming itself into a whirling mass of shattered rubble.

The entire escarpment appeared to rise momentarily as it disintegrated into pulverised granite and boulders. The blast vomited hundreds of tonnes of shattered rock, which began to crash back down in a crushing tidal wave.

An instant later, the shock wave hit the two watchers, rocking the car alarmingly on its springs and tearing at Kammler's cap and his thick leather coat before hammering into the forest to their rear. It was followed almost immediately by the sound wave, an impossible roaring and snarling that broke over them and bored into their heads.

Eventually it dissipated and Kammler straightened up. The sheer power of the explosion had sent him into a defensive crouch – not that he or Scharführer Weber had been in any great danger. He brushed down his coat, removing the thin film of white dust that had been carried with the blast.

He kept his eyes glued to the mountainside. When the air finally began to clear, he found himself marvelling at what he saw. Just as he'd intended, it looked as if a massive rock slide had obliterated one entire side of the mountain.

Here and there a dark slash of red indicated where a rich vein of minerals – iron, perhaps – had been torn asunder and slewed down the slope. Uprooted trees lay like heaps of scattered matchwood, crushed under the weight of the rock. But crucially, there was no sign – not the barest hint – of the tunnel complex that now lay hidden behind the wall of debris, not to mention the sixty young soldiers entombed therein.

Kammler gave a satisfied nod. 'Good. We go,' he announced simply.

Scharführer Weber slipped into the driver's seat and blipped the throttle. Kammler clambered in beside him and, with a last look at the dust-enshrouded scene, signalled the staff sergeant to move off.

The dark forest swallowed them. For a few minutes they drove in silence, or at least comparative silence. Even at this hour the hollow crump of artillery could be heard in the distance. The cursed Americans: how they loved to flaunt their military superiority over the Wehrmacht.

It was Weber who broke the quiet. 'Where to, Herr General? Once we make the metalled road?'

'Where indeed, Konrad? Where indeed?' Kammler mused. 'With the Americans and British to one side, and the Russians to the other, where do we of the Schutzstaffel turn?'

For a long moment Weber seemed unsure of how to answer, or even whether an answer was expected. Finally he must have presumed that it was.

'To the Werewolves, Herr General? To seek out their headquarters?'

'Indeed, Konrad, a good thought,' Kammler answered, staring out of the window at the dark trees. 'A fine suggestion. That's if they had one. A headquarters. But I suspect that no such thing can be found.'

Scharführer Weber looked puzzled. 'But Herr General, a

movement such as the Werewolves . . . Surely . . .'

Kammler glanced at his driver. The younger man was doubtless fitter too, so he would need to be careful. 'Surely what, Konrad?'

Weber's hands gripped the wheel more tightly. 'Well, Herr General, how long can our Kameraden beneath the mountain hold out? They will need to be relieved. Dug out of there. As we promised they would be.'

'No, Konrad. Correction. As I promised. You promised nothing.'

Weber nodded, keeping his eyes on the route ahead. 'Of course, Herr General.'

The track swung down to cross a rock-strewn riverbed. Scharführer Weber would need to be extra careful not to get a puncture here, or damage an axle.

Kammler stared ahead, eyes piercing the gloom of the dawn forest. 'If you could pull over, Konrad.' He feigned a smile. 'Even an SS general has at times the need to pee.' He gestured at the river crossing. 'Perhaps when we make the far side.'

'Of course, Herr General.'

They crawled across the rough ground, the car groaning and bucking with every turn of the wheels. Once over, Weber pulled to a halt and Kammler climbed out of the car, taking several paces into the forest as if to relieve himself in private.

Once he was out of sight, he eased the Walther PPK out of its holster and cocked it. He was ready.